PRAISE FOR
M. K. LOBB

Praise for *To Steal from Thieves*

★ "The tension never lets up in this **electric tale** that's equal parts clever heist, searing romance, and pulse-pounding action-adventure." —*Publishers Weekly*, starred review

"**Insightful and fun**, *To Steal from Thieves* spins a **clever, unforgettable narrative** about how desperation forges us into dangerous people—and how to reconcile and love those parts of ourselves anyway." —Kamilah Cole, bestselling author of *So Let Them Burn*

"**Utterly immersive**, this book will plunge you straight into the grimy alleys of London for a high-stakes adventure that's **impossible to put down**." —Amie Kaufman, *New York Times* bestselling author of *The Isles of the Gods*

"Sparking with delicious cons, impossible heists, and an infuriatingly twisty romance, *To Steal From Thieves* is **a jewel of a novel**—one every reader will want to make off with!" —Kika Hatzopoulou, bestselling author of *Threads That Bind*

Praise for the Seven Faceless Saints Duology

"With lush prose, gripping characters, and an intricate lore that will keep you turning the pages, *Seven Faceless Saints* is **an absolute hit**."
—Adalyn Grace, #1 *New York Times* bestselling author of *Belladonna*

"A dazzlingly sinister tale of magic, mayhem, and murder. **Lobb's debut has truly got it all:** exquisitely drawn characters, an opposites-attract romance with top-notch pining, and a world so immersive, you'll want to wander the Palazzo's every shadowy corridor and uncover its every horrible secret. **Prepare for your next obsession.**"
—Allison Saft, *New York Times* bestselling author of *A Far Wilder Magic*

"A satisfying conclusion to Lobb's Seven Faceless Saints duology, *Disciples of Chaos* is **equal parts heartbreaking, propulsive, and achingly romantic**."
—Kelly Andrew, author of *The Whispering Dark*

TO
STEAL
FROM
THIEVES

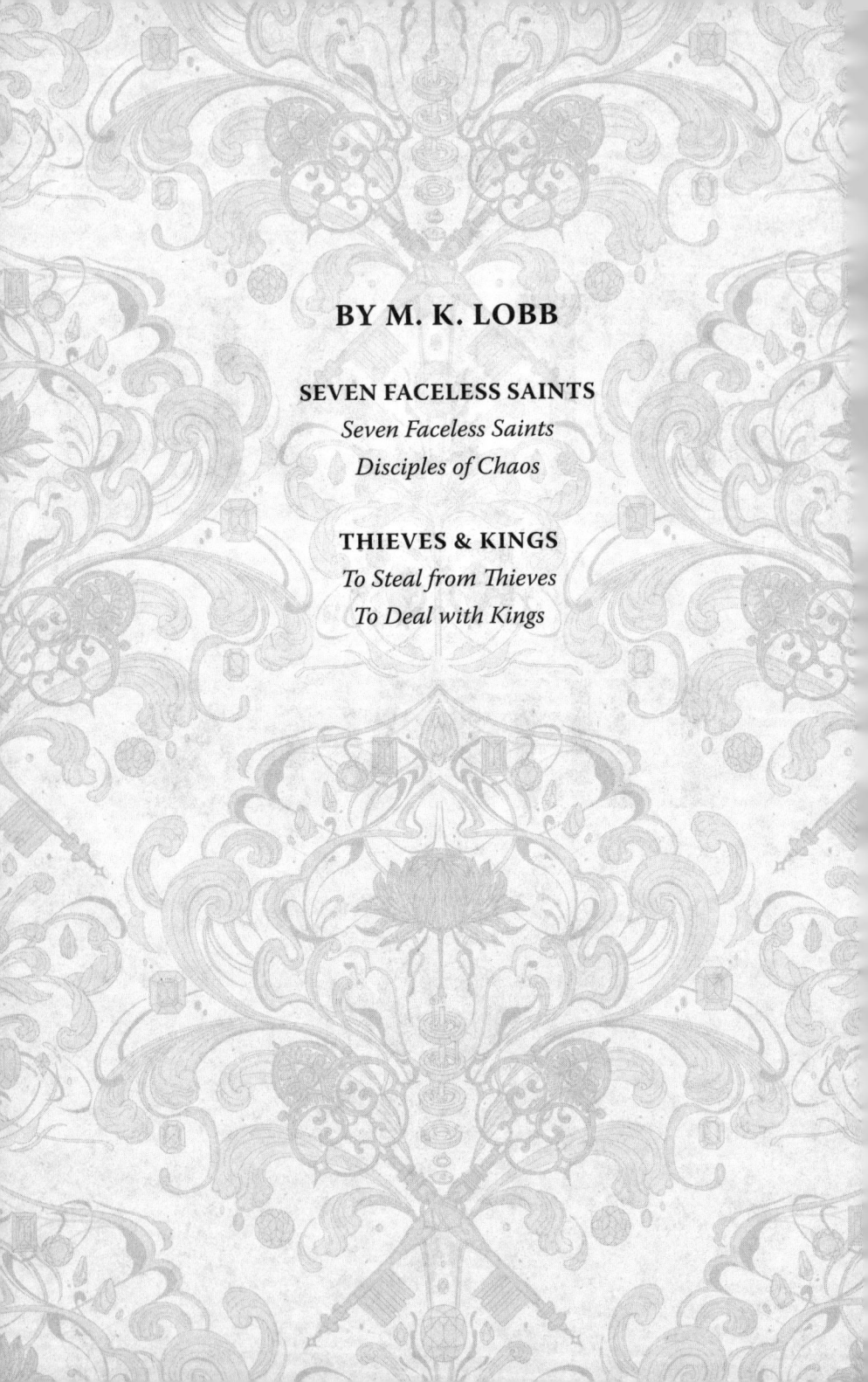

BY M. K. LOBB

SEVEN FACELESS SAINTS
Seven Faceless Saints
Disciples of Chaos

THIEVES & KINGS
To Steal from Thieves
To Deal with Kings

TO
STEAL
FROM
THIEVES

M. K. LOBB

LITTLE, BROWN AND COMPANY

New York   Boston

Little, Brown and Company
Hachette Book Group
1290 Avenue of the Americas, New York, NY 10104
Visit us at LBYR.com

Originally published in hardcover and ebook by Little, Brown and Company in March 2025
First Trade Paperback Edition: February 2026

Little, Brown and Company is a division of Hachette Book Group, Inc. The Little, Brown name and logo are registered trademarks of Hachette Book Group, Inc.

The publisher is not responsible for websites (or their content) that are not owned by the publisher.

Little, Brown and Company books may be purchased in bulk for business, educational, or promotional use. For information, please contact your local bookseller or the Hachette Book Group Special Markets Department at special.markets@hbgusa.com.

The Library of Congress has cataloged the hardcover edition as follows:
Names: Lobb, M. K., author.
Title: To steal from thieves / M. K. Lobb.
Description: First edition. | New York : Little, Brown and Company, 2025. | Audience: Ages 12 & up. | Summary: "A con man and a magical inventor join forces to rob the Great Exhibition in 1800s London, each determined not to benefit their partner in crime." —Provided by publisher.
Identifiers: LCCN 2024009124 | ISBN 9780316575485 (hardcover) | ISBN 9780316575508 (ebook)
Subjects: CYAC: Magic—Fiction. | Swindlers and swindling—Fiction. | Love-hate relationships—Fiction. | London (England)—History—19th century—Fiction. | Fantasy. | LCGFT: Fantasy fiction. | Novels.
Classification: LCC PZ7.1.L6224 To 2025 | DDC [Fic]—dc23
LC record available at https://lccn.loc.gov/2024009124

ISBNs: 978-0-316-57549-2 (trade paperback), 978-0-316-57550-8 (ebook)

Printed in Indiana, USA

LSC-C

Printing 1, 2025

*For anyone who has ever been willing
to risk it all*

ZARIA

ZARIA MENDOZA EMPTIED A VIAL OF BLOOD INTO THE FLAME. Rather than sputter out, the candle burned brighter, a column of orange stretching to the workshop's low ceiling. There was a sparkling quality to the illumination—a result of the soulsteel Zaria had added prior to the blood. The ashy powder still clung to her fingers, and a distinctive grit filled her mouth as the flame continued to burn. She focused on it with narrowed eyes, waiting for the transformation to occur.

Perhaps it was the late hour, but the reaction seemed more sluggish than usual. Zaria felt a single drop of perspiration track a line down her temple. There was no room for failure. Not when she'd left everything until the last minute.

As she had this thought, the candlelight appeared to condense, blood and powder melting into one. Relief shot through Zaria like a well-aimed arrow. She dropped heavily into her chair, grasping the tiny crimson shard that crystallized into existence the moment the flame flickered out.

Primateria. The physical embodiment of magic was warm to the touch as Zaria rolled the gemlike object between her fingers, eyeing its faint yet enduring glow. It was weak magic—limited magic—but that was the only form there was. Nonetheless, its creation always leached her strength. Exhaustion unfurled in Zaria's veins as the high faded, and for a moment, the world around her seemed a little less tangible.

Another tiny piece of herself gone, channeled into her work. Lapped up hungrily by the processes that made her creations what they were. It was the price you paid when magic was made, not inherent. Blood and soulsteel, soulsteel and blood.

Heart thumping in her ears, she turned to the revolver on her side table. Objectively, it was a beautiful thing: Its inner workings were visible through the intentional cracks in its alloy exterior, the cogs and gears moving like clockwork. She suspected it was sleeker than any gun the Metropolitan Police had in their possession, and stroked it fondly before prying open a hidden compartment and depositing the primateria. It clicked into position, embraced smoothly by the rest of the inner workings. Light flickered along the metal like tiny bolts of lightning—it was always enjoyable to watch magic force its way in—then settled. Zaria's stomach gave a satisfied lurch as her shoulders relaxed.

"Lovely," she murmured, and stepped back.

The revolver was not merely a weapon, but an entity of whirring parts and careful calculations. Alchemology—the creation of magical items—was a difficult study. One wrong measurement or maneuver could result in disaster. Despite its being a learned skill, some people were more innately capable of alchemology than others. It took years of practice. Of learning to retreat deep into your own mind while maintaining multiple threads of focus. Most people never achieved it at all.

Then again, few tried. Alchemology was illegal in Britain, considered an occult practice by Parliament and the monarchy. Even if it *had* been a respected trade, errors were common, and most practitioners either died or quit before they mastered it. As someone prone to making errors, Zaria was *very* careful with her work.

Her father, though, had commanded alchemology the way a skilled artist commanded a paintbrush. Itzal Mendoza's arrival in 1830s London saw him catapulted to the heights of dark market demand, and he'd taught his daughter everything he knew. He'd been forever frustrated by her lack of focus, her poor attention to detail, and her penchant for leaving things unfinished. When she *could* focus, though, she worked for hours at a time, neglecting all else in favor of her creation. With Itzal gone, it was how she made her living. But in a world where the inexplicable was considered satanic, the products of alchemology were only trafficable by certain channels.

Usually illegal ones.

Zaria traced the barrel of the gun with a finger. Her father had died last year, leaving her with nothing but dangerous knowledge and an absurd number of unfinished commissions. Commissions that *needed* to be seen through, because everyone knew how risky it was to disappoint a dark market client. She had no choice but to continue her father's work. Though she tried desperately to navigate the market the way Itzal had, she lacked his organization, his easy charm. His lingering reputation simply wasn't enough to bolster hers. Then, of course, there was the fact that men dabbling in criminal transactions didn't often trust a young woman. Not with magic, and certainly not with their money. But these were the slums, and Zaria tried to make it work. What other option did she have?

A light knock sounded on the doorframe, slicing the silence. Zaria turned, her attention immediately compromised. "Oh. Hi, Jules."

Framed by the entrance to her workshop was Julian Zhao, son of the pawnbroker who owned the building. He was also her closest friend. Zaria wasn't great at friends. She tended to approach people the same way she did alcohol: She kept them around while they were fun and shoved them out of sight when they gave her a headache.

But Jules was an exception. He couldn't be shoved out of sight, though his slight stature might have suggested otherwise. With a shock of black hair turned brassy by the candlelight, he might as well have been part of the house itself.

"Your twelve o'clock is here," Jules said slyly, thrusting his shoulders back as if to mimic a high-society butler. "Two of them. They're waiting for you in my father's office."

Exhilaration surged through Zaria's veins. She blew out the last candles in her workshop, casting the blueprints papering the walls into darkness. "It's never just one, is it?"

Then she strode across the dirt floor toward Jules, the scent of smoke thick in her nostrils. He moved aside to let her emerge into the dusty hallway that connected the pawnshop with the rest of the tiny brick house. It was far from a charming property, but compared to the rest of the slum, it may as well have been a manor. Of course, operating a business in this area also meant you owed a weekly debt to the kingpin for his crew's protection—whether you wanted it or not.

"Don't look so nervous," Jules said archly. "Think of the money."

Zaria raised her eyebrows. She knew she didn't look nervous, even if her stomach was in knots. She was wearing what Jules called her *business face*—which was to say, no expression at all. She was good at putting on whatever mask served her best. If anyone looked apprehensive, it was Jules. He was a twitchy sort of creature, his emotions presenting themselves in flashes that disappeared as quickly as they came.

"I'd like more money than they're going to offer," Zaria said bitterly, and Jules gave a thin-lipped smile.

"You'd like more money than you could carry."

Who wouldn't, Zaria wondered, in a place like this? When the nights were cold and people were forced most months to choose between food and rent?

"Enough money to fill a man's pockets and drown him."

"I can think of worse ways to go," Jules said.

Zaria couldn't argue with that. "Your father's not around, is he?" she asked as they ascended the crumbling staircase. She could hear the tightness in her voice and made an effort to shove her nerves further down. Her head still spun with the painful sensation that always followed the creation of primateria, and she squeezed her eyes shut. When she blinked them open again, the world righted itself, though a low throb still pulsed at the base of her skull.

"He had business on Drury Lane. Why?"

"It'd be awkward if he found me doing dark market dealings in his office, now wouldn't it?"

Jules gave a soft laugh devoid of humor. "Perhaps. But it's not as though his hands are clean."

That was true. After all, George Zhao ran a pawnshop in the heart of a London slum; he couldn't very well be expected to have a strong

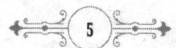

moral compass. He did what it took, and Zaria didn't begrudge him that. If you ever ceased trying to claw your way up in society, you'd be trampled in a heartbeat.

Jules caught up with her as she rounded the corner at the end of the hallway. The flickering candlelight lit his angular face in a strange way as he forced Zaria to hold his gaze. His dark eyes were made for seeing through falsities. "Are you sure you don't want me in there with you? They'll have guns."

"And if they want another one, they won't shoot me. I'll be fine."

In this part of London, women didn't have the luxury of relying on people to do things for them. If their husbands weren't dead from disease, then they were neck deep in drink or else slinking off to some brothel. Zaria Mendoza made her own deals, and she would see them through.

Jules spread his hands in good-natured surrender. "All right. Well, scream if anything goes wrong."

"If you hear screaming," Zaria said, "I assure you it won't be coming from me."

She watched with some measure of disconnect as Jules disappeared back down the stairs, then glanced down at her cracked pocket watch. Twelve-fifteen in the morning. Her meeting was supposed to have been at midnight, which meant she'd kept them waiting long enough so as to be fashionably late. She took a steadying breath. It had been so much easier when her father was alive. Not only because his commissions kept them afloat in the grime-encrusted belly of the slum, but also because he'd been the one to do the actual transactions. No matter how many times Zaria met with a client—or one of their hired grunts—she felt inadequate somehow. They always looked at her with confusion or distrust. As if her appearance would somehow impact the quality of her work.

Luckily, her work had gotten far better over the years. So she endured the gibes, the sideways glances, the far-too-low offers. Word of mouth was how any dark market vendor built a reputation, so satisfaction was crucial. If that meant accepting less money for the time being, then fine. She simply needed to be patient. The right deal would come along, and once she'd fulfilled all her father's commissions, perhaps she could be free.

Besides, things were already looking up. Tonight, her buyer was one of the most powerful men on this side of London.

Zaria took a deep breath. Then she shook her hair back, stood up straight, and shoved open the door at the end of the hall.

She sauntered into George Zhao's office, ignoring the two men who hovered on the far side of the room. It was always vaguely embarrassing to meet here, where her patrons could see the walls stained by water damage and the items cluttering every available surface. Where they might notice how much dirt caked the floor no matter how often Jules tried to sweep it aside.

But what mattered most in transactions like these was how you presented yourself. So Zaria stalked over to the chair behind the desk, sank into it, and propped her feet up. Only then did she make eye contact, forcing an expectant kind of confidence onto her face. "Evening, gentlemen."

Now that she had deigned to look directly at them, she examined the men with interest. Both were tall and dark haired, though not in a way that made her suspect they were related. The older of the two was balding, with an angry face and thick eyebrows. The younger had a sharp jaw and straight nose, his expression bemused. They were clad in all black, their trousers and overcoats made of thick linens. Those who risked their necks to deal on behalf of the rich—provided they didn't steal anything—were well compensated. And if they *did* steal something, it wasn't difficult to find someone else willing to hunt them down.

Zaria leaned back in her cushioned chair, positioning the revolver wordlessly on the desk.

The older man grunted. "Is that it?"

"Yes."

He started forward, eyes narrowed in distrust. "Looks more or less like a regular firearm."

Zaria raised a brow, and even the younger man shot his companion a disdainful glance. The expression looked comfortable on him, complementing his high collar and the vaguely amused curve of his mouth. If trouble wore a face, Zaria thought, it was undoubtedly that of the boy before her.

"That's the point." She drew out the words as if speaking to a fool. "Unless you wanted to draw questions from the coppers, I suggest you thank me for my ingenuity."

The man's face reddened.

"Relax, Larkin," the younger man drawled. To Zaria, he added, "Show us."

Zaria shrugged, taking the gun in one hand. The thing about her style of revolver was this: It wasn't a revolver at all. You didn't have to go through the inconvenient, menial task of loading it every time you fired more than a few shots. The cylinder spun as it should, but that was merely for show. Her guns didn't fire bullets; they fired magic.

Real magic was nothing like the stories described it—its sole use was manipulation. As long as you had the right tools and materials, you could use primateria to modify an object's purpose into one that should otherwise be impossible. Simple, more common examples included perpetually burning lamps and unbreakable glass, but the dark market wasn't concerned with items like that. People wanted *weapons.* So that was what Zaria made, because anything she didn't get paid for was a waste of energy.

She pointed the revolver lazily at a thick panel of wood leaning against the wall—already riddled with holes from prior demonstrations—and pulled the trigger.

The gears whirled as light flashed from the barrel of the gun, leaving a barely visible shimmer in its wake that hung in the air, filling the space with a lightly acrid smell. There, in the panel across the room, was a fresh hole. Magic fired from a gun ate away at material in the same way a highly concentrated acid might. It worked faster, though. Much faster.

And unlike bullets, magic left no trace.

Zaria turned back to her audience expectantly. The younger man tipped his head back and laughed; there was something sharp about the sound. He ambled over to the wooden slab, dragging a finger over the new indent. Dark eyes found hers across the room.

"It's not very big."

Now it was Zaria's turn to laugh, long and low in her stomach. "That a line you hear a lot?"

His brows lifted, though he continued to look more amused than anything else.

"*Kane,*" Larkin said chidingly, making the single syllable a long-suffering sound before addressing Zaria. "Fifteen shillings."

Anything below three pounds struck her as an insult, but Zaria knew how to play this game. She didn't respond, only let out a small laugh as she crossed her ankles on the desk. Her blood raced in the silence that followed. Their opinions didn't matter; all she needed was for the gun to make it back to their boss, who *would* be impressed.

Larkin huffed. "Fine. A pound."

She kept waiting.

"Two."

Zaria dropped her feet back to the floor, sliding the chair forward to fix the duo with the full weight of her glare. "Does Lord Saville want this or not? If he can't afford it, then get out of my house." She scoffed. "Because I feel sorry for you, I'll settle for three pounds."

This time Larkin laughed, and Zaria did not.

"You don't quite understand what I have here, do you?" she said. "You must be new to dark market paraphernalia. This is a weapon like nothing you've ever seen. It never needs loading, will never rust. It puts other market revolvers to shame. Hell, it'll put the inventions in the Great Exhibition to shame."

"How does a girl like you know what'll be in the Great Exhibition?" Larkin said, his voice dripping derision.

"A girl like me always does her homework." Besides, it was hard to miss the gossip. The docks were filled with ships as of late, each one supposedly delivering impressive feats of art and technology from all over the world to be displayed in London's Crystal Palace. With them came slews of patrons who rarely talked about anything else. It was driving Zaria rather mad, though the rest of the city seemed abuzz with excitement. She suspected that had to do with the ongoing publicity campaign—the event had been continually redefined through posters, press releases, and handouts until the public response turned more favorable. Zaria wasn't so easily convinced, suspecting it an excuse for British industries to flaunt their success.

"And you think you can compete with professional inventors, do you?"

She refocused on Larkin. "Yes."

He grunted. "Two's the final offer."

Zaria crossed her arms. At the same time, something twisted

deep in the pit of her stomach. "Don't pretend your boss isn't prepared to pay for it. He knew full well what it was going to cost. I'll give you three seconds to accept my offer, or I'm going to find someone willing to pay double. Trust me—it won't be hard." She held up three fingers, then flicked one down. "Two seconds."

Larkin looked furious, though the younger man—Kane—quirked his mouth. He was handsome, Zaria conceded to herself, though in the way of someone fully aware of it.

"One." She stood as if to leave. The tension in the air was palpable, but she let it wash over her. She didn't have another buyer, but they didn't know that. What did it matter? She had the upper hand. She'd grasped it with ease.

"Good evening, gentlemen." She gave them a curt salute.

Larkin slammed three pounds onto the desk.

She scooped the coins up lightning quick, tossing him the revolver in return. "Nice doing business with you. Oh," she added as the pair made for the door, "and don't get caught with that."

Larkin thrust the gun at Kane, who handled it with the caution one might show a newborn baby. Zaria watched them go. They could find their way out alone.

She collapsed back into the chair, money clutched between her fingers, and let her forehead rest against the cool surface of the desk. The world spun behind her closed eyelids. How much longer would she be able to do this? She needed to make a living, and the dark market allowed her to do what she did best. But alchemology had a cost—or, rather, the creation of primateria did. It *took* from a person. Zaria had seen that much firsthand.

Her father had died after giving too much of himself to his craft. Zaria had been forced to watch him wither away, his skin turning paper-thin, his face desiccating into a skeletal likeness of the man she'd known. Yet even as he'd drawn his last breath, he hadn't believed his love of alchemology was killing him. Denial had been his downfall.

Zaria still had time. She was barely eighteen. But creating magic was like a drug, and the more she did it, the faster she would burn out. There was a reason people didn't commit to a life like this. And what did she have to show for it?

Three pounds. Three pounds wasn't enough. Not when rent was due and alchemology supplies cost nearly as much as a finished product. She had promised Jules they'd leave this place—that he wouldn't have to waste away like his father, relying on the desperation of others, on the come and go of clients on redemption day.

There was no life to be had in the London slums.

Either you died here, or you got the hell out.

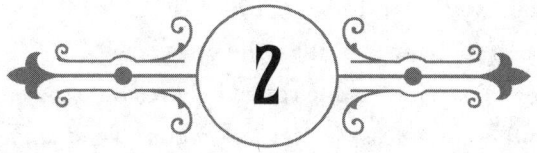

KANE

KANE DURANTE WAS TIRED OF LARKIN'S COMPANY. HE'D SPENT days with the man, conducting dark market business like a hired grunt, yet he hadn't learned anything useful. Frustration and impatience formed a poisonous concoction in his veins as he tossed the revolver from one hand to the other, marveling at its lightness. Unlike every other magical firearm he'd seen, it was sleeker, quieter, and if Kane wasn't mistaken, more deadly accurate.

Magic wasn't harmful by default, but it could certainly be made that way. Once laws forbidding alchemology had pushed practitioners into the shadows, the dark market had snapped them up, and now magic was all but synonymous with destruction. That's the way it had been for centuries, and he couldn't see things changing anytime soon.

For his part, Kane had never attempted to create magic. If you wanted to actually *do* anything with it, you had to understand mechanics and chemistry, physics and mathematics, and his smarts were more of the street sort.

"Put that away," Larkin said, a hiss that sliced the night. "You heard what she said. Besides, if Saville saw you—"

"No one will see me." Kane rolled his eyes but stowed the gun in his waistband nonetheless. "As far as I'm concerned, once we deliver it, Saville can shove it firmly up his—"

"*Kane.*"

Kane gave an easy smile, if a little impish. Larkin was a large man, all broad shoulders with an expression to frighten children, but he wasn't the fool Kane had hoped for. Rarely did he reveal anything of use.

"You'd best watch your mouth, Hunt," Larkin growled, saying Kane's false surname with all the confidence of someone who didn't know it was false. "If Saville heard you talking this way, he'd have your body in the sewers with a knife in the throat."

"Your loyalty to Saville is truly admirable." In fact, it was getting on Kane's nerves.

Larkin snorted. "What do you know about loyalty? You've been working for him for—what? Five minutes?"

"Five *days*," Kane grumbled. Five whole days, and he was no closer to finding the necklace. It was meant to be arriving on a ship from Ireland soon, then to be displayed in the Exhibition in two weeks' time. The event had been advertised for months now by posters proclaiming THE GREAT EXHIBITION OF ALL NATIONS—1ST MAY, 1851! Once the necklace was in the public eye, stealing it would be next to impossible. Kane needed to work fast. If he failed, Saville would be the least of his worries.

It shouldn't have been difficult. All Kane needed to know was which ship the necklace would be on and when it was arriving. Since Saville's company oversaw the city docks, Saville was the perfect mark. It had been easy enough to get hired by the lord, but labor at the riverbank had quickly turned to less savory deeds. They weren't something Kane was unused to, but running dark market errands gave him less time to keep an eye on the river. Less time to search Saville's numerous offices or manipulate his other employees into talking. All Kane really needed was a schedule—a ledger—*something*. But Larkin, Saville's longtime grunt, either didn't know shit or was careful not to let anything slip no matter how many times Kane manipulated the conversation to that end.

And right now, Larkin's eyes were a warning. "He won't keep you if he finds out you're talking like that."

"Who's gonna tell him?" Kane goaded. "You?"

"I ain't no snitch, but not everyone's as nice as me."

Kane made a sound in the back of his throat. Larkin may not have *been* a rat, but he was about as nice as one. He said nothing, though, as they made their silent way down the street. The cobblestones were lined with shallow trenches carrying vile liquid matter to the cesspools, and one had to swerve every so often to avoid horse dung or buckets of human piss tossed from windows. London's rich could afford brass piping and shower basins, but the only clean water here came from a single standpipe in each building. This particular slum was known as Devil's Acre. It was a place for criminals, and for people so poor their morals had long since fled.

It was also the place they were to meet Lord Saville's messenger, who would give them money if they showed up and put a price on their heads if they didn't.

Or, at least, so the rumors went.

Kane preferred to avoid Devil's Acre at all costs. No matter the season or time of day, the area was wet, loud, and generally gag inducing. Unsupervised youths went barefoot as they slunk between the crowded rows of terraced housing, and the overall state of *filth*

was indescribable. If death could be a physical place, it was undoubtedly Devil's Acre. Even being here for a short time was nauseating, and Kane set his teeth as he averted the sunken gazes of its unhoused occupants, a pit forming in his stomach.

The sulfurous stench was overwhelming as he followed Larkin down an alleyway, fighting the urge to cover his nose. The slum was a good place to conduct business, though, if only because the coppers had long since given up trying to force it into any semblance of order. The dark pressed in alongside the ammonia-stained buildings, which became tighter and more uniform. A beggar flung himself at Larkin's feet, murmuring something about coin and blessings, and Larkin kicked him away.

"Can't get nowhere around here," Larkin said as Kane's hand twitched to the knife in his waistband. "Not without being accosted by scum or guttersnipes, anyway."

Kane wasn't sure he shared the sentiment, but he could admit the desperately poor were sometimes vicious. He sidestepped a second man with a dirt-encrusted hat, scanning the shadowy street. "Where is he?"

Larkin shrugged. "We were late meeting the girl. He should've arrived before us."

The alchemologist. Though he was aware of Mendoza's reputation, it was the first time Kane'd had any dealings with her. He was still reeling from both the quality of her work and her obvious youth. He'd been picturing an older woman, not one on the cusp of adulthood. It was her overall presence, though, that had struck him most. Slim but somehow imposing. Mousy brown hair and a face like a predator, calculating and fierce. A little hungry.

Kane wondered what, exactly, she was hungry for.

Larkin rumbled, "There he is," and Kane glanced up to see Fletcher Collins slink around the corner like the snake he was.

Kane knew from experience that rich lords tended to put their trust in one of two types of men: the charming, self-important bastard or the dangerous gentleman with no time for good humor. Kane played the first type, Fletcher the second. It had quickly become clear Saville preferred the latter, so Kane's fellow con man had ended up in the role of confidante. No matter how hard Fletcher tried, however, he hadn't been able to get Saville to divulge anything of import. And now Kane was wasting time fetching dark market weapons, of all things.

He did enough of that as Kane Durante. It was rather tiring to do it as Kane Hunt, too.

"Did you get it?" Fletcher said by way of greeting. He was blond with high cheekbones, his speech stilted to cover his Irish accent. It was a far more believable act than it had been when he and Kane were younger. When they'd pulled cons simply because they'd wanted to.

Things were different now. That was the way it was, Kane supposed, when you were the adopted son of the most feared man in Devil's Acre. When you were the most loved, trusted, and depended upon of his circle.

But being loved by Alexander Ward, kingpin of the dark market, was like trying to escape the jaws of a wolf. A constant struggle and one you couldn't possibly win. So you were forced to wait, poised among the teeth, until eventually you learned to use your own.

"Of course we got it." Kane pulled the revolver from his waistband with a wink. "What are you going to give us for it?"

Larkin's eyes bulged, but Fletcher ignored the barb. "The real question is, what did you end up giving her?"

"Three."

There was a pause as Fletcher digested that. "Seems like a lot."

"Saville gave us five," Larkin pointed out. He'd made no secret of his disdain for Fletcher, and frankly Kane couldn't blame him. Fletcher had gained Saville's favor with inexplicable speed while Larkin was still a glorified errand boy. Much to Kane's chagrin, Fletcher had been summoned away from the docks almost immediately. He supposed it was penance for having the build of a bodyguard and the poker face of a politician.

"Besides," Larkin went on, "Mendoza was being difficult. Said she could sell it for twice as much if we didn't accept."

"That's what everyone selling something says," Fletcher snapped. He snatched the revolver from Kane's hands. "You two are fools."

"You don't need brains to do someone else's business" was Kane's smooth retort. "We got it, didn't we? And it's the best of its kind, at least from what I've seen. I'll eat my hat if Saville isn't proper chuffed."

Larkin's face was wary, and Kane didn't blame him. With his impassive eyes and sharp tongue, Fletcher put on an intimidating act. You never knew he was angry until his fist was already in your mouth.

Kane had a decent punch, but he had an even better smile, so he tended to use that more. He flashed it now, purely in a show of annoying his friend.

Fletcher glowered. "You each get five shillings."

"*Five* shillings?" Kane repeated the words with mock incredulity but accepted the money. The little pouch was heavy, linen-smothered shillings rolling over his fingertips. Larkin opened his and peered inside, but Kane slipped the coins into his pocket without hesitation.

Fletcher arched a brow. "You're not going to count it?"

"I trust you."

Fletcher's mouth twisted to hide his amusement. A few raindrops had begun to spatter their heads, and Larkin turned up the collar of his frock coat.

"We're done here. Kane, go back to whatever hole you crawled up out of."

"Until next time," Fletcher agreed.

With a salute in Larkin's direction, Kane slipped into the shadows, resigned to making the walk alone while Fletcher went to hand off the revolver. His detour took him past the Romney Street pub, where he often found patrons passed out in the gutters. This usually afforded Kane the opportunity to pluck their knives and what little money they had on their person. Tonight, though, the only men outside were a too-sober pair who watched him pass with more suspicion than he felt was warranted.

If they knew who he was, perhaps they'd avert their gazes. *Ward's golden boy*, they might murmur to each other once he'd passed. *Touch him and you'll lose your hand.*

But Kane took care with his identity. After all, no matter how many names he donned, he couldn't help the fact that he wore the same face. Best to be recognizable to as few as possible.

Patrons stumbled out of the pub, circumventing him with loud guffaws, and that was enough to convince Kane there was nothing here for him. Not tonight. He wasn't in the mood for alcohol accompanied by conversation or girls grasping at his sleeves and lapels. He didn't care to lose himself in a smoky haze surrounded by strangers.

Instead, he made his way toward the docks. The streets of the slum gave way to factories, which in turn gave way to abandoned warehouses with smashed-in windows. The air tasted like gravel dust and reeked of the tainted river. It was a miserable place, especially when the overhead moon was shrouded by fog and factory fumes. Which, Kane thought wryly, was much of the time.

That said, it was familiar in its misery. The air rang with the distant hollers of the dockers and the accompanying thuds of crated cargo being heaved from ship to shore or vice versa. The port was always busy, but it was positively packed with steamships as the Exhibition drew nearer, delivering people and exhibits and all manner of goods. It seemed to Kane that London's population doubled daily, especially with the new rail lines leading into the city. It was driving him mad. Everywhere he turned he was reminded of his task, and how little time he had left before the necklace wound up in the Crystal Palace.

Kane made a concerted effort to avoid the riverbank, opting instead to duck down a narrow alley that widened a short time later at the entrance to an abandoned factory. Painted white letters above the door declared it MOORE & SONS, though time had left the words faded and barely legible. Kane shouldered the door open, momentarily obscuring the arrow carved into the wood. The crude symbol matched the tattoo on his neck in shape if not starkness. As he entered, he unconsciously brushed his fingers over the skin there, feeling the slight ridge where it hadn't healed smoothly.

I am the archer, and my men are my arrows, Ward was fond of saying. *It's an honor to win my trust, Kane. And you barely had to fight for it, did you?*

It never felt like a compliment, nor something to be proud of. It always felt like a threat. Being part of Ward's crew was an honor. It brought you safety. Power. It brought you dark market connections, a place to live if you were lucky, and protection from the law.

But it also brought you Ward.

"There you are." Fletcher's voice echoed from the other end of the room. The floor of the abandoned factory had been converted into something of a living area, despite the telltale lofty ceilings and posts set at odd intervals in the middle of the space. A coal stove burned in one of the corners, its elaborate iron grate the focal point.

Kane crossed to where Fletcher lounged in a shabby armchair, all ease and impassivity. Despite the chill, his friend had removed his collared waistcoat, and one index finger skillfully twirled a silk hat.

"How did you get here before me?" Kane demanded.

"The good Lord granted me speed," was Fletcher's wry response. His Irish accent was back, drawling and playful.

"You mean Saville? Or you talking about God?"

Fletcher grinned, and Kane knew that if the good Lord saw it fit to grant either of them anything at all, it would be a one-way ticket to hell.

"I'm only joking. I passed off the revolver pretty quickly—Harrison was closer than I'd thought."

"Ah." Kane recognized the name as belonging to another of Saville's confidantes. There was a short lull as he got to his feet, then poured two glasses of whiskey and set one in front of Fletcher. The alcohol burned his throat in a way he never particularly enjoyed, though something about the sensation relaxed him. Perhaps it was the promise of eventual inebriation.

"Cheers," Fletcher said, then sighed. "I still haven't learned anything about the damned boat, nor when it's expected to arrive. The only time I've been in Saville's office at the docks was when he was with me. And every ship already in the harbor looks the same."

Kane nodded. He'd expected as much.

"Larkin and the other men don't seem to like me," Fletcher continued. "I was at Saville's Piccadilly house yesterday and convinced one of the maids to talk to me, but she didn't let anything slip." He cast his gaze at the ceiling, taking a long swig of whiskey. "Maybe I should offer to work as a maid instead. No one pays attention to them."

"You *would* look fantastic in an apron."

Fletcher swatted Kane's knee. "What does Ward want with this necklace, anyway? If it's because of the dark market resale value, there are easier things to steal."

Kane grimaced. How was he to know what went on in Ward's mind? His demands were endless, often dangerous, and failure meant dire consequences. Although Kane didn't think Ward would ever *kill* him, that didn't mean the kingpin couldn't hurt him in other ways. Fletcher-shaped ways, specifically.

Kane collapsed into the chair across from his friend, trying to ignore the deepening pit in his stomach. "Ward doesn't tell me things like that."

Not anymore. The older Kane got, the harder he fought against Ward's demands, until the two of them had become engaged in an ongoing, relentless power struggle. He could never escape, though. It simply wasn't an option. The kingpin would find Kane wherever he went, and in any case, Kane wasn't sure he wanted to leave. Ward was the only family he'd had in years. The only parent he could remember clearly.

He hated the man, yet he needed him. He longed to impress Ward almost as much as he longed to kill him.

So Kane stayed, which meant Fletcher stayed as well. It was a fact that rendered Kane both relieved and paranoid. Fletcher was the one thing he couldn't bear to lose. They'd been inseparable as brothers since the day Kane brought him into Ward's crew five years ago, Fletcher then a homeless youth sent to London to escape the Irish famine. Ward quickly made it clear he had no love for Fletcher—not least because of his distaste for Catholics—but he let him stay nonetheless. At the time, Kane had thought it a kindness. Only in recent years had he come to understand the truth.

Fletcher was the perfect way for Ward to ensure Kane played nicely. He was unending leverage.

And Kane could never, ever tell him as much.

"Ah, well," Fletcher said, shaking Kane from his thoughts. "Tomorrow's a new day, and the Exhibition's in just under two weeks. If we're lucky, Saville might get us to help with the preparations. No way the Royal Commission is doing everything alone."

Kane took another swallow of whiskey. The back of his throat had gone numb to the burning. "I can't imagine he'd get us to help with something like that. For all intents and purposes, we're hired hands. Dark market runners. I say we head to the main port tomorrow and see if we can learn anything for ourselves. Maybe some of the dockers will have information."

Fletcher inclined his chin. "Good idea. I don't much fancy having to steal the necklace once it's on display in the Crystal Palace."

"Don't even say that." The prospect already gnawed incessantly at him, such that Kane had begun to plan heists in his sleep. He closed his eyes and saw prison; he opened them and saw Ward. He wasn't sure which was worse.

"At least it's small. I heard one of the main exhibits is some kind of telescope, and that it's as long as three men lined up head to toe. Can you imagine trying to steal such a thing?"

Kane managed a wry smile. It hurt his face. "I wouldn't put it past Ward to ask."

"Relax." Fletcher refilled both their glasses, easily interpreting Kane's expression. "We'll get that godforsaken necklace. There's nothing Kane Durante and Fletcher Collins can't steal."

His stoic confidence was contagious as he used their real surnames, and Kane drained his drink in a single swallow.

"You'd better be right about that."

3

ZARIA

ZARIA SAT ALONE IN HER WORKSHOP, A VIAL OF BLACK LIQUID rolling lazily across the table.

Six candles illuminated the space, flickering unevenly as she lit a seventh. This one she set before her, bowing her head until she felt heat on her face, a stinging caress. Using an eyedropper, she transferred the black solution into the flame. Aleuite, the substance was called. Once heated, it could be bonded to create a number of different alchemological compounds. Tonight she would use it to create a magical explosive. It was one of two dozen outstanding commissions that required her attention, and the sooner it came together, the sooner she got paid. Over half of the money from the revolver had already gone to George Zhao. Zaria owed him more rent than she cared to remember.

The thought made her cheeks burn. George let her stay here out of lingering respect for Itzal, but Zaria knew her presence frustrated him. She wasn't a gambler the way Itzal had been, but given the soaring prices of alchemological supplies—and her woeful inability to keep track of payment dates—she was scarcely any better where her finances were concerned.

Zaria shook the thoughts away. Her aleuite was ready; she only needed the primateria. She took the last of her soulsteel in trembling fingers, already craving and dreading the ache of creation in her bones. The powder dissipated upon touching the flame, which turned a more vivid orange, burning valiantly ever higher. She extinguished the rest of the candles in the room. Immediately, the darkness made the scent of must and ash seem heavier. It smelled like her childhood. Like hovering by Itzal's worktable, watching in awe as her father's deft fingers shaped wood and steel. Like his accented voice in her ear, muttering a warning that never managed to dissuade her.

The tendril of flame appeared to undulate instead of flicker—an indication that everything was ready. Her vial of blood was empty, so she took a knife to the fleshy part of her thumb, wincing as the sharp tip coaxed beads of crimson to the surface. She let them drip into the flame in a slow trickle. Then she closed her eyes and retreated deep, deep into herself. Into her mind.

Real magic lived inside of you. You only needed to know how to access it. That was the reason alchemology was outlawed—people believed primateria was created using bits of one's soul and that was why the process weakened them over time.

The first person to discover primateria had done so accidentally. A man named Philippus Hohenheim uncovered the magical properties of soulsteel more than three hundred years ago while attempting to use it for medicinal purposes. He'd hoped combining it with his blood would cause a sort of transmutation to happen, resulting in a universal solvent. Instead—according to his writings—he felt

something wrenched from his very soul. He devoted several years to experimenting with his findings, but once the papacy was informed, the practice rapidly became forbidden across Europe.

That was Zaria's favorite thing about alchemology—there was always more to learn. You couldn't simply insert primateria into something and hope a change took place. No, you had to know *exactly* how you wanted the magic to interact with the mechanism surrounding it. Technical knowledge was a crucial prerequisite, since you needed to understand the inner workings of...well, everything. More difficult—at least for Zaria—was focusing on these planned interactions while you attempted to dredge the magic up from your own depths. It was a meditative sort of thing, and she'd never been very good at narrowing her thoughts.

It wasn't Itzal who had eventually guided her to success. He hadn't the patience to repeat instructions as often as she required. Instead, it was his temporary assistant, Cecile Meurdrac, who had explained the process in a way that eight-year-old Zaria could wrap her mind around. Cecile had been a woman of few words, but she was gentle where Itzal was abrupt. Tolerant where he grew increasingly exasperated.

You will know when you find it. Cecile's soft voice echoed in Zaria's thoughts. *It is not an image, not something you can deliberately conjure up, but a feeling. Something your unconscious mind will come across if only you keep searching.*

She found it more easily these days. It had taken years, and far too many impatient tantrums, but eventually she recognized the path to magic. It was there if only you knew where to look.

Breath slowing, Zaria imagined the complex chemical interactions that would take place in the aleuite explosive. There was a jolt like a skipped heartbeat, and her focus narrowed to a single point.

What followed was strange, blissful relief. It was a stomach-plummeting, heart-clenching, throat-tightening sensation. For a fleeting moment, there was only the feeling she had come to know as *magic*. Nothing else was important. Zaria wondered, not for the first time, if this was what the men who frequented the opium dens were chasing. If they yearned to be lost the way she did. But their endeavor was a pointless one—there was nothing to be achieved from it. She, on the other hand, was creating.

Suddenly, there was lightness, both of sensation and color.

She extended her mind, reaching for that light, continuing to push. It was like trying to topple a wall of stone with a single finger, but she needed only to find the weak point. When she did, it seemed an infinite rush.

Zaria gasped, lurching forward. Her vision cleared, and each breath was a shudder. The candle flame was a wisp of dead smoke. But there, within a cooling divot of wax, was a glittering, crystal-like red object.

Light is found in the depths of the human psyche, Cecile had told her. *Descend into your own mind. Only when you go deep enough can the vital force of the universe—the one that makes up your soul, your energy—be projected into matter. Into magic.*

All at once, the euphoria was replaced by nausea. Zaria's head spun with a horrid ferocity, and she bucked sideways in her chair as she upended the meager contents of her stomach onto the floor.

She supposed this was what she got for creating magic two days in a row. Was this what her father had wanted for her? The same bitter thought unfurled in Zaria's mind as she rested her sweaty cheek against the table, heartbeat throbbing dully in her ears. How could Itzal *leave* her like this? He'd known he was dying and had set her up to follow the same sorry path all the same. He'd gambled his savings

away, leaving her alone and destitute, and saddled her with the work he'd left behind.

When making primateria finally killed her, she'd track him down in hell.

"Ah. I see you've reached the stage of vomit and self-loathing."

A voice sounded from the door, and Zaria didn't have to look to know it was Jules. Without lifting her head from the cool tabletop, she said, "I am begging you to shut up."

His footsteps drew closer. A heartbeat later, his face entered her field of vision, sideways and flush with concern. He set a glass of water down with a *clunk*. Zaria considered it as she breathed in, then out. The idea of picking it up seemed like far too much effort just now. She could feel what the magic had cost, as if some tiny, crucial piece of herself was missing, another fragment sliced away.

"Is that an explosive?"

Jules's voice was at her ear, tense and bordering on irate. Zaria removed her magnispecs and shot him a withering look.

"Well, yes, but it's not explosive *yet*. Relax, would you?"

"I will not," Jules said, eyeing the mess before her. He picked up a particularly ugly clock, examining it in disdain. "Did you nick this from the shop?"

Zaria plucked the clock from his hands. It didn't appear to be working, but the parts were in decent shape. "Maybe. Do you think your father will notice?"

"Yes. He keeps a log, and you know that, so get that scheming look off your face."

"I am not *scheming*. The thing doesn't even work."

"Put it back."

She grunted, conceding. "Fine."

"What type of bomb is this, anyway?"

"The type that only destroys live tissue."

Jules grimaced. "That's the worst kind."

"Yeah, well, I'm not playing morality police. Crowley is growing impatient, as you well know." Zaria referenced one of her father's former clients with a sigh. Just last week, he'd sent his lackey along with the warning that the next time he saw her without the explosive in hand, he'd break both of hers. "And he's not the only one, but I've just used the last of my soulsteel."

"Shit."

"Shit," Zaria agreed, using the desk to push herself up. Her hands vibrated against the wood, and she squeezed her fists tightly, hoping Jules wouldn't notice.

It was a futile hope. His eyes snapped downward, lips clamping together to form a tight line. "Maybe you should stop for a while."

"Stop what?"

"You know what. Do you really want to end up like your father?"

Zaria didn't want to have this conversation again. It had been a while since Jules last suggested she cease practicing alchemology, but her frustration surrounding the topic hadn't diminished. So what if her mouth was still bone-dry and the back of her throat tasted like bile? Apart from Jules, magic was all she had. If she suddenly quit, who knew when the kingpin—who ensured the terms of dark market deals were adhered to—would darken the pawnshop's doorstep?

What she needed was a primateria source. Though the price and availability of soulsteel was prohibitive enough, Zaria's more pressing concern was the toll creating primateria took on her health. She didn't want to die the way her father had: drained, weak, and with little to show for her efforts.

There was a theory that Hohenheim had created three sources of magic before his death, desperate for his discovery to live on after

his passing. In fact, many alchemologists believed that this was what had killed him. Despite Itzal's wholehearted belief in the sources, Zaria had always been skeptical. Her father had spent years trying to track one down and never came across anything of note. Eventually, his obsession had faded to acceptance, and one fateful night he'd destroyed all his research in a rage.

Now, years too late, Zaria understood his feverish hope. She had dozens of commissions to fulfill, and they were pulling life from her faster than she could create them. If she could create magic without drawing from her own energy, it would change everything.

"I can't just *stop*," she told Jules, injecting all her frustration into the words. "I owe your father money. I promised you I'd get us out of Devil's Acre. Would you rather I take up a job in a factory making a shilling a week? Do you want my clients to keep knocking at our door?"

"My father might be more understanding than you think."

"We both know he doesn't like me. Besides, he can't be understanding if he's dead."

Jules crossed his arms. "And what if *you're* dead, Zaria? How the hell does that help either of us?"

It didn't, of course. "That's a risk I have to take. You know full well there's no other option."

"We could just…run. Go anywhere else, even if we don't have a plan."

"With no jobs, no money, and no clientele base? Are you prepared to leave your father on his own, vulnerable to whoever comes here searching for me?"

Jules sank heavily onto Zaria's bed, and she knew that she had him. It brought her no joy.

"I'm sorry." She meant it. She possessed the unfortunate tendency to speak before thinking, her thoughts forever poised on the tip of her tongue. "But I know my limits, and I need you to trust me."

His only reply was an exceedingly rude gesture. Zaria swatted his arm, flopping down on the bed beside him. The familiar warmth of his body was a comfort. She and Jules had spent many a night here after Itzal's death, backs pressed together as his breath lulled her to sleep. That was before George Zhao declared them too old to be sharing a bed and banished his son back upstairs. After that, Zaria had slept alone with an ever-present candle to drive the demons away.

But now, with her friend's slim frame silhouetted by the dark, she could almost imagine he'd never left. Suddenly, they were ten again, telling secrets in the orange-limned dark, voices pitched low so as not to wake Itzal.

The collar of Jules's shirt was threadbare, the sleeves a little too short, and Zaria was struck all at once by just how tired he looked. She wasn't the only one working hard. She wasn't the only one suffering. Jules worked long hours in the pawnshop, dealing with all manner of unpleasant folk, and saw his future stretched out before him like some grim shadow in a looking glass.

Jules's grandfather had started the pawnshop years ago; he had been a sailor from mainland China who had brought his family to settle in London upon growing weary of the sea. Both Jules's grandparents had lived on the top floor of the pawnshop until the fever took them six years ago, his *nai nai* within a month of his *ye ye*. Zaria had never known anyone to work harder and remembered them both fondly. But running this place in the heart of the slum made for a difficult life, and Zaria knew Jules dreamed of more.

And yet. *And yet.* She couldn't abide his incessant worrying about her—didn't want him to point out the things she was trying so very hard not to think about.

"You're running yourself ragged," Jules said, as if he could hear her thoughts, pressing his bony shoulder into hers. "You can't blame me for not wanting to watch you destroy yourself. But I'll try to trust you. Just...promise you're not doing it for me."

Zaria's head was still spinning, her muscles one generalized ache, but she cracked a wry smile. "Not everything is about *you*, Jules."

He rolled his eyes. "My poor ego."

It was a lie, though, Zaria thought. Of course everything was about Jules. How could it not be? He was all she had. He kept her sane and gave her a reason to wake each morning. She would not allow herself to die, because she couldn't abide the thought of leaving him on his own.

"If we could leave right now, where would you go?" she asked, tilting her chin toward the ceiling. "If money wasn't an object and you could go anywhere you pleased."

Jules was silent for a moment, considering. His onyx eyes were serious.

"The country," he decided eventually. "Somewhere with grass. A place with nobody else around, where you can look out your window and see for miles. Somewhere you can always see the sun."

Zaria nodded, though she could scarcely picture such a thing. "Would I be there?"

"Of course." Jules nudged her shoulder again. "There's a big house that's all ours, and we don't have to worry about kingpins or rent. It has a yellow front door. In the summertime, we sit outside and look toward the forest. There are more trees than you've ever seen. Maybe I write a book, and you invent something genius and impossible just because you can."

"Hmm." Zaria wished she could see it as clearly as he did. That she could dream without an oppressive sense of melancholy. "Why is the front door yellow?"

Jules situated himself more comfortably beside her. "Why not? It's a nice color. You see it from a distance and know you're home."

How simple, Zaria thought. A world of grass and sunshine, of trees and yellow doors.

"I see it," she murmured, surprised to realize that it was abruptly true. She saw herself free from this place, from the stink of the river and the cries of the miserable, and wanted it with a voracity that made her ache in places she'd forgotten existed within her.

You see it from a distance and know you're home.

What would it be like, she wondered, to feel at home?

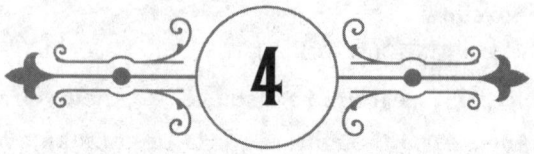

KANE

THE NOTE HAD ARRIVED EARLIER THAT DAY LIKE A PUNCH TO Kane's stomach.

It was folded in half, his name scrawled on the front alongside a drawing of an arrow. The sight of it had made Kane drive his fist into the wall, and he now sprawled on the sofa in furious pain as Fletcher stared at him sardonically.

"Did that make you feel better?"

Kane stretched his throbbing fingers. They were already starting to swell, an ugly purplish sheen on a couple of the knuckles. "Yes."

Fletcher snorted. "Lying bastard."

Stress rose like bile in Kane's throat. The note had contained nothing but a single line of script in Ward's hand: an address. One Kane knew to be in the most miserable part of Devil's Acre. He didn't need any more information to know what he was supposed to do.

"Want me to come with you?" Fletcher continued, though he had to know what the answer would be.

"God, no." Kane lifted his head, mouth twisting. "Did you see who delivered it?"

"It was on the table when I got back."

Kane swore, soft and low. He leapt to his feet, grabbing the glass and bottle he'd abandoned the previous night, and poured himself a drink. It burned viciously going down, and he inhaled through clenched teeth. Fletcher's eyes were a relentless weight as Kane refilled his glass. He pretended not to notice. Only when he'd finished did he yank his coat on, flipping the collar up to hide his neck. His head was already spinning.

Fletcher followed him to the door. "Kane—"

"I'll meet you at the docks," Kane drawled. He'd meant to come off as nonchalant, but even to his own ears he sounded resigned. "One hour."

"Be careful."

"When am I not?"

Fletcher's answering expression was so withering, Kane might have laughed if he hadn't felt like screaming.

The air outside was chilly, heavy with the scent of recent rainfall, but the alcohol warmed his insides as he hurried to the outskirts of Devil's Acre. He felt his inhibitions lower. Not enough to make him happy about playing the role Ward most preferred him in, but enough to make him wonder whether a fight wouldn't be the worst thing in the world if it came to that.

Kane didn't like collecting money from people. Didn't like the way they looked at him—as if he were more monster than boy. Didn't like the person he became when he was forced to defend himself against someone who was only trying to protect what little they had.

But what could he do? Kane had to protect what *he* had. He could still starkly remember being fifteen and failing to shake payment out of a young shop owner. He'd returned expecting trouble, yet Ward had been eerily silent about the whole thing.

The next day, one of Ward's errand boys—Abe, his name was—accosted Fletcher and sliced his cheek. When Kane had gone to Ward in imploring fury, the kingpin's face had been cold and empty. That was when Kane knew Abe's attack hadn't been random.

Fletcher still bore the scar from his left temple to his top lip. It made Kane furious every time he looked at it. And yet he was the reason Fletcher had joined Ward's crew in the first place. Kane had thought it safe at the time—somewhere a boy could go when he didn't have anyone else. After all, that was what Ward had given *him*, wasn't it?

Kane had met Fletcher purely by accident. Orphaned in the first few years of the Great Hunger, Fletcher had been slated to sail to British North America alongside thousands of other child migrants, but he had snuck aboard a ship set for London instead. He'd done so in hopes of tracking down his younger sister, who'd been sent to England the month before. Fletcher never found her. Instead, he'd wound up homeless in the country that had persecuted his people and outlawed his religion—up until the day he attempted to pick-pocket Kane Durante.

Poor choice of mark, you dumb Paddy, Kane had said, drawing his knife as he hurled the pejorative term he'd heard Ward use countless times.

Fletcher, nearly double his size and surprisingly quick for it, had snatched Kane's blade with an impish grin. *Aye, but I seem to be doing fine all the same.*

Something about that grin had made Kane crack one in return, and in the end, he'd brought Fletcher home with him. *He's a huge bloke, a decent pickpocket, and he'd make a good confidence man* was the pitch he'd given Ward. *Besides, you always say the Irish only trust their own.*

Even if they hadn't become as close as they were now, Kane would have still felt responsible for Fletcher. Would have still done what he could to repent for bringing him into this life that he was far too good for. As it was, the least he could do was keep Fletcher alive for as long as possible.

His heart rate kicked up a notch, accompanied by a surge of energy that had nothing to do with exertion. Desperation was like a spreading poison in his blood. It made him want to slice his skin and let it leak out, slowly, until his mind settled again. Now that it was daylight, people in the slum took note of him. Though they didn't know Kane, something about his appearance marked him inherently as one of Ward's. Something he couldn't see when he looked in the mirror. He pulled his collar closer to his neck as if that might stave off the fearful glances. Everyone knew the kingpin. After all, this was Ward's turf, and the people here paid their dues one way or another.

Eyes narrowed to keep his gaze from swimming, Kane scanned the soot-stained buildings for the one Ward had described in his note.

All these godforsaken houses—if you could call them that— looked the same. But he singled it out a moment later, and people parted to let him through as he made his way to the wooden front door. It was cracked in places, barely holding on by the hinges. Kane kicked it open with little effort.

The interior of the house managed to be both bare and cluttered. Black grime clung to every surface, and a distant part of

Kane—perhaps the more sober part—was horrified to see a single makeshift bed on the wooden floor. It was lacking even a gas lamp, and the sole window was stuffed with rags to keep out the elements. It wasn't the first time he'd been inside such a place, but the misery—not to mention the putrid stench—never ceased to disturb him. All in all, it was scarcely better than a doss-house.

"Hello?" Kane put a hand to the knife in his pocket. Ward had gotten him a dark market revolver for jobs like this, but it struck him as unfair to bring a gun to what would surely be a fistfight. People in Devil's Acre didn't have magical weapons or, indeed, weapons at all. They couldn't afford such a thing.

A man loomed in the poorly lit space, his shoulders seeming to fill the entirety of the apartment. He wore a threadbare jacket and hat, and exhaustion was etched into the lines of his dirty face. A factory worker, mostlike. Kane's stomach hollowed.

"Get out of my house," the man snarled, though there was fear in his eyes.

Kane calmly folded down the collar of his jacket. An unnecessary action; the man knew why he had come. But something about the kingpin's mark tended to aid compliance. "I understand you're owing."

The man's lips trembled, and suddenly he was brandishing a knife. Where the *hell* had that come from? Perhaps Kane was drunker than he'd realized.

"You get the hell outta here. I've got no money."

Yes, Kane thought, tilting his chin. That was evident. People were expected to pay for the protection that came with living in a kingpin's claimed territory, but what they *really* paid for was the privilege of being left alone. "You don't get to live on Ward's turf for free."

"You think I *want* to live here?" The man bared his teeth. "I got no choice. I'm barely keeping my—my family—"

He lunged before completing the sentence, rusted knife flash-ing. Kane stepped deftly aside. Ward's instructions were always the same: *Take fingers if you have to. If they don't have the money, make them pay regardless.*

But he didn't intend to do that today. "Stop this."

The man ignored him. The knife came again, and Kane blocked it with his own, like the tiniest of sword fights. He used the contact to rotate the tip of his blade into the fleshy part of the man's hand, right beside the thumb. The rusty knife clattered to the floor.

"Bastard," the man growled, grasping his wrist as blood welled up.

And then his other fist collided with Kane's jaw.

It was a clever move. Kane, thinking him distracted, hadn't seen it coming. Pain sparked along the nerves of his face and radiated down into his neck. The blow rattled his composure, and all at once, he'd had enough. Damn it. He'd been trying to make things *easy*. When the man raised his fist again, the action woke something in Kane. Something dark and ugly and ignorant of consequences.

He spun so fast that he was barely aware of his body carrying out the movement. His hand wrapped around the man's throat, thumb hooking beneath jawbone, and suddenly he was slamming the man up against the wall. It didn't matter that Kane was slighter. He knew where to press. How to make it hurt.

The man blinked at him, eyes wide, fingers scrabbling at Kane's hand on his neck. Kane only squeezed harder. That dark, animal rage coursed through his blood, and he felt almost gleeful.

"I gave you a chance," he breathed in the man's ear.

The man gasped a word, and Kane loosened his hold slightly. He regretted it a moment later when he registered what that word had been.

He used his grip on the man's throat to slam him into the wall a second time. Skull collided with brick, and the sound reverberated through the room. *"You motherf—"*

But he didn't finish what he'd been about to say. Because at that moment someone peeked around the corner, eyes enormous in the shadows. Someone with a small face, whose head barely reached Kane's waist.

Oh, *hell.*

It was a little girl. She couldn't be more than three. Those large eyes found Kane's hand on her father's neck, and her lips parted as someone reached for her from the other side of the wall.

"Lizzie, *no.*"

The child pulled away, and a woman appeared. Despite the child hovering between them, she was scarcely older than Kane himself. Everything about her was still distinctly girlish. Her expression was pinched as she took in the scene before her, attempting once more to drag the child back.

"Please forgive us."

Kane's heartbeats collided with one another. The man had stilled in his grasp. *Please forgive us,* she'd said, when he was the one who had barged into their home. The one strangling her husband right in front of her.

God, he *was* a monster, wasn't he?

He loosened his grip. The man slid down the wall, slumping against it. His hand went to his neck, and his face was wild, terror mingled with confusion.

Kane's face was nothing at all.

There was a long moment during which no one moved an inch. Or perhaps it only felt like an eternity to Kane. His mind whirled aimlessly, and he regretted the drink. What did they see, these people, when they looked at him? He must be their nightmares realized.

Their fears in the form of a wild-eyed, knife-wielding boy. But he couldn't hurt the man further; not like this. Not in front of a wife who would shut her eyes when the blade came down and a daughter who wouldn't know to do the same.

And yet he couldn't return to Ward empty-handed.

"If you can't pay," Kane said, his voice an unrecognizable hiss, "then be gone within the hour. Or I assure you someone worse than me will come to collect, and they won't just be looking for money."

"But—" the man began, and his wife shushed him with a breathless shriek.

Kane knew what he'd been about to say: *Where will we go?* It was a fair question. But homelessness was better than death, at least for now.

The man still looked as though he might argue. That was a problem; Kane needed them to agree. Because if he returned without the money, weaving tales of a family who'd fled, and Ward discovered he was lying…

The room was impossibly quiet as Kane knelt, lips at the man's ear. "This is a gift," he breathed. "This is *mercy*. I assure you, you will not get it twice."

Finally, blessedly, the man nodded.

Kane's muscles relaxed. He straightened, readjusting his collar. "Be out by dusk. Don't return."

The little girl's eyes locked with his, just for a moment, and he imagined the alcohol in the pit of his stomach burning anew.

When he left, he did not look back.

"Fletch!"

Kane called his friend's name, ducking his chin to avoid the

putrid spray of the river. Fletcher stood at the edge of the docks, surrounded on three sides by shipping containers. Workers scuttled past with hats drawn low over their faces and vests soaked through. Their hollers and the *ch-chk, ch-chk* of their carts over stone were all but swallowed by the wind. It was crowded despite the weather, but Fletcher, being taller than Kane—who was quite tall—veritably towered over everyone else.

He raised an eyebrow as Kane approached. "Had some trouble, I take it?"

Kane ran a hand over his swollen jaw, wincing. "This is going to sound mad, but people aren't keen on debt collection."

"That does sound mad. I'm sure you were ever so charming."

Kane made a noncommittal sound in the back of his throat. He'd forced a family into homelessness today. A *child*.

Fletcher's brows knit together. "What's wrong?"

"Nothing. Look—a few ships are docked up ahead."

It wasn't as though he'd just noticed; they were, after all, fairly large. Stares from the dockworkers held a tangible heat as they navigated the throngs, but Kane didn't care. It was Fletcher's gaze he felt the most, dissecting his expression as if any moment he might say, *Wait. What are you hiding?*

A bird screeched somewhere overhead. It sounded like a warning. Kane skirted two men arguing over some kind of cargo marked with the words SAVILLE SHIPPING CO., lifting his chin as they neared a ship bearing the matching logo. He tried not to dwell on the time they'd spent working for Saville—time they'd *wasted*—only to learn nothing of import.

"The necklace wouldn't have arrived on one of Saville's boats, though," Fletcher muttered thoughtfully. "It was coming from Ireland, right? Courtesy of George Waterhouse and Co."

Kane inclined his head. "Saville's company employees would have dealt with it when it arrived. They would have decided where it should dock." He swallowed an impatient sigh. "Maybe we should have gotten hired on here. I figured Saville's personal crew would know more than the dockers. That we might be able to track down some kind of ledger. But…"

"You couldn't have known," Fletcher said. "It was a good idea. I doubt the dockers know anything about which ships are carrying what exhibits. Besides, people are clamoring for these jobs, and they're picked at random. You can't con your way in."

Kane sighed. Those had been his exact words when he'd convinced Fletcher they were better off conning their way into Saville's inner circle. And even now, when it seemed he'd made the wrong choice, Fletcher still supported him without question. What had Kane done to deserve such undying loyalty?

He knew the answer: He hadn't done anything. Other than condemn his friend to a lifetime of servitude.

"Ward has never wanted something this much," Kane said darkly as they continued down the docks. "At least not that I can remember. I'm afraid of what he'll do if we fail."

There. He'd said it.

Fletcher cast him a sideways glance. "You're important to Ward. Everybody knows that." He elbowed Kane lightly in the ribs. "That's why I hang around you. For the safety."

Kane felt as though someone had injected ice directly into his bloodstream. He forced a painful grin, unable to bring himself to respond.

A number of ships had been anchored away from the main docks, some of them bearing words Kane didn't recognize. Partially due to impatience—and partially because he couldn't bear to continue the conversation he and Fletcher were currently having—he grabbed the arm of a young docker walking past.

The boy started. He couldn't have been more than twelve, Kane saw now, with a shock of reddish hair and dirty cheeks. When he cursed, though, it was with the vocabulary of someone far older.

"Calm down," Kane barked, trapping the boy between himself and Fletcher. "I only want to ask you something. And I'm not going to hurt you," he added, "so relax. Do you know if any of these ships came from Ireland?"

"It's important." Fletcher's arms were crossed, his face damp from the misty wind and the river spray. The boy shied away from his towering form, a seemingly automatic reaction.

"I—I don't know," he said. "It's busy round here as of late. There might've been such a ship, though. If there was, I ain't telling you for free."

Kane made a noise in his throat. "Fair enough. Here's my offer: You answer the question, and *he* doesn't chuck you in the river." He tilted his head at Fletcher, who was stone-faced.

The boy blanched, then glowered. "Blazes, fine! That one at the end arrived this morn. Some of the older guys were saying it had come from round those parts. That it was full of expensive shit. A bunch of fancy-dressed toffs and coppers came by as it was being unloaded. I stayed back, mind you; father tells me not to trust men like that. That's all I know."

Kane's stomach plummeted. Could that have been the Irish ship transporting the Waterhouse exhibit? He hoped not, given that everything on board had apparently already been moved. With his luck, though, he wouldn't be surprised.

"That might well be it," Fletcher said, echoing Kane's thoughts. He peered in the direction the boy had gestured, easily able to see over the heads of everyone else in the vicinity. "It's certainly a fancy enough vessel. I think we might be in trouble, Kane."

Kane roared his frustration into the wind, spurring the boy to run like hell. Panic and helplessness rendered him speechless for a moment, and he yearned to hit something as he dragged his hands through his hair, yanking at the roots. Everything they'd done up until now had been to avoid this very outcome, and it had all been for naught.

"We're going to have to steal the blasted necklace from the Exhibition, Fletch." To Kane's horror, his voice held a quaver.

"Okay," Fletcher said, staring out over the fog-shrouded river. The set of his mouth was determined. "Okay, that's not ideal, but it's fine. We'll make it work. You always have a plan, right?"

A laugh bubbled like hysteria in the back of Kane's throat. Yes, he did tend to have a plan, but this wasn't supposed to be happening. He wasn't supposed to *need* a backup plan. Sure, he'd spent sleepless nights imagining how he might steal from the Exhibition if it came down to that, but those had been stress-induced exercises in futility.

He forced himself to take a steadying breath. Fletcher's life was on the line. And just as they'd said a hundred times before, there was nothing the two of them couldn't steal.

"Yeah," Kane said, even as his stomach continued to churn. "Yeah, Fletch. I've got a plan."

KANE

THE FIRST TIME KANE SAW WARD, HE'D BEEN CRYING.

Kane, that is. Not Ward. Maria and Cristian Durante had been yelling at each other in irate Italian and had ushered Kane from the room and slammed the door, so he'd been forced to listen to their voices from behind a wooden barrier. It hadn't made much of a difference, though Kane could no longer remember what they'd been arguing about. He only knew it had frightened him. His mother, too, had been frightened—he could hear it in her voice. And so he'd stuffed his fingers in his ears and cried, even knowing his father would say he was too old to be doing such a thing.

That was when the silhouette of a young man appeared in the hall. For a heartbeat, Kane had thought the man was a specter; no one had knocked on the door, and certainly no one else shared their apartment. The man must have seen Kane's fear, because he'd put a finger to his lips, which had turned up in a smile. His eyes were too light a brown—almost yellow—and when he spoke, his soft voice was audible even over the yelling.

"Don't be afraid. What's your name?"

Canziano, Kane must have said, though the only part of the conversation he remembered clearly was the part that came next.

How the man had helped him to his feet and said, "I'm Alexander. If you like, you can call me Ward."

Kane and Fletcher had spent the rest of the previous evening trying to learn where precisely the cargo from the docks had been moved. The ship from Ireland had definitely been empty—once the coast was clear, they'd peered through the portholes to confirm the boy's story—which meant the Waterhouse exhibit must have been taken to the Crystal Palace directly, just as Kane had feared.

Stealing the necklace would be complicated. The palace would be packed with patrons, and while Kane planned to use that to their advantage, the reality was that the building was made of *glass*. What they needed, he reasoned—as he racked his brain for the plan he'd told Fletcher he already had—was a way to hide from view, if only for a few moments. A way to grab the necklace and make a quick escape. A mere diversion wouldn't be good enough—not with so many pairs of eyes present. They needed a distraction nobody would recognize as such.

Once, Kane knew, Ward had commissioned a peculiar item from a dark market vendor. It was an explosive of sorts, though it left no damage in its wake. Rather, it had provided a brief cover of opaque smoke just long enough to commit whatever unsavory action Ward had intended it for. Or, at least, so Kane had heard. He hadn't actually been there to see its effect, but if Ward still possessed such a thing, it could make Kane's impossible task far less daunting.

Problem was, he didn't expect the kingpin to be in a good mood today. He knew Ward would inquire after the money he'd been tasked to retrieve, so he figured it was best to pass information along as soon as possible. *The place was abandoned*, Kane would say, hoping to hell it would be true when Ward inevitably sent someone to confirm the claim. *They must have known I was coming.*

How strange it was, to be both feared and afraid.

Kane slunk through the slum like a skittish phantom, heading away from the river. It was obvious the moment he entered the area inhabited by the wealthy: People rushed through the gas lamp–lined streets in spotless frock coats and silken dresses, and the sound of stagecoach wheels rattled against the inside of Kane's skull. Awnings were drawn out over shop fronts, and the architecture shifted to something grander, less uniform. Through the soot-stained windows, he could see all manner of items for sale. There were emporiums of dresses stitched from the finest imported fabrics. There were gleaming swords and pistols, burnished gold and silver vessels, and shelves chock-full of everything from confectioners' supplies to remedies that promised to cure every imaginable ailment.

At the side of the road, a ruddy-faced man selling sheep's feet cursed at a barefoot beggar, spittle flying. The beggar ducked his head and disappeared into the bustling crowd, only to be spat back out again when another stagecoach came clacking by. This part of London, Kane thought, was where wealth collided with extreme poverty. It had never been so evident as of late, when an unmistakable air of excitement lay thick over every crowd as the Exhibition neared. The city had always done its best to force the poor to the outskirts, but scarcely had it been quite so obvious. For an event spearheaded by the prince consort—who was said to be socially conscious—it certainly struck Kane as an odd use of public funds.

He ducked past a group of men with clay pipes between their teeth and rounded the corner. It was quieter down the side street, with rows of magnificent multilevel houses set into the same block. Kane stopped outside a particularly ornate front door, shoving his way through the cast-iron gate enclosing the property. A row of many-paned windows faced him, shrouded by heavy velvet curtains, and he knew as he mounted the tapering steps that he was being watched.

Sure enough, the door opened before he had a chance to knock. This wasn't a surprise. Regardless of where the kingpin was staying, the alchemological device bracketed to the doorframe detected any movement by the entrance. The high-pitched sound it emitted was soft but earsplittingly metallic, and Kane cringed as a beady-eyed man appeared on the threshold, his fingers occupied with resetting the device.

"Tom," Kane said when it was blessedly silent once more.

"Durante." The ginger-haired man flashed a grin. He seemed to stand a little taller, as if expecting Kane to berate him for slouching. That was the way people were around Kane; they behaved as though they thought Ward's power extended to him. In a way, he supposed, it did. But it didn't mean Ward treated him any better.

Tom moved aside to grant Kane entry. The entryway was magnificent: The ceilings vaulted high above their heads, and a gleaming staircase curved to the second floor. The walls were heavily papered with some dark, expensive-looking pattern, and an enormous chandelier hung from the ceiling on a chain, crystal pieces tinkling softly in the wind before the door slammed shut. In the adjacent parlor, a small group of men were playing cards, their drunken guffaws carrying through the house.

Overall, it didn't look like a place Ward would live. It was too... blandly pleasant. Kane wondered how long he would stay here.

"What brings you by, Durante?" Tom asked. Tension edged his voice. It annoyed Kane, who had enough tension of his own.

"Need to speak with Ward," he grunted, wondering what other reason Tom thought there could possibly be for his presence here. "Is he in?"

"Aye, should be in his office. He expecting you?"

Kane narrowed his eyes. "Does it matter?"

"No." The man was quick to backtrack. "Just curious."

Damn it all. Kane was aching for a fight with someone who deserved it.

Tom led Kane toward the stairs, their footsteps echoing in the enormous space. This house wasn't quite as nice as the last one, but it was certainly nicer than the one before. Ward had a number of places in the city and moved around as he saw fit. Kane supposed that even with a handful of coppers in your pocket, being the dark market's kingpin wasn't exactly the safest occupation.

They walked almost the entire length of the second-story mezzanine before Tom jerked his finger in the direction of a door. Kane nodded to show he understood, his tongue dry against the roof of his mouth. He didn't thank Tom but waved the man away with an impatient flick of his wrist.

Tom thumped back down the stairs, but still Kane didn't open the door. He took a breath. Stilled his heart. He hadn't seen Ward in more than a week, and it felt simultaneously like an eternity and no time at all.

He turned the brass handle.

The windowless room he entered was deceivingly large, illuminated by an odorous gas lamp and boasting a mahogany cabinet of curiosities. Alchemological concoctions, tiny skulls, and insects pinned to a board were displayed behind the glass, but Kane hardly spared any of it a glance. He was looking at the man sitting behind the desk in the center of the space. A man with rich brown hair and golden eyes like a fox.

Alexander Ward.

Despite the aura of power that surrounded him, he wasn't an imposing man. Slim, late thirties, and too handsome to be allowed, Ward looked like someone who ought to be obeyed. His brows were a few shades darker than his slick hair, the eyes beneath them stern and long lashed. He had a cruel mouth that demanded trust and adoration whenever it deigned to smile. Kane was all too familiar with that smile. It had the ability to turn his stomach and was always accompanied by either a blessing or a curse.

"Kane. My boy." Ward's voice was smooth and breathy as he tasted the sound of Kane's name on his tongue. He made the endearment that followed it sound dangerous. "I wasn't expecting you."

Kane felt his face twist and fought to reset it. "Well, here I am."

Ward held out a hand, palm up, indicating the chair facing him. "Sit."

Casting a sidelong glance at the dart gun on the kingpin's desk, Kane sidled over and sat. He was familiar with the weapon; it was similar to a regular alchemological gun, though far less likely to be lethal. Rather, the magic-infused darts lodged beneath the skin and hurt like absolute hell. Kane had been hit with one only once, and he thought death might have been preferable to the extraction. Wariness overtook him, but he took extra care to keep his expression cool, letting a smirk play at the corners of his mouth.

Ward leaned back in his own chair. His expression mirrored Kane's, as if he knew exactly what he was doing. "I hope you're here to deliver good news. And yet, something tells me otherwise."

"The address you sent me to was empty." Kane's voice was steady. That was one good thing about the education Ward had given him: No matter what turmoil plagued him on the inside, he knew how to con a man. How to speak in way that made people believe you. That made them *want* to believe you.

But this was Ward, and he might as well have invented conning.

The kingpin tapped his index finger against his chin, a contemplative action. Kane knew Ward was letting him stew. Giving him time to explain why he'd come unannounced. But Kane held his silence, because although Ward was many things, patient wasn't one of them.

Sure enough, Ward gave a huff through his nose. A small victory.

"You know, I sent Dickens to follow up," he said silkily as Kane froze. "The family was indeed gone. And only just recently, by the looks of things. Isn't that interesting? *Convenient*, one might say."

Kane swallowed. It took considerable effort. "They must have known I was coming."

"The only way they could have known you were coming, Kane, is if you told them." Ward leaned back in his chair, eyes flashing darkly. "And we both know you didn't do that."

It was a test, and Kane's stomach clenched even as he said with confidence, "Of course I didn't."

Technically, it wasn't a lie. The family *hadn't* known he was coming. Ward stared at him, hard, and Kane stared back, refusing to be cowed.

"What happened to your face?"

Ah. That. Kane gave a self-conscious tug on the collar of his overcoat. By now the bruising at his jaw had begun to purple, and there had been no hope of Ward's not noticing. "Got into it with a beggar on the street."

"What street?" Ward murmured, pulling a piece of parchment across the desk toward himself. "I'll send someone to take care of the vermin. Unless you already did."

"I did."

"Is there a body?"

"I didn't kill him. Just won the fight."

"Ah." Ward's tone was laced with skepticism. "You know I have several constables on my payroll."

Kane bit the inside of his cheek. "It would have been an inconvenience."

And the lies were already piling up. He should have taken a finger when that man in the slum couldn't pay his dues. Damn his wife. Damn his little girl. Why had Kane bothered telling them to leave? He wasn't *nice*. He didn't shy away from bloodshed. He wasn't supposed to care about things like that.

"I see." Ward crossed his arms, tapping a finger against his bicep as he studied Kane's face. "You know, I'm glad you came to see me. I was about to send for you."

"Why is that?"

"You've got bigger problems than a missing slum family. Did you know the exhibit from Waterhouse and Co. arrived in London yesterday? That it's already been unloaded and set up in the Crystal Palace?"

Of course. Of *course* Ward already knew. Sweat beaded on Kane's brow as he digested the questions. How was he to respond? Ward never asked a question he didn't already know the answer to.

Ward wasn't looking at Kane anymore, but was examining his fingernails, frowning as he slid the tip of his knife beneath one dirt-free crescent. "Silence won't help you, Kane. Not with me. You know that."

It struck Kane as a nonsensical thing to say. What *would* help him where Ward was concerned? There were no right answers here. Once Ward had decided to be angry with you, nothing you said or didn't say was going to make any difference.

"Yes," Kane said eventually, a low growl. "Yes, I knew. I was going to tell you."

Ward's brows ascended his forehead. "You were? Well. You'll forgive me if I find that hard to believe." He leaned across the desk so that he and Kane were eye to eye. "Your plan didn't work, you incompetent bastard. Thought you could charm Saville, did you? Learn everything you needed from his men? I gave you free rein. I can see now that this was a mistake."

Kane could sense the coming storm. He swallowed, hands fisted in his lap.

Ward's lip curled back from his teeth as he went on. "When I suggested Saville as a resource, I didn't mean for you to waste time acting as his errand boy. This wasn't to be a simple con job. Sometimes I forget you need constant, specific instruction in order to be useful."

"I'm still working on it." Kane shook his head once, a curt gesture that sent lightning through his skull. "This isn't a regular job. You asked me to steal something priceless. Something of international acclaim. It's taking longer than usual because I'm trying to be careful, okay?"

"I need you to be careful and *efficient*."

Kane forced his next question out—if he didn't ask it now, he knew he never would. "Do you still have those alchemological explosives? The ones that create the smoke? I was thinking I could..." He trailed off. Ward was *laughing*, though not a single sound left his mouth.

"You mean to ask me for further assistance?" the kingpin said, his smile fading with alarming quickness.

"If you want the necklace so badly, then surely—"

"Your audacity"—Ward cut him off—"is astounding as always. No, I will not help you, Canziano. Not with this."

"Don't." Kane's reply was the crack of a whip. "Don't ever call me that."

The name struck a painful chord within him, and it sounded all wrong on Ward's lips. After his parents died, Kane had left Canziano Durante behind—the first name for a saint, the second for his father—and became Kane Hunt. The perfect identity for a boy trying to pass as British. He'd slowly started using his true surname again, and now went by Durante unless pulling a con, but he never wanted to be called *Canziano* again.

Canziano had died alongside his parents.

Kane remembered only flashes of his previous life. Ten years had faded into clouded memories of soft hands and lyrical Italian. Of brightly colored art in a tiny dark house. Maria and Cristian Durante had been traveling statuette makers, but Kane couldn't remember how they'd ended up in London. He'd stopped trying to recall his parents' faces, perhaps due to unconscious self-preservation. All of it—the hands and colors and faces—had been replaced by Ward.

Ward fixed Kane with a glare that turned his insides to ice. When the kingpin spoke, his voice was dangerously soft. It was the voice he reserved for telling people they'd disappointed him. The voice that was, more often than not, the last thing they heard.

"I can call you whatever I wish. I *own* you. Or have you forgotten?"

Kane had not forgotten. He clenched his jaw so tightly that it was a wonder the bones stayed intact. "I'm...sorry."

"Ah, don't sell me a dog." Ward snorted, pushing himself to stand. His movements as he rounded the desk were agile, almost feline. "You're not sorry. But you should be."

Kane stiffened in his chair as Ward's hand snapped out to encircle his wrist. He could feel blood pumping through the veins there as the kingpin withdrew something from his pocket. It was a tiny device, custom-made by some long-dead alchemologist, no doubt. One end was marked by tiny whirring gears—the other boasted a horribly sharp point.

"I'll get it," Kane said breathlessly. "I swear. You don't have to do this."

"Okay." Ward shrugged, releasing him. "Send Master Collins along instead then, would you?"

The moment stretched taut between them. Kane glared, hoping the heat of his gaze was palpable. This was how it always went—how it would always go. Ward knew his weak spot, and he would poke and prod at it until Kane snapped or Fletcher died.

A sound like a growl built in the back of his throat as Kane shoved his right sleeve all the way up. "We both know that's not happening."

Ward leaned close, taking Kane's chin between his thumb and forefinger. "You are lucky," he crooned. "Lucky I love you like a son. Lucky I give you so many chances."

A familiar sharp pain bloomed on Kane's arm. He refused to flinch as Ward drew the *x* without looking, those amber eyes unwavering.

I don't want you to forget, Ward had said the first time, back when Kane was twelve, *the number of mistakes you make. The number of chances I give you. The rest of my men are not so lucky. And so, you see, I want you to remember each and every time I could have punished you but didn't. Let it not be said that I am not merciful.*

Ward stowed the device back in his pocket as Kane's eyes flicked down to his arm. The black ink had a glittering quality to it, and after a moment, the crudely drawn shape began to burn with excruciating vigor. It would continue to do so, Kane knew, spreading throughout his body for the next several hours. It was no normal ink, and Ward did not deal normal punishments. The alchemological substance in the needle moved through one's system like a poison, doing no real damage but making one seriously reconsider whatever they'd done to piss off the kingpin.

Kane shoved his sleeve back down. What a foolish thing. He didn't need ink in his skin to know he was lucky not to be dead.

Of course, Ward marked his disappointment on the rest of the men, too—more than once Kane had seen them trying to carve away the top layer of skin, desperate for the pain to stop—but most only received a handful of x's before Ward disposed of them. No one had as many as Kane, and yet here he was. Still.

Always.

He flexed his hand, trying to ignore the lingering agony.

"This necklace is more important than you know," Ward hissed in Kane's ear. "I even let you bring Collins along, hoping a second pair of hands might compensate for your idiocy. Do you *hear* the words I say? Do I need to be right beside you at all times, feeding you commands to ensure you get things done properly?"

"I told you, I'll get it."

"You'd better. I am accustomed to getting what I want, Canziano. Keep me waiting too long, and Master Collins might find your next job to be far, far worse. Please me, and I'll consider letting him go."

This dragged Kane from his haze. Hope settled in the rhythm of his rapid heartbeats. "You'd let him leave your employ?"

"That's what you want, isn't it?" Ward's gaze was sly.

Kane had never told Ward that. Didn't realize he'd so much as implied it. And yet he wasn't surprised to discover Ward knew precisely what cards to play to guarantee Kane would do as he wanted. "Do you mean it?"

Ward's teeth flashed. "You know I never make a deal I won't uphold." He let the words hang in the air before snapping, "Now go."

It was true. Ward was terrifying, and he lied with ease, but he kept his promises. He paid his debts.

Kane couldn't leave fast enough. He shoved wordlessly past Tom before hurtling into the descending night, gulping breaths of cool air. The pain had crept up to his shoulder, and his head was beginning to throb. What the hell was he going to do now?

He knew the answer, of course. He was going to have to steal the necklace from the Great Exhibition, and it was going to be impossible.

But as Kane passed through Smith Square, a short distance from Horseferry Road, he remembered Mendoza. The alchemologist with the keen gaze and an edge to her voice. The way she'd pointed that impossible revolver at the wall, sending a streak of dark magic into the wood. How she'd scowled and said, *You must be new to dark market paraphernalia.*

That was what Kane needed. Someone who knew how to create the things Ward wouldn't give him. A diversion was only the start— if he could align himself with a skilled alchemologist, every problem he encountered in his bid to steal the necklace could be solved.

Perhaps he ought to pay Mendoza another visit.

6

ZARIA

"Hat's not enough," Zaria snapped, eyes fixed on the tiny pouch the chemist was currently weighing.

The woman shrugged. "That's what twenty shillings gets you. You want more, bring more money."

Zaria pressed her lips together, glancing out of the dingy window to where Jules stood keeping watch in the rainy street. This wasn't the first time she'd completely run out of soulsteel, but she tried not to let it happen often. She had another client coming to pick up a commission tonight, and as of right now, the second explosive still wasn't finished. It wouldn't work properly without primateria, and Zaria couldn't create primateria without soulsteel.

She liked Louisa Hoffman just fine, but the chemist was notoriously inflexible. She never offered discounts, and she didn't accept debts. The shop she ran with her husband received a small shipment of soulsteel from Switzerland biweekly. Although the mineral was naturally occurring, it wasn't sold via any legitimate channels; instead, it was being illegally mined in the Alps and shipped worldwide. Few were using it for legitimate alchemological purposes; it had become something of a curiosity, and vials were purchased for absurd reasons that encompassed everything from rumored healing properties to warding off evil. Then there were those who bought it simply to display. Demand was increasing rapidly as more people began collecting these so-called *curiosities*, and Zaria was getting priced out of her own damned market.

"You're screwing me over," she grunted, snatching the pouch from the counter and pushing a pile of shillings across to Louisa. "I thought we had an understanding."

The woman gave an apologetic shrug. "I said I'd have it available for purchase every two weeks. I never said I'd only sell it to you. The price reflects the demand, Zaria. I'm sorry."

Zaria knew it was unfair of her to be angry. Louisa was trying to make a living just like she was. But a chemist always had patrons, and Zaria couldn't help feeling resentful at the ease with which the Hoffmans kept their business afloat. "It's fine. I'll take what I can get."

She shoved the pouch of soulsteel into her pocket and ducked back out into the rain. The clean, soapy scent of the shop was replaced at once with the pungent stink of the streets. Even outside of the slum, the roads were covered with all manner of foul matter, the rain churning up what ought to have remained undisturbed.

"Well?" Jules said when Zaria reached him. She held up the tiny pouch in reply, and he inhaled through his teeth. "Is that going to be enough?"

"It'll have to be."

They walked in silence for a time before Jules asked, "Who's the commission for?"

Zaria sighed. "Nobody we're familiar with. Mister Vaughan, his name is." Her clients were all beginning to blur together. "Another explosive. I'm already late completing it, and if I don't have it ready for pickup tonight, I'm in trouble."

"You'll be fine," Jules said confidently. "You're excellent under pressure."

That tended to be true, but it didn't mean Zaria liked it. She squinted through the rain as they headed back into Devil's Acre, already considering how she might make the soulsteel last. A dark sludgelike substance had formed in the divots at the side of the road, and she swerved to avoid it, slamming into a boy around her and Jules's age.

"Sorry," she muttered, but the boy was already ducking away, a flicker of beige passing through his fingers before he shoved them into his pocket. It took Zaria a moment to comprehend what she'd seen—a small linen pouch. *Her* small linen pouch.

He'd stolen from her.

"*Jules!*" she bellowed, already sprinting after the pickpocket. She kept her gaze on the boy's cap as he wove in and out of the crowd, short and lithe enough that he was difficult to keep track of. Her boots slipped in the disgusting sludge, but she was heedless of the muck that spattered on her skirts. "Stop that boy!"

The call was to the citizens at large, but no one paid her any mind. Most scarcely glanced up. Petty theft was common here, and people weren't inclined to get involved in what they considered to be strangers' business. Zaria came to a halt, breathing hard, a deep ache pinching one side of her chest. Distantly, she was aware of Jules hurtling past her—he had always been faster, and besides, he wasn't weighed down by skirts—but she caught up to him a moment later, blood trickling from his nose as he swung a fist at the thief who had evidently decided to turn and fight.

Zaria shoved her way past the few nosy onlookers who had already stopped to observe, wincing as Jules's knuckles made contact with the other boy's face. The thief cursed colorfully, stumbling backward into a couple of onlookers, then used the entire force of his body to slam Jules to the ground.

Zaria didn't stop to think. She was on the thief in an instant, wrenching at his arms in an attempt to stop him from pummeling Jules. Someone in the crowd screamed as the boy turned and elbowed her in the stomach, but Zaria barely felt it. She scrabbled for her knife. Jules grunted as he took a punch to the side of the head, and then Zaria drove the blade into the meat of the thief's shoulder, clenching her teeth with the effort it took.

The boy screamed, whirling for her once again. His eyes met hers, wide and furious, the scleras tinged red. His unfamiliar face was gaunt and speckled with grime. Zaria yanked the knife out and leapt back, her entire body trembling from the sudden rush of energy. She bared her teeth.

"Give it to me," she hissed. The fingers clenching the blood-slick knife felt numb. "The soulsteel. Give it back."

The thief made an offensive gesture, spat at her feet, then took off at a run. Zaria made to follow him, but a hand grabbed her arm, pulling her back.

"Zaria, *no*."

She turned to glare at Jules, chest heaving. Blood still dripped from his nostrils, and discoloration was already starting to spread beneath his eyes. His hair was in disarray, damp from rain and sweat, and his coat was rumpled, torn near the collar. His expression was exhausted and utterly forlorn. Zaria's anger abruptly dissipated at the sight of him.

With the small crowd having dispersed, she pulled him into an embrace. Tears blurred the corners of her vision. Not tears of sadness, but of frustration. Of helplessness and anger and fear. She might have crumpled to the ground in that moment had Jules's steadying arms not kept her upright.

"I'm sorry, Zaria," he rasped. "I understand how important the soulsteel was, but he's clearly not giving it back without one hell of a fight. You're better off letting it go."

She wiped at her eyes. "Don't apologize. It's not your fault."

"I know." He still looked miserable, though. "What are you going to do now?"

"I don't know." Zaria winced as she studied his busted face more closely. "But you should go back to Louisa. Get her husband to take a look at your nose." Gert Hoffman was a former apothecary with a great deal of medical knowledge, though these days he sold drugs more than he administered them.

"Your commission—"

"Don't worry about that. I'm not going to get in any trouble. The explosive will still work."

Jules appeared doubtful but capitulated. "Fine. I won't be long. If you need anything, my father should be in his office."

Zaria nodded. As she watched Jules walk away, though, she wasn't nearly as confident as she'd claimed.

The explosive *would* work—just not the way it was supposed to. Not unless she got her hands on more soulsteel.

And it was too late for that.

When Zaria returned to the pawnshop, soaked to the bone and caked to her knees in muck, her misery had hardened well and truly

into anger. Was some unseen force conspiring against her? As if she wasn't already having enough trouble fulfilling her father's outstanding commissions, now she was down twenty shillings with nothing to show for it. She couldn't afford to keep living like this. George was lenient with her when it came to rent payments, but she was still barely keeping her head above water. Even her most impressive commissions didn't yield enough of a profit.

Then there was the fact that Jules could have been seriously hurt, and it was all her fault. She knew full well that pickpockets were rampant in Devil's Acre, and she hadn't been careful enough. The theft never should have happened in the first place. It had, though, and now Jules was the one paying for it. When would he finally stop trying to help her? He had to know it was hopeless. That she was merely putting off the inevitable.

Once she had changed and retrieved the unfinished explosive, Zaria made her way to the pawnshop proper to wait for Jules. With George in his office, she wouldn't be able to meet her client's representative there, so she settled herself behind the shop counter and trained her gaze on the door. Her thoughts revolved in an infinite loop, each one more miserable than the last.

For God's sake, she'd *stabbed* a man today. Had stuck her knife into his flesh like it was the most natural thing in the world. She was always prepared for the eventuality that she might need to defend herself—and this wasn't her first time doing so—but she couldn't stop thinking about the onlookers. The ones who had simply... watched. The people in the slum had become hardened to all manners of violence, and was she any different? Was she destined for a life where such things were the norm?

Blessedly, she was released a moment later from her hypothetical spiral by a small shape darkening the pawnshop door. It opened with a gentle protestation of hinges as a young woman squeezed through, shutting it behind her. Zaria relaxed her stance. Whether in disappointment or relief, she wasn't entirely sure.

"Apologies," she called out, "but the owner's busy. You'll have to come back later."

The young woman snorted. She looked around Zaria's own age—perhaps a year or two younger—with a knot of reddish-blonde hair and narrowed dark eyes. Though her hips were narrow, her shoulders were broad, and she stood at least a head taller than Zaria in stature. "Don't be obtuse. I'm here to collect."

"I—oh." Zaria knit her brow, pushing back from the counter to straighten up. "Forgive me."

The girl's mouth twisted. The result wasn't quite a smile but something wry and derisive. "One of the only female alchemologists dealing on London's dark market, and you're surprised when another girl comes to pick up a commission? Please."

"It's not exactly commonplace," Zaria said, schooling her expression to impassivity. She knew of a single other female seller; the woman supposedly sold weapons up near Christchurch. Luckily, their clientele didn't seem to overlap.

"Do you have it or not? Mister Vaughan has waited long enough. He's disappointed by the amount of time it took, by the way. Would rather like his deposit back."

Zaria huffed a laugh. Not only at the audacity, but also at the impossibility of the suggestion. The deposit from Mister Vaughan—whoever he was—had been long gone for months. "Your boss made a request, and I delivered. There's no reason for me to return his deposit."

The other girl drew herself up tall. Her dress, although deceivingly simple, was clean and well-made, allowing for ease of movement.

Despite her youthful face, she was threatening, with a glint in her eye Zaria neither liked nor trusted. "I didn't come alone, you know. I've two companions waiting just outside. If your work is anything less than impeccable quality—"

"Why don't you take a look at it?" Zaria snapped, shoving the linen-wrapped explosive across the counter. "I don't *do* less than impeccable quality."

The girl's features remained cool as she picked up the device. She didn't say a word as she unwrapped it, but it was obvious she had a practiced eye. Zaria was tense even as she crossed her arms in a show of impatience. So *this* was why such a young woman had been sent on Vaughan's behalf. Somehow, one way or another, she had knowledge of alchemology. Strange—it wasn't a skill that good, God-fearing citizens taught their children, and that applied twofold where women were concerned. Zaria hoped that the girl wasn't practiced enough to notice something was missing.

On the outside, her commission appeared fine. Excellent even. The inner workings were carefully contained in a smooth casing, a few metal pins protruding from one side. Mercury fulminate had been injected into the pins, and significant contact to any of them—say, someone throwing the explosive onto the floor—would result in immediate detonation.

The girl tapped one of the pins now, her fingernail clicking against the metal. "I take it I'd better not drop this."

"I wouldn't," Zaria said dryly.

"It'll only affect organic matter, though, correct?"

"Yes." The lie slipped out too easily. Had she gotten the soulsteel, she would have used primateria to alter the function of the mercury fulminate, imbuing it with magic to ensure the resulting chemical reaction aligned with her intentions. Instead, all she had to offer was a regular explosive.

There was a tense silence as the girl turned it over in her hands. Had she tilted her face closer, she might have noted the absence of the faintest glow surrounding the base of each pin, but it appeared her examination was complete. Zaria let a long breath out through her nose.

"Satisfied?"

The girl pursed her lips. She was really quite pretty; how unusual that she'd ended up in this line of work. "I believe I am. It's Mister Vaughan, though, who will make the ultimate determination."

Zaria nodded. "I'd offer to demonstrate, but you can imagine why that would pose some complications."

"Indeed." A pouch of coins skidded across the counter once the girl had returned the explosive to its wrappings. "For your sake, I hope the product makes up for the long wait."

Zaria smiled tightly. Then the girl was gone, two figures detaching from the shadows and following her into the night.

Hell. Now she only had to hope Mister Vaughan didn't use that explosive until she was well out of London.

As she made her way down the corridor, more than ready for a decent night's sleep, she came to an abrupt halt. Voices were emanating behind the door to George's office, sharp and impatient. Unease crept into the back of her throat as she pressed her ear to the wood.

"It's a matter of business," a man was saying. His voice had a snide, nasal quality about it. "You're in debt, George. Ward has extended a considerable amount of clemency, but he's running out of patience."

Zaria had to strain to hear George's reply; he spoke more softly and must have been farther away from the door.

"He asks for a different amount every time, and always more than the time before. How am I meant to plan for that?"

"You keep your own books, don't you?" the other man responded. "You'd best figure it out."

George muttered something Zaria couldn't quite hear, then a second unfamiliar voice cut in.

"You wouldn't know how to beg if your life was on the line, huh? You always did have more pride than a bloke like you ought to." Zaria could almost hear his sneer. "That said, for reasons I don't understand, Ward quite likes you. Believes you do good work, and that your shop's a fixture in this area. So here's his offer: You have a fortnight to pay everything you owe, or one of two things is gonna happen. One, you lose your precious family business. Or two, he'll let you keep it, but your son is gonna work off your debts. Ward could always use a few more in his crew, you see. Choice is yours."

Zaria bit down hard on her lower lip, suppressing a gasp. Given the silence beyond the door, she could only assume George Zhao was equally aghast. Ward, the dark market kingpin, also controlled a significant portion of Devil's Acre. Anyone who lived in the slum paid for his crew's protection—either from the coppers, rival gangs, or the crew themselves. Business owners, however, were expected to contribute far more than most, and on a monthly basis. Last year a brothel owner had refused to pay up, and a week later he was discovered to have offed himself. Or, at least, that was the story. The business was now run by Ward's crew.

The kingpin had his uses, though. When it came to the dark market, he kept buyers and sellers alike in check. Anyone who had an issue with undelivered commissions or payments could appeal to him, and he would have his men deal with the problem discreetly— for a percentage. He also helped rich buyers track down the right alchemologist for a job. Though Zaria knew Ward must be aware of her existence, she hadn't had any personal dealings with him yet. She feared it was only a matter of time before one of her clients invoked his services. Vaughan almost certainly would once he realized he'd been duped.

Overall, the kingpin was a notorious presence in London, and neither Parliament nor law enforcement cared to interfere. If the rumors were true, this was because he had contacts in both places.

Given that Zaria lived and worked in the pawnshop, she and George had an agreement that she cover 25 percent of his dues. She didn't know exactly how much debt he was in, but he prodded her for payments with enough desperation that she was sure the amount wasn't negligible. It *must* be considerable if the local kingpin was threatening to take the entire pawnshop.

Well. The pawnshop, or Jules.

The idea of Jules being forced to join the kingpin's crew was almost too horrible to bear. Not only because of the type of work it would entail, but because Zaria knew her friend would do it. Regardless of what George chose, once Jules knew what the options were, he would give himself up willingly. That was the type of person he was—his loyalty to his family meant he would never allow his father to give up the business if there was another alternative.

"You're not taking my business *or* my boy," George said finally, his voice unsteady, and Zaria realized she was digging her nails into her palms with enough ferocity to sting.

One of the men laughed; by now, Zaria was too distracted to tell them apart. "You get the money and that won't be a problem, will it?"

"You ought to be thankful," the other man said. "Anyone else woulda been homeless already."

"Or fingerless," his companion put in, guffawing.

"Two weeks is hardly enough time." This was George, his reply barely audible.

"Two weeks is all you get. Be grateful it ain't two days—that was my recommendation."

Zaria was struggling to hold her tongue. Part of her wanted to burst through the door to George's office and—what? What could she possibly hope to accomplish that wouldn't make everything exponentially worse? The injustice of it all was infuriating, but nothing she said or did would make a difference. What did Ward or his men care for justice? It was common knowledge that the kingpin requested more money each month just because he could. That Zaria hadn't seen this coming was the most ridiculous part of all.

The sound of footsteps interrupted her mental spiral, and she scrambled away from the door in the seconds before it opened, slipping into the pawnshop and hoping to hell the kingpin's men went out the back way.

She only relaxed once a full minute had passed, letting her shoulders slump as she considered what to do next. She yearned to confront George. To ask him what he would do if he couldn't get the money in time. Did he plan to tell Jules? Should *Zaria* tell Jules? She knew George was a proud man, and he wouldn't be pleased to know she'd eavesdropped on that particular conversation. But even if he wasn't likely to have told *her* what had happened, she had to imagine he would tell his own son.

She would give him time to do the right thing. And if he didn't, Zaria would have to decide whether to tell Jules herself.

7

ZARIA

THE NEXT DAY PASSED IN A BLUR OF ANXIETY. BETWEEN THE deal involving the faulty explosive and what she'd overheard from George's office, Zaria felt trapped in a corner. Jules had stopped by her room shortly after she'd gone to bed, showing her the salve the Hoffmans had given him for his swollen nose, and it had taken every ounce of her self-control to force a grim smile when he reassured her—once again—that they would find a way to get her more soulsteel.

She hated keeping things from Jules. The weight of all she wasn't saying was a physical sensation pressing down on her from every angle. George had left shortly after the kingpin's men last night, and Zaria had pretended nothing was amiss, returning his curt nod as he swept outside. She'd wondered where he was going. If there was any possible way he would be able to pay his debts in a mere fortnight. She sincerely doubted it. George's capacity for outright denial was unmatched. If she knew him at all, he would pretend last night hadn't happened and carry on as he always did. Not for the first time, she considered talking to him, but she knew from experience it wasn't likely to make a difference.

In the end, she'd spent much of today simply trying to avoid Jules. It turned out to be easy; he was still contending with all the items that had been pledged yesterday. Every week followed the same pattern: People from all over the slum made their pledges on Monday, then returned Saturday to redeem them. By then, they would have received their weekly wages, and as a result, Saturday was known in pawnshops as redemption day.

Would that cycle come to a halt in two weeks' time? It went without saying that Zaria would rather see the pawnshop close than see Jules forced to work for the kingpin, but the idea still unnerved her. No matter how she tried to convince herself it could be a positive thing—wasn't she always looking for an excuse to get out of here?—she knew that it would only make their lives worse. They'd end up homeless, forced to sleep in filth and pick up low-paying factory jobs. Penniless, they likely wouldn't even make it out of Devil's Acre.

Nausea festered in the pit of her stomach as she watched Jules organize the shop's meager offerings. She'd come to help him close up, just as she always did, but her lack of focus was blatant.

"You okay?" Jules asked, wiping dust on the front of his trousers as he finished with a shelf of dishware.

Zaria nodded. "Just tired."

It was the truth—she still hadn't recovered from the previous week's work. But Jules knew her better than that. He snatched a gilded cane from one of the shelves, eyes narrowing as he pointed it at her. "A porkie if I've ever heard one."

"I'm not lying!"

"See, here's the thing," Jules said, letting the cane drop. "It makes no sense for you to deny it when we both know I'm smarter than that. I *know* you're not okay, Zaria. I get it. But we'll get through it like we always do."

She nodded again, trying to push away the mental image she couldn't stop conjuring: one of Jules pointing a *real* weapon, expression cold as he carried out the kingpin's warped version of justice.

"You know what I think?"

But Zaria never did find out what Jules thought. He trailed off, consternation twisting his features, as the door to the pawnshop gave an audible *click*.

They both froze in place. Jules's eyes, as wide as dinner plates, met Zaria's through the candlelight.

Wind? he mouthed.

She gave a single shake of her head, hissing, "You locked it. I'm certain."

Thieves in the slum didn't limit themselves to picking pockets, and Zaria had forgotten her knife in her workshop when she'd changed clothes earlier. Her heart was frantic as she took a step closer to Jules, scanning the shelves for something to use as a weapon.

The door swung open, a whip-quick motion.

A shadowy figure stepped inside. It was clearly a boy: Tall and lean, clad all in black, and when the light caught the angles of his face, Zaria realized she *knew* him.

"Who the hell are you?" Jules demanded. "We're closed, and it's well past visiting hours."

The only response was a soft laugh. The boy shut the door and moved more fully into the candlelight's illumination. Yes, Zaria thought, that slicked-back hair, those sharp features, the overconfident set of his shoulders...it was one of the dark market lackeys from the other night. His elder companion was nowhere to be seen, but Zaria didn't doubt he was close. Men like this rarely worked alone.

Zaria shot Jules a look, indicating he should be cautious. Taking a step forward, she said, "I don't know what the hell you're doing here or why you've broken our door, but Saville isn't getting his money back."

The boy tilted his head. Kane—that was his name, she remembered now. He had a face made for smirks and knowing glances. The kind of face that said, *I do stupid things purely out of curiosity.* Beneath that, though, his jaw was clenched, his forehead slightly furrowed. He was as handsome as she recalled. A gal-sneaker, Zaria supposed. Typical.

"I didn't break the door," he said. The timbre of his voice was low, as smooth as silk. "I just picked the lock. It was disconcertingly easy, by the way. And I'm not here for money."

"Then why *are* you here?" Zaria demanded. Her blood pounded in her ears.

Dark eyes flicked to her face. "I'm here for you, alchemologist."

Zaria tensed, confusion and misgiving warring in her chest. Whatever reason Kane had to be looking for an alchemologist, she was certain it couldn't be good. "Was there something wrong with the commission?"

"What?" Kane flicked a brow upward. The high collar of his black coat was askew, Zaria noticed, a contrast to his unruffled appearance three days prior.

"Don't be coy," she bit out. "I recognize you from the other night. I assume your partner's around here too somewhere, isn't he?"

Kane frowned, seemingly perplexed. The expression didn't suit him. "Partner?"

"The man you came here with before?"

"Oh. Larkin." An eye roll. "He's not my partner."

Zaria exchanged a glance with Jules, thrusting her chin at the door to indicate he should leave while he had the chance. Jules gave a stubborn shake of his head, and Zaria watched in horror as he withdrew a serrated knife from somewhere behind the counter. Its edges were rusted, clearly dull, but he pointed it at Kane without wavering. "Get out of my shop. Now."

Kane blinked in amusement. "That is, without a doubt, the most ancient knife I have ever seen. Do you intend to make me sit for a quarter of an hour while you saw through my skin?"

"I'm not against the idea."

"I assure you, I've no interest in your shop or anything in it." Kane raised one hand, reaching inside his coat with the other. Before Zaria could process the movement, he had withdrawn a revolver—similar to the one she'd handed him the other night—letting it dangle from a finger as he thrust it toward her. "Here."

She narrowed her eyes, studying him in distrust. Had he commissioned such a weapon on his own, or did Saville value him more greatly than she'd realized? "Why would I want your gun?"

"I'm working with the assumption you'd prefer me unarmed," Kane drawled. "If you're saying that's not the case—"

Zaria snatched the gun from his loose grip. When she pointed it at him, he didn't look remotely surprised. The weapon was still warm from being against his chest. "Whatever you came to say, say it quickly."

"Perhaps we could talk somewhere more private?"

"Absolutely not," Jules said before Zaria could answer. She didn't miss the way he shifted his body in front of the cabinet where George kept the pawnshop's money, but somehow she didn't think Kane was lying about his disinterest in the shop. He didn't look as though he had need for money—at least not compared to the customers Zaria was accustomed to seeing. That, combined with the dark market weapon, made her curious about what he had to say.

"We can talk," she decided. "Briefly. But I keep the gun."

Kane tilted his head, flashing the ghost of a grin. "Lead the way."

Zaria sidestepped over to the door, never lowering the revolver. She heard Jules hiss her name, low and furious, and she directed an apologetic shrug his way. "Don't worry about me. I'll shoot if I have to."

She said it mostly for Kane's benefit, but he appeared unperturbed even as Jules added, "She will."

"Right," Kane said, now with an air of impatience. "You're both terribly threatening. If I may?" He indicated the door.

Zaria ushered him through. Without a candle, the corridor was dark as pitch, but Kane didn't miss a step. He was a great deal taller than she was, which irked her unnecessarily.

"Are you always this mistrustful?" His murmur stretched into a wavering echo.

"Only of people like you."

A short laugh. "And what are *people like me*?"

Zaria gave him another light jab with the gun, glaring at what she imagined was the middle of his back. "Slippery. Practiced liars. Willing to sell their souls."

Kane gave a hum low in his throat. "To whom am I meant to have sold my soul? The devil?"

Zaria didn't put much stock in the devil. "People like you work for either the highest bidder or the man who threatens you most."

"People like me do whatever it takes," Kane said as they crossed the corridor and entered her workshop, rotating to face her. His eyes weren't as dark as they'd looked from afar—they were more of a hazel. "And so do people like you, I suspect, or you wouldn't be talking to me right now."

Zaria scowled, lighting a candle in the corner of the room. As it flared to life, she tried to imagine her workshop from Kane's perspective. It was crammed full of an odd assortment of pipes, valves, brackets, and tools. Half-finished projects lined the shelves, along with chemicals in welded-shut containers. Glass bottles large and small held a number of different powders and liquids. She caught Kane eyeing them curiously and indicated that he should step away from a particularly sparkly one.

"Get to the point," Zaria said, shivering as orange light licked up the side of Kane's face to settle in the hollow of his cheek. "Jules will worry."

His lips quirked in a way she supposed he thought was charming. "I take it that's your unpleasant companion upstairs?"

"He's not unpleasant."

"Agree to disagree." Kane extended a hand before Zaria could continue arguing. "Kane Durante, if we're finally doing proper introductions. I work for Alexander Ward."

Zaria felt the blood drain from her face. It took her a moment to find her voice, and when she did, the words came out strangled. "Alexander Ward? *The* Ward?"

"That's the one."

She knit her brow. "Wait. I thought you worked for Saville."

"That was a short-term arrangement. Part of a job."

Zaria had seen members of Ward's crew before, and Kane didn't quite fit the bill. The men who always came to collect dues were middle-aged and broad shouldered, seeming to share one brain between

them. Kane, though, was different. He was young and lithe, for one, but also distinctly calculating. He seemed accustomed to getting what he wanted and moved as if nothing ever cowed him.

"Prove it," she said.

"Prove what, exactly?"

"That you work for Ward."

Kane's answering expression was withering as he reached up and yanked the collar of his jacket aside. Without knowing why, Zaria flinched. For a heartbeat, she had the wild impression her reaction had hurt him; his face tightened perceptibly. But perhaps it was only her imagination, for the tension was gone the next moment, as she saw what was inked on the pale skin of his neck.

"You're marked by him," Zaria said, a needless observation.

"Well spotted."

The kingpin's mark was a crude thing, stark against the striations of blue-tinged veins. It was too harsh when compared to the delicate hollow of his throat, the angled juts of his cheekbones. Kane Durante was a proper *criminal*. He was no different than the men Ward had sent to threaten and intimidate George.

Zaria was abruptly possessed by the desire to hit him.

She forced herself to take a breath, another question occurring to her. "Was it *Ward* who commissioned the magic revolver?"

"No."

"Oh." Those who made dark market purchases rarely used their real names, and though Zaria had no love for the kingpin—hated him even—she couldn't deny the idea of Ward's owning one of her creations was a thrill. "Why are you here, then?"

Kane scrutinized her workshop, taking in her unfinished commissions and the organized chaos around them. When he finally answered, it was without meeting her eyes. "A very good question.

You see, I've been attempting to get my hands on something important. An artifact that's going to be displayed in the Great Exhibition. Conning the owner of a shipping company—*that's* who commissioned you—was supposed to ensure we could steal it before it went on display. Alas, it didn't quite work out."

"We?"

"My friend and I," Kane clarified, finally turning to face her. He adjusted the collar of his jacket as he did so, covering both the mark and the pale skin of his throat. "Not Larkin. Someone else. Given the security detail and sheer number of people who will be attending the Exhibition, it's going to be very, very difficult for us to steal this item without landing in prison. That's where you come in."

Zaria hardened her expression even as unease tightened her throat. "I don't follow."

"I come with a proposition. You see, an alchemologist could be very useful to me."

There was a beat of silence as she chewed that over. "Do you have the money for a commission?"

"I'm not looking for a single commission."

"Then what do you *want*?"

Kane caught his tongue between his teeth, considering her through a half-lidded gaze. "I won't be able to do this alone. And I think you and your clever little magic would be very helpful indeed." He held up a hand, stopping her protest before she could voice it. "I've seen your work. It's better than anything else available through the dark market at present. You may not realize it, but you've built yourself quite the reputation. Everyone wants your inventions, and yet you're notorious for not delivering on commissions."

That sent an unpleasant jolt through her. Sweat began to bead at the back of her neck. "I—I've a reputation?"

"Don't tell me you didn't know."

Zaria blew out a breath, trying to process this. Here she'd thought herself of little import to the kingpin. "And now you're asking me to help you *steal from the Exhibition*?"

"I suppose you could put it that way."

"That's mad."

"Is it?"

"I'm not a thief! I'm... an inventor." Perhaps it wasn't exactly the right word, but it fit better than most.

Kane gave an impatient flick of his hand. "You wouldn't have to do the actual stealing. But you can make *magic*, and I've seen what your creations are capable of."

"Alchemology is about manipulating function, as I expect you well know. It's about changing an existing mechanical process, an existing chemical reaction. It's not as simple as you make it sound. The limitations are endless."

"Right. But the limitations depend on the alchemologist, and you have fewer than most if my information is correct."

"Why don't you ask..." Zaria fought to recall the name of the alchemologist who lived just outside Devil's Acre. "Étienne?"

"He specializes in security devices, which is essentially the opposite of what I'm going for. Besides, he's, like, ninety years old."

The man was nowhere near that, but Zaria didn't think it prudent to argue. She frowned. "So you want me to... what? Create items to help you do the job?"

"In a sense." Kane's voice turned impatient, and it caught her off guard. She kept very still, watching as a muscle ticked in his jaw. He had a wild, frantic energy about him she hadn't noticed at first. "I would prefer if you worked with me as I assess the situation, and we can go from there. To start, are you familiar with those exploding devices that fill the room with thick smoke? The kind that's impossible to see through?"

"Aleuite explosives," Zaria snapped, then gave her head a baffled shake. "You're asking me to help you commit a crime by working for *free*?"

"Of course not," Kane scoffed. "Nobody does anything for free. Not here."

"Then what are you offering?"

His eyes glittered as he shook his head. "I don't make offers. I let people tell me their price."

"You're insufferable."

"I'm not sure that's relevant."

Zaria thrust a finger at the door, vaguely indicating the direction of the pawnshop. "Ward is threatening to kick us out of the building. His men—your *colleagues*—make our lives a living hell. Why would you possibly think I'd want to work for you?"

"*With* me," Kane corrected her. "Hate Ward all you like. Lord knows it's warranted. But don't let the company I keep prevent you from getting what you want."

She paused, uncertain. What could Kane possibly have that she wanted? She didn't know him, and anyone who worked for the kingpin could hardly be trustworthy. But she saw the fine fabric of his jacket, considered the slick sheen of his boots. Somehow, by whatever unsavory means, he had money. His connection to Ward also afforded about as much protection as one could hope for in Devil's Acre. What if this was the opportunity Zaria had been waiting for?

"Come now," Kane said, arching a brow. The expression was cocky on him. "Don't tell me you're unsure. You're a dark market vendor. And yet you live"—he waved a dismissive hand—"*here*. Do I take it your business venture isn't exactly going well?"

She felt her face heat. "What's it to you?"

"My point is, if it's money you want, I'm good for it."

"I'm sure you are. You have the hard-earned quid of everyone who lives in this part of the slum, don't you?"

"I have little to do with the collection of dues."

"But you have something to do with it."

Kane inclined his chin, mouth a cruel line. "And you're too morally pure to deal with someone like me, is that it? The terror of Devil's Acre. Empty on the inside." Sarcasm was heavy in his voice. "Perhaps I am all those things. But it doesn't quite dissuade you, does it?"

Zaria shook her head as if that might clear her spinning thoughts. "How much can you give me?"

"Tell you what—you help me get to the necklace, and I'll take whatever else is in the display with it. The exhibit was sent by an Irish jeweler named George Waterhouse, and I guarantee every piece will fetch more in resale than you've seen in your entire life."

Damn it all, but he made it so tempting. Though Zaria tried not to look, his words painted a picture of hope. She could settle her debts to George *and* make sure he had enough to pay Ward. They wouldn't lose the pawnshop, and Jules would escape the kingpin's grasping claws. They could finally leave London. They could buy a house in the country, and she would paint the door yellow herself.

But there was one more, rather important, element.

"How can you be sure we won't get caught?"

Kane bared his teeth—grinned?—as he tilted his head toward the ceiling. He took a step forward, then another, until the barrel of the revolver was pressed firmly against his chest. She had the urge to move away, but didn't, gritting her teeth at the heat of his body so close to hers. It was utterly inappropriate, the proximity at which they were standing. To her horror, it sent her pulse leaping, and she tilted her chin up. The candle on her worktable flickered, tendrils of fire reflecting in the depths of Kane's eyes.

"I joined Ward's crew when I was ten years old," he said softly, running a finger over the curve of his neck. The tattoo there. "He taught me everything I know. I don't *get* caught."

Zaria's nerves sparked to life at the note of danger in his words. It shouldn't have been enough to convince her—really, it shouldn't have—but she couldn't help being convinced nonetheless. He was clever, this boy. He knew what she wanted, and had reeled her in so seamlessly that even being aware of it didn't make a difference.

"Okay, Kane Durante," she said, moving the gun away from his chest so as to offer her hand. "You've got yourself a deal."

KANE

KANE HADN'T ALWAYS BEEN SOMEONE TO FEAR.

When Ward had first taken him in, he'd been swiftly alienated from the rest of the crew. Unlike them, Kane hadn't had to win Ward's trust—it was simply given to him. He looked like Ward's deceased son, the older men whispered behind his back. That was the only reason Ward liked him. Everyone knew antagonizing Kane was dangerous, as it risked Ward's wrath, so the younger boys took to bothering him at night. They were upper-class youths, with fathers who collected rent from the families on Ward's behalf. They thought themselves untouchable.

Or at least they did, until the night someone attacked Kane in the dark.

Upon seeing Kane's bruised face the next day, Ward called a meeting and demanded the culprit come forward. When no one did, he whipped out his dark market gun and fired a streak of blazing magic through every window in the room.

"I'll ask *once more*," he'd bellowed, "and if I don't get an answer, I start aiming for heads."

When Bobby Martin took a shaky step forward, Ward shot him.

"You are always my priority," he'd told Kane later that day. "They are my men, but you are my heart. They know that. And a man is always more dangerous once he learns how to aim for the heart."

But if Kane had learned one thing about Ward's crew, it was that they'd never respect a boy who didn't fight his own battles. They were like wolves, constantly battling for their place next to the alpha.

So the next time someone took it upon themselves to try to dispose of Kane, he didn't wait for Ward to pull the trigger.

Once he'd finished retching, he'd expected Ward to be angry. You weren't supposed to kill your allies. To Kane's surprise, though, Ward seemed almost delighted. His mouth tilted up in a cold smile, and his eyes took on that eerie gleam with which Kane had become so familiar.

On that day, the rest of the crew learned two very important things: One, that Ward would allow Kane to kill whomever he wished. And two, that Kane would do it.

He hadn't retched since. Instead, he'd hollowed himself out, little by little, until all that remained were wry grins and bottomless self-hatred.

"I've refined the plan," Kane told Fletcher the next morning.

He'd scarcely slept a wink for the second night in a row, though

this time pain wasn't the culprit. Blessedly, Ward's punishment had long since worn off. No—he'd spent the rest of the evening in the sitting room reflecting on his conversation with Mendoza.

Zaria, his brain supplied. That was her given name. It suited her, somehow, in the way it rolled swiftly off the tongue. Kane could still feel the press of the gun against his chest, the heat of her dark gaze on his face. Had he made a mistake, seeking out her help? She was clearly hesitant to trust him. But she was the kind of girl who *wanted*—Kane could taste it simply by being in her presence. And who could blame her? She lived in the slum with a pawnbroker and his son. Her father had left her nothing save a reputation that, by the sounds of it, had quickly deteriorated.

And her *work*—Kane had taken a good look at it when she'd led him into her workshop. Though he knew little about the process of alchemology, he could discern when the product was well-made. Zaria Mendoza's inventions were created with meticulous care. No wonder she was in such high demand.

"Are you *drinking*?" Fletcher said, stifling a yawn. "It's barely past dawn."

Kane drained the last of his whiskey. He'd long since forgotten about it, and it was unpleasantly warm. "I went to see Ward the day before yesterday."

"Ah. I wondered why you seemed off." Fletcher snatched the glass from Kane's hand and took it over to the table, where he sank into one of the hard-backed chairs. "You didn't tell him, did you? That we were too late to get the necklace?"

"He already knew."

Fletcher's face turned masklike. His hesitation was tangible as he asked, "Was he very angry?"

"Yes," Kane said. "Yes, Ward was angry." The words sounded dull even as they threatened to choke him.

"Are you okay?"

Rarely. "Of course."

Fletcher dragged a hand over his chin. "You can tell me, you know. If he hurt you again."

Kane's face heated as his friend trailed off. More than once he remembered arriving home with blood on his shoes or bruises on his face. Ward preferred to hurt Kane by making him hurt others. But on the few occasions he'd lashed out himself, seemingly unable to control his rage, it had been...

Well. Kane's memories were fogged by shock and time.

"I'm not hurt," he said shortly. "Merely added to the collection."

Fletcher knew what he meant without Kane's having to roll up his sleeve. "That's not right."

"Almost makes you wanna leave this hell, doesn't it?" *Say yes. Please, God, say yes.*

But Fletcher shook his head. "Stop dreaming about escaping when you know we never will. You'll only torment yourself."

You can escape, though, Kane thought. *Soon.* He would make sure of it. Somehow this job, this place, hadn't yet broken Fletcher's spirit, and Kane was determined it never would. After they delivered the necklace to Ward, Fletcher would be free to go, and Kane could suffer in peace. Could spend his days bloodying those who owed Ward money and pushing families with small children out of their homes. Perhaps when there was no one left to whom he could confess his guilt, he would cease feeling it at all.

It was something he hoped for. But it was also something he feared.

"Tell me what you came up with," Fletcher said when Kane remained quiet. "I assume Ward's demands haven't changed. The Crystal Palace is huge, and once it opens, it'll be difficult to steal from. There'll be far too many witnesses, not to mention security measures."

"I'm aware." Kane grunted, wishing for his glass back even as his head pounded. "But I've found someone to help."

"Who?"

"Do you remember the alchemologist Saville commissioned the revolver from? Zaria Mendoza?"

Fletcher's brows came together. He crossed his ankles beneath the table, causing the hems of his trousers to rise up slightly. "I mean, obviously I never met her myself, but I remember. Everyone knows about her. You think she could help us?"

Kane rose, crossing the room to reach for the whiskey on the opposite counter. Fletcher beat him there, grabbing the liquor and tossing him a dismayed look.

"Again, it's *dawn*. Answer the question."

Kane sighed dramatically. He pulled his fingers through the dark mess of his hair. "I went to visit her last night."

"And how did that go?"

Kane briefly recounted the evening, noting that Zaria had been on his mind since Ward refused to be of any help the day before. He described the things she could make and what he'd seen in the cramped quarters of her workshop last night. "She's clever. Really clever. And if we're going to pull this off, we'll need magic."

Fletcher tugged at the lapel of his jacket but didn't argue. "I never said she wasn't clever. I saw that revolver."

"You should've seen her demonstration. Trigger smooth as butter and a firing speed you wouldn't believe. No kickback whatsoever."

"Can she be trusted, though?"

"Anyone can be trusted if you're making the best offer."

"And what was yours?"

Kane huffed a short laugh. "I said that if she helped us get to the necklace, I'd give her the rest of the Waterhouse display. Told her it would go for thousands of pounds."

Fletcher's eyes widened, mouth thinning perceptibly. "God above, Kane. Do you know how much harder that's going to make things? The theft of a necklace might not draw attention right away, but stealing the entire *exhibit*? And just how do you figure we'll be able to get out of the Crystal Palace without getting caught?"

"Relax."

"*Relax*? Kane, you're an apt thief, but you're not a god."

"I never claimed to be," Kane said, a resigned sort of calm settling in his bones. "I have no intention of stealing the Waterhouse jewels. I'm not mad."

Fletcher shook his head, lips parted as understanding took hold. "You're going to double-cross her."

"It's perfect, don't you see? I promised her something I can't possibly deliver until the task is already complete. That way there's no backing out. We get the necklace, we escape, and she's none the wiser until it's far too late."

"So it's a con."

"Of course it's a con." Kane would do what he could to keep Zaria happy while she worked with them, and then he'd cut her loose. What other option did he have? Ward had made it clear he wouldn't tolerate further delays. "Don't tell me you're suddenly turning *moral*."

Fletcher's mild gaze tracked Kane's progress as he paced the length of the room. "Never. But if you ask me, a girl who deals on the dark market isn't the kind of girl who will be easy to trick."

"She may deal on the market, but she's just a regular girl," Kane insisted. "We've tricked far more dangerous people than her."

There was a long pause before Fletcher said, "All right. If you think it'll work. If you really think she can help."

"I know she can."

His reply came out harsher than he'd meant it to. Light slanted across the table, dulled by the grit-stained window, and the moment that followed was too quiet until Fletcher made a sound in the back of his throat. "Don't, Kane."

"Don't what?"

"Make that face. It's your self-hatred face."

Kane wondered how his friend could tell the difference between that and his regular expression. "It is not."

"This isn't about Mendoza, is it? What's the problem?"

No, it wasn't about Zaria. She didn't matter; she was merely another moving part for Kane to contend with.

"I'm just tired." He set his jaw against the lie. He *was* tired, but that wasn't the problem. The problem was this: He and Fletcher were about to embark on their last job together. They'd either fail, and Fletcher would die, or they would succeed, and Fletcher would leave. If it was the latter, Kane would be glad, but he would also be alone with Ward once more.

Sometimes Kane toyed with the thought of killing the kingpin. Of watching his eyes glaze over and feeling his body go cold. Of leaving this hellscape of a city and never looking back.

But Kane knew that wherever he went, Ward would follow, at least in spirit. He manipulated Kane's life the way a puppeteer pulled strings. Somehow Kane had spent so much time despising Ward that the man had become an integral part of him. Was that love? It didn't feel like it. It felt like something slimier, something far more painful.

It felt like self-destruction.

"When do we meet with Mendoza, then?" Fletcher said, and the

soft lilt of his voice made Kane wonder if it wasn't the first time his friend had asked the question.

He stopped pacing, eyes darting to the door. Outside, rain fell in an even sheet. He could hear it echoing against the converted factory roof.

"I told Zaria we'd meet tomorrow to discuss what we need from her," Kane said eventually. "We can't do much but take it step-by-step."

"And where exactly are we meeting?"

Despite everything, Kane couldn't help a smirk. "Every job starts with a stakeout, Fletch. Surely you know that."

Fletcher inclined his square chin. "So we need to pay the Exhibition a visit ahead of time."

"Yes. And I think it would be rather nice if we had security on our side, don't you?"

Dusk swelled above the rooftops as Kane and Fletcher slunk into the streets. They'd spent a good few hours discussing a course of action—Kane had always been good at improvisation, but he preferred preparation whenever possible. He knew what he wanted from Zaria Mendoza, and he knew how they were going to gain entry to the Exhibition. They all had a role to play, including Zaria, though she wasn't yet aware of it. Kane suspected she wouldn't be thrilled when she found out what that role was.

Now he needed to ensure the coppers didn't get in their way.

He pulled his lips back in a grimace, shoving his hands deeper into the pockets of his coat. The rain was cold and stinging, and it slipped down the back of his neck as he pushed damp hair out of his face. Unlike Fletcher, he hadn't thought to bring a hat.

"Do we know for certain Price will be on duty?" Fletcher asked. He had to raise his voice slightly to be heard above the *tap-a-tap* of rain against the cobblestones.

"If I remember correctly."

"You usually do."

Richard Price was an inspector who worked out of the Westminster Division. He was a humorless sort of man and had been with the Metropolitan Police since they took to the streets twenty-two years prior. Despite having been dirty for at least half of that, he'd retained the job long past his physical prime and now oversaw handfuls of sergeants and constables. Richard was Ward's preferred contact, but that was not the man to whom Kane was referring. No—he was much more familiar with Richard Price Junior, whose name gave him even more power than his sergeant status. It was him Kane would be looking for. A young chap in possession of more confidence than experience, he would be far easier to manipulate.

They walked to Westminster in the type of silence reserved for thieves or companions deeply familiar with each other. As it happened, Kane and Fletcher were both. Kane barely saw where his feet were taking him, but it wasn't that he was familiar with the route—he rarely frequented this part of London—rather, his mind was too occupied. It was filled with plots, with plans, with the guardedly hopeful expression on Zaria's face when she'd agreed to their deal. He couldn't help wondering what she might think when he shared the plan with her. Whether she might catch a whiff of his intended betrayal. If there was one thing he knew about Zaria already, it was this: She looked at everything like she was dismantling it methodically, piece by fragile piece. Kane found he did not care for it at all.

Once, when he was younger and a markedly different version of himself, his mother had commented on how easy he was to read.

When you're sad, the house is sad with you, she would tell him, a croon in lyrical Italian. *I can feel it grow colder.*

Kane remembered very few things about his mother. Perhaps his mind had hidden them from him in unconscious self-preservation, or perhaps he had deviated so far from the boy who had known her, he no longer retained anything that was not Ward. Now, when Kane was sad, he held it inside himself like some explosive substance. Harmless when left alone, but dangerous if it came in contact with the wrong thing.

He very much hoped Zaria Mendoza was not that thing. He did not want to be seen, did not want to be known, and certainly did not want to be understood.

Despite the hour, the city surrounding Whitehall Place—the location of the police headquarters—was a bustle of bodies and sound. People in smart black coats hurried to and fro as a newsboy hollered some indecipherable fact about the most recent headline. This part of London boasted a considerable amount of recent construction, but Kane knew that not far from here terraced slum housing crowded the perimeter. He squinted through the rain, picking out the building occupied by the Metropolitan Police Force's Westminster Division. It was a nondescript reddish brick, set back from the crowds either by conscious design or by virtue of the fact that it was currently occupied by law enforcement.

A middle-aged officer stood outside the Great Scotland Yard entrance, a clay pipe held between two of his fingers in a way that struck Kane as rather dainty. He raised his head as they approached, gaze slipping to Fletcher the way gazes tended to do.

"Price Junior in?" Kane said before the copper could address them.

The man cut them with a look that made it clear he thought them up to no good. Rainwater slipped down the bridge of his nose, which must have been broken at some point. He never took his attention off Fletcher; though, between Kane and Fletcher, the latter was less likely to do something rash and potentially violent. "What's it to you?"

Kane hooked his thumbs through his belt loops. The smile he gave was not a nice one, but before he could speak, he heard his name hollered from the building's entrance.

"Hunt! Get over here."

Kane didn't have to turn to know the speaker was Richard Price Junior, who was shrewd enough never to use his real surname. Broad faced and stern featured, Price crooked a finger at Kane and Fletcher, beckoning them closer. Though the action was one of confidence, there was something about the set of his mouth that betrayed his discomfort.

"We'll talk in my office. Follow me."

Price led them away from the other officer and up the steps leading into the police headquarters. His office was near the entrance, and the colleague waiting inside was sent away with a wave of his hand. Fletcher shut the door with an ominous *click*. Kane motioned for Price to sit down at his desk.

"Please," Price said stiffly, "feel free to take a seat as well."

Kane and Fletcher did not sit.

Price sat. Perhaps it was due to the fact that no one save him had spoken thus far, but there was the beginning of a nervous sheen across his forehead. He hid his anxiety well, though, Kane had to admit. He always did.

"Junior," Kane said, knowing it would annoy the man. "How are you?"

He deliberated two ways of approaching the situation. The first was to play nice with a dirty copper, offer him money, and hope he didn't betray you. The problem with making a deal with men like this, however, was the possibility always existed that someone would offer them a better one. Hell, they might take your money, *then* betray you. This was how Ward dealt with Richard Price Senior, because he trusted the inspector as well as Ward ever trusted anybody. They were on the same page more often than not.

Which was precisely why Kane did *not* trust Richard Price Senior. So he'd come to his son, who always responded better to a little threatening.

That was the second way.

"What do you want, Hunt?" Price said, sounding tired in a way Kane could nearly empathize with. "Did Ward send you?"

Kane's grin was bitter. "Ward doesn't dictate my every move, you know." He might as well have, but Price didn't need to know that.

"Don't be coy with me. Get to the point—I was about to go on patrol."

"Ah." Kane turned to smirk at Fletcher, who stared stonily back. "Someone's confident today. Don't worry, I only came to ask a simple favor. I suppose your lot are going to be contributing security to the Exhibition?"

Price's eyes narrowed. He didn't look all that impressive, the only one of them seated, like a child who had been told to relax. The wall behind him was papered with certificates of obvious import, each one depicting his name in fancy penmanship—no doubt a nod to his work-related escapades.

Kane was not impressed by paper. Kane was impressed by those who made deals with confidence and exceeded expectations. Alas, his expectations for Price were not high, but he was going to have to make it work.

He dropped into the chair opposite the man. "You and your father have cooperated with Ward for quite some time. As such, you know what people like me can offer you." He flashed his teeth, eyeing the fountain pen Price tapped against the inside of his wrist. "But you also know what people like me are capable of."

"You're only boys" was Price's acidic response. His furtive gaze slipped to Fletcher, then back to Kane, cheeks coloring. Evidently, he was deciding not to acknowledge that Fletcher was a good head taller than he was. "Being part of Ward's crew may make you feel important, but you're not. And you certainly don't understand the intricacies of the law."

Kane leaned back in his chair, arranging his face in a frown. "Fletch, do we know anything about the law?"

There was a pause as Fletcher pretended to think. "You know what? I think—I *think*—I remember hearing you're not supposed to take bribes or look the other way when something illegal happens."

"That sounds right. But if someone *were* to start taking bribes, don't you think it's in their best interest to keep that information quiet?"

"Oh, certainly." Fletcher was the portrait of seriousness. "Especially when the man paying out those bribes keeps a *very* comprehensive list of names and dates. It's important to remember where your money went and when."

Kane nodded at the ceiling. "That it is."

"I *get it*," Price snarled, now looking more like an angry law enforcement officer and less like a boy playing at one. He half rose from his seat, fingers splayed across the desk. "What, specifically, do you want from me?"

Kane leaned forward until he and Price were almost nose to nose. He grinned. "Nothing."

"Excuse me?"

"I want you to do nothing. Hear nothing. See nothing. I want you and your most charmingly corrupt colleagues to do whatever it takes to get placed inside the Crystal Palace, as close as you can get to the Waterhouse exhibit, and then I want you to do *absolutely nothing.*"

Now Price simply looked dubious. "The Duke of Wellington has upward of ten thousand troops on standby, and we've recruited an additional thousand officers. I only have control over my own division, and I've no idea where the Royal Commission will want my men."

This had occurred to Kane already. It might have been a problem, but if he could be certain of one thing, it was that powerful men were suggestible when it came to other powerful men. "Then stand by the exhibit yourself and put your rank to good use for once."

"And what do I get out of this, Hunt?" Price crossed his arms over the brass buttons carving a line down the front of his black uniform. "Besides watching someone other than me catch you in the middle of whatever stunt you're trying to pull."

Kane ticked the answers off on his fingers. "One, you know Ward is good for money. If everything goes well, you'll see it. Two, your family's dirty little secrets stay buried. And three, Fletcher won't kill you."

The wooden floorboards creaked as Fletcher shifted his weight in the corner. He wasn't much of a killer, but Price didn't need to know that. What mattered was that he was large, intimidating, and *looked* like he might kill you if it suited him.

"I don't think even Ward would dare have a copper harmed," Price said, the final shred of his bravery laid out between them.

Kane snorted. He couldn't help it.

"God help you, Junior," he said. "We both know who really runs this city, and it sure as hell ain't the coppers."

ZARIA

ZARIA'S FATHER HAD NEVER BEEN WARM.

Itzal Mendoza was the type of man who taught you how to be clever, how to navigate situations, and how to survive. He hadn't wasted much time on love and affection, though Zaria hadn't particularly minded. She was desperate to be clever in a world where women were told they didn't need to be. She yearned to take what she wanted from people who didn't want to give her anything. And of course, above all else, she wanted to survive.

Perhaps it was that Itzal had spent too much time grieving her mother. After immigrating from Spain to England, he'd met Aurora Clarke, a middle-class woman who fell for his handsome face and smooth accent. But Itzal's heart was broken when Aurora left him for a Welshman, turning up only once nine months later to deliver a child.

If she'd known her mother at all, Zaria might have been hurt that the woman hadn't wanted her. Of course, Itzal hadn't wanted her, either—he'd told her as much. He had loved Aurora and gotten Zaria instead. A poor consolation prize. But during the years that Cecile was around, Zaria hadn't felt quite so alone. She had been something of a mother figure, though she was only about a decade older than Zaria. Cecile had taught her more than just alchemology—she'd taught her how to be a woman in a man's field. How constantly being underestimated was a series of chances to prove yourself. With Cecile at her side, Zaria had nearly stopped resenting her father.

For a while.

Now that they were both gone, she remembered what it was to be angry.

So really it didn't matter that Itzal might not have loved Zaria, just like it didn't matter that her mother had abandoned both of them the moment she had the chance. Thanks to Cecile, Zaria was equipped nonetheless with the tools she needed. What she hadn't committed to memory, she could learn on her own. She hadn't needed Itzal's help then, and she didn't need it now. What she *did* need, though, was a primateria source.

Tonight she was looking through her father's work for the first time in years, brushing dust from the pages. Helping Kane steal from the Exhibition was surely the equivalent of taking on several new commissions, a fact that had only occurred to Zaria once he'd left. Had she made a vow she couldn't keep? She had no soulsteel. No free time. No *energy*. And yet what other choice did she have?

"What's this?" Jules asked as he entered the room, squinting at the myriad notes spread across Zaria's desk. Some of them were her own, scrawled onto paper that had been folded and unfolded more times than she could count, but most had been written by Itzal.

Those covered the yellowing sheets of a poorly bound book—the only book he hadn't set aflame—meticulously sketched and carefully preserved. There were drawings of gears and levers, cogs and gauges, recipes for various potions, and mathematical equations. In the margins were jotted notes and brief descriptions, some circled, others stroked out with aggressive dark lines.

"I'm trying to see if my father left anything about his search for the primateria source," Zaria said, not lifting her gaze from the page she was skimming. She'd been sitting here for hours already, her back beginning to ache from leaning over the worktable, but once she was determined to do something, the devil himself couldn't pull her away.

"I thought he burned all his research on that. You've looked before," Jules reminded her, as if she didn't know.

"I'm looking again. Maybe I missed something."

Jules peered over her shoulder as she ran a finger down the rough parchment. A cloud of awkwardness hung in the air between them following their argument the previous night. He hadn't been pleased when she told him about the deal she'd made with Kane, calling him a number of names that would have been scandalous in polite company. Zaria couldn't exactly blame him. Kane was, after all, working for the man who ensured the pawnshop rarely made a shilling that didn't go to his crew.

Though he still didn't know the whole truth, Jules eventually admitted the payment was too good to pass on. The problem, he rightfully pointed out, was whether Zaria would be able to give Kane everything he requested. Each time she created magic lately, it seemed to take more from her. Earlier today Jules had found her passed out on the floor of her workshop, unable to recall whether she'd fainted or simply fallen asleep.

So here she was, scouring Itzal Mendoza's yellow-edged notes. The endeavor was proving futile, but if Zaria was going to work for Kane, she needed to get her hands on a primateria source. It was becoming more difficult to ignore the impact creating magic was having on her body. She knew little about Kane, but it was obvious he wasn't the patient type.

Without speaking, Jules sat down beside her, pulling a stack of notes over to his side of the table. Zaria shot him a tight but appreciative smile. For a while, they simply sat in companionable silence, the shuffling of papers the only sound in the room. Zaria was determined not to miss a single page. She scanned a messily scrawled ledger, her stomach hollowing. Each time he took a commission, Itzal noted a brief description of what the person had purchased, their last known address, and the amount of money received. The commissions were impossibly close in date, the prices higher than anything Zaria ever managed to get. She worked too slowly. She could be a poor negotiator, given that oftentimes she was too blunt, too impatient.

"I don't understand what any of this means," Jules sighed, shoving a handful of onyx hair off his brow. His face was skeletal in the dim light. "I'm not convinced I would know if I *did* find something important."

Zaria shared his frustration. Even with her experience, her father's scribbles were hard to decipher. "You don't need to help me."

He ignored that. "Are we sure these magic sources even exist? I mean, they could just be a legend."

"Of course we're not sure. But Hohenheim was the original alchemologist. If anyone could create such a thing, it was him."

"Create them from *what*, though?"

Zaria shrugged, squinting at a cramped bit of handwriting instead of looking at Jules. "His own life force, supposedly. It was

his greatest work—a complicated series of chemical processes. I'd understand it better if I could find one."

"If they do exist, though, they could be anywhere in the world. This is mad, Zaria."

Christ. He was right. She was in danger of adopting her father's lifelong obsession, and it was a futile quest. The list of names, of prices and places, seemed suddenly to mock her. Seized by sudden fury, Zaria swept the stack of parchment aside, watching blindly as the sheets pirouetted to the floor.

It does not matter what you dream, Itzal had told her once. *It matters only what you accomplish.*

"And what difference did it make, Papa?" she murmured to herself, hands tightening into fists. "You died nonetheless."

Jules stared at her. "What did you say?"

"Nothing."

What was wrong with her? Zaria stooped shakily to pick up the notes, and Jules bent down to help her. She couldn't resist examining them, running her fingers over the familiar script. Remembering the *scritch-scritch* of Itzal's pen in the dead of night, long after he'd said he was going to sleep. Line after line flashed before Zaria's eyes. Some written sideways, some covered after the fact by sketches. She arranged the papers into a pile, then paused, heart slamming against her ribs.

Because there, in the margin of the sheet she was holding now, was handwriting she recognized. Handwriting that was indubitably not Itzal Mendoza's. It was too slanted, too narrow, too neat.

Source: disguised?

"Look at this." She shoved the piece of parchment under Jules's nose.

He recoiled in surprise, brows drawing together as he tried to focus on the tiny script. "What am I meant to be seeing?"

Zaria pointed at the words. "This isn't my father's writing. It's Cecile's."

"You think 'source' could be referring to a primateria source?"

"What else? She would have been working with my father around the time he was looking for it. I never imagined him involving her, but…"

Itzal and Cecile had worked well together, but their relationship had been fraught, hence its short duration. Itzal had a tendency to believe he always knew best, and he certainly wouldn't have wanted to risk someone else finding the source before he did. Zaria could recall the tension in the house the night Cecile had left. Her departure had been abrupt; she'd wrapped Zaria in a quick but tight one-armed hug, shot Itzal a glare, and slammed the door behind her. Even years later, Itzal had refused to explain what they were arguing about.

Jules thumbed his collar to loosen it. His interactions with Cecile had rarely gone deeper than basic pleasantries, but he knew she'd been important to Zaria. "Do you have a way to get in touch with her? If we can find that source, it won't matter what Ward's errand boy wants you to create."

Zaria rotated the sheet of paper, as if looking at the writing from another angle might yield more information. "Why do you think I've been combing through all this stuff? Problem is, I haven't a clue where Cecile might be. I haven't seen her since the day she left, and she didn't tell us where she was going."

"I thought you two were close."

Zaria wasn't sure *close* was the right word. Regardless of the time they'd spent together, she knew little about Cecile and hadn't offered much about herself in return. Their closeness had been, if anything, a quiet companionship. "I think she was too afraid of my father to tell me much," she admitted to Jules. "But also, I was a child. Perhaps she feared I'd go looking for her."

"You wanted to," he reminded her. "You told me as much."

A hollow sensation gnawed at Zaria's stomach. It was true. She remembered feeling guilty when, after Itzal's death, she realized she'd been less upset to lose him than she had Cecile—and Cecile hadn't even died. Of course, Zaria had grieved in both cases, but the loss of her father was more about fear. The sensation that the world had abruptly been placed on her shoulders, and her not knowing what the hell to do about it.

"I wouldn't have known where to start," Zaria said eventually. "I still don't." How could she know so little about the woman who had taught her so much? With Zaria's luck, Cecile might have gone all the way back to France.

"We could ask my father," Jules suggested. "Itzal might have mentioned something to him at the time."

Zaria glanced at the clock in the corner of her room. It was late, but George Zhao kept strange hours. She'd been avoiding the man these past couple of days, knowing she wouldn't be able to help confronting him if they were in the same space for too long, but that didn't seem to matter anymore. She wouldn't be able to sleep until they spoke with him.

For years, she'd told herself not to bother with futile hopes. If even her father couldn't find a primateria source, how could she? Now, though, she *wondered*. If Itzal had allowed Cecile to assist with his research, maybe it didn't matter that he had burned the results. Maybe some of what he'd learned still existed in the mind of his first and only assistant. And maybe, if Zaria could find her, she would finally have a lead.

"Yes," she said. "Let's ask your father. Right now."

The stairs creaked as they slunk upstairs, the sound ominous against the fragile silence. Jules's candle was a bloom of light in the corridor outside George Zhao's office, and he paused outside the door, twin flames in the depths of his eyes as they met Zaria's. "Try not to be upset if he can't help."

She blinked in impatience. "I don't get upset."

"No, you don't always get *visibly* upset," he corrected her. "It's not the same thing."

"Don't be absurd." But Zaria knew Jules was right. She was too reactive, too emotional—Itzal had always told her as much, and thus she'd spent years learning to push it down. To hide her excitement, her misery, her frustration. She was quick to anger and even quicker to snap unkind words. When she was disappointed, it dropped like a stone in the pit of her stomach and hollowed everything else away. Better, she had learned, not to let anyone know what she was feeling at all.

And yet Jules had always been able to see through her. At times, he arrived in Zaria's room before she'd even fully realized she was sad. She didn't know *how* he knew—how his emotional intelligence was so many leagues above her own—and sometimes she feared she was failing as his friend. Steady Jules, who wasn't afraid to express himself and took everything in stride. Who was always there to be her comfort yet rarely seemed to require anything in return.

Zaria couldn't help but feel it was a lopsided relationship. It was why she was so desperate to give him the world. A better one than this, preferably.

With that thought, she knocked on George's office door.

"Come in."

So George *was* awake. Good.

He was at his desk when Zaria and Jules entered, poring over what appeared to be a ledger of numbers. Something to do with the shop, no doubt. He was very like an older, balding version of Jules. He had the same searching gaze, the same thin build, the same melancholy smile. But one of his incisors was missing and there were crow's-feet stamped on the corners of his eyes. A clay pipe was poised between his teeth, though no smoke emanated from it—he claimed he simply liked the feel of it in his mouth. Besides, tobacco cost a fair bit of money.

"What are you two doing awake at this time of night?" George grunted, motioning for them to enter the office farther. He seemed utterly at ease, which set Zaria's teeth on edge and only reinforced that she'd been right to accept Kane's offer. *Someone* had to take the kingpin's threat seriously. How could George look his son in the eye, knowing what was at stake?

Jules shut the door. "We could ask you the same question."

"Lots to do in preparation for redemption day."

"Hmm." Jules led Zaria over to the other side of George's desk. "We wanted to ask you something."

George set down his pen, which Zaria took as assent. Jules shot her a look, indicating that she should be the one to speak. She cleared her throat.

"Cecile Meurdrac. You must remember her."

George frowned at them. "That's not much of a question."

"Do you know where she went when she left us?"

George set the pipe down, and Zaria was struck by how long it had been since she and Jules's father had engaged in direct conversation. They occupied the same space, yes, but rarely bothered interacting. George Zhao was simply a fixture of the pawnshop. Zaria accepted his presence, and he accepted hers. Their silent point of contention, she knew, was Jules—George wanted his son to take over the shop. Zaria wanted Jules to get as far away from it as possible.

"Why?" George said just as the pause was becoming uncomfortable, drawing out the single syllable. "Why now?"

Jules cut in before Zaria could reply. "So you *do* know."

"You tell me why you're asking, and then I'll decide how much to say."

Frustration heated Zaria's cheeks, and yet she couldn't help being struck by how much George looked like his son when he set his jaw. Damn these men and their stubborn streaks.

"Because I miss her," she blurted out, at once a truth and a lie. "I'm looking for Cecile because I miss her. Apart from you and Jules, she's the closest thing I have to family."

George visibly softened, relaxing back in his chair. "Don't think I'm not sympathetic, Zaria. To be as grown as you are without parents or any marriage prospects"—he returned the pipe to his lips and spoke around it—"it is unfortunate, to be sure. But Cecile can't help you. In fact, I'd be surprised to learn she's still alive, given where she was headed."

"And where was that?" Zaria pressed, ignoring the remark about her admittedly woeful lack of prospects.

The thin line of his mouth twisted. "She went to work for Alexander Ward."

"*What?*" She and Jules spoke at the same time. Zaria felt as if someone had cuffed her upside the head, her thoughts reeling. Kind, quiet Cecile had left to work for the most dangerous man on this side of London?

Why did everything seem to involve the kingpin as of late? He was becoming inextricably twined with every part of Zaria's life.

"I don't know why you're surprised," George said. "Ward has always held a deep fascination for alchemology. Why do you think he situated himself in the dark market? He all but popularized the magic trade in London."

Zaria shook her head. "I'm not surprised he wanted Cecile to work for him. He had his eye on my father for years. I'm surprised she *went*, is all."

Though working for Ward would surely have afforded him both money and safety, Itzal had turned the kingpin down more than once, resolutely declaring that he didn't answer to anyone save himself. Ward had enough influence that Zaria was certain he could have forced her father to create whatever he demanded, but for reasons she wasn't clear on, that had never happened. Not that she knew of, at least.

George gave a half-hearted shrug. "You know I held a great deal of respect for Itzal, but he was a difficult man to work with. I suspect Cecile grew weary of him, and Ward could offer her so much more."

"Does she work for him still?"

"I've no idea. Like I said, I'd be surprised to learn she's still alive. The kingpin is demanding, and Cecile had an impertinent streak, not unlike yourself."

Zaria lifted her chin but didn't argue. It was Jules who said hotly, "Having an 'impertinent streak' is the only reason Zaria has been able to help pay our dues. Her clients are forever trying to shortchange her, and she doesn't take it."

George beheld his son with an impassive expression. "You'd do well to adopt that skill yourself. It's not becoming for a woman to act in such a way, but for a pawnbroker it is a necessity."

Jules flushed, and this time it was Zaria who bristled. When

Jules was behind the counter, he wasn't quite as firm in pricing as his father, instead electing to work with what people required or could afford. In a place where everyone was struggling, he'd told Zaria more than once, he couldn't bear watching patrons' eyes cloud with dismay when they realized they wouldn't reach an arrangement.

He doesn't want to be a pawnbroker, Zaria wanted to snap. *And that's if the shop even survives long enough for him to get the chance.*

But she held her tongue. She understood how important family was to Jules, and to his father as well. The years George had spent caring for his ailing parents was proof of that. Despite her gripes with the man, she knew Jules's dream of leaving the slum included his father, and she would never stand in the way of that. Whether George *would* leave, though, was another question entirely, and a barrier she wasn't sure how Jules would deal with.

George's eyes had drifted back to his work, and Zaria knew the conversation was over. That was fine by her; she'd gotten what she came for. She could tell Jules was still grinding his teeth, and she put a gentle hand on his arm.

"Thanks," she told George curtly, pulling Jules from the room as he added, "Good night."

George inclined his head.

"You're not a disappointment," Zaria said to Jules the moment the door closed behind them, knowing where his thoughts were. "You know you're not. He expects a lot, but he loves you."

Whether that love was enough for George to keep his son from Ward, though, she wasn't sure.

Jules's smile was faint, bitterness thinning his lips. "Yeah. I guess."

Once back in her workshop, the two of them stretched out on

Zaria's bed, cocooned by the darkness. Zaria still clutched the paper in her left hand, as if prolonged contact with Cecile's words might foster some deeper connection to the woman.

If she could find Cecile, perhaps she could find a primateria source. And if she found a primateria source, she wouldn't have to worry about what acquiescing to Kane's demands would do to her. She could create without limits. Then, when she had the jewels Kane promised her, they would have everything they needed to save this place—or leave it behind.

"Too bad about Cecile and Ward," Jules murmured eventually, his soft voice shattering the fragile quiet. "But we'll find another solution. Don't worry."

To her swiftly deteriorating state, he meant. Zaria grunted. "I'm not worried."

Not yet, at least. Whereas Jules had seen George's mention of the kingpin as a dead end—or, at the very least, one too dangerous to pursue—Zaria saw it as the key. She *was* going to find Cecile.

And, much to her dismay, she knew who might be able to help her.

ZARIA

THE MOMENT JULES'S BREATHS EVENED OUT BESIDE HER— Zaria hadn't the heart to send him back to his own room—she leapt from the bed and donned her coat. As she did so, feeble moonlight through the grimy window caught the sketch she'd been working on earlier. It wasn't a concept for an invention or even a blueprint; it was the face of Itzal Mendoza, cast half in shadow the way it had always been when he'd bent over the desk upon which his very likeness now rested.

Zaria could still remember the first time Itzal had created magic in her presence. She'd been young—too young to recall the exact words her father had used to describe the glistening stone before them. And perhaps *stone* was the wrong word for it, but in the foggy crevices of her memory, that was what it had been. Something so small, so simple. Itzal had been sitting at his worktable. Light streamed in through the window, illuminating the creases of his sun-weathered face. He'd turned to Zaria and smiled, and she remembered it because it was a rare thing.

Then he'd handed her the primateria.

It hadn't been warm, exactly, but rather the perfect temperature of her skin. Zaria wanted to know what it was at once. Even back then, she'd hungered for knowledge with a desperation that sunk claws into the cage of her chest. He'd told her about magic then. Not in the broad sense, or the way of stories, but the real thing.

Why hadn't he told her more?

As she ducked out into the street, something hot burned in the pit of her stomach. An impatience. A fury. A *need.* People howled drunkenly from the gutters, and in the distance, she could hear what was almost certainly a fight. Someone had started a small fire at the end of Horseferry Road, and Zaria swerved to avoid the putrid scent of whatever they were burning. She clutched a small lamp that, in appearance, looked scarcely any different than a regular gas lamp but—thanks to a combination of soulsteel and a combustible liquid called solanum—could last weeks without burning out. It was one of the very few dark market items she'd allowed herself to keep over the years.

What was she doing? Seeking out Kane Durante, especially in the dead of night, could only be a mistake. Venturing into the kingpin's territory without a clear destination in mind—that was also a mistake. But if Kane wanted Zaria for her alchemological prowess, helping her find that primateria source—and therefore Cecile—was in his best interests. And who better to ask than someone who spent his days at Alexander Ward's side?

The river was a roar in Zaria's ears as she neared the docks. Its waters were black beneath the foggy shroud of night, inscrutable and horribly infinite. Some of the kingpin's men lived near the docks in a place known colloquially as the barracks, and although she wasn't sure of its *precise* location, that was where Zaria hoped to find Kane. She rubbed her clammy palms on the front of her jacket. It was ridiculous to be nervous, and yet she could feel each pulse of her heart beat. She bit the inside of her cheek and picked up her pace, scouring the fronts of industrial buildings as the slum disappeared behind her.

"There you are."

A voice from her left made her whirl around. The greeting was one of familiarity, but Zaria didn't recognize the figure that slunk out of the shadows between two decrepit buildings. It was a man, tall and sporting a hat, his face half-concealed by a kerchief. The glint in his eyes had her free hand snapping to the knife hidden at her waistband. As the clouds moved aside to reveal a sliver of moonlight, she could see her reflection in the smashed window behind him, disfigured by a spiderweb of tiny fractures. She looked afraid. It made her furious.

"Beg your pardon," Zaria said, hand tightening on her blade as she set down the solanum lamp. "I don't believe we're acquainted."

The man moved more fully into the moonlight. He looked to be nearly double her age, with a mustache and broken teeth. "A bricky thing, aren't we?"

"I'd kindly ask you to leave me alone." She kept her voice cool, scanning him for weapons all the while. The bulge in the front of his black coat suggested he might be carrying a gun. It was a nice coat—far too nice for him to be a vagrant or a simple pickpocket. That didn't bode well. A dawning sensation of horror crept over Zaria like a chill.

The man cackled. It sounded oddly akin to a dog's bark. "I admit, I'd have thought you more difficult to track down. It ain't often a lass goes out alone after dark 'less they're a dolly-mop looking for coin or trouble."

"I'm not for hire, and I assure you I'm not looking for trouble."

"Well, you've found it anyway." His face was a leer. "You don't much look like an alchemologist."

"Beg pardon?" she gasped, but he didn't repeat himself. Suddenly, his earlier words clicked into place—he *knew* her. Knew she was an alchemologist.

She was a *target*.

Zaria began to back away, hoping to put some distance between them in case she had to fight. Fear was metallic in the back of her throat, her heart rising to meet it. Was it worth fighting or was it better to run? How good was his aim in the dark?

The man slipped a hand into the front of his coat, and Zaria stopped thinking. She lunged at him, barreling into his sturdy body with all the force she could muster. It was foolish. So, so foolish. But all she could think was that if she could trap his arm against his chest, he might not be able to draw the gun she was sure he was reaching for.

They struggled for a second that felt like an eternity. Her hair came loose around her shoulders as he shoved her to the ground, the breath rushing out of her. Gooseflesh rose on her arms. She felt sick. What she could see of the man's face was smug fury as he pointed the gun, ignoring the desperation with which she tried to scrabble away. In that moment, she only had a single thought.

Jules, I'm so sorry.

"Oi! What the hell's going on here?"

Zaria tensed as a new voice split the air, this one louder and angrier. It bounced off the factory walls, echoing in a way that indicated the speaker had no qualms about being overheard.

The man glanced over Zaria's shoulder, mouth forming a grimace as his eyes lit with what might have been…recognition? He stowed his gun back in his coat, then took off into the shadows.

A mixture of relief and dismay washed over Zaria as she realized who had spoken. She took a deep breath, shuttering her eyes and flexing her fingers for a moment before scrambling shakily to her feet. Of *course* Kane would find her.

She didn't move as he halted a few paces away, though she let her gaze flick to his face. The collar of his jacket was turned up to hide his tattoo, and his hair was slightly mussed. His expression was cold and impassive, though the corners of his mouth hinted at danger in a way that she was coming to recognize as his signature.

"What the fuck are you doing here?" Kane spoke without looking at Zaria. His attention was on the place where the man had disappeared, and if his words hadn't made it exceedingly clear he wasn't happy to see her, his voice did. "Who was that?"

She took another deep breath to calm her racing heart. It felt like something alive in her chest, rattling around wildly in a bid to escape. "No idea."

"He would have killed you."

"Probably." Zaria didn't know how she managed to sound so nonchalant. She wanted to scream. Perhaps it was the fact that Kane had hired her for her competency, and it wouldn't have inspired confidence if she let him see how shaken she was. Working for the kingpin, he had to be accustomed to seeing people nearly get killed. So she tried to match his perceived energy just as she always did when she wasn't sure how to navigate an interaction.

Kane frowned. Tonight the green in his eyes seemed brighter, ringed by a dark brown. "That doesn't concern you in the slightest?"

"When did I say I wasn't concerned?"

He shook his head, glancing skyward as if to appeal for patience. "Never mind. You still didn't answer my question."

"I can't remember what it was," Zaria admitted.

"What. Are. You. *Doing here?*"

"Oh, that. I was looking for you, actually."

"What a very, very stupid idea." Kane showed his teeth in a way that almost passed for a smile but was just a little too unsettling. "I'm not easy to find."

"And yet I found you, didn't I?"

"No, you didn't. *I* found *you*, and if I hadn't, you'd be dead right now."

"I had everything under control," she lied, unable to abide his self-righteousness.

"Really?" He laughed without a trace of humor. "Because it looked as though you were about to be shot by a man twice your size. What were you thinking, coming here by yourself in the middle of the night? You don't even know where I live. Were you planning to wander aimlessly until you happened across me? When we came to an agreement, it was for us to work together. Not for me to rescue your sorry ass in the dead of night."

"I didn't—"

"I sincerely doubt I'm going to get any kind of *thank you*, but you'd best be glad I showed up when I did. Now, if you please, I'd be interested to know who has it out for you. If we're going to be working together, it could pose a bit of a problem."

His dismissive curtness had Zaria's back up before she could think better of it. She knew she'd been foolish. She *knew* that. But it sure as hell didn't mean she wanted to hear Kane Durante say it. "I didn't ask you to rescue me, and I don't know who that man was, okay? His face was mostly covered." Her next exhale was uneven. "He knew me, though. I think he was sent to find me."

Kane's eyes were slits. "Start listing your enemies."

"I don't have any."

"Everyone has enemies, whether they know it or not. Swindle any clients lately?"

Zaria scowled. "I'm not *swindling* anyone, but my father used to require that his clients pay a deposit up front. Maybe someone thinks I don't intend to deliver." It was why she couldn't simply ignore the deals Itzal had made before his death. He'd taken the money and gambled it away, leaving her with debts she had to pay with her life.

"You're fulfilling his outstanding commissions," Kane surmised. "If someone put down a lot of money and still hasn't gotten what they asked for, that's a good reason to kill you. But there's more, isn't there?"

Zaria worried at her lower lip. She was loath to admit what she'd done, especially to Kane of all people.

"Tell me, Miss Mendoza."

"Fine." The word was a hiss. "I gave someone an unfinished commission the other night. I was out of soulsteel, but they'd made it clear they wouldn't wait any longer."

"So the item doesn't work properly."

"Correct."

Kane whistled long and low. "Once again, what the *hell* were you thinking? You don't mess around with dark market buyers. You've put your own life in jeopardy."

"Why do you care?"

"As you might imagine, your death would inconvenience me greatly."

That stung, although it shouldn't have. "Because you need something from me."

"Because," Kane corrected her, "we have a mutually beneficial agreement."

She scanned the lines of his face, looking for some evidence that he was being disingenuous. He had seemingly perfect control over his features, which just now appeared hewn from granite. She found her focus drifting down to his mouth and wondered vaguely whether he'd become a con because he was handsome enough to sell water to a drowning man.

"Miss Mendoza?" he said, and Zaria realized she had missed his next question.

"Yes." She forced her gaze back up to his. "What?"

"I *said*, what was this client's name?"

"Oh—Vaughan. I've no idea if it's an alias or not."

"Interesting. Well, I'll make sure this Mister *Vaughan*'s apparent bloodlust doesn't impact our deal."

Zaria lifted her chin. "Speaking of our deal, I'd like to discuss the terms."

There was an indecipherable shift in Kane's expression. "Not now. Let me escort you home. You almost died tonight, and it's far too late to talk business."

"We're not going anywhere."

A cavalier shrug. "All right then."

She watched in disbelief as he leaned against the nearest soot-stained building and procured a small pipe. Not clay—metal and wood. Of *course* he would be able to afford something like that. He watched her slyly over his hands as he lit it with a solanum lighter, then tilted his head back, chin jutting toward the dark sky. His gaze seemed to flick among what few stars were visible through the smog,

and if Zaria hadn't known better, she might have thought he was tracking constellations. She figured his preoccupied silence was as much of an invitation as she would get.

"I actually came to ask you a favor," she said after a beat.

Kane puffed smoke into the air. The look he gave her was incredulous. "*Did* you, now? Well, you're ever so charming, I can't imagine I wouldn't oblige."

"Are you going to listen or not?"

"Have you noticed Orion's Belt is visible tonight? Unusual, that."

Zaria was beginning to think she'd never met a more frustrating person. Every barbed remark was poised perfectly to infuriate her. But she forced herself to think of Jules's face. Of pockets full of money. Of leaving London and never seeing Kane Durante's dagger-edged smirk again. She could manage for a week or two.

She hoped.

"I don't care about Orion's Belt," she said, though she indeed glanced up, automatically seeking the trio of stars. "I need help finding someone. A woman who used to work for Ward. It was years ago, and I don't know if she's still in the area"—*or alive*, her brain supplied—"but it's imperative that we speak."

Kane surveyed her with mild irritation. "You're asking me to get Ward involved in a manhunt just so you and some woman can *speak*?"

"No," Zaria snapped, too quickly. "I don't want Ward involved at all. And it's not a manhunt. But I would think you have the same resources he does, right?"

"We already have a deal, Miss Mendoza. Are you certain you wish to make another?"

"It's not a deal. Besides, it helps me help you."

"Does it, now?" His expression was appraising as he pivoted to face her straight on. "Who is this woman to you?"

Zaria didn't answer right away, treading carefully. "I believe she might have important information. Information that can help me with my work."

Kane's face hardened. She could *see* him thinking, unraveling the pieces. After a moment of silent consideration, he leveled an accusatory finger at her. "You're looking for a magic source."

Damn it all. Zaria should have known he would be able to guess as much. He was familiar with the dark market. He knew what alchemologists coveted, what legends they believed.

"Good luck with that," he went on, voice scathing. "I'm not convinced those even exist. Why do you think there aren't exactly an abundance of dark market alchemologists?"

"Because most people don't have a prayer of mastering the craft. If I didn't know better, I'd think you were envious, Kane."

He lowered his pipe, bending at the waist so as to lean in closer. "Ward once told me that creating magic is like falling in love. You want it at first, but then it begins to hurt, and you can't bring yourself to stop. You can't be compelled to draw away. And finally"—he smiled winningly, wickedly—"it kills you."

Perhaps it *was* like love—at least from what little Zaria knew of such things. She knew the way her father's love for her mother had left him a bitter shell of a man. But it turned her cold to hear Kane describe it so.

"I didn't ask for your input," she ground out. "Can you help me find her or not? It's in *your* best interests, you know. If she does have a magic source, I'll be able to create everything you ask of me without difficulty. Stealing the necklace will be easy."

Kane made a noncommittal sound in the back of his throat, peeling himself away from the wall. The smell of his pipe was acrid in Zaria's lungs. "What's her name, this woman?"

"Cecile Meurdrac."

"Meurdrac," Kane echoed, the hint of his accent shaping the syllables somewhat differently. He stared into the middle distance as though he'd abruptly forgotten Zaria's presence. Then he added, "I'll do my best. But you owe me a favor in return. No questions asked, at the time of my choosing."

Zaria swallowed. The action took more effort than usual. "What kind of favor?"

"No idea. I suppose I'll know when the time comes."

"Absolutely not. Tell me now."

Kane tilted his head, teeth gleaming in the moonlight. He looked rather haunted like this, shadowed on one side by the looming factory. "Ever so bold, Miss Mendoza."

"Zaria is fine."

He didn't correct himself. "You asked me for a favor. I don't do favors—I negotiate." That cursed pipe was at his lips again, and he blew a short puff of smoke in her direction. "Take it or leave it."

Leave it, a voice hissed in the back of her mind, and it sounded distinctly like Jules. But Zaria had never been one to shy away from risks. Everything she had ever gotten, she'd gotten by playing the game, no matter what that game might be.

"Fine," she said, her mouth twisting around the word. "I'll take it. But only if you're successful in finding Cecile."

Kane shook her hand for the second time that week, yanking her close so his tobacco-laced breath was at her ear. "I assure you, *Zaria*—nobody hides from me."

As she ripped free from his grasp, heart beating in her throat, Zaria believed him.

"Now," he said, shaking the contents of his pipe out and stowing it in his pocket. "Let me escort you home."

"That won't be necessary." But a chill slipped down her spine as she considered the prospect of being accosted once more by her attacker, and she didn't argue as Kane trailed her all the way back to the pawnshop, relenting to her unspoken—but obvious—desire for silence. Only when they reached the door crowned by its trio of golden orbs did Zaria deign to address him again, pivoting to find him far closer than she'd anticipated. Her next exhale tangled in her chest.

"Are you planning to follow me everywhere from now on?" she managed to force out.

"If I need to. Don't go out alone. At the very least, bring your unpleasant friend along."

"His name is Jules" was her automatic reply. "But fine."

"So you *are* capable of doing as you're told."

"This may surprise you, but I have very little interest in being killed."

"Good. I need you." Kane tilted his head, his gaze serious, piercing. A lock of unruly chestnut hair had come loose from its normally slick style, and it curled against his brow, the darkness turning it nearly black. Zaria stood motionless, pinned to the spot, entirely unsure what to make of that. A heartbeat later, Kane straightened, winking. "Because of our agreement, of course. Speaking of which, don't forget that we start tomorrow. Hyde Park, two o'clock. Don't come alone. Dress nicely."

"Don't forget about Cecile," Zaria said.

"Oh, I'll find the woman, just as I'll find the man who wants you dead. And when I do"—Kane smiled unpleasantly—"someone will be very sorry indeed."

Only after he was gone did Zaria remember how to breathe again.

ZARIA

A s Zaria emerged into the gray afternoon the next day, Jules at her side, she couldn't help but feel guilty.

She hadn't yet told Jules about the second deal she'd made with Kane Durante. His stupid wink still lingered in her mind; it was the last she'd seen of him before he disappeared like a phantom into the night. Jules had made it clear from the start that he didn't like Kane. Neither did Zaria, to be fair, but she wanted what Kane could give her more than she hated the way he conducted himself.

That was what she tried to convince herself, at least. It was hard to look at him, knowing he worked for Ward. She wanted to ask him more about it, but at the same time, she knew it would only make her angry. Kane was the reason people in Devil's Acre lived in fear. Not the only one, certainly, but the things he did contributed to the general sense of hopelessness.

Zaria couldn't imagine Jules doing those things. And she was desperate to ensure he never had to.

She looked over at him now, guilt churning within her. He would be disappointed she'd gone to Kane without telling him and made a bargain without his input. More to the point, she didn't think she would be able to weather his wrath when he found out she'd nearly been killed. And he *would* find out in the event that she attempted to recount the tale, because she'd always been terrible at lying to him. An argument would ensue, and Zaria could already imagine how that would go: They would bicker, Jules's fear manifesting as rage. He would blame Kane, claiming that Zaria had been perfectly safe until he'd walked into their lives. It wouldn't be untrue, but Jules would refuse to listen to sense, and it would spiral into a debate about whether they should be working with Kane at all.

And she had to keep working with Kane. It was the only way to get the money they needed.

Zaria gave herself a shake as she and Jules picked their way through the slum. Per Kane's directions, she'd dressed in the nicest thing she owned. Still, it was nothing ostentatious: a simple maroon dress with an embellished neckline and layered skirts. Beside her, Jules wore his least-frayed coat and hat. Together they made a rather sad display, but if Kane said a single derogatory word about it, Zaria was committed to knocking his teeth in.

Despite the weather, their street seemed more crowded than usual. People in patched clothing held armfuls of meager belongings, and neighbors shoved one another aside, harsh voices echoing down the alleyways. All had hollow eyes and cheeks. Some were undoubtedly homeless. Zaria watched, heart sinking, as a small boy hunkered down beside a scum-covered ditch at the side of the road.

"Miss Mendoza! And Master Zhao!" A woman in a filthy overcoat waved, scuttling over to the child. She pulled him to his feet and proceeded to wipe dirt from his face as she addressed Zaria and Jules. "Still keeping an ear out for me, I hope?"

"Aye, Lottie," Jules said heavily. "But neither my father nor I have heard of any place to rent. Nothing that wouldn't cost an arm and a leg, mind you."

The woman flashed missing teeth in some version of a strained smile. "God bless, Master Zhao. I pray something turns up before the cold returns."

Jules shook his head as they continued on, a familiar hopelessness in his expression. London seemed to grow more crowded every day with the recent industrial boom, and the chances of someone like Lottie finding a place were slim.

The reek of the river was carried over on a gust of wind, and Zaria wrinkled her nose. The streets had begun to widen and give way to brothels, and she spied more than one pair of eyes leering at her and Jules from the shadows. After last night, every unwanted glance had her on edge, and she stuck closer to her friend than usual.

Could you kill a man, Zaria? Itzal had asked her once as they worked on an invention together. *If you had to, could you kill a man?*

By then Zaria had known her father well enough to not be startled by the question. *If I had to.*

He'd smiled, then. A strained, rare smile. *Good.*

It wasn't the only time he'd asked, and still Zaria hadn't the occasion to find out whether she'd spoken honestly. Could she have killed her attacker, she wondered, if Kane hadn't shown up? She wanted to believe the answer was yes. Truth be told, she didn't know.

By the time they approached Hyde Park, the light rain had begun to dwindle. Zaria scanned the lush grass and the slew of well-dressed men patrolling the area as they hollered instructions to one another.

Holding the Exhibition here had been a controversial decision; until recently, the park had been an area for the wealthy, *respectable* members of society to ride horses and do whatever it was rich people did. Now the Crystal Palace loomed in the near distance, dazzling and futuristic, dominated by a gargantuan glass arch in the middle. It had been erected right in the center of Hyde Park—they hadn't bothered removing any trees, building the structure around them instead. At first, it had struck Zaria as a preposterous idea, but now she thought it perfectly reasonable. She couldn't imagine anything wouldn't fit in the Crystal Palace.

Nonetheless, exhibits spilled out into the park. Set up on the grass was an array of elaborately carved statues, machines with moving parts, enormous deposits of coal and other minerals, and what looked like a small house set against the glass backdrop. Though the Exhibition wasn't set to officially open for another week, the Royal Commission had clearly put a lot of effort into preparations.

"I'm not sure this is a good idea," Jules said for what must have been the thousandth time today.

"Hey, Jules?" Zaria said, gaze tracking a rich-looking couple as they passed. "Can I ask you something?"

"Sure."

"Do you think this is a good idea?"

He scowled at her. "It just feels like a rather conspicuous meeting place."

She didn't disagree. Throngs of people milled about in the park, come to gawk at the exterior of the Crystal Palace. There were rich and poor folk alike—a testament to the work the prince consort had put into making sure the event was accessible to all. It was a move that had surprised Zaria given his wife's general disdain toward the lower classes, evidenced by her unwillingness to support social

legislation that would benefit the less fortunate. No matter how the queen's government tried to portray her as a ruler who cared about all her people, the poor knew the truth. They felt it.

Zaria scanned the unfamiliar faces as she and Jules moved through the crowd, but none of them were Kane. So she thought, at least, until she heard a familiar, disingenuous laugh from a short distance away.

She pivoted, eyes narrowed at the back of the boy who had uttered the sound. He stood facing a handsome, rotund older gentleman, and—to Zaria's abject horror—a police officer. Surely Kane wouldn't keep such company? He was a criminal, for God's sake.

But when the boy turned, she no longer had any doubts. She knew that indulgent grin, that straight nose. She even recognized the carefully arranged hair beneath that black hat. The enormous blond copper glared at Zaria over the older man's head, and she was quick to drop her gaze. What was Kane *thinking*? Interacting with law enforcement outside the very building from which he intended to steal?

"There he is," Zaria said to Jules now, nudging his elbow. "There's Kane."

Jules followed her line of sight, distrust wrangling his features into something unpleasant. A heartbeat later, it was replaced by horror. "Why's he with a copper?"

"No idea."

"Maybe we should just leave."

"We're not *leaving*. We walked all the way here." Indeed, the excursion had taken the better part of a half hour. She sidestepped Jules, ignoring his protests, and walked directly up to Kane. After all, they hadn't done anything illegal yet, had they?

Zaria raised a hand to tap Kane on the shoulder, but he turned in

the heartbeat before she could make contact. It was as if he'd somehow sensed her presence. He flashed a devilish grin and, to Zaria's bewilderment, pulled her tightly against his side.

"Here she is," Kane said smoothly. "The lovely woman we were just speaking of. Mister Taylor, Officer Sullivan: my fiancée, Eleanor."

Zaria was too stunned to speak. She blinked at Kane in fury, but he was focused on Taylor, the firm hand encircling her waist his only acknowledgment of her shock.

"Ah, yes. Honored to meet you." Taylor took Zaria's hand, and she would have recoiled had the officer's stare not communicated such a blatant warning. Who *were* these people?

She glanced over her shoulder, catching a brief glimpse of Jules's horrified expression before Kane's voice dragged her back again.

"My apologies, sir. You see, she's a bit—"

"*Overwhelmed*," Zaria interjected, smiling beatifically. "I'm just so thrilled we're finally meeting. I've heard *so* much about you from my husband-to-be."

If nothing else, it was worth it to see the look on Kane's face as he processed her response, then worked to regain his composure. If he was going to catch her off guard, she was going to return the favor.

Taylor boomed a laugh. "Oh, Theodore's too kind, the charming bastard!" He tipped his hat in Kane's direction, then gestured at the Crystal Palace. "My congratulations again on the excellent work you've all put into this feat of architecture. I'll send for you the moment I hear anything, will I?"

"Please do," Kane said warmly. His grin was all teeth.

Taylor, though, either didn't notice or didn't mind. He tipped his hat once more before strolling away through the lush grass.

The moment his back was turned, Zaria pulled away from Kane, fixing him with a look she could only hope aptly communicated her fury. "What the *hell* was that?"

"That," Kane said as Jules approached them, "was Ambrose Taylor. Politician, collector of artifacts, and member of the Royal Commission for the Exhibition. He's kindly offered to do me a favor. Why did you bring *him*, by the way?"

This was clearly in reference to Jules, who grimaced. Zaria, however, didn't answer the question. She couldn't help her gaze darting apprehensively to the enormous blond officer.

Kane heaved an impatient breath. "Relax, would you? He's not a real copper."

Of course he wasn't. She ought to have known.

The man—boy?—in question extended a hand to Zaria. "Fletcher Collins. I've heard quite a bit about you, Miss Mendoza." His voice was low, a little rough.

Zaria stared at his outstretched hand. "Do you work for Ward, too?"

"I do. Unlike Kane, though, I doubt my reputation precedes me."

"How unfortunate for you."

"Oh, I prefer it that way." Fletcher's grin was lopsided, seemingly genuine. He withdrew his hand and nodded at Jules, apparently realizing there would be no regard for niceties. "And you are?"

"That's irrelevant," Jules muttered at the same time Kane said, "Julian Zhao, son of George Zhao, the pawnbroker down on Horseferry."

Jules gaped. "I never told you that."

"I do my research." Kane's lips tilted up in a smug grin.

Zaria believed him. Beneath that careless facade, she had the impression Kane was deathly clever and calculating. She wondered if his smile was intended to distract his marks from the moment he finally stabbed them in the back.

"If you don't *mind*," Zaria said, steering the conversation back around, "I'd be interested in knowing why I was pretending to be your wife."

"Fiancée," Kane corrected her mildly, as if it made a lick of difference. "Conveniently, Mister Taylor believes I'm none other than Theodore Wright, apprentice to Charles Fox."

Zaria knew the name. Charles Fox was one of the engineers who'd assisted Joseph Paxton in designing and constructing the Crystal Palace. "I'm assuming he believes that because you told him as much."

"Correct."

"That's not what *convenient* means."

"Well, it's certainly been convenient for me," Kane pointed out. "You're here to assist, not to question my methods. Anyway, Theo just got engaged, poor bastard, so it's lucky you arrived when you did. Taylor's a big family man," he added, seeing Zaria's less-than-impressed expression. "Besides, I think we make a striking couple."

She didn't deign to respond to that. She still wasn't clear what they were doing here, and she itched to ask Kane whether he had any news of Cecile. But she couldn't broach the topic in front of Jules, so she held her silence.

Jules said, "Don't you think it's a bit foolish to meet outside the building you plan to steal from?"

Kane's mouth twisted in what might have been amusement, but it could have been distaste. Instead of answering, he said, "I don't recall inviting you."

"*I* invited him," Zaria snarled, wishing she could point out that it was Kane who had told her not to go anywhere alone. She tensed, wondering if he would bring up the previous night, but he only clicked his tongue.

"Yes, and I don't recall inviting you to invite him."

"Then I suppose it's a good thing you're not really my fiancé. Jules goes where I go."

"Can he be trusted?"

"Of course I can," Jules said acerbically.

"*Kane*," Fletcher intoned. He said it in the way of someone who was accustomed to telling Kane off, and Zaria wondered if perhaps Fletcher Collins was not so bad.

Kane gave a long-suffering sigh. "Fine. We're meeting here, Master Zhao, because there's a private viewing of the exhibits taking place today. I managed to get Fletcher onto the force, thanks to one of Ward's contacts, and Ambrose Taylor has kindly given us two tickets to said private viewing." Indeed, he brandished two slips of paper with a flourish. "It's invite only, for organizers and those who've contributed to the anticipated success of the event. Hence my alter ego, Theodore Wright." His smile was self-satisfied. "The real Theo Wright has no plans to attend the Exhibition just yet."

Zaria grimaced. "Did you *do* something to him?"

"Absolutely not," Kane said, as if such a thing contravened his high standard of moral integrity. "Merely a fortunate happenstance. Anyway, because of the limited guest list, the palace will be less crowded, which means we can move around more easily. We'll be able to get a decent look at the necklace and the layout of the building. Think of it as a reconnaissance of sorts."

Fletcher inclined his head toward the unoccupied turnstiles at the Exhibition's entrance. "It looks as though we won't have to worry much about exterior security."

"Not yet," Kane agreed.

It was interesting, watching the way the two navigated each other. Kane was undoubtedly the leader, but Fletcher's confidence was obvious. As if Kane's presence bolstered him, bringing him into focus rather than overshadowing him.

Jules turned to Zaria. When he spoke, it was as if Kane and Fletcher weren't present at all. "You can't seriously want to do this."

Zaria hesitated—she didn't particularly want to have this conversation in front of the others. As it turned out, she didn't have to, because Kane addressed Jules first.

"If you've come along solely to try to dissuade her while shooting me dirty looks, consider yourself unwelcome here."

"Stop it." Zaria turned her glare on Kane as Jules's teeth came together with an audible *click.* "You can't blame him for being concerned, given...everything about you."

"And yet," Kane said, "I suspect our agreement benefits him as well." His gaze slid to Jules. "Am I wrong?"

Something icy coalesced at Zaria's core. Did he *know*? It would only make sense that the kingpin's crew knew what their associates were doing. Was that why Kane had come to her when he did? Did he know she would be easy to convince because of what was at stake?

Jules, to her relief, didn't so much as blink. "I haven't decided whether or not it's worth it."

"You live in Devil's Acre."

"Yes. And every day we're one visit from *your* crew away from homelessness." There was a slight quaver in Jules's voice, but he didn't back down as he met Kane's eyes. "Can you really blame me for not liking you?"

Zaria watched Fletcher's hand migrate to Kane's shoulder, as if he feared his friend might do something rash, but the precaution was unnecessary. Kane merely tilted his head, expression icing over into something cool and thoughtful.

"You know what, Zhao?" he said. "You've got a set of morals on you. I don't like it, but I respect it."

Nobody appeared to know quite what to do with that, at least until Fletcher cleared his throat. "I think I see Price. I'd best be going. Security duties await." Hand still lingering on Kane's shoulder, he gripped it tightly—a brief, familiar gesture—and shot Zaria and Jules a wink. "Nice to meet you."

And then Fletcher was gone, his tall frame engulfed by the crowds as he wove his way toward a pair of officers waiting by the turnstiles.

This left Zaria and Jules alone with Kane, the latter alone in appearing unbothered by the development. He worked his jaw, gaze tracking the progression of a gilded carriage like an animal might watch its next meal.

Zaria took a breath, trying to organize her thoughts. What difference did it make, really, if Kane had taken advantage of her desperation? It was one job. By this time next week, it would all be over. She'd have more valuables than she knew what to do with and, with any luck, a primateria source in hand. She and Jules would no longer have to worry about what the future held, and she'd never have to see Kane Durante again.

"I suppose we should get going as well," Kane said after a beat. "See you later, Julian."

Zaria's brows slid up of their own accord. "Excuse me?"

"It's *Jules*," Jules said. "And I'm coming with you." He stood shoulder to shoulder with Zaria, arms crossed.

Kane tsked, shaking his head. "You're not. I only have two tickets,

and even if I had a third, we'd look ridiculous attending as a trio. Besides, your outfit is abysmal. This is a private event, and we need to look like the height of upper-class London."

Zaria glanced at Jules's threadbare ensemble, then to Kane's outfit: a well-trimmed black frock coat, black trousers, and shoes in which she could all but glimpse her reflection. She rolled her eyes where Jules could see. They didn't all have dark market money for custom-made suits.

"The height of upper-class?" she scoffed at Kane. "You look like you're about to swindle money from a rich old woman."

"That is so incredibly specific." He scanned her from head to toe, an almost dismissive action. "I suppose you, at least, are passable."

Zaria looked down at herself. *Dress nicely*, Kane had told her last night. She'd obliged as best she could, but it had been a foolish request in the first place. "No one is going to believe I'm upper-class."

Kane waved a dismissive hand. "No one's going to be looking at you," he said. "You'll be with me."

She had the sudden desire to smack him.

"And just what the hell am I supposed to do while you're inside?" Jules demanded. "Stand out here by myself?"

Kane shrugged. "What do I care? Go to the shops. Sit on a bench. Make a new friend."

"You've got to be joking."

Zaria glared daggers at Kane, her stomach tightening. She hadn't planned on doing this without Jules. Hell, she hadn't planned on doing this at all. "He's coming with us. You're a con man, aren't you? Figure out a way to make it work."

Jules was already shaking his head. "Whatever. If it's going to make things difficult, I'll wait outside." His eyes flicked to Kane, their depths reflecting the gray-blue skies overhead. "If you get any funny ideas, though—"

"Yes, yes," Kane drawled. "I'm sure you'll stab me, or shoot me, or some alternate manner of painful retaliation."

"No. Zaria will, though." Jules gave her a measured nod, concern in the lines of his mouth.

Zaria returned it and couldn't help the ghost of a smile that crossed her face at his words. It was true. Jules wasn't much for violence, but then he'd rarely needed to be. Zaria was the angrier one. The unpredictable one. The one who acted first and regretted later.

"Somehow, that does not surprise me." Kane wasn't looking at either of them; his attention was on the entrance to the Crystal Palace, and in one hand he clutched a silver pocket watch on a chain. There was eagerness in the way he held himself. A kind of energy Zaria suspected had to do with the thrill that prefaced the execution of something unsavory.

She felt it, too. Though she could scarcely admit it to herself, she did. It was a delicious kind of anxiety, and the moment it reared within her, she made an effort to push it back down. She wasn't like Kane. She would not delight in this as he did.

"Be careful," Jules murmured in her ear, a needless warning he could always be counted on to provide.

"You can trust me."

A rough laugh escaped him. "It's not you I don't trust."

He gave Zaria's arm a last squeeze, the pressure a grounding sensation, before Kane took it and led her into the fray.

ZARIA

ZARIA LET KANE CLEAR A PATH THROUGH THE CROWDS, WHICH he did with surprising ease. His hands were occupied with placing hers in the crook of his elbow, and it felt horribly intimate. The warmth of him was tangible even through the fabric of his jacket. Every one of her muscles was tense, but somehow she managed to take step after step, letting him guide her. The worst bit was how utterly comfortable Kane appeared.

"Could you relax a little?" he said, directing a winning smile at someone Zaria didn't bother to take note of. "You're meant to like me, you know. I'm not leading you to the gallows."

"I am not interested," she muttered through her teeth, "in pretending to be your fiancée. Can't I be your—your cousin, or something?"

This got Kane's attention. As they passed through a turnstile, he looked down at her, brows drawing together in abject horror. "No, you may not be my *cousin*."

"And why not?"

He inclined his chin to where a man stood at the Exhibition's entrance, laughing loudly with two people who must have been organizers. Zaria recognized him immediately. He was the chap Kane had been speaking to a short time earlier. Ambrose Taylor, if she recalled correctly. A member of the Royal Commission.

"If you're going to help me pull this off," Kane purred in Zaria's ear, "you're going to have to work on your acting."

"What's my name again?"

"Eleanor."

"And yours?"

"Theodore," he replied, turning that sickly charming grin on her again. Why was he always *grinning*? "But my friends can call me Theo."

"In that case, I'll stick to Theodore."

Kane uttered a mocking laugh, though it turned into the real thing as they approached Taylor and his company. There was another man with them now. He was portly with a rather bulbous nose, deep-set eyes, and a beard that started where his chin ought to have stopped. Something about the way he held himself made Zaria suspect he was important.

"Mister Cole!" Kane disentangled his arm from Zaria's, flashing teeth as he extended a hand toward the newcomer. "An absolute honor. I didn't realize you and Mister Taylor were acquainted."

Zaria's heart skipped in her chest as she fit the pieces together. Henry Cole, chief administrator of the Royal Commission for the Exhibition? She wouldn't have recognized the man, but she knew

he was a rather prominent civil servant who'd been instrumental in planning the event.

Cole drew himself up tall. He did not, Zaria was unnerved to see, appear won over by Kane's overindulgent greeting, though he allowed the handshake nonetheless. "And you are?"

"Master Wright," Taylor was quick to inject, giving a half bow as he gestured in Kane's direction. "And his charming future wife."

Zaria felt heat climb her face. The next moment Kane had set a hand on the small of her back, and she bit the inside of her cheek so hard that she tasted blood.

"Please," Kane said, still addressing Cole, "call me Theo. I'm apprentice to Charles Fox—I'm sure you're familiar. How wonderful it is to stand before this magnificent feat of architecture and engineering." He spread his arms wide to indicate the palace. "And may I offer you and the rest of the commission my congratulations? You have truly outdone yourselves in organizing this event so quickly."

Cole considered Kane the way someone might consider a plate of food before deciding whether or not they wanted to eat it. "I didn't know Mister Fox had an apprentice."

His demeanor set Zaria on edge. She shifted her weight, fearing he might somehow mark Kane as not, in fact, being Theodore Wright. Kane flashed another easy smile.

"That's the rub, isn't it? We must work in the shadow of the more accomplished man until we possess the skill required to rise through the ranks. In this case, however, working under men such as yourself and Mister Fox is no hardship at all. It's truly a privilege. Although," Kane added, "I daresay you don't need to be told about the value of hard work."

"I certainly don't," Cole said gruffly, but Zaria could see that he was softening. "Well, I won't hold you up any longer. Taylor will take your invitations. Enjoy yourself."

Kane's teeth flashed again. "I appreciate it, sir. God bless."

He managed to make it sound genuine as he shook Cole's hand once more, and Zaria forced her expression into what she hoped was reminiscent of a smile.

Then Cole was mercifully gone, his short stature engulfed by the slew of patrons.

Taylor took the two slips of paper Kane procured from his pocket. "Thank you very much, sir. Ma'am." With a wink, he indicated that they should pass through the next turnstile.

And the Great Exhibition opened up before them.

The interior of the Crystal Palace was beyond imagining. The impossibly high ceilings were paneled in the same glass as the walls, allowing the sunlight to stream in, and mezzanine-like structures jutted out to form a second story. Above it all, a glass dome arched to make room for several lush elm trees. Once Zaria managed to tear her gaze downward, she noticed a towering pink crystal fountain splashing joyfully in the center, the noise a backdrop to the excited chatter of the wealthy patrons who surrounded it.

The building's iron framework was visible everywhere she looked, but it didn't detract from the experience. How could it? For around her were *colors*—more than she'd known existed. Red banners declared the names of companies and their respective countries. Blue woven carpets hung from the walls. Gilded furniture and ivory statuettes sat beside printed glassware. There were carriages and clothing, art and animal skins, pottery and porcelain items. And *machines*! For manufacturing, for science, for transportation and medical applications.

It seemed humanity's creative genius had been condensed into

a single space bursting at the seams with ideas and veritable *worth*. It was so overwhelming, so impossible, so…absurd. That moment of wonder shattered to the ground around her, a delicate glass orb slipping from clumsy fingers. Once she managed to digest the sight, she saw it for what it was: audacious. The empire's flagrant boast. The Exhibition had been promoted as a unification of sorts, but Zaria suspected the goal was unification only insofar as it remained inherently, inextricably British. And yet how many of these things weren't British at all? How many had been taken by force from faraway places in the name of expanding an empire? While they were building the Crystal Palace, filling it with priceless items, how many people in the slums had starved?

"This entire event," Zaria said under her breath, "is just an elaborate way of showing off."

"I could have told you that from the moment I saw the first pamphlet," Kane returned, though even he couldn't quite hide his astonishment. "It's a global competition. An attempt to be the best. The most progressive, the most enlightened."

All her earlier wonder melted away, replaced by a sense of profound injustice. "What are we waiting for? Let's steal from this place."

"That's the spirit," Kane said mildly. "Though perhaps lower your voice a bit."

Despite the overwhelming number that had gathered in Hyde Park, the Crystal Palace itself was fairly empty. Small groups of people milled about, each more rich and important-looking than the next.

"I thought it would be busier," Zaria said, and Kane loosed a short laugh.

"I told you, this is just a private viewing. The Royal Commission will be here, along with their families, and all those involved in constructing and organizing the Crystal Palace and exhibits. As long as we don't run into Mister Fox, nobody should notice I'm not Theodore Wright."

"Do we know what Fox looks like?"

Kane's shrug was remarkably unconcerned. "More or less. Don't speak to anyone but me, and everything should be fine."

Zaria refrained from noting that she didn't particularly want to speak to *him*, either. When she'd woken this morning and prepared to meet Kane in Hyde Park, she hadn't imagined she would be thrust into his world—a world of cons and scheming—right off the bat.

"You could have told me we were going to be doing this," she said. "Pretending to be other people, I mean."

"Ah, but would you have agreed?" Kane pointed out. "You would have gotten in your head about it, and everything relied on my ability to con Ambrose Taylor."

"Everything relied on *me* not selling you out, you mean."

"I wasn't worried about that."

"Why not?" Zaria demanded hotly.

He ran his free hand through his hair, looking amused. "I'm good at reading people. I was almost positive you'd do better if I didn't let you worry about it ahead of time. You're good in stressful situations, but you panic if you know they're coming. Am I right?"

She lifted her chin, a bit miffed. He *was* right, but she wasn't pleased he'd managed to ascertain that after meeting her only a handful of times. "*Almost positive* isn't going to cut it when we have to do this for real."

"Let me worry about that."

"How could I not worry? Do you see how much security there is already?"

"Yes, and we've planned for it. As a special constable, Fletcher

will be briefed over the next week, taking note of the planned security rotations. There are hundreds of officers on the payroll, but the ones we can trust—I say that loosely, of course—will be positioned near the necklace. Of those men, Fletcher will find out which ones need to be avoided; plus, he'll map out the floor plan and all the most accessible escape routes."

That sounded reasonable, Zaria had to admit, though she didn't say it aloud. She only wanted to find what they'd come for and get this excursion over with. "Do we know where the Waterhouse exhibit is supposed to be?"

Kane rotated in place, pulling her along with him as he squinted at their surroundings. "The whole building is shaped like a cross. See?" He indicated with an arm. "It's divided into machinery and mechanical inventions, decorative manufactures, sculptures and architecture, and raw materials. In this direction are the exhibits from Britain and its dominions. All the foreign countries are the other way. Since Waterhouse is Irish, the necklace should be...this way." He pointed.

Of course they had divided the British from the foreign. A proverbial line drawn in the sand, separating the represented nations into a clear hierarchy. It was, Zaria thought, an odd way to approach unification.

As they walked, she dragged her attention away from Kane to the myriad items that made up the Exhibition. The walls had been painted in garish shades of red, blue, and yellow, and somewhere an organ played a triumphant tune. As they drew closer to the sound, she yearned to cover her ears. There was just so *much*: a second fountain, this one sporting a statue of a boy holding a swan; an enormous ivory throne; an entire gazebo; a taxidermy elephant upon which sat a beautifully embroidered howdah. It was ostentatious in a way that bordered on infuriating.

"Everyone will be attending the Exhibition," Kane told her under his breath. "Not only people from all across London, or even Britain, but people from all over the world. And it's not only for the wealthy— when I say everyone, I mean *everyone*."

"Then why try to steal from it during the day?" Zaria hissed back. "Every single patron becomes a potential witness."

"Because at night there's nobody here except security. Try stealing from a display when a copper is looking directly at it. The crowds may be inconvenient, but they also lend anonymity. Also, on the off chance we need to make a quick escape, it'll be easy to get lost."

That, too, made sense. Still, Zaria chewed on her lower lip. She couldn't imagine trying to do *anything* covertly surrounded by this many people. And this was merely a private viewing—it would be even busier when the Exhibition opened to the public.

"Besides," Kane continued, "that's where you come in. I know alchemologists can create explosives that emit a substance to provide cover, if only for a few moments. And I shouldn't need much longer than that."

Zaria tapped the fingers of her free hand together in a rapid, repetitive rhythm. She knew exactly what Kane was referring to, but her mind raced as she considered all the problems they could encounter. "I can't just carry an armful of explosives into the Exhibition."

"No, you can't," he agreed, but said nothing more.

They passed a few foreign displays on their way to the British ones: Greece and Turkey, Spain and Portugal. Zaria stopped to gawk when they reached France. It was the largest exhibit thus far, with

tapestries and textiles far more beautiful than anyone else had to offer. Next was Belgium, which had provided a statue of a man on a horse; the German states had sent glassware; and Russia's exhibit was empty, given that the ships carrying their contributions had apparently gotten stuck in ice and hadn't yet arrived.

The scene changed to reveal Trinidad and its fragrant spices, Canada and its well-crafted canoe, and something called a Tempest Prognosticator, which somehow predicted storms using leeches. That one intrigued Zaria greatly.

"Have you quite finished?" Kane asked, and she ripped her gaze away from the prognosticator. She hadn't even realized she'd come to a full halt.

"It's interesting."

"Yes. And you know what's even more interesting? That." Kane jutted his chin toward what appeared to be an overlarge bird cage, all thin brassy lines culminating in a tapered point. Within the cage was a glass box, and within the box was an array of beautiful jewelry. There were brooches and earrings, necklaces and cuffs. It was all far flashier than anything Zaria had seen even the richest Londoners sport.

"Is that it?" she said, a chill abruptly crossing her skin. "The Waterhouse exhibit?"

"Yes." Kane's voice was reverential. He led her closer, eyes shining in a way that, had anyone else cared to look closely, would surely have given him away as a thief. "Yes, this is it. And that"—he pointed—"is the necklace."

It was lovely, to be certain. Set behind the glass upon a soft cream-colored cloth, it was the center of the display. A point of pride for George Waterhouse, the famed Irish jeweler, it looked far too heavy to wear. Shining white rocks that must have been diamonds sat within individual frames of elaborate gold filigree, and in the very middle was a beautiful bloodred stone—the largest gem Zaria had ever seen. It was perfectly cut, shaped like a teardrop.

That said, she couldn't imagine why Kane wanted it, other than perhaps its inconceivable *worth*. But so many items in the Exhibition had to be priceless—why this one specifically?

It didn't matter. The rest of Waterhouse's display would be Zaria's, and here it was, so close that she could barely refrain from stretching out a hand and grasping the bars of the display. For an echo of a moment, she saw it all again: the house in the country, the calm silence of a place without squalor and suffering. Jules's smile, free from strain as it hadn't been since their youth.

In one week, everything would change.

KANE

KANE'S MOUTH WENT DRY AS HE STARED AT THE NECKLACE. The one thing standing in the way of saving Fletcher's life. The main source of his current conflict with Ward.

It was larger than he'd imagined. Even more stunning. The longer he looked at it, though, the more he understood why Ward wanted it so badly. It was a piece fit for a queen, and it was surely priceless. Finally, *finally*, Kane had found it. Now he only had to take it.

The necklace sat within a glass case that in turn sat inside a rectangular iron cage. One side of the cage was dominated by what appeared to be the brass-plated front of an ordinary safe. It was an unusual display, and Kane frowned, tracking a slow semicircle around the setup.

"It's locked," Zaria said needlessly. For a moment, her words scarcely registered with Kane. She had a strange look on her face, as if something had shocked her and she hadn't quite recovered. Perhaps she was merely overwhelmed by the sheer number of things in the Crystal Palace. Despite the rather dreary day, light streamed through the angled glass ceiling, picking up the gold in her hair, the gold flecks in her large brown eyes. Kane could tell she was self-conscious about her simple attire, but here, all sun gilded and swathed in crimson, he couldn't imagine how she felt like an outsider.

He gave his head a shake, refocusing on the Waterhouse display. He had picked countless locks in his life—it was a skill most of Ward's crew had—and he'd expected to encounter one here, but this lock…it was clearly different.

"Son of a bitch." He exhaled the curse, glancing over his shoulder to ensure nobody was watching. A few feet away, a group of patrons marveled at some beautifully woven tapestries, and just past that, a man chuckled jovially as he pointed at a longsword. None of them were looking at Kane and Zaria.

He could steal it now, Kane thought, if not for the lock. Could smash that glass case, grab the necklace, and run.

But he pushed the idea from his head. It was a foolish thing to entertain. Even if the necklace hadn't been locked up, he wouldn't make it more than a few steps before he got a bullet in the head. Officers milled around the perimeter of the Exhibition, and Kane didn't know their rotations. Not yet. That was Fletcher's job. That was why they had a plan in place. Posing as Theodore and his fiancée, Kane and Zaria would enter just as they had this morning, paying their shillings and getting lost in the crowd, which would be far larger than it was today. The queen and the prince consort would each make a speech not long after the doors opened, which would divert enough attention to allow Kane to pay a visit to his very own contribution to the Exhibition. It wasn't here yet, of course, but it would be. Once he got his hands on it, that was.

What he *hadn't* planned for was this particular lock. Kane could pick a simple lock in seven seconds. A more complicated one typically took between two and five minutes. He knew from Ward that an alchemological smoke bomb provided complete opaqueness for around three minutes and gradually diminished in the seven minutes following.

Three minutes to work at the lock, seven to escape. Those were the numbers Kane had been relying on. But this? He didn't have a goddamned clue what to do with this.

"Mad, isn't it?" The man who had been examining the longsword came to stand between Kane and Zaria, arms crossed over his narrow chest. He wore a suit and top hat of some luxurious fabric, and he didn't seem to notice the tension in the air.

Kane forced a vague smile onto his face. "What's mad?"

The man shrugged, eyes on the exhibit. "Why, the lengths at which they've gone to in order to keep the Waterhouse jewels safe. See, they've got one of those new American permutating locks on the cage. Seems a bit unnecessary, what with all the security milling about."

"You never know the kind of things people might try to steal," Zaria said, and Kane shot her a withering look behind the man's back.

"What's so special about this lock?" he said, hoping to distract from Zaria's comment.

The man brightened. He was the kind of person who liked to be asked about his knowledge, Kane saw. That boded well.

"Why, it's a new design patented by Day and Newell—the most complicated one yet! America entered the design, and their representative has teamed up with Waterhouse to showcase both the lock and the jewelry in one display. You see, it requires a parautoptic key, which can have as many as fifteen changeable bits. The owner of the key can rearrange the bits however they'd like prior to each insertion, and the lock will adjust without any manual reordering of the levers." The man adjusted the hat atop his graying hair. "The brass plate in front is to hide the levers from view. Impossible to pick, they say!"

"Fascinating," Kane said, though his blood ran cold. He'd never heard of such a thing. "How is it you happen to know about this?" He tried to lace the question with interest as opposed to suspicion. In his experience, only those who were up to no good knew this much about lock picking.

The man gave a self-deprecatory wave. "It's a special interest of mine. I read something about it in the paper when the American exhibitors arrived in the city."

"I've something of an interest in locks myself," Kane said smoothly. "It's an unusual hobby, isn't it? How nice to find someone who shares it." In his periphery, he saw Zaria roll her eyes, but he ignored her. "I suppose the Americans intend to do a demonstration at some point?"

The man nodded, the wrinkles in his brow deepening. "Oh, certainly. Like I said, the parautoptic key is especially interesting in the way it can be reset."

"I can imagine." Kane grinned. The action felt mechanical. "I look forward to it."

The contraption featuring the permutating lock had thrown him off. It was a variable he hadn't factored into his mental plan. But knowing there was a key around here somewhere . . .

"Rumor has it the Americans aren't only here for the Exhibition, but also to tour the country picking their competitors' locks," the man told Kane confidentially, his voice softening. "A curious marketing tactic, isn't it?"

"Very curious," Kane agreed. "Enjoy the rest of your day, sir." He dipped his head, flashing a last grin at the man, then motioned for Zaria to follow him over to Canada's exhibits.

"What was all *that* about?" she said, lips thinning. "Did you know him?"

Kane pretended to be interested in the birchbark canoe that hung suspended above their heads. "Not at all. But sometimes the most pertinent information is given willingly."

"Whatever you're talking about, can you say it in plain English?"

"The lock on the Waterhouse exhibit? I'm not going to lie; it throws a wrench into the plan. I wasn't expecting to have to contend with a new design." Bitterness flooded Kane's mouth as he spoke. "But the man I was speaking to over there—didn't you hear what he said? You only need the proper key."

"I'm pretty sure that's the case with every lock."

Kane ignored her tone. "This one is different."

"What are you thinking?"

"Nothing. Yet. Stay here for a moment, will you? I've got to find Fletcher."

Zaria cut him with a look, but it seemed more exasperated than hateful. A lock of hair had escaped its intricate knot, brushing the curve of her cheek, and Kane clenched his hands into fists. Maybe he was imagining it, but something about her demeanor had shifted since they'd entered the Exhibition and found the necklace. Perhaps it was the anxious excitement of seeing the very object they were after. It made everything more real. Perhaps Zaria was finally beginning to realize that he *did* know what he was doing. Either way, Kane thought he liked the change.

Unfortunate that he was going to betray her in the end.

He stayed close to the center of the palace's long corridors, avoiding the guests of import clustered at each of the major exhibits. As he moved, Kane took note of the places people congregated. What drew their attention? What was arranged so as to block their line of sight? In which corner could he stand and go more or less unnoticed? People in crowds, he had learned, tended to move in a predictable way. They were like sheep. They stayed with the majority, took cues from their peers without even realizing they were doing it.

Because the palace was so grand, it took Kane longer than expected to track down Fletcher. He eventually spotted his friend among the foreign exhibits, positioned a short distance away from France.

"Nice," Kane said as he approached, indicating Fletcher's newly acquired constable's hat.

"Shut up. Price gave it to me." Fletcher spoke from the corner of his mouth, keeping his attention fixed straight ahead. "What's going on? I thought we weren't going to meet up until later."

Kane pretended to be very interested in a woven carpet as a laughing duo passed them by. "I need you to look into something for me."

Fletcher waited, an invitation to continue.

"The Waterhouse jewels—they're in a cage. A fancy display case that's essentially a safe, featuring a new type of lock that's being shown for the first time. I've never seen anything like it before."

Some of the color leached from Fletcher's already pale face. "That's... not ideal."

"To say the least. Apparently, though, it was sent by some American company called Day and Newell. If my information is correct, each lock corresponds to a parautoptic key with up to fifteen bits."

"Where did you *get* that information?" Fletcher asked, and Kane shrugged.

"Right place, right time. I need you to find out how many bits are on the key to the Waterhouse exhibit. That'll tell me how many levers are inside the lock. It's impossible to see the interior workings—the design specifically makes sure of that."

"Why don't we just try to steal the key?"

"Because the second someone notices it's missing, they'll either change out the lock, increase security, or move the exhibit. I don't want to risk that."

Fletcher gave a long-suffering sigh. "I'll see what I can do. Naturally, this couldn't be simple."

"Nothing ever is," Kane said. He pulled out his pocket watch, grimacing when he saw the time. "I'd better get back to Zaria. She'll wonder where the hell I've ended up. This place is a maze."

"How's it going?" Fletcher wondered, too innocently. "Has she stopped glaring at you yet?"

"I think we're getting there."

"*Kane.*"

Kane turned. "What?"

Fletcher shot him a meaningful look. "I know you love a challenge, but don't convince her to like you. It's not in either of your best interests. You can't give her any of what you're promising."

For some reason, Kane didn't think Fletcher was referring only to the money.

He kept his voice light. "I don't think I'm in danger of her liking me."

"I'm just saying."

Kane gritted his teeth. It shouldn't have bothered him, but it did. Getting people to like him was part of his unofficial job description.

Zaria, though, was different. She'd known who he was from the very beginning, and Kane hadn't bothered doing much in the way of convincing her otherwise. Why should he? They'd made a deal. They both wanted something, and he suspected they'd both do whatever they needed to in order to get it. Zaria Mendoza was temporary. Kane's desire to win her over was borne of habit, nothing more.

"Well, *stop* saying," he said to Fletcher. "I'll see you later."

Fletcher touched the brim of his police-issue hat, a clear indication that he wouldn't broach the subject again, but Kane didn't miss his friend's eye roll.

Now that he knew more or less where he was going, it didn't take him long to find Zaria. She'd moved, but not far, her attention on an enormous telescope angled toward the ceiling far above their heads. It was at least three times as long as Kane's entire body, shiny and intriguing. For a fleeting moment, he ached to put his eye to it. To see whether it really did allow one to cast their gaze into space and track the movement of the stars.

"You're back," she said as Kane came to a halt beside her. "That took a while."

"I'm not sure if you've noticed, but this is a fairly large building."

He expected her to snap a retort. To roll her eyes or make a dismissive sound in the back of her throat. Instead, though, Zaria smiled.

It was an insidious thing, that smile, and it stole Kane's breath away. It occurred to him that he hadn't yet seen her smile—not at him, not really. It changed the entire structure of her face somehow.

Kane thought of Fletcher's warning. He shouldn't let Zaria soften toward him, not with what he was planning. But he was, after all, a selfish boy.

So he gave a small smile back, a ghost of the real thing.

"What do you think of the telescope?"

Zaria's question came unbidden, another thing catching Kane off guard, and for a heartbeat, he wasn't sure how to respond. He was no longer thinking of the telescope at all. He was thinking of perilous plots and dangerous betrayals and all the things he wanted but didn't deserve.

"It's interesting" was the reply he settled on. He wasn't about to tell Zaria how he'd always been intrigued by space—how he loved to be able to see the stars on those rare clear nights, because they made him feel small, and lately he felt far too big for his corner of London.

Zaria's gaze was fixed on a well-dressed man gesturing animatedly at the telescope, his voice a wavering boom as he provided a lengthy explanation to a middle-aged couple. "It *is* interesting, isn't it?"

There was a sly note in the way she spoke, and Kane stared at her, hard. It wasn't often he encountered someone he couldn't decipher. Some sixth sense told him Zaria was hiding something. But what?

Before he could settle on a response, an unwelcome voice drifted over to them.

"Hunt?"

Kane stiffened, careful to react as little as possible. He knew who he would see even before the man who had spoken drew up beside him.

"Lord Saville." He turned, plastering a grin onto his face.

Saville was a tall man, thin shouldered and bespectacled. Kane ought to have expected he would be here, yet the prospect hadn't so much as crossed his mind over the last few days. *Fool*, he chided himself as Saville's sparse brows drew together.

"How the hell did you get in here? Conned your way in, did you, the way you conned me?" The lord's scowl deepened. "I don't appreciate men who enter my employ only to disappear. I'll have you know, I'm not inclined to—"

Kane grabbed Saville's elbow, steering him away from the crowd before his voice could carry any farther. The weight of a dozen eyes was tangible. "You must have me confused with someone else," Kane said loudly, injecting a jovial note into his laugh. Then he hissed, "My lord, I really must insist you keep your voice down."

Anger flashed in Saville's eyes—he was quite clearly unaccustomed to having anyone insist anything of him. He puffed his chest out, wrenching his arm from Kane's firm grip. "Hunt, I can get you thrown out of here faster than you can flutter your lashes."

"You don't know what you're talking about," Kane said, head spinning as he fumbled for a plan. Had Saville been anyone else, he would have killed the man. He couldn't have anyone here knowing he was not, in fact, Theodore Wright. But Lord Saville, owner of Saville Shipping Co., was a complicated problem, and one Kane couldn't simply dispatch. Had he seen Fletcher, too, and recognized him despite the constable's uniform?

And with that thought, a solution came to Kane.

This was the thing about cons: You had to commit to your character in order to truly sell it. If your character was impatient, your impatience had to be such that no one would dare question it. If your character was confident, the type who didn't take no for an answer, you had to make it clear that refusal wasn't an option. Kane had always been good at that. He slipped into a role with little to no trouble at all, and had no difficulty imagining how he might behave if he were truly that person. Perhaps it was that he longed not to be himself, if only for a moment. Perhaps it was the fact that he forgot, for a moment, the persistent sensation of wanting to claw his way out of his own skin.

"Listen, my lord," he murmured to Saville, pitching his voice even lower. "I didn't think it would come to this, but since it appears we can't avoid it...I hope we can rely on your discretion the way you're going to have to rely on ours."

"And just what is *that* supposed to mean?" Saville said, drawing himself up tall.

Kane gave an audible sigh, beckoning Saville over to one of the glass windows where no one would be within earshot. "Mutual discretion," he reminded the lord firmly before continuing. "Fletcher and I are part of a special task force put together by the Metropolitan Police to investigate dark market vendors. Magical items are a rarity, as I'm sure you well know, but they're becoming more common as demand increases. Luckily for *you*," he intoned, because Saville showed signs of wanting to interrupt, "we're not focused on buyers right now. Our instructions are to go directly to the source. Walk with me."

Saville opened his mouth, then closed it again, appearing not to know what to say. Kane couldn't tell whether the lord believed him, and his question was answered a heartbeat later.

"You're *boys*," Saville hissed, overlarge eyes narrowed in suspicion behind his spectacles. "You expect me to believe the police entrusted *you* with such a thing?"

"We're older than we look. It's part of the job, you know, to appear unassuming. And before you say anything else, my lord, I would suggest you not encourage us to rethink our policy of not prosecuting buyers."

"I'm not—" Saville sputtered, face reddening. "What I mean to say is, I'm not *buying*—"

"Don't make a fool of yourself. We both know exactly what I saw and heard while in your employ."

Saville quieted, fury still lingering in the lines around his mouth. "Say I pretend to believe you. What are you doing *here*, at the Exhibition's private viewing?"

"Why, my lord." Kane pretended to be miffed. "I think we both know that to be none of your business."

Saville snorted, an indelicate sound. When Kane came to a halt, so did he, rotating so their gazes locked. "And I think we also both know I'm never going to believe this little charade without proof."

"You're right," Kane allowed. "You're the type of man who doesn't accept anything at face value. I expect that's why you've had so much success." He flashed a cold smile, indicating with his chin. "It's also why I've brought us here."

Saville followed Kane's gaze. It was clear the moment his eyes found Fletcher: They bugged out even more prominently, shock entrenching itself between his brows as he took in the uniform. "I—"

"Say nothing," Kane said. "Say nothing to anyone. Even if you do, they will pretend not to know what you're talking about. Do I make myself clear?"

Saville nodded, never looking away from Fletcher. "With regard to my own involvement—"

"*Nothing*, my lord. You're a powerful man, and we aren't looking to meddle. But keep a low profile from now on, would you? You can never be too careful when deciding who to trust."

Saville nodded a second time.

"Now go," Kane urged him. "And remember—mutual discretion." He made it a warning.

"You've made that very clear," Saville said smoothly. "You needn't worry."

Kane didn't relax until the lord was gone, swept into the slews of important patrons. One potential disaster averted.

How many more would he have to contend with before this was over?

14

ZARIA

Zaria lost track of the hours they spent in the Crystal Palace. Kane was unrelenting in his need to know every detail of the place, and it somehow seemed even larger on the inside. Fletcher was in charge of learning about security, Kane told her, but it didn't stop him from marking the places coppers seemed to congregate or how often they left their stations. He took note of every exit, and there were fewer than Zaria would have anticipated for a building of this size.

"You ought to be paying attention, too," Kane told her as they passed the crystal fountain once more. "Given the escape plan, I mean."

"I assume the plan involves running for the door."

He looked affronted. "I didn't join forces with an alchemologist so we could sprint for a public exit. You can create a chemical compound that melts glass, correct?"

"I'm not an amateur."

"Trust me, I'm aware. I'm thinking a pane of glass on the north side of the building will have to go. It's close to the exhibit but not too close, and with the smoke, security won't have a good line of sight. I just need to examine it from the outside."

Zaria considered the adhesive device she'd have to create and the chemical compound she'd need to imbue it with. Manipulating glass was a basic skill in alchemology, but Kane's demands were adding up quickly. Now more than ever, it was crucial that she spoke with Cecile. "What happens if we're caught?"

"We won't be. But if we are, then you hope to hell I can bribe the coppers under Ward's thumb to let us go."

From his tone, Zaria suspected arrest wasn't the only potential repercussion, but Kane's mouth soldered into a line so firm that she let the subject drop. Better to badger him when they weren't surrounded by people.

As they exited the Crystal Palace, it became clear she wasn't finished with Kane for the day. Shoving through the turnstiles, she turned away in her eagerness to be rid of him, but Kane grabbed her arm. The wind was frigid after spending hours in the trapped-sun warmth of the glass palace, and already his cheeks were stained lightly with pink.

"Midnight. The converted factory on the corner of Millbank and Wood. Meet me there, and don't you dare come alone. I've found what you're looking for."

Zaria recoiled in surprise, excitement pooling in her stomach. "Cecile? You've tracked her down already?"

He merely arched a wicked brow, striding away before she could reply. She kept her eyes trained on his back until he disappeared into the crowd, her glee quickly souring. It was unlikely Kane had managed to search London so quickly, which meant he must have known where Cecile was all along. That or he'd asked Ward. Was it possible he'd only feigned ignorance to force her into making a second deal with him?

She couldn't be sure either way, but Zaria ultimately resolved to keep her guard raised just a little higher when she was around Kane Durante.

So she'd spent the evening in the pawnshop with Jules, impatience gnawing through her insides as she tried to focus on relaying the day's events to her friend. Truthfully, there wasn't much to tell, and she must have seemed distracted based on the suspicious looks Jules kept tossing her way.

It felt like an eternity before dusk fell. At eleven o'clock, after Jules had gone to sleep, Zaria shrugged on one of his coats and swept into the night, unable to bear the anticipation any longer. She kept her head down and moved quickly, keen not to draw any attention from would-be murderers. It was dangerous, she knew, but the walk was short—less than ten minutes—and she was resolute that Jules wouldn't be involved in this particular scheme. With his frock coat and her hair tucked up inside one of George's hats, she undoubtedly looked like a factory boy finishing a late shift.

The converted factory Kane had described was easy enough to find. It was a place to be leery of, Zaria was certain, with its blacked-out windows and towering entrance. Faded letters on the exterior wall declared it to be MOORE & SONS.

She hovered outside it a moment, feeling foolish. Kane was nowhere to be seen, but then, she was far too early.

Wind swept her hair around her face in a flurry of dark strands as she removed her hat. Zaria exhaled through her teeth, pressing her back against the brick in an attempt to avoid the cold. This part of Ward's territory was quiet compared to the constant tumult of

Devil's Acre. She wondered if the kingpin was nearby, wondered how much he saw with eyes that weren't his own.

There was a feeble whine as the door to the old factory was thrust open, and Zaria leapt away from the wall. Her heart pounded a frantic tattoo until she heard Kane's voice say, "For God's sake, Miss Mendoza, I told you not to come alone."

He cut a lone figure in the darkness, glass of whiskey in hand, silhouetted by the faint glow of a candle on the other side of the door. The top few buttons of his shirt were undone. Shadows traced the line of his mouth and congregated in the hollow of his throat, and fury emanated from him like something physical.

"Yeah. Well—" Zaria swallowed, injecting more confidence into her voice before starting over. "Jules fell asleep, and I didn't want to wake him. Besides, I was out and about anyway."

"Is that so? And are you commonly out and about at"—Kane procured his silver pocket watch, frowning down at the tiny hands—"eleven twenty-three in the evening?"

"Sometimes."

"Have you quite forgotten that someone is trying to *kill* you? And it's not Mister Vaughan, by the way."

"How can you be sure?"

Kane scoffed delicately. "He doesn't exist. That is to say, whoever commissioned you gave a false name. I'm sure there are, in fact, many Mister Vaughans, but he's not one of them."

"Oh." That shook Zaria a bit, although using an alias to do dark market business wasn't uncommon. "Well, regardless, I took precautions." She gestured down at her outfit.

"If this person knows where you live—who you live with—then it won't make a lick of difference. You're too short to be Julian, even if you're wearing his clothes. Which, by the way, look positively absurd on you."

Framed that way, the words made unease rise within her. She shoved it down. "It's sweet that you're worried about me."

He snorted, but something in his gaze made her swallow as he said, "If you're not going to involve Master Zhao, then I'll be forced to escort you everywhere, and somehow I doubt either of us wants that."

"I'm not forcing you to do any such thing. But since I'm here now, it would be polite if you asked me to come inside."

Kane took a very long drink, as if he'd decided he couldn't bear to deal with her sober. His tone was dry as he said, "I suppose you'd better."

Zaria took hesitant steps to the doorway as he moved aside, beckoning her into the entryway. Somehow the place managed to be very *Kane*. There wasn't a lick of color to be seen, and the furniture was arranged in a way that struck her as rather random. A painting portraying a wintry landscape hung above an unlit fireplace, and beside that was a pianoforte.

A pianoforte. In a converted factory a mere few blocks from the slum. It was shoved into the corner, shrouded by the darkness, which was why Zaria hadn't noticed it at first. Now, though, she couldn't seem to look away. Only rich folk had such things.

"Where did you get this?" she asked softly, running a hand across the keys. They were a fine ivory, not a trace of dust to be found on their smooth surface. It wasn't just for show, then. Someone cared about the instrument very much.

Kane must have known what she was referring to without looking. "No idea. Ward had it here before Fletcher and I moved in."

So Fletcher lived here, too. Interesting. "Do you play?"

Kane paused a beat too long. "No."

"Oh." Zaria frowned. "Does Fletcher?"

"No. Don't touch it."

She snatched her hand away, more out of shock than anything else. He had to be lying, but why?

"A drink?" he asked, turning away.

"I didn't come here for a drink. I came here for Cecile."

Kane might have sneered, though it was difficult to tell until a second candle flared to life before him. "Well then," he said, "you ought to have come at the time I specified. *I* am having a drink. Whether you decide to join me or not is up to you. You may wish you had, however, when you see where we're meeting your mystery woman."

Zaria watched as he folded into a nearby armchair, long legs stretched out before him. Scowling, she took a step farther inside, still refusing to take off her coat. Doing so felt like capitulation somehow. "And where is that?"

"Someplace no one would expect to find us."

Zaria waited.

"Church," Kane clarified eventually, lips inches from the rim of his glass. "I have the impression it's not a place you frequent, either."

"And how would you know?" Zaria said, hating the way he addressed her while staring at the wall on the other side of the room. She stalked into his line of sight.

Kane regarded her from beneath half-lidded eyes. "You strike me as someone angry at God, Miss Mendoza."

"Takes a heathen to know one, I expect."

"Hmm." A noncommittal sound in the back of his throat.

Zaria felt her mouth twist into reluctant amusement. Here she was, standing in Kane's home, watching him sip whiskey with that formidable expression. He must have sensed the press of her attention, because the next moment his smile returned with a disarming vengeance.

She'd never felt closer to hell.

"Aren't you?" she asked softly, though she hadn't meant to humor him. "Angry sometimes, I mean?"

Kane's eyes looked blacker than ever. "To be angry at God, I would have had to expect something from him in the first place."

Now that—*that*, Zaria understood. She wasn't about to say as much, though. She didn't want Kane to know her. How she felt about the divine. How heretical thoughts scurried across the surface of her mind whether she invited them or not. She was already damned, was she not? If magic was unnatural, then surely she was beyond saving.

"I have always thought it best," she said haltingly, "not to have expectations of anyone save yourself."

Kane tilted his glass in her direction. "I would agree."

He didn't seem inclined to expand on that, and Zaria suddenly didn't know what to do with herself. She didn't want to sit down— that, too, felt like giving in—but she also didn't want to hover in the middle of the room. Heart thrumming in her chest, she made a slow circle around the perimeter, coming to a halt at the end of the sofa. "I've changed my mind about the drink."

Kane's harsh brows lifted in suspicion, but he inclined his chin. "Glasses are over there."

Poor hospitality, Zaria thought, but she made her way to the counter nonetheless. Her hand was unsteady as she poured the whiskey, causing a few drops of it to splash over the rim. She wasn't a fan of alcohol, but she needed it to take the edge off, if such a thing was possible.

She was made of edges, and Kane of razor-sharp points. No matter how many deals they struck, Zaria couldn't shake the idea that they were in no way meant to fit together. Not even for a short time. And yet here they were, a con artist and an inventor, combining their wildly different skills in hopes of committing an impossible crime, adjusting to accommodate each other's corners.

"So," Kane said as she perched on the edge of the hard-backed wooden chair opposite him, "what makes you think Cecile Meurdrac knows anything about primateria sources?"

Zaria took a sip of whiskey, wincing as it burned the back of her throat. "What do you want with the necklace from the Exhibition?"

"We're not talking about me."

"Then we're not talking about me, either."

To her surprise, Kane smiled at that—really smiled, instead of that wry mask he usually wore—and said, "Fine. I want the necklace because if I don't get it, lives will be on the line."

"Whose lives? Yours?"

"No. I don't know." Kane's smile disappeared. "That remains to be seen."

"Fletcher's?" Zaria said.

She knew she was right the moment Kane's jaw tensed. He tried not to make it obvious, and it was an admittedly subtle shift, but Zaria saw it all the same.

"Why would you say that?" he demanded.

Because, Zaria thought, she was familiar with the brand of desperation that came either from needing to save your own life or the life of someone close to you. But she only said, "Who else is there? You don't strike me as someone with many trusted friends. So if it's not your own life you're worried about, it must be Fletcher's."

"And you think I'd risk everything for him, do you?"

"Yes" was her immediate response. "I'd do it for Jules." She *was* doing it. "He's like family. I can tell you and Fletcher are the same."

Kane pushed a breath from between his teeth. He set down his glass with one hand, clawing through his hair with the other. At the same time, something in his face darkened further. It was a haunted look, reminding Zaria oddly of the way her father had looked on his deathbed. Like he was being destroyed from the inside out. An unidentifiable twinge shot through her, snatching the air from her lungs. It was the face of a man who was trying to fight, but deep down had already accepted his own fate.

"Does Fletcher know?" Zaria asked, though she suspected she already knew the answer.

"No."

She nodded slowly. "Someone's threatening his life, and you didn't think it pertinent to tell him? That's fucked-up, Kane."

"It's none of *your* goddamned business." His teeth were suddenly very prominent in the dim light. "Especially given that you're doing the exact same thing."

"What's that supposed to mean?"

"Come now, Zaria. You think I don't know about Ward's ultimatum?"

Zaria felt her cheeks heat. "I'm giving George time to tell Jules. I wasn't even supposed to know—it shouldn't come from me."

"Somehow I doubt Julian would agree."

"It would kill him to know his father kept this from him. I'm still hoping George does the right thing."

"But it's better if *you* keep it from him, is it?"

"At least Jules's life isn't in danger," she hissed, even as a sick sensation unfolded in her stomach.

Kane's eyes glittered. "That remains to be seen. You think

working for the kingpin is safe? He kills his own, Zaria." A pause. "Sometimes I do it for him."

Her mouth went dry. She tried to swallow, but the muscles of her throat seemed to have stopped responding. Perhaps she shouldn't have been surprised, but she was. To learn both that even being part of Ward's crew didn't keep you safe from him, and that Kane had been involved in killing his own associates. He had an undeniable air of danger about him, but he didn't strike Zaria as a *murderer*.

"Is that why you came to me?" she said eventually, voicing the question that had been weighing on her all day. "Did you know what was at stake and that I'd be easy to persuade?"

Kane shook his head. "No. I mean, I knew George Zhao was in trouble, but that's not why I came to you. I came to you because you do good work. For all I knew, you didn't care *what* happened to the pawnbroker and his son. All I'm worried about is getting this damned necklace and saving Fletcher. Understood? You only need to worry about your role."

"And will my life be in danger as well?" Zaria demanded.

"No," Kane shot back. "He has no idea you exist. You have no reason to be afraid."

Her chest tightened. "When you say *he*, do you mean Ward?"

There was a beat of silence. Kane worked his jaw. Eventually, he sighed, the mask seeming to fragment and fall away from his face. In that moment, he was not a thief, not a con artist, and not a kingpin's lackey. He was just a young man sharpened by fear and swathed in desperation, his expression as transparent as the glass walls of the Crystal Palace.

"Yes," he said hoarsely. "Yes, I mean Ward. Mad as it may sound, he cares for me, and he wants that necklace more than anything. He doesn't know you're helping me, but even if he did, you'd still be safe.

I swear it. Fletcher is his way of keeping me in line, that's all." For a heartbeat, Kane seemed almost uncomfortable. Then he stood, went to grab his coat, and threw it on with considerable drama. "It's about time we left to meet Cecile."

Zaria spoke without truly intending to, the words slipping out in a rush. "Cecile used to work with my father. There was a time when he was obsessed with finding a primateria source, but he gave up and destroyed all his research. I'm hoping Cecile might remember what he learned, because I haven't a clue where to start looking. And I'm... I need it. I can't go on this way forever, and what will happen to Jules if I die? He'll never escape this hell."

Kane blinked, seeing her admission for what it was—an offering. One painful truth exchanged for another. "You'd do anything for your friend." It wasn't a question.

"Yes."

"So would I."

"I know."

They stared at each other, strangely hesitant in the face of mutual understanding. Could you truly be so terrible, Zaria wondered, if you were willing to lay down your life for another? If you cared about someone enough to want to give them the world? Kane Durante may have been mysterious, but he was no enigma. He simply wore his pain like an undercoat, donning layer on layer overtop.

"It's hard," Zaria whispered, "to care about someone you don't deserve."

She swore she saw Kane recoil and feared she had let her guard drop too much. But then his shoulders sagged, and he lifted his eyes to hers. They weren't shadowed anymore; rather, they were the color of warm honey, the irises ringed in green. "If I can steal this damned necklace, Ward will cut Fletcher loose. He'll free him from this life I dragged him into—a life he's far too good for. How he's managed to *stay* good despite everything, I haven't a clue, but what I do know is that I need to make sure it never breaks him." The column of Kane's throat shifted as he swallowed, the inked symbol there standing out in stark relief. Vulnerability pinched the corners of his mouth. "Help me make sure it doesn't break him. Please."

The breath fled Zaria's lungs. When she'd agreed to work for Kane, she'd assumed his motives were selfish. Just another criminal after something precious, prepared to take down everyone in his way. Now, though, he seemed human. Someone she could relate to whether she liked it or not. If she was in Kane's place—if Fletcher had been Jules—wouldn't she do whatever it took, no matter the cost?

The answer came readily.

"I'll help you," Zaria told him, and meant it. "But first, take me to Cecile."

15

ZARIA

THE SKY OUTSIDE WAS AN OMINOUS BLACK, LACED WITH LOW fog that settled around the rooftops. Zaria followed Kane back toward the slum, where inebriated men with soot-smeared faces hobbled down the street, casting them wary looks. More than once she swerved to avoid unidentifiable puddles that had accumulated in the slopes and divots of the cobblestones, leaching a putrid stench into the air.

"Which church are we going to, exactly?" Zaria asked as they turned into Smith Square, tearing her gaze away from the ground.

"St. John's," Kane responded, pointing straight ahead. His chin was tilted skyward, and he looked rather like a beast scenting the air.

Zaria had seen St. John's before, though she'd never had occasion to actually enter it. It was an imposing stone building constructed in the Baroque style, all columns and cornices with four thick towers protruding from the roof in a square formation. Zaria had always thought there was something dark about the place. It reminded her of a mausoleum, and she had the sense there ought to be gargoyles or faceless stone angels at its entrance. Something about the towering walls with their crowning pediments demanded silence—or perhaps reverence.

Nerves coalesced at her core like a snarl of tangled wire. Desperate as she was to see Cecile again, Zaria hadn't let herself dwell on what that meeting might actually look like. Neither of them had ever been particularly good at showing emotion, and she was braced for the awkwardness that might ensue. If she had learned anything about herself, it was this: Her reaction to small things was too big, her reaction to big things too small. She could never quite seem to strike the right balance, and any attempt to do so felt horribly contrived.

Cecile never judged you, Zaria reminded herself, mentally swatting aside the plethora of possible reactions she'd begun to consider just so she could be sure to choose the correct one. *Anyway, she's not like that. It doesn't need to be some big moment.*

But the flutter of her stomach didn't appear to be listening.

She trailed behind Kane as he ascended the wide front steps. When he reached the entrance, his figure cast into shadow by the supported overhang, he paused. "Have a weapon ready just in case."

He already had his slick revolver in hand, and raised it with all the confidence of someone who'd pulled a trigger many times before. Zaria shoved the barrel of the gun down. She'd taken to carrying a gun of her own given the recent attempt on her life, but they didn't need weapons for this. "Cecile isn't dangerous. And just so you know, I'm talking to her alone."

The look Kane leveled at her could have cut glass. His vulnerability from earlier was gone; in its place was a boy hewn from stone. "I don't think so."

"I'm not interested in having you eavesdrop on our conversation."

"Something to hide, Miss Mendoza?"

"No." Zaria bit the word out too quickly, though it wasn't a lie. She simply didn't want an audience. "Just wait outside, will you?"

Kane stared at her for a long moment, moonlight catching the sharp angle of his jaw. There was a coolness in his expression, and Zaria tensed against whatever would follow. But he only said, "Fine. Once you're inside the church, head to the back left corner of the sanctuary. Open the door. Go down the stairs. Take a right, and you'll find yourself in the crypt. The message I sent Cecile instructed her to meet you there."

"You're joking." Zaria crossed her arms, but he remained deadpan.

"I assure you, I am not. I've held many a meeting here—it's discreet, you see, and nobody but me will even know you're inside. People don't expect criminals to meet in a place of worship."

"But a *crypt*?"

Kane shoved his gun back into his coat, clasping his hands in front of him. The wind tumbled down from the rooftops, sending a few strands of hair whipping across Kane's forehead, and he brushed them away with a curl of his lip. "Thou detestable maw, thou womb of death—"

Zaria cut him off. "Don't quote Shakespeare at me."

"If you're going to go, you'd better not linger," Kane said. "I doubt Cecile will wait long."

St. John's church was just as enormous on the inside, filled with gray light that streamed in through the arched windows. Like the exterior, it was devoid of color. There was no stained glass, no smiling angel babies woven into bright tapestries. The barrel-vaulted ceiling was high, the room simple and polished. It was quiet in a way that made Zaria feel like she was waiting for something. She could imagine ghosts filling the pews, watching mournfully as some broken saint prophesied.

The silence itself seemed to echo, and Zaria was almost grateful for the sound of her own footsteps as she made her way across the sanctuary. There was a podium facing the pews, a Bible splayed open atop it, and behind that was a framed painting of what could only be an artist's rendition of Christ. Zaria cast it a cursory look as she passed.

Church was not comforting to her. It was not *for* her, though she couldn't have said precisely why. She merely knew it to be true each time she stepped foot inside a place of worship, though she would never dare say such a thing aloud. To others, God was morality, virtue, and everything in between. Her doubts often left her feeling so terribly alone. Even Jules preferred not to discuss it, claiming such things were not to be spoken aloud. In fact, Kane was the first person Zaria had felt truly understood her on that front.

Perhaps there was a god, or perhaps not—it didn't seem to make much difference. Either way, Zaria didn't think she would find him here.

She found the door Kane had mentioned with ease and opened it to reveal a descending staircase. Low brick ceilings greeted her, so different from the level above, and she wrinkled her nose at the stench of must and rot. Cecile must be here somewhere: Candles had been lit in the sconces lining the walls, dripping pale wax into curved brass. It was a foolish thing, but Zaria swore she felt a weight pressing in around her.

Then again, perhaps it was just the dark.

She kept a hand on her revolver as she moved forward, gaze narrowed and darting around the space. A chill threaded along her bones. Kane had said he conducted meetings here often—what if the same was true for other unsavory characters, and someone else was already down here? Perhaps he ought to have come along after all.

Lack of experience does not equal inability, Itzal had told Zaria once. *Just because you have not done something doesn't mean you are incapable of it.*

It was true enough. She didn't think there was much she wouldn't do, should necessity demand it.

If you had to, could you kill a man?

Zaria knew the moment she reached the crypt. The ceilings—although still low—arched above her head, separated by pillars. What appeared to be rectangular stone deposits were set back against the walls, nearly the perfect height for one to seat themselves on, but Zaria knew instinctively that they were burial vaults. Other than that, though, the space was empty. There were no coffins. No relics.

No Cecile.

Zaria stepped across the dusty floor. When she reached the other side of the crypt, she turned around.

And froze.

Her light had settled on a pair of feet only strides away from where she stood. Black shoes. The frayed hem of a dress. Heart beating relentlessly in her throat, Zaria lifted the lamp and her gaze.

Cecile stared back, at once a stranger and undoubtedly herself. This version of Cecile was no longer full cheeked but deathly thin, clad in gray. She seemed to have appeared from nowhere, as though hell itself suddenly decided to purge her from its depths. The

flickering light illuminated her pale face, making it appear drawn and skeletal. Though by now she would have been about thirty, her graying hair and fragile bones made her seem older. The result of years of creating magic, likely. Itzal had looked the same way, Zaria realized with a jolt, though seeing him daily meant the transformation appeared far more gradual.

"Cecile," Zaria said, a hitch in her voice. She felt like a child again, yearning for the woman's quiet comfort, a companionship that wasn't weighted with expectation. She hadn't allowed herself to acknowledge how much she missed it until this moment. Of course, she'd always had Jules, but Cecile had fulfilled a different role. She was like a mother, a mentor, an elder sister.

Cecile Meurdrac smiled, the action stretching the papery skin of her cheeks. "Zaria. My, you've changed since I saw you last. You look very well, and so much like your father."

Her voice sounded exactly the same, and time seemed to distort around Zaria, who bit her lower lip. "I've missed you."

She couldn't tell whether it sounded genuine—though it was—but Cecile didn't question it. She knew Zaria said what she meant. "Would you mind if I embraced you?"

Zaria shook her head. Then Cecile's thin arms were around her, holding firmly the way she knew Zaria preferred. She smelled like florals, her touch a repressed memory. Zaria rested her head in the crook of the other woman's cool neck, emotions warring within her. Joy. Overwhelm. Frustration. A thousand questions gathered in her throat, but the one that slipped out had nothing to do with the pri- materia source.

"Why did you leave me?"

Her voice sounded small, and her cheeks reddened as Cecile pulled back, mouth turning down at the corners. Regret danced in her blue eyes. "I'm so sorry, Zaria. I thought it would be for the best. Where I was going…it wasn't safe."

"Because you went to work for the kingpin, you mean."

Cecile's thin brows shot up. "You knew?"

"I only just found out," Zaria admitted. "George told me. Until this week, I'd never thought to ask him. You two didn't seem to have much to do with each other."

"That's true," Cecile said. "But I expect Itzal told him what happened."

"Which was what?"

The other woman sighed. "Our parting wasn't exactly amicable. I don't wish to cloud your opinion of your father, especially now that he's gone."

"I don't care about that," Zaria insisted, though a cold sensation trickled through her blood. It wasn't like her opinion of Itzal wasn't already tainted, but something about the way Cecile spoke made Zaria wonder whether she wanted to hear what came next.

Cecile's gaze darted around the space. "Why don't you first tell me why you went to the trouble of tracking me down? From what I've been told, it sounds like you've commenced a rather dangerous search."

The last thing Zaria wanted was to hear Cecile warn her away from seeking a magic source—to remind her what that obsession had cost Itzal. How to make the woman understand? "I was going through my father's documents recently, and I came across a notation in your hand. I was trying to find out what he knew about primateria sources." She gritted her teeth. Saying the words aloud brought her frustrations to the surface all over again. "He was desperate to find one. Though he wasn't successful, I'm positive he must have learned something of use. And I *need* to find one, Cecile. He left everything to me, including his list of commissions."

Cecile's eyes flashed with perturbed comprehension. "Oh, Zaria."

"I need to finish them. I can't pay back the deposits, and his clients aren't exactly understanding. I think—I mean, I'm worried they'll come after me." There was no point telling Cecile it was already happening. "But I'm so afraid that—"

"That you'll work yourself to death just like he did," Cecile finished in a hushed tone. "The deposits . . . he lost the money, didn't he?"

Zaria didn't answer. The question seemed a rhetorical one.

"I'm not surprised." Cecile coughed a dark laugh. "That's why I left, you know. We worked so hard, put so much effort into our creations, and then he would lose it all. His share *and* mine. It was during this time that Alexander Ward was trying to recruit your father to work exclusively for him. Itzal Mendoza was a well-known name on the dark market, but your father wouldn't budge. To get Ward off his back, he offered him the next best thing." She sighed wearily. "Me."

"What?"

"Your father told Ward I knew everything he did. That I was a better choice because I was without a child to distract me." Cecile's expression turned sympathetic, and Zaria stilled. Was that what she'd been to her father? Nothing but an inconvenient distraction from his work? It was the impression he'd given every day of her life, but she never thought she'd hear proof he'd said it aloud. Acid climbed the back of her throat.

"I accepted Ward's offer," Cecile said. "What other choice did I have? Itzal was no longer paying me, and life in the slums is difficult. I don't have to tell you as much. It was a dangerous escape, but one that gave me everything I needed. I left without saying a thing, mostly because I didn't want you to come searching for me, but also because I didn't want you to think poorly of me."

"I wouldn't have," Zaria said hoarsely. Even back then, she'd understood desperation. How the need to survive could trump all else. "You're not working for Ward anymore though, right?"

"No, I'm not."

There was a heavy pause. It felt as though the crypt air grew heavier around them. "How come?"

Cecile stepped closer, the fabric of her dress whispering across the stone floor. Her eyes reflected the candlelight like twin flames. "I'll tell you something about working for that man, Zaria," she said. "It is very, *very* difficult to stop."

Zaria swallowed. "Because he didn't want to let you leave." It wasn't a question.

"Of course he didn't. When you work exclusively for someone, you learn a lot about your employer. With every piece of information I picked up, I knew I was digging myself a deeper hole. Eventually, it became clear there was no turning back. Knowledge is a dangerous commodity. More dangerous than anything we create in our workshops."

"But you *did* leave."

Cecile splayed her long fingers out before her, staring at them contemplatively. The shape of her mouth was melancholy. "I did. After less than two years, in fact."

"How?"

"I believe the more pertinent question is why. Truly, I might have been content to stay. The pay was good. I always had work doing what I loved. It was the ideal arrangement, at least on its face. And yet things were not so perfect." Cecile's stare turned glassy. "One day, about eight years ago, I went to Ward's office. I had an idea that I was excited about. You see, Ward wasn't interested in the search for a primateria source; he wanted me to *create* one, the way Hohenheim once had. He was growing weary of the limits to my creation. He was growing weary of *me*, and resented his own need for my skill. He wanted to wield magic in his own right, but he couldn't master it. He wanted a primateria source.

"I worked tirelessly trying to unravel alchemology's Magnum Opus—the process used to create a primateria source, as you'll remember. I was attempting to work backward, so to speak, and I hit countless dead ends. I grew weak, sickly." Cecile gestured down at her thin frame. "I forgot where I was for hours at a time. On the day in question, however, I thought I was having a breakthrough. I left my workshop and ran to Ward's office at once, intending to let him know.

"The front doors were unguarded." Her eyelids fluttered half-closed. "That should have been the first sign something was wrong. But I was so excited, I scarcely noticed. I barreled up the stairs. I could hear voices coming from Ward's office and recognized his at once. The door was cracked, just slightly, so I shoved it open the rest of the way."

Zaria had to remind herself to breathe. The silence turned oppressive, absolute, until she found her voice. "And then?"

"Then." Cecile said the word as if it were an entire sentence on its own. A moment encapsulated by a single word. "Then I saw them, lying on the floor of his office. A man. A woman. And—" Her voice cracked, sputtering out. What she said next was a mere croak. "And a young boy. He wasn't on the floor; someone had lifted him onto Ward's desk. His face was turned toward the door, toward me, and it was as pale as anything I'd ever seen."

"They were dead," Zaria said quietly.

"The man and woman had been shot. The boy—God only knows whether he was still alive at that point. There was blood all over the floorboards. It was fresh, spreading toward the door where I stood. In the center of it all, standing casually as if they'd been discussing the weather, was Ward and two of his men. He looked up at me, met my eyes, and I saw that his were..." Cecile exhaled a shaky breath. "They were empty. So *horribly* empty. That was when I decided to leave."

"And he let you?" Zaria said, her stomach churning as she tried and failed not to imagine the scene Cecile described.

"He did. I still don't know why—perhaps it was easier that way. I got a place near Regent's Park, far outside of his territory. But he found me, of course, and to this day, he sends me small sums of money in exchange for my silence. I suspect he *likes* it, knowing I live in fear of him and that I'm reliant on him. Alexander Ward likes control far more than he likes killing." Cecile's throat bobbed. "I haven't touched alchemology since. I wanted to get in touch with you so many times, but I feared it wasn't safe."

A strange ache took up residence in Zaria's chest. "Can we...I mean, will you contact me now? I'm no longer a child. I'm willing to take the risk." Hell, she was already taking so many.

Cecile's face softened. "Yes," she said. "Yes, I think so."

Zaria bit her lower lip to hide her smile. For the first time in years, she felt warm with optimism. She owed Kane Durante, frustrating bastard though he was.

"When it comes to your father," Cecile continued—and Zaria was grateful for the change of subject—"he did much of his research alone. That said, he was positive magic sources *did* exist, and he was convinced there was one in Britain. The difficulty lay in finding it. You see, nobody's quite sure what the source would even look like. Some believe it can take the shape of nearly anything. And if your father knew anything for certain, that was a long time ago."

Zaria's heart sank. "So you can't tell me anything more."

"I'm sorry," Cecile said, her brows drawing together. "I really am. But your father was not one to confide in others no matter how well he knew them. We worked together for a time, yes, but our relationship was purely business. Any side projects he may have had, he did by himself."

It was what Zaria had expected, but it still hurt to hear. Rediscovering Cecile had been a beacon of hope. A promise that she hadn't yet exhausted all possibilities. Now she had hit another dead end, and the expression of the woman before her was full of such pity that she could scarcely bear it. Gathering her determination, she made one last-ditch attempt.

"Your note—it said something about the source possibly being disguised. Were you doing research of your own?"

"Ah. Yes," Cecile said, an emotion Zaria couldn't decipher lighting her face. She leaned closer, voice low and furtive, one hand reaching into her pocket. "When it comes to primateria sources, I have suspicions of my own, but I need you to be *smart* about this, Zaria. I debated whether or not to even share this with you. You see, I believe—"

Suddenly, the sound of footsteps grew audible above their heads, echoing through the crypt walls. Surely it was too late for even the most devout to pay the sanctuary a visit. What had Cecile been about to say? Frustration swelled in Zaria's chest alongside the panic.

The voices came next, and her eyes locked with Cecile's.

"Did you bring someone else?" Cecile said, a barely audible whisper, and Zaria shook her head. Her heart pounded against her ribs like a caged animal trying to escape. She could feel sweat beginning to bead on her upper lip. The footsteps belonged to more than one person—it couldn't be Kane, then. Or, at least, not Kane alone. She set the lantern down, intending to extinguish the flame, when it snagged on a duo of silhouettes at the entrance to the crypt. One of them lifted something. Zaria's vision wasn't clear, but she suspected she knew what it was.

A masked man swam into view. When he spoke, his low voice held the echo of a smile.

"Miss Mendoza," he said. "Regret working with Kane Durante yet?"

His finger twitched, and several things happened simultaneously.

Zaria reached for her own gun, screaming Cecile's name as the woman lunged, moving with astonishing speed. She shoved Zaria harshly aside, causing her to stumble just as a single shot reverberated through the crypt. There was a flash. A cry that might have come from her own lungs. The ashy, bitter scent of magic.

Then silence.

16

KANE

K ANE CLAWED HIS WAY FREE WITH A GRUNT.

He had been trapped firmly beneath the body of a man twice his size, hand outstretched in pursuit of his gun, which lay a few feet away. His opponent was masked, armed with only fists and a knife: Kane had wrested the man's revolver from him at the start of the fight and chucked it a considerable distance down the street, only to get his own gun knocked from his grip in return.

The man and his companions had caught Kane unawares outside the building as he unloaded and reloaded his gun, waiting for Zaria to emerge. At first, Kane had wondered what the hell they were doing here. It wasn't unusual for criminals to be lurking around at night—*he* was here, after all—but something about the way they'd approached the church had raised his proverbial hackles.

It was immediately obvious they hadn't come for him. Kane doubted they would have bothered with him at all had he not shouted as they ascended the steps to the church's entrance. Perhaps the move had been a foolish one, but he hadn't been able to help it. A single, desperate thought had cycled through his mind on a loop: that Zaria was *in there*. He didn't even know whether she was armed.

Realization had hit then, followed by a searing jolt of panic. Just like the masked figure who'd accosted Zaria in the alley near Kane's home, they'd come for *her*.

He'd launched himself at the men before logic could hold him back. The largest of the three had turned to face him while the other two darted into the church.

Hence his current situation. Even as he fought his way free, the fact remained that Kane was not nearly as strong as the brawny man with whom he was engaged in combat. Distantly, he reflected that he ought to have brought Fletcher for backup. He'd told his friend about his second pact with Zaria, but after thrusting Fletcher into Exhibition security duty, he figured this was something better dealt with alone.

Now he was having serious second thoughts.

The man slammed into him again, and Kane coughed an exhausted laugh. He was fighting poorly. His mind was on Zaria, on the other two men who had sprinted into the church, their own guns raised. He shouldn't have cared. It was a distraction, and a foolish one at that.

"Let me—*go*," Kane hissed through clenched teeth as he struggled out of a choke hold. His fist connected with the man's temple, and he whirled once more for the gun as that thick arm refastened around his neck.

The man gave a grunt of frustration as Kane slipped free a second time. "This ain't about you, idiot boy."

They were the first words his opponent had spoken. His voice was low, gravelly—that of a man all too familiar with a pipe.

Kane had made it to his gun. He stooped to pick it up, never dropping his eyes from the man's shrouded face, and raised the weapon. "Unfortunately for both of us, you *made* it about me. And I'll admit, I don't much like you and your pals meddling in my business."

"Shoot me then." The man's eyes were alight with mockery. He took an exaggerated step back, then another. Kane moved with him. He was coming woefully close to the gun Kane had tossed at the commencement of their fight. If he bent down, he would be able to retrieve it.

Urgency stabbed at Kane, low in the pit of his stomach. He didn't have time to play games. Two other men were in the church, both armed. And though Kane hoped Zaria could hold her own for a short while, he also knew it was a fight she would ultimately lose.

"You touch that gun," Kane snarled, "and I *will* shoot you. Don't test me."

The man held his gaze as he bent his knees. "Oh yeah?"

"I'm serious."

As he spoke, the man swiped a hand toward the ground. No sooner had his fingers wrapped around the gun than Kane fired.

They were quiet, these dark market guns, and Kane never quite got over the thrill of seeing the way magic streaked through the air and buried itself in skin. *Ripped* apart skin. Tendrils of light furled outward from the man's chest like bright smoke, followed by a thick stream of blood. His eyes flew wide as his weapon clattered to the road, the sound distant in Kane's ears. Tinny. The smell of ash permeated the air. Kane watched as the man pressed a hand to the left side of his chest, red pulsing from between his fingers.

When he fell, it was as if in slow motion, the remnants of magic swept away on the wind.

"I told you not to test me," Kane said icily.

Then he sprinted away from the pooling blood.

His grip was deathly tight on his revolver, and his fingers didn't want to let go even as he clawed open the church door. It had been some time since he'd killed someone, but the tension that came afterward was horribly familiar. He pushed it aside. The man would have killed *him* had he been given the chance. It was why Kane had fired without a second thought.

If Ward had taught him anything at all, it was this: When you encountered obstacles, you removed them. If something was in your way, you got rid of it—no matter what it took.

The church was even darker than the night-shrouded streets. Kane didn't know how long it might have taken the man's companions to find Zaria and Cecile, but he hoped to hell the crypt hadn't been the first place they'd looked. He sprinted between the pews in the sanctuary, shoes skidding across the shiny wooden floor, and darted down the stairwell leading to the crypt.

It had been years since Kane had come to St. John's for anything other than business. Once upon a time, though, he'd come here to pray. To kneel on the hard floor and stare up at the beautiful artwork of godly figures, hoping he might find...what? Comfort? The memory of his dead parents? Proof of the divine?

He'd found nothing but stiff muscles and a sense of impending misery, and thus hadn't bothered returning. What Kane had told Zaria was the truth: He wasn't angry at God. He didn't expect anything from him. Not anymore.

But he had, once. And he'd been let down.

Kane was only partially down the narrow stairwell when he heard the gunshot. Horror seared through him as though he'd been the target, and he leapt over the remaining half-dozen steps, heart hammering in his chest. *Don't let her be dead* was the thought that prevailed as he barreled through the arching entrance to the crypt, his own gun raised, blood pounding in his ears.

It took him a moment to digest the scene. Two figures stood facing away from him, revolvers out. They were both pointing, Kane saw with dismay, at Zaria. She was kneeling, positioned oddly. One of her hands clutched a gun. The other was bloody, fingers splayed atop the prone form of a woman Kane recognized as Cecile Meurdrac.

She was certainly dead. A dark stain spread out from a wound in her stomach where her rib cage flared. Her skin was papery, whiter than a sheet, though something about her willowy build and gaunt face made Kane wonder if that wasn't only a consequence of being deceased.

He took all this in very quickly, a fraction of a second passing before he lifted his own gun and fired.

Light blazed through the air, accompanied by a scream and the telltale scent of ash. He'd hit the taller man in the back, purposely not aiming for the spine. This time, he wasn't shooting to kill. Because the second man—Kane saw as he turned around, confirming his suspicions—was not a man at all but scarcely more than a boy. Scrawny and half a head shorter than his companion, the part of his face Kane could see suggested he wasn't much older than thirteen. Whoever was after Zaria, they had youths doing their dirty work. Someone with gang affiliations perhaps? It wasn't unusual for homeless juveniles to be entrenched in the criminal underworld.

Kane was not a good person, but he also wasn't a murderer of children.

"Get the fuck out of here," he bellowed, the sound earsplitting in the small space. The boy didn't need to be told twice. He took off, sprinting past Kane and up the steps. The man followed on his heels, breathing labored and blood dripping in his wake.

Kane lowered the gun, trying to collect his wits. He felt as if lightning had shot through his veins and had yet to fizzle out. He couldn't process what had just happened and thus reverted to his coping mechanism of choice: not processing it at all. His gaze roved over Zaria's crouched form, and for a moment, he felt nothing save a sensation of acute relief.

"You're okay," he said, and Zaria straightened ever so slightly to face him. Her eyes were shiny, her cheeks flushed, but she appeared unharmed. Why had he been so terribly afraid for her?

Because you need her, the snide voice in his head pointed out. *You should be worried about losing her skills—nothing more.*

"Is that all you have to say?" Zaria replied, her voice barely a whisper.

He took three more steps into the crypt. "God, Mendoza. I was afraid they had killed you as well."

There—he'd called her by her surname. That was good. That suggested he was maintaining some level of detachment.

Zaria got to her feet, the action requiring considerable effort. Her body was shaking. "As well? *As well?* Did you *know* those men were coming here to kill Cecile?"

Kane shook his head, frowning. How could she ask him that? "I wouldn't have brought you here if I'd known. I promised Cecile safety." The woman's current address had been in one of Ward's many logbooks—the kingpin kept track of everyone with whom he'd ever had a meaningful interaction—though he'd never mentioned her in Kane's presence. She'd been perplexed when he showed up at her door, then fearful, but Zaria's name had been the key to her cooperation.

"You were standing directly outside the church!" Zaria raised her voice until it echoed throughout the stone enclosure. The sound was an assault on Kane's ears, and he couldn't help his wince. "You let them in!"

"I didn't let anyone in," he said, surprised to hear the words come out evenly. "There was a third man with them, and we got in a fight. But don't worry; he's dead now."

"Oh, excellent," Zaria snarled. "So *you* killed someone as well. Really excellent."

"I didn't exactly have a choice."

Zaria shook her head as if trying to clear it. She ran her fingers through her hair, smearing Cecile's blood across her face, though she didn't appear to notice. She turned away from Kane. Her gaze was fixed on the wall, or perhaps something in the middle distance. It took another moment for him to understand that her shaking wasn't the result of shock or distress.

No. She was furious.

"*You.*" Zaria spun back around, pointing a vibrating finger in his direction. "You had something to do with this. Do you know what that man said to me before you shot him? He asked me if I regretted working with you yet."

Kane went rigid. He became aware that his gun was still raised, which likely wasn't helping; he lowered it. "He mentioned me by name?"

Zaria gave a wild sort of scoff. "Don't act surprised."

"Tell me exactly what he said."

"Just what I told you. He said, '*Regret working with Kane Durante yet?*'"

Kane's blood iced over. Only a limited number of people called him by his true surname. People who knew him as himself, and not one of the many roles he played for Ward. He narrowed his eyes. "If I wanted you dead, Mendoza, I would have done it myself. And I certainly wouldn't have missed."

He knew at once it was a foolish thing to say. Zaria lunged, closing the space between them, and shoved Kane hard against the crypt wall. His back collided painfully with stone, and he was too startled to do anything but blink as her arm formed a barrier across his throat. She jammed the barrel of her revolver into his stomach, not dissimilar to the way she had that day in the pawnshop.

"Don't try to deny it. You're somehow connected to whoever's trying to kill me."

"That's—" Kane cleared his throat in an attempt to force the words out. "That's not true at all."

Zaria was past listening. She shook her head, hair whipping from one side to the other. "Cecile is *dead*. She stepped in front of me, and now she's dead. The only person besides Jules who's ever bothered to give a shit about me." She cut off, swallowing as a tear slipped down her cheek. "I was so grateful you'd found her, did you know that? For one single, *stupid* second, I thought everything might be okay after all."

The pain in her voice was sobering, and it took another moment for Kane to register her words. "Cecile stepped in front of you?"

"That's what I said." There was a sharp jab in his ribs as Zaria shifted the revolver.

His jaw tightened until it was physically painful. It all made sense now: her desperation to believe this was his fault. That he had been the one to lead those men here, and that Cecile had died as a result of something *he'd* done.

Because if it wasn't Kane's fault, then it was Zaria's. She didn't want to blame herself, so she was blaming him, no matter how illogical that was.

"You can say you don't believe me," Kane forced out through clenched teeth, "but I'm not the one who can't deliver on commissions. I'm not the one people want dead. Not enough to act on it, at least." He offered her his bitterest smile. "Cecile is dead because someone's after *you*. Because she gave her life to protect *you*. And I know that's a lot to digest, but don't try to pin it on me just because you can't bear to accept the truth."

It was harsh, and Kane knew it. But life was far harsher, and sometimes people died because of you, even if indirectly. He was responsible for enough terrible things; he didn't need more accusations flung at him.

The barest twinge of regret lanced through him as Zaria's lips quivered, then pressed together so tightly they turned white. When she spoke again, it was a whisper. "You're an asshole."

Kane didn't have a response to that. It wasn't as though she was wrong.

They stood there for a long moment, chest to chest, both breathing too rapidly. Tears still beaded along Zaria's lower lashes, but the upward tilt of her chin was obstinate. She smelled like lavender and something metallic. Her hair flowed around her in golden-brown waves, and though Kane knew the style wasn't considered respectable, he couldn't help being enraptured by it.

He could almost forget she was holding a revolver to his chest, because he was a goddamned idiot.

Finally, Zaria unleashed a curse and let him go. Her face was a mask of grief and fury as Kane stepped away from the wall. He could have moved earlier—could have bent Zaria's arm and shoved her

back with ease—but suspected that would have done a poor job of convincing her he posed no danger.

That was the reason he gave himself, at least.

Zaria slipped her gun back into her waistband, and Kane caught a glimpse of a corner of parchment protruding from her pocket.

"What's that?" he couldn't help asking, and the look she directed at him made it clear he'd overstepped. She seemed a diminished, broken version of herself, as if Cecile's death had siphoned something vital out of her.

"None of your business. I'm getting the hell out of here." Her voice broke on the next words. "Can you—I mean—what are we going to do with her?"

Kane grimaced, knowing Zaria meant Cecile. The man he'd killed in the street could stay there—it wasn't all that unusual to die in a midnight skirmish, and someone would collect him eventually—but Cecile's corpse couldn't remain inside a functioning church. It seemed he wouldn't be getting any sleep tonight. "The body I can deal with, but you're not going anywhere without me."

Zaria was already tucking her hair back up into her boy's hat. She moved gingerly, shoulders so taut it was a wonder she didn't crumble. "I was perfectly fine on my way over here. If anything, the common factor in my near-death experiences is *you*."

Kane scowled disbelievingly at her. "I'm the common factor in you making it out of those experiences alive, you mean. And do I get a single thank-you? No. Instead, you threaten to shoot me."

To Zaria's credit, she looked a bit chastised, but the next moment she was glowering again. "Thank you *so* much for your concern. I'm sure it has nothing to do with the fact that I happen to be useful to you." With that, she turned to go, the set of her shoulders stiff.

"Wait," Kane said. "Did Cecile have the information you wanted?"

"As if you care," Zaria shot back, already heading for the stairwell as the dark reached out to envelop her.

Kane ground his teeth. But his irritation didn't stop him from following her all the way home, keeping a respectable distance, just to ensure she indeed made it unscathed.

Only because she happened to be useful to him, of course.

17

ZARIA

THE MOMENT ZARIA ARRIVED HOME, SHE UNFOLDED THE PIECE of paper she'd taken from Cecile's cold hands.

The other woman's shoving her aside had saved her life, but it also meant Zaria was slow to retrieve her gun. The second she had it pointed at their two attackers, she'd crawled on her hands and knees toward Cecile's prone form.

Cecile's fingers had been scrabbling against the fabric of her dress, and for a moment, Zaria thought she was attempting to stop the flow of blood.

"It's going to be okay," Zaria had said, focus trained on the two men as she pressed her free hand to Cecile's wound. She knew the words were a lie. She'd told her father the same thing on the last night of his life, only to wake at dawn and find him unresponsive in his bed, skin already purpling as lividity set in. She didn't know why she'd said it again tonight. It was a foolish human trait—the desire to insist that everything was fine no matter the circumstances.

Cecile had made a weak sound that Zaria was forced to lean in to interpret. It was then that she realized the woman wasn't trying to stop the blood flow—she was trying to get something out of her breast pocket. The same pocket she'd been reaching into right as they were interrupted.

"Get back," Zaria had snarled at the men, who'd stepped forward upon realizing Cecile was still alive. Her finger shook on the trigger. She didn't know how long the impasse would last. *Could* last.

"Take this," Cecile had gasped, all the color leaching from her lips as Zaria chanced a glimpse of her face. "I don't know what information your father had, but...I've managed to ascertain what a source might look like." Her next breath was a rattling thing. "I don't know if it'll be of any use. Despite what happened with Itzal and I...I want to...see you continue his work."

Zaria hadn't known what to say. Her attention was diverted, and anguish sat like a rock in her stomach. Her mouth didn't seem to be able to form words. If they'd had more time, if she'd only been here alone, there were so many things she would have asked Cecile. So much she wanted to know about her father, about their partnership, about alchemology in general.

Since Itzal's death, Zaria hadn't known another alchemologist. Hadn't interacted with another person who understood the struggle, the elation, the fear that the craft inspired. There were rival alchemologists involved with the dark market, of course, but it wasn't as if she knew any of them personally. You didn't interact with your competition. Even amateur alchemologists kept to themselves for fear of being exposed.

Cecile had drawn her last breath as Kane entered, and Zaria took advantage of the chaos to stuff the piece of parchment into her own pocket.

Looking at him had been the thing that finally caused her to snap. The way he'd stood in the entryway, hands steady on his gun, perfectly at ease. He was a nightmare walking, that boy. He was sin with a smile.

"You're okay," Kane had said, almost no inflection to his voice. A statement of fact—she couldn't even tell whether he was pleased about it.

For a beat, Zaria hadn't known how to respond. But then something had opened up within her, a crevasse at the bottom of which only rage dwelt, and it all came rushing upward. In Kane's world, everything was a game. In Kane's world, people were pawns, and it didn't matter if they died.

Regret working with Kane Durante yet?

In that moment, everything had felt like his fault. He'd dragged her into his life of schemes and thievery, asking more of her than she could reasonably give. Enough that she'd sought out help, sought out Cecile, and in doing so condemned the woman to death.

She had no hard evidence it was Kane's fault. Logically, Zaria knew that. Perhaps it was *her* fault, just as he'd said. Someone was targeting her—perhaps more than one person—and the people around her weren't safe. Getting involved with Kane had almost certainly been a mistake, but it had also made her more cognizant of all the reasons she needed to get out of London. Even if by some miracle she managed to finish all her father's outstanding commissions, was it already too late? Had she invoked the kind of wrath that couldn't be escaped so long as she stayed here?

The more she thought about it, though, the less certain she was

that this was about the commissions at all. She'd dealt with impatient clients before, but she'd never been in true danger until her path crossed Kane's.

The way he had stood there, seeming completely incognizant of the fact that her heart was cleaving into two...how could she align herself with someone so unaffected by death? Kane had *killed* a man outside, he'd said. Like it didn't even matter. Like it was normal to be hunted down by would-be assassins and murder them before they could do the same to you.

Zaria could barely remember what she'd said to him, what words she'd flung as she took out her revolver, desperate to finally—*finally*—find some weak spot. She wanted to see that impassive facade crumble. She wanted to know how it felt to knock Kane Durante off-balance.

As she sat at her workshop desk, the pit within her only deepened. Now that the rage had been released, she felt empty. She longed to sleep but knew it was futile. She wanted to stare into the fathomless dark until unconsciousness dragged her into a more bearable kind of emptiness.

But then she flipped over the parchment Cecile had given her and saw what was etched on the other side.

She'd been expecting words. A location, perhaps, or a description of some kind. Instead, though, she was greeted by a drawing.

It looked to have been taken out of a catalog of some sort. One edge of the parchment was jaggedly ripped, indicating it had been removed from a larger document.

Zaria recognized the item immediately. How could she not?

It was a drawing of the necklace from the Waterhouse exhibit. The necklace Kane was trying so desperately to steal.

The pendant had been hastily circled, and beneath the drawing was a single word in what Zaria now recognized as Cecile's hand.

Carmot?

It took a moment for the word to register. Everything hurt, and not because of her fall to the crypt floor. Her heart hurt. Perhaps that was why it took a moment for the pieces to click together. Carmot was the—possibly mythical—substance from which primateria sources were supposed to be composed.

I don't know what information your father had, Cecile had said, *but I've managed to ascertain what a source might look like.*

Then there was the note Zaria had found among her father's records: *Source: disguised?*

For whatever reason, Cecile thought the necklace in the Waterhouse exhibit was a primateria source.

Zaria remembered it perfectly: an enormous crimson rock set in gold filigree surrounded by diamonds that managed to pale in comparison. It was approximately the same size of the primateria she created herself, and she supposed it was possible a skilled alchemologist had used transmutation to make it appear more jewellike and less…magical. Could that crimson rock be *carmot?*

If Cecile was right—if this was true—it would make sense why Ward, kingpin of the dark market, wanted the necklace so badly. Why he didn't appear to care about the rest of the display. According to Cecile, Ward had long wanted a primateria source.

He wanted to wield magic in his own right, but he couldn't master it.

Zaria wouldn't let Kane see her growing reservations. Let him think she was nothing but another person he had charmed and managed to con. Suddenly, the most important thing was the maintenance of Kane's trust—she couldn't have him cutting her out of the deal. Not when she now so desperately needed to be a part of it.

Not when she intended to take the necklace from him the moment he stole it.

KANE

"WOULD YOU PAY ATTENTION?"

"Sorry." Kane gave his head a shake, squinting through the dim at Fletcher's scowling face. "What did you say?"

Fletcher had just returned from acting as reinforcement for a particularly unpleasant eviction, so he wasn't in the best of moods. Given that, Kane hadn't wanted to launch directly into the previous night's sequence of events. Besides, he wasn't in a good mood himself. He couldn't stop picturing Zaria's face when he'd found her in the crypt kneeling beside Cecile's body. If she'd decided to back out of their deal, she hadn't said as much, but Kane couldn't help but worry she was thinking about it. Last night, he suspected, had led Zaria to a revelation about just how fucked-up he really was.

Who wanted her dead? And why, for the love of God, had they invoked his name?

"I *said*, where the hell were you last night?" Fletcher's tone was irritated. "You weren't here when I got home from the Exhibition. I never even heard you come in."

"Ah." Kane felt his face twist. "Remember when I told you I'd promised to help Zaria find someone? A woman named Cecile, in exchange for a favor?"

"Yes."

"Well, things didn't go...smoothly."

Fletcher's pale brows drew together. "What the hell did you do now?"

That was rather presumptive. After all, *Kane* hadn't initiated what chaos had ensued. He took in Fletcher's state of considerable disarray: the blood on the sleeve of his white shirt that undoubtedly wasn't his, the disturbed ruffle of his hair. For once the two of them seemed equally miserable.

"I found Cecile," Kane said after a moment. He got to his feet as he spoke, suddenly feeling the strong need for a hit of tobacco. As he readied his pipe, he continued. "And I took Zaria to meet her at St. John's church."

Fletcher twirled his hat on the tip of his index finger. "Okay. The problem?"

"She wouldn't let me come with her—she wanted to talk to Cecile alone." Kane shook his head. Everything about Zaria was intense. Rash. And yet she thought *him* difficult to trust. "So I waited outside."

"You're kidding."

"I didn't care much either way. About thirty minutes later, though, we ended up with company. The murderous kind."

Fletcher stopped twirling the hat. "Beg pardon?"

"Someone wants Zaria dead, and they've hired the most incompetent blokes to carry out the deed. Don't ask who," he added,

because Fletcher had opened his mouth, presumably to do just that. "I have no idea. The problem is, it seems there's no shortage of people she's pissed off. Her father took a ton of deposits from rich clients without delivering a product, then he went and died, leaving her to fulfill the commissions. Except she's not very fast at it."

"And now she's being targeted by a client who thinks the Mendozas swindled him."

"That, or it's the one client she actually *did* swindle. She delivered a faulty commission last week." Kane didn't know what his expression looked like, but Fletcher appeared to read his face without difficulty.

"There's more, isn't there?"

He sighed, sinking back into his chair as he passed Fletcher the pipe. His friend took it but didn't put it between his lips, instead staring at Kane with an intensity that made him feel like a naughty child. "Yeah, there's more. Cecile's dead, and whoever killed her knew my real name."

"What?"

Kane launched into the story of how he and the large man had gotten in a fight while the man's two companions went into the church. How Kane had killed his attacker before finding Zaria hunched beside Cecile's body with a gun in her hand, trapped in an impasse.

"Wait a moment," Fletcher interrupted. "You murdered someone at *church*?"

Kane gave a dismissive flick of his wrist. "We were in the street. It's not like I shot him at the foot of the cross."

"You can't kill a man so close to God's house. It's not right."

"Lord save me." Kane groaned, tilting his head back. Fletcher's Catholicism was a little more deeply embedded than his own tattered faith. "We're sinners, Fletch, and you know it. Anyway, I took Cecile's body to Roberts's factory and was up nearly all night."

David Roberts was on Ward's payroll and thus offered up the use of his factory's enormous coal-fired ovens for dealing with remains. He was a rich businessman, gruff and aloof, with a strict *don't ask, don't tell* policy.

Fletcher gave a slow shake of his head. "Well, better hope Zaria got what she wanted out of Cecile before she was murdered." At long last, he put the pipe between his lips and gave a mournful puff.

"Mm-hmm," Kane agreed. "She never told me either way. She was too busy trying to rip my head off. She thinks I have something to do with the danger she's in."

"Maybe you do."

Kane blanched, scowling. "I thought you were supposed to be on my side."

"Think about it, Kane. Someone could know she's useful to you. But since they can't seem to kill her, maybe they're trying to turn her against you."

"Nobody apart from you knows she's useful to me. Besides, who would care enough to do that?"

Fletcher shrugged. "It was just an idea. You've no shortage of enemies. Do you think Zaria's going to call the deal off because of it?"

"No," Kane said at once, then hesitated. He was beginning to suspect Zaria wasn't as predictable as he initially thought. "I don't know. She was pretty upset about Cecile's dying. That woman was important to her for some reason."

"Then is it possible you came off a little bit…cold?"

Kane sat up, wrinkling his nose. "What do you mean?"

Fletcher made a humming sound in the back of his throat. "You're pretty good at acting like death doesn't bother you, that's all.

People like you and me are used to it, but I'd hazard a guess she isn't. She's probably scared, Kane, even if she didn't admit it. Not to mention sad. Did you even try to comfort her?"

"Did I try to—?" Kane cut himself off. "No. I was too busy being relieved *she* wasn't dead." Was that what Zaria had wanted? Comfort? Some kind of emotional reaction from him? It wasn't like he understood her well, but Kane had gotten the impression that this was the last thing she'd been looking for. Furthermore, she lived in Devil's Acre; surely she'd seen no shortage of terrible things. "Just... tell me your evening went better, would you?"

"Actually," Fletcher said, straightening, "it did. I managed to get my hands on the pamphlet they're going to be handing out at the Exhibition once it officially opens." He thrust a folded piece of paper at Kane's chest. Kane opened it; it appeared to contain a small map of the Crystal Palace as well as a list of the main exhibits.

"Very useful. Was Price able to give you an idea of the security rotation?"

Fletcher tilted his head to one side, then the other. "More or less. He wasn't very forthcoming, but I got the sense it was because security isn't very organized yet, not because he was trying to hide something from me. He managed to get his officers stationed near the Waterhouse exhibit, and he pointed out the ones we can trust to keep their mouths shut. They're more loyal to Price than the institution as a whole."

They were going to have to take Price's word for that, Kane thought. He didn't like it. "And the lock? The parautoptic key?"

Fletcher held up a finger, his mouth curving into a rueful smile. "I was getting to that. Turns out a lot of people know about the Day and Newell display. The company is trying to show up the British

Detector lock, and so far, it seems to be working. Problem is, it's never been picked before."

"So I've heard." Kane didn't bother to hide his impatience. "The key, Fletch."

"I talked to a number of people—just making casual conversation, you know—and from what I can discern, the lock Day and Newell's exhibitor will be using in their demonstration has fifteen levers. That's as complicated as it gets. Which makes me suspect the one on loan to Waterhouse will have fewer."

"But you don't know how many."

"This might come as a shock to you, Kane, but most people don't go around discussing the number of bits on a parautoptic key." Fletcher crossed his arms. "Why did you need to know, anyway?"

Kane ground his teeth, though his frustration wasn't directed at his friend. "If I know how many levers we're dealing with, I think I can get Zaria to re-create the key."

Fletcher's brows drew together. "How would that work?"

"Whoever has the key can rearrange the bits, and when they go to lock the safe, the interior levers shift to accommodate the new arrangement. It's constantly changing, which is why it's so hard to pick. An alchemologist like Zaria could come up with a design using magic—one where the key bits could shift to fit the required arrangement. I might still be able to pick it, but it would take ages and far too much guesswork."

"And there won't be time for troubleshooting," Fletcher murmured. "Especially when there's no guarantee you'll even be successful."

"You see the dilemma. Plus, since it's a brand-new foreign design, there's nothing for me to practice on." Kane hated problems

he couldn't solve and questions he didn't have answers to. Heists involved an element of calculated risk, and although he had no qualms with risk, he couldn't very well calculate it if he didn't have all the information he needed. It felt like standing just a little too close to the edge of a precipice, fearing the fall but at the same time yearning to peer at what lay below.

"If Zaria can make a design where the bits adjust," Fletcher said, "then get her to make one where the *number* of bits adjust, too. Assuming you haven't scared her off completely."

Kane said nothing. He didn't yet know whether he had or not.

"Keep her happy, Kane. Even if it means pretending to have real human emotions."

Kane dragged his gaze to the window. The last dregs of sunlight were fading into the west, leaving behind a night saturated with fog. It shrouded the building across the way so it looked like some looming, liminal place. "She's going to lose her mind once she realizes we've tricked her."

Fletcher shrugged again, this time with a simultaneous wince. "Yeah, well. By the time she figures it out, it won't matter, will it?"

19

ZARIA

Zaria was going to con Kane Durante.

She sat at her desk that evening, working on the aleuite explosives, trying to reconcile with that fact. He and Fletcher were meant to be here in less than an hour's time. Kane would finally tell Zaria exactly what he needed from her. He would outline whatever steps he'd come up with in order to get into the Exhibition, take the necklace, and get out.

He would not, however, touch on the part where Zaria snatched it from under his very nose.

Guilt flared within her as she recalled what Kane had told her about Fletcher's life being on the line. She wasn't responsible for whatever happened once the deed was done, right? Any consequences involving Ward or Fletcher would not be her doing. Besides, if Kane was as close to Ward as everyone said he was, then certainly Ward's threat must be nothing more than a bluff.

Zaria refocused on the materials in front of her. Every explosive required an oxidizer and a fuel source, but in this case, the aleuite would act as the latter. Combined with an oxidizing agent, it would still explode, though not in a way that destroyed. It could be dangerous if you got too close, but otherwise it should leave the Exhibition's displays—and themselves—unharmed. Alongside her chemicals, she had already fitted together the outer casing, and now the difficulty lay in the insertion of the impact fuse.

Well. That and getting her hands on more soulsteel.

She couldn't focus. Her head was full of the expression on Kane's face when he'd told her how much he cared for Fletcher. Zaria sighed, leaning back in her chair. Fragmented light streamed through the dirty window, turning her desk a dappled gold. When she shut her eyes, the pattern was imprinted on the back of her lids, fading as the seconds slid past. It was only dusk, but already she was tired. The kind of tired that seemed to linger in her bones no matter how much rest she got.

A light knock sounded on her door, and she pushed her chair back with a grating sound. "Yes?"

Jules stuck his head inside. "Are they here yet?"

"No. Soon, though." She didn't want to see Kane and Fletcher again. Didn't want to be nice to Kane's face while he stared smugly down at her, thinking he had the upper hand. It rarely shifted, that smug expression. Not when he'd laid eyes on Cecile's dead body. Not even when Zaria had pressed a gun to his blackened heart.

"What are you making?" Jules inclined his head toward the assortment of chemicals and metal bits on the desk. Wax had pooled around the bottom of a candlestick, engulfing the corner of a sheet of parchment that had the misfortune of being too close.

Zaria's eyes stung. Her head was full of Cecile, of the necklace, of so much anxious energy she didn't know how else to expel it. She had craved the sweet release of creating magic and the kind of pain that didn't originate inside her head.

Because there was so *much* pain, even though she hadn't seen Cecile in years. It was like the woman's presence had caused something inside her to ease only for that contentment to come crashing down around her, the emotional shift so abrupt, it gave her whiplash. It felt like losing her father all over again. Was it foolish, at eighteen years old, to yearn for an adult she could rely on? Itzal may have been cold, but he'd always *been* there, a steadfast presence always available to provide advice no matter how harsh and impatient his approach.

"I was just working on commissions," she told Jules, then gestured at the mess on the table before her. "This one, though, is for Kane."

He shifted his weight, mouth soldering in what she recognized as determination. "I've been thinking…you should teach me to help you."

The readiness with which he spoke left Zaria stunned. He'd never suggested such a thing before. It was an absurd offer—he knew how difficult alchemology was to learn. Zaria was an impatient teacher, and most important, she didn't *want* this for him. "Absolutely not."

Jules didn't cower beneath her disbelieving stare. "You can't keep creating this much magic on your own. You know that. Your body— your soul—won't be able to withstand it."

Zaria's cheeks heated. She didn't like to speak of souls. Didn't like to imagine a part of her existed over which she had no control. "I'm fine."

"You're not. Kane wanted your help because he knows how good you are. His expectations are high, and I think we both know he

doesn't understand your limits. What happens when he inevitably asks too much of you? The Exhibition is less than a week away. You won't be able to create everything he needs in time."

"I'll be able to do it. On my *own*."

"But I'm saying you don't have to."

"And I'm telling you to drop it!"

"Why the fuck won't you let me *help you*?" Jules all but hollered the words, making Zaria go motionless, blood stilling in her veins. Jules never yelled. He especially never yelled at her. Sure, they sniped at each other every so often, but always with the understanding that neither of them was truly angry.

"Because," Zaria whispered once she had collected herself, remembering how she'd urged Kane to be honest with Fletcher. The word felt shaky on her tongue, and she swallowed, trying again. "Because it's dangerous, Jules, and you're already in enough danger."

The silence that fell in the wake of her admission was taut, threatening to snap. Zaria recoiled as she felt a wall slam down between them. Jules narrowed his dark eyes, nostrils flaring. "What the hell is that supposed to mean?"

Zaria felt like she was being submerged in water too deep to tread. She felt herself withdrawing, her overwhelming emotions becoming a dull, jumbled hum in the back of her mind, as if her brain was anticipating the fallout and trying to disconnect. She fought to remain present—she *deserved* this. The pain that accompanied the way Jules was looking at her right now.

And then, haltingly, it all came tumbling out. The conversation she'd overheard between George and Ward's men. The real reason she had been so desperate to take Kane's offer. How she'd gone to find Kane with the intention of asking him to track down Cecile, only to be accosted by the man with the gun. Cecile's death and her murderer's mention of Kane. Kane saving her life not once but twice, and how furious she was at him anyway, because he treated everyone like they were expendable.

Everyone but Fletcher—and her. For now.

She gave Jules each and every truth, all her good intentions crumbling down around her. A dozen different emotions flitted across Jules's pale face. Horror. Relief. Disbelief. Fury. He eventually settled on betrayal, studying Zaria as if he were seeing her for the first time. "I don't know where to start. Were either of you ever going to tell me?"

She braced herself, regret coursing through her. She wished she'd done this so very differently. "I thought your father would. Or I hoped he would, rather."

"My father doesn't tell me anything important," Jules snapped. "You know that, Zaria. How could you keep that from me?"

"I was going to tell you once I was certain he hadn't! But then everything with Cecile happened—"

"Yeah, let's revisit that. What the hell are you on about? Someone's after you, and they killed Cecile, and you didn't tell me *that* either?"

Although they were questions, the words slammed into Zaria like a brutal statement of fact. *They killed Cecile.*

"I was trying to spare you! Someone is trying to kill me, and I don't want you involved!" Zaria was on her feet now, eyes stinging. "I definitely don't want you learning alchemology—you might as well ask me to put a damned target on your back! You're the one person left who I care about. Can't you see that I'm just trying to keep you safe?"

"By cutting me out?" Jules shook his head in disgust, a vein bulging at the side of his neck. "You get frustrated with me whenever I

ask you not to *work yourself to death*, and meanwhile you're lying to me because you think I need protection? We're supposed to be a team, and we could have dealt with all of this together. Don't give me this rubbish about wanting to keep me safe. Nothing about our lives is safe. You've taken it upon yourself to play savior, and its bullshit."

Anguish speared through her anew. "That's not what I'm trying to do! I just can't lose—"

"You can't lose me?" He interrupted her harshly, a strangled laugh escaping his throat. "I'm practically a grown man, Zaria, not a child you need to protect. If you were as committed to getting out of the slum as you claim to be, you'd know we need to work together. You want that better life so badly? Stop making impulsive choices that only make everything worse. Be *patient.* I've been squirreling away shillings for months while all you've done is lose money, just like your father did."

Zaria flinched as the shock and hurt drained out of her, giving way to numb disbelief. "That's not fair."

"No. Dreaming of a better future together while lying to my face as you pursue it? *That's* not fair." Jules's hands were clenched at his sides, his lips trembling. "You know it's not, or you wouldn't look so fucking guilty right now."

They simply stood there for a moment, warring dark gazes locked, breaths coming fast. Zaria didn't know how to respond. There didn't seem to be anything left to say. The world felt like it was collapsing around her, and she wished the ground would yawn open to swallow her up.

"I'd better go meet Kane and Fletcher," Zaria said finally, her voice toneless. Dead. "You don't have to come. We both know you don't want to anyway."

Jules only kept staring at her, his face unreadable. How had everything changed so fast? How had a few unspoken words fractured their friendship with such swift efficiency?

"Yeah," he said eventually. He sounded as empty as Zaria felt. "Yeah, I *don't* want to. I'll see you later."

And then he was gone, the door slamming hollowly behind him.

A short while later, Zaria sat on the front stoop of the pawnshop, solanum lamp flickering beside her. Regret was a sickness in the pit of her belly. True to his word, Jules didn't join her.

Kane Durante was the last person she wanted to see just now. His presence confused her emotions, and she was already emotional enough. Once this next week was over, she wanted to erase all thoughts of him, to wipe the slate clean. For tonight, though, she only had to be civil and maintain his trust.

Someone in the area had started a fire—the air was acrid with the stench of burning rubbish, and a group of rowdy youths were mafficking at the end of the block. Zaria couldn't imagine what they could possibly be whooping about, and she found herself growing more irritable as the minutes pressed on, mustering a grim smile only when Lottie and her son passed by.

As dusk's fading glow gave way to night, the unmistakable shapes of Kane and Fletcher rounded the corner. Zaria recognized them even in her periphery. Fletcher was taller than anyone else she knew, and Kane was...well, she swore she could *sense* his presence and hated herself for that fact.

She stood up as they neared. Fletcher was sporting a black frock

coat and gray trousers while Kane wore a pair of suspenders over a white shirt unbuttoned at the collar. He looked exactly like a boy who might try to rob you.

Zaria could scarcely bear to look at him.

She had never deluded herself into thinking she was a particularly good person; after all, she supplied London's most dangerous citizens with magical weapons and devices. But she was beginning to realize that she wasn't bad in the way Kane was bad. At least she had a conscience, husk of a thing that it was.

"You look terrible," Kane said by way of greeting.

"Thanks." The single word was clipped.

Fletcher tsked. "You're not supposed to say things like that to a lady."

Zaria said nothing, though the prospect of being considered a *lady* was absurd. She returned Fletcher's nod of acknowledgment, trying to ignore the tiny resurgence of guilt that followed. Trying to ignore the possibility that, if she had things her way, he might just die in six days' time.

"Where's your shadow?" Kane asked her, scanning the street.

"Excuse me?"

"That scowly creature you always seem to have around. Julian."

Zaria frowned even as she was aware of the irony. "I suspect you're thinking of *your* shadow. And if I recall correctly, his name is Fletcher."

"Hey," Fletcher objected.

They both ignored him.

"*Jules,*" Zaria said through the restriction in her throat, "is busy tonight."

This evidently irked Kane, who shot a terrifying look at a dirty young man slinking by. He waited until the man was out of earshot before saying, "My plan takes him into account."

"I never said he was going to be a part of this."

"You didn't have to. Aren't you two a package deal?"

Zaria bit down hard on her bottom lip as Jules's words came back to her. *We're supposed to be a team.* "He's busy, okay?"

Kane raised his brows, and Fletcher studied her with a too-discerning gaze, as if he could see the truth right there in her face.

"Fine," Kane said. "We'll do it without Master Zhao, then. Leave the lamp—I don't want to be spotted. Let's get going."

"Going where? I thought we were meant to be discussing the plan for"—Zaria lowered her voice, glancing around to ensure they were indeed alone—"you know what."

Kane removed his hat, smoothing back his hair. "If you'll recall, you owe me a favor. I'm cashing it in."

Incredulity lanced through Zaria. She knew what he was refer-ring to, of course, but the fact that he had the gall to ask... "I would have thought this *favor* became void the moment Cecile bled out on the floor of the crypt."

"I don't think so," Kane said. "There were no terms to our agree-ment apart from my request, to which you so kindly acquiesced."

"Don't talk like that," Zaria snapped.

"Like what?"

"Like you think you're so pompous and clever."

Fletcher shifted his weight, visibly impatient. If Kane noticed, he didn't acknowledge his friend. "I *am* clever. It's not my fault you made a deal you'd later regret. Now, I'd have preferred a fourth set of hands, but I suppose the three of us will have to do." Kane gave his hat a twirl, then set it atop his head once more. "Shall we?"

"We shall *not*," Zaria said. "Taking part in one of your schemes is already more than enough."

"Ah, now, don't be like that. Helping me tonight is going to help you in the long run. You want those jewels, don't you?" Kane's expression was knowing. "Last I checked, the pawnshop was looking fairly drafty. And you did make a promise."

Zaria could scarcely believe her ears. The absolute *gall* of Kane Durante to try to cash in a favor as though nothing had happened. As though Zaria hadn't left the church that night with Cecile's blood on her hands.

"Fine," she said, forgetting about the necklace. Forgetting she needed Kane to trust her. "*Fine.* You can cash in your favor. I can play nice, if that's what you want. But if you think I won't hate every moment of it, you're sadly mistaken." She set her teeth. "I *know* you had something to do with Cecile's death even if you won't admit it. I hope it haunts you."

Kane came to stand before her so they were face-to-face. His eyes looked green today, Zaria saw, then resented that she'd noticed. The heat of him was tangible as he leaned down, pausing with his lips inches from her ear. She stiffened.

"I can assure you," he murmured on an exhale, "it won't."

Vile. He was *vile*. For a moment, Zaria couldn't speak, couldn't find the words to communicate her fury. She wanted to say something that would hurt Kane Durante. Wanted to fling words to puncture that unruffled demeanor of his. But she couldn't think of anything, and in any case, Fletcher quickly stepped between them.

"As much as I'd enjoy watching you two argue all night, I believe we have a plan to execute." He cleared his throat with an air of pointed impatience. "Kane?"

Kane nodded and relaxed as if nothing had happened. "Of

course. We're headed to the Piccadilly area," he said in response to Zaria's unspoken question. "Just follow me."

And so Zaria did, trailing behind the two of them as they skirted the edge of the slum, the air growing thick with the familiar reek of decay. Chest-high brick walls separated the buildings, ropes functioning as clotheslines strung up between them. Down one of the corners, a man who was clearly intoxicated dunked his head into a barrel of dirty water, only to be screamed at by a woman doing her washing.

Kane and Fletcher moved with dutiful briskness, Fletcher's stride just the slightest bit longer. Once again, Zaria considered what Kane had told her—how he was stealing the necklace in order to try to keep Fletcher alive. She wondered if Fletcher had any inkling of that truth. Wondered if, when he found out, he might grow to resent his friend.

It would be well deserved, she thought as she glared at Kane's back. As if he felt the weight of her gaze, he glanced over his shoulder, hazel eyes guarded.

"You'd best keep up," he barked, then turned around.

Bastard, she thought, pulling the collar of her jacket closer to her skin.

About twenty minutes later, Kane and Fletcher came to a halt. They stood before a mansion-like building, surrounded by more greenery than was common in the inner city. Nearly a dozen windows faced the road, the stonework arranged so as to embellish each one, and a balcony stretched above Zaria's head. The house took up nearly half the block: a ridiculous, extravagant display of wealth. A cast-iron fence surrounded it on every side, but no gate sealed it off from the rest of the street.

At night, it was more evident than ever how different the slum was from wealthy areas like this; Piccadilly was quiet, almost unnervingly so. Though people like Zaria couldn't afford to pay much attention to etiquette, she was aware that this—walking around at such an hour with two young men—was decidedly improper.

"Who lives here?" she demanded, fearing the worst. Could this be Ward's place?

"Nobody," Kane said. "At least not right now."

Fletcher had disappeared from his side, Zaria realized. A moment later he appeared again, dragging what looked to be two wooden pallets on wheels. She frowned. "What are those for?"

Kane ignored her, stalking up to the front door. He bent over the lock, his body shielding Zaria's view of whatever he was doing, but she was able to guess. Sure enough, a moment later there was an audible *click*. Kane gave the door a shove, and it swung open.

"Nice," Fletcher said, beginning to drag the wooden pallets up the front steps. The wheels clunked dully on each subsequent stair.

Zaria watched in blatant confusion. "Would one of you mind telling me what, exactly, we're doing here?"

Kane stared at her from the doorway, eyes half-lidded. One side of his mouth tilted up, and there was more amusement in that look than Zaria would have liked.

"Haven't you guessed?" he said. "We're committing a crime, Miss Mendoza."

20

ZARIA

Zaria stared at Kane. Her thoughts were all a jumble—she didn't know if she was waiting for more information, for her feet to start moving, or for Kane to tell her he was joking.

She knew he wasn't joking, though. It was Kane. She supposed this was just another evening for him. That he did illegal things all the time covered by the shroud of night. Whenever Zaria looked at him, it was an effort to remember what she wanted. The primateria source. The Waterhouse jewels. His continued trust—or, at the very least, enough of it to keep him from noticing anything was amiss.

She focused on those things. Let strategy quash emotion. Let logic override the way her breath caught when his gaze met hers, always seeming to communicate a challenge. And then, once she was certain she had her head on straight, she followed Kane and Fletcher into the house.

It was the most beautiful home she had ever been inside. The main entrance had impossibly high ceilings and gleaming surfaces; a wide staircase in the center of the room ascended to the second level. A glittering crystal chandelier hung above their heads. The air smelled like polished wood and held all the silence of a place protected from outside noise. There was very little furniture; it felt less like a place where someone lived and more like an exquisite display. It was a building that should have held a dozen staff. Yet tonight, it appeared, not another soul breathed within these walls.

"Whose house is this?" Zaria asked again, keeping her voice low.

Kane took no such precautions. "It belongs to a widowed duchess," he said, the words echoing through the space. "Or, at least, it did."

"Where is she now?"

"Dead."

Zaria whirled from where she had been examining a painted vase. "Did you *kill* her?"

The question escaped her mouth before she could think better of it, and Fletcher gave a throaty laugh.

Kane merely smirked. "We did not. By happy accident, she died earlier this week."

"Natural causes," Fletcher added. "She was elderly."

Zaria wasn't prepared to be quite as blasé about a woman's death as they were. Despite Kane's and Fletcher's words, she wasn't entirely convinced they *hadn't* killed her. "And why are we here, snooping through her house? What's the crime, apart from trespassing?"

Kane didn't answer right away. He had strolled purposefully into the adjacent room, squinting through the dim as if in search of something. Whatever it was, he must not have seen it, because he re-emerged a moment later into the entryway, brow furrowed.

"We're stealing something" was his matter-of-fact reply as he made his way to the next room over. His footsteps echoed in his wake, an eerie, hollow sound. Zaria followed on his heels.

"Stealing what, exactly?"

Kane paused, beckoning past her to Fletcher, whose eyes lit up. He came to join them in what Zaria realized belatedly was a drawing room, dragging those ridiculous wheeled pallets along behind him. She couldn't tell quite what they were looking at; everything in here must have been valuable. Sofas and chairs were arranged around a shiny wooden pianoforte, and the walls were covered with portraits and artwork that, for all Zaria knew, could have been priceless. An unlit fireplace with an elaborate mantel occupied the far wall, and a beautiful woven tapestry hung above it. She hated it, this ostentatious display of wealth while so many went hungry in the slums.

"We are stealing *that*." Kane pointed, a self-satisfied smile playing across his lips. Zaria felt her jaw slacken.

"You're joking."

"I most certainly am not."

"The *pianoforte*?"

Kane crossed his arms as Fletcher wheeled the pallets onto the patterned carpet. "Yes, the pianoforte. Keep up, would you?"

The pallets made sense now, Zaria realized, watching Fletcher push them up against the instrument. It was admittedly beautiful: ivory keys unchipped, wood finish gleaming. "But you already have one of these."

"Yes," Kane agreed.

"Why do you need another?"

"I don't, technically speaking." He strode past Zaria to assist Fletcher, not deigning to provide any more of an explanation. When she didn't follow, he pivoted to quirk a brow at her. "Are you going to help?"

This was utterly ridiculous. She'd figured Kane wanted her assistance with something dark market related or perhaps within the realm of alchemology. She had not, however, foreseen his wanting her manpower. All at once, Kane's disappointment over Jules's not joining them made sense.

I'd have preferred a fourth set of hands, he'd said.

Preposterous.

"We're not going to be able to lift that," Zaria said, staring dubiously at the pianoforte. "Even with the three of us, it'll be far too heavy."

"Ah." Kane tapped his temple with a finger. "But that's why we have Fletcher."

Fletcher winked, beginning to unbutton his coat. A moment later, he stood before them in nothing but a white shirt on top, and Zaria felt her cheeks heat. She'd never seen so many muscles on a person. The steep taper of his neck to shoulders alone was ridiculous, and frankly, she was surprised that his shirt was enough to contain his biceps. Everything about this was astonishingly improper, even to someone like Zaria, who had seen more than enough partially clothed men in the slum.

"I don't want to ruin my coat," Fletcher said, perhaps misinterpreting her stare as horror. "Sorry."

She set her jaw, mouth a firm line as Kane came up beside her.

"Ready?"

He had rolled the sleeves of his shirt up to the elbow. He was muscular in his own way but leaner, more sinewy. Even in the relative darkness, she could see dark markings along his forearms. More arrow tattoos? She tilted her head slightly, trying to make them out.

Kane caught her looking and shoved his sleeves back down, scowling.

"What are those?" she couldn't help asking. "On your arms."

"Nothing," he snapped back. "How strong would you say you are?"

Zaria only continued to stare at him. She'd obviously knocked Kane off-kilter, though she couldn't figure out why. What was he hiding? Had he worked for someone else prior to Ward? Someone with a different way of marking their most trusted men?

But no, that didn't make sense: Kane said he'd been with Ward for years. He was too young to have had a previous employer.

So Zaria let it go. What difference did it make?

"I'm strong enough," she said defensively, though it wasn't like she had much idea either way; women didn't often do this kind of labor. "That said, I don't think I'm the lift-a-pianoforte kind of strong."

"Do your best," Fletcher said from around the other side. "I'll be doing most of the work anyway."

And that was how Zaria ended up shoving the world's most unwieldy instrument up a makeshift ramp and onto the wheeled pallets Fletcher had supplied. He hadn't lied—he was definitely doing most of the work—but sweat beaded on Zaria's upper lip as she braced a shoulder against the wood. The pianoforte had three legs—two in the front, one in the back—and at Kane's direction, they managed to get the front two onto the first pallet, the back one onto the second. The pedals, Zaria saw, were attached by a harp-shaped bit of wood attached to the underside of the instrument. Had she known anything at all about music, she might have thought it was beautiful. It certainly had to be expensive.

When they had finished, Zaria slumped against the wall, a dawning horror washing over her.

"Wait. How the hell are we going to get it down the front steps?"

Kane shoved back a handful of sweaty hair. His shirtsleeves had ridden up again, and this time Zaria could see the shape of a tiny black *x* against the skin of his wrist. She stared at it a moment but didn't dare wonder aloud what it meant.

"You think we didn't plan for that?" Kane said. "We're going to back slang it. There are double doors leading out into the garden. It'll fit," he added before Zaria could ask.

Well then. "You've been here before."

"Of course we've been here before," Fletcher cut in, shrugging his coat back on. "We plan ahead. Surely you know that by now."

Zaria watched them wheel the pianoforte through the entryway and past the staircase, to the rear of the house. Kane didn't ask for her help, and she didn't offer it. She wished Jules was here. He'd roll his eyes at these two, equal parts horrified and amused by what they were doing.

She hated that she'd hurt him. Her whole life, her instinct had been to hide her fears and weaknesses. When you grew up in Devil's Acre, that was what you learned. Even those who suffered the most strove to maintain their pride. Jules, though, was different. He'd always been vulnerable, at least around Zaria. He told her the truth even when she didn't want to hear it.

All you've done is lose money, just like your father did.

He'd been right, though, hadn't he? No matter how inadvertently, Zaria was struggling the same way her father had. She was a burden to Jules and George, and she'd potentially endangered both their lives.

"You can stay here if you like," Kane called back to her, "but I really wouldn't recommend it."

Her head snapped up. Kane and Fletcher were already maneuvering the pianoforte through the glass doors, moonlight gilding the

bone-white keys. She followed, pausing amid the shrubbery. The air smelled like damp leaves, the scent of factory smoke imperceptible for once. It felt like a fever dream, standing in a well-maintained garden beneath the shroud of night, a rolling pianoforte atop the grass. It seemed impossible that they wouldn't get caught. But then again, who would be keeping an eye out for pianoforte thieves?

"All right." Kane rubbed his hands together. "Ward owns a warehouse just across the street. Don't worry," he added, perhaps in response to Zaria's grimace. "He rarely frequents it. That's where we're going to store this thing."

Together he and Fletcher shoved the instrument across the grass—that part seemed to take some effort—and through the iron gate at the perimeter of the garden. Zaria felt her whole body tense as they crossed the dark road, but she didn't see another soul in the vicinity. In this part of the city, properties were large enough that the buildings were far away from one another. And thank God for that; they must have made quite the odd sight pushing a pianoforte on wheels down the street.

"Don't worry," Fletcher said jovially, catching Zaria's wince at the clacking of wheels against the cobblestones. "It sounds just like a stagecoach. If anyone happens to overhear, they won't think anything of it."

She suspected he was probably right, but it didn't make the situation any less strange. She was relieved when they stopped outside the doors of the warehouse and Kane—unhurried, unbothered—procured a key from somewhere on his person. Once the lock clicked, Fletcher yanked it ajar, holding the door open for Kane in a gesture that seemed automatic.

"Thanks, Fletch," Kane said, shoving the pianoforte through. "I'll take it in. You can stand guard."

Zaria folded her arms across her chest. "And me?"

Kane glanced over his shoulder at her, an afterthought. "Come or stay. It doesn't make a difference."

And then he was gone, Fletcher slamming the warehouse doors behind him with an upheaval of dust. The Irishman leaned against the exterior of the building, long legs crossed at the ankles, staring into the smog. After a beat of uncertainty, Zaria did the same. Something about the way Fletcher glanced sidelong at her made her suspect he had something to say. But perhaps he thought better of it, because he remained silent until Zaria said, "What is it?"

He breathed a laugh, directing a grin into the night. "You're perceptive."

"You're easy to read. If there's something you want to say to me, just say it."

Fletcher turned to look at her now. "Kane. You're angry with him, and you have the right to be."

"I know that." The words came out defensive, though Zaria had tried to keep her voice calm. She gritted her teeth as Fletcher considered his response.

"Where Kane goes, trouble tends to follow. That said, I can promise you he never meant for Cecile to die."

"So he told me."

"You don't believe him?"

That startled a laugh out of Zaria. "Should I? Tell me, has Kane Durante ever been honest a day in his life?"

"He tells the truth more often than you might think. But I also know he won't waste much time trying to convince you of it."

"Because he doesn't care what I believe as long as he gets what he wants in the end?"

Fletcher ran an agitated hand through his hair. "No. Because he thinks it's better to let everyone detest him."

It was harsher than Zaria had been expecting, and she swiveled to face Fletcher, her lips parted. She didn't think they were talking about her or Cecile any longer. She didn't quite know *what* they were talking about, in fact.

"Whether he intended it or not," Zaria said coldly, "Cecile died because of Kane. The man who shot her *named* him, Fletcher. Said his name like I should have known better than to ever get involved with him. And he was right, though I suppose it's too late now. I'll see our agreement through, but only because I keep my word."

And, a voice in her head supplied, *because you're going to help me get what I need.*

A moment of silence fell between them. She was braced for Fletcher to argue, but to her surprise, he didn't. He worried at his lower lip, abruptly looking very tired.

"Don't tell Kane I said this," he mused, "but I think he rather *likes* working with you. Having someone besides me around. But I also think the moment he starts to feel truly content, he tries to destroy it."

Zaria narrowed her eyes, searching the lines of Fletcher's face. She didn't know why he was telling her this. "Is Kane going to...do something? Something that will make me regret our arrangement?"

"No," Fletcher said, and the single syllable was heavy. "I only wanted you to keep it in the back of your mind."

"Why?"

"Well, you're angry at him now, and I'm sure you'll be angry at him again."

"Ah." Now Zaria understood. She relaxed the weight of her body more fully against the door. "You're making excuses for him."

Fletcher shook his head. "I just think—"

Zaria cut him off. "Are you the only person he hasn't driven away yet?"

"He could never drive me away. I would never let him."

"Why not?"

Fletcher hesitated a moment. Above them smog mingled with the moonlight, turning the sky a murky gray. "Kane has always been Ward's favorite. He convinced Ward to let me join his crew when I was young. He thought he was helping me, and he was at the time. But Kane doesn't see it that way. He doesn't see the fact that I'd be on the streets—or possibly dead—without him. He doesn't see how badly a young Irish boy, starving and separated from his family, needed a friend. All he sees is the fact that he damned me to a life governed by Ward's rules. And nothing I say will change his mind. For whatever reason, he thinks I'm too good for this life."

Zaria took a beat to digest Fletcher's words. She didn't want to relate to Kane, who blamed himself for being a poor friend. But she knew what it was to look at the person you cared for most and wonder if you could have done better by them. "And what do you think?"

Fletcher was quiet again, and at first, she thought he wouldn't answer. Eventually, he said, "You know, my parents were the most optimistic people I knew. We had so little, and yet they never made me feel like I was wanting for anything. My father used to say this Gaelic proverb—*Níor bhris focal maith fiacail riamh*. It means 'A good word never broke a tooth.' You don't lose anything by being kind, essentially." He sighed. "I've done a lot of things that would have disappointed my parents. For the most part, though, I try to imagine what they would have done in my place. I have good memories to draw on, and they ground me. Kane doesn't have that. I'm not convinced he knows how to be positive. He blames himself for everything, including where I ended up."

"That's foolish," Zaria said decisively. "It makes it sound like you didn't play any part in your own life."

Fletcher tilted his head back, gazing up at the sky. "You're not wrong. But I can't be angry at him for it. Because if the situations were reversed, I suppose I'd be furious at myself, too. He's my brother. He thinks misery is all he deserves."

"Well." Zaria pushed away from the door. "Maybe he's right."

Neither of them said another word.

21

KANE

KANE STARED AT THE PIANOFORTE.

It was beautiful, all sleek lines without a chipped key in sight. Far lovelier than the one he and Fletcher had back home. Not that it made a difference: He hadn't touched the instrument. It simply sat there collecting dust that he every so often swept away, a reminder of the place he'd lived before Ward.

His life, Kane was coming to realize, was separated into *before*s and *after*s. *Before* was sitting on a bench beside his mother, legs not quite long enough to touch the floor, copying the deft placement of her fingers as she taught him the difference between sound and music. It was the constant skitter of Baroque pieces in the background—his mother's favorites when she was in a good mood—or the steady lull of a nocturne when she was feeling particularly reflective. *Before* was Kane learning to replace her music with his own. It was the way his racing fingers slowed the racing in his head, and the pride he felt whenever he added something new to his repertoire.

After was an imperfect cadence, discordant in its inconclusiveness.

After was silence.

Kane traced a finger over the keys the way he so often did at home. *Do you play?* Zaria had asked him the other day.

No, he'd said.

No. Don't touch it.

Having the instrument was a comfort. Something that had always been around no matter where he was or what was happening. But Kane did not play—not anymore. He couldn't bear the sound. Music held far too much feeling, and he didn't want to feel anything at all.

He turned away, an unbearable restlessness creeping through him as he stooped to pick up a sheet in the corner of the room. His hands fisted in the fabric as he unfolded it, then cast it over the pianoforte like a funeral shroud. The material took longer to settle than he would have anticipated. When it did, he stood there a moment, the lone living thing in a hollow space devoid of light and sound.

Ward rarely used this warehouse. He'd more or less allowed Kane to do what he wished with the place, though this was the first time in ages that he'd come here.

He shoved his hands in his pockets, loped back over to the door, and hurled it open to find Zaria staring directly at him.

"Christ," Kane said, sidestepping her as he reached for his pipe. He surveyed her over the end of it as he drew up beside Fletcher, who was leaning against the side of the building. "Were you missing me?"

The look Zaria shot him was pure derision. It made Kane feel more tired than he already was. "What took you so long?"

"I took precisely as much time as I needed."

The deed had gone better than anticipated, especially given that Julian Zhao hadn't deigned to join them. Not that Kane had expected any issues. The late widow's home they'd stolen the pianoforte from had been empty for nearly a week. Her eldest son had an estate in the country, Kane knew, and hadn't yet arrived to deal with all his newly inherited belongings. Hell, he probably wouldn't even notice anything was missing.

Zaria exhaled through her nose. "Have I fulfilled my favor to you, then?"

Kane pretended to think about it, rocking the pipe between his middle and index fingers. "I suppose."

"I can't believe *that* was what you decided to ask for."

"Oh, I knew what I was going to ask for the moment we made our deal," Kane said, and it was the truth—the success of the heist relied on the instrument. "It's always best to plan ahead."

He saw Zaria's shock betray her for a moment, but she clamped down on it almost immediately, refusing to meet his gaze. "Unbelievable. Can you escort me home now, then?"

Fletcher gave a slow shake of his head, amusement in the shape of his mouth. He unfolded his large frame and pushed away from the wall. "We still hoped to start going over the plan for the Exhibition's opening."

Zaria shifted her weight, glancing into the distance, then back again. The feeble moonlight caught her hair, gilding the strands.

"What?" Kane couldn't help saying. "Do you have someplace else to be?"

"I assumed the planning session was canceled given the *theft*." She hissed the last word, though there was no one around to hear them.

"We don't have a lot of time to pull this off," Fletcher pointed out.

Kane wasn't inclined to be quite so amicable. "A deal's a deal," he told Zaria. "And I want to ensure this one goes smoothly. So, if you have other plans, cancel them. If you don't have time, *make* it. It's not up for negotiation."

This time Zaria did meet his gaze, and Kane immediately wished she hadn't. Her eyes were dark in the dim light. Dark and furious and bottomless. Looking into them was like being thrust headfirst into black waters and forgetting which way was up.

"Don't speak to me like that," she snarled, rounding on him. The air seemed to thrum with the force of her anger, and perhaps it should have made Kane contrite, but...he *liked* it. He felt alive even as he forgot how to breathe, and he thought that if this was what it was to drown, he would let the water fill his throat willingly.

Anger, Kane was beginning to think, was better than nothing. Better than the horrible emptiness that clung to his insides and lashed through his bloodstream. He liked to be near Zaria in the same way that he sometimes craved danger. He liked the taut curve of her jaw, the harsh line of her mouth, the twin juts of her brows as she stared him down in a way that would certainly make a lesser man cower.

Hate me, Kane might have told her, had honesty been a feasible thing just then. *Hate me, so that we both know what it is to feel something.*

But he was not an honest man. He was not even a kind man.

"I'll speak however I like, Miss Mendoza," Kane said. His voice was deathly quiet, balancing on a knifepoint. "This is *my* operation. Right now, you work for *me*, or you can forget the second half of our deal. Do not test my temper."

He had known it would rile her up—had suspected he might

suddenly be fielding curses—but Kane didn't much care. He didn't care that Fletcher had just uttered an audible sigh or that the street abruptly felt far too small for the both of them.

"Kane—" began Fletcher's attempt at interference, but Kane held up a hand, effectively cutting him off. He turned back to Zaria. Daring her to say what she so clearly longed to.

Something crystallized in her gaze, and she took a step closer, chin tilting up to look him in the eye. For a heartbeat, Kane wondered if she might hit him. The line of her mouth thinned further, and the edge to her voice could have cut glass when she said simply, "You're unbearable."

Yes, Kane thought. *Yes, I suppose I am.*

He was the first to look away, and it felt infuriatingly like surrender.

Zaria didn't speak all the way back to Moore & Sons. She walked sullenly behind them, her fury a tangible thing that prickled the back of Kane's neck. He ignored it. The buildings on either side of them narrowed as they passed close to the river, then away again as they weaved through the alleyways. Shadows stretched long and ominous across the road. Kane could feel Fletcher trying to catch his eye, probably to shoot an exasperated look his way, so Kane pretended not to notice.

The night seemed to have grown colder by the time they arrived. Zaria's shoulders were hunched as she shoved past Fletcher, not bothering to thank him for holding the door. Kane followed behind her, lifting a brow as Fletcher's gaze finally met his.

Relax, Fletcher mouthed, and Kane only grimaced.

"Take a seat," he said to the room at large, bringing a candle to life and setting it in the center of the dining table. He lit two more as Zaria slunk stiff-backed into one of the chairs, eyes never wavering from his face. It was difficult not to stare her down as he said, "Okay. Let's take it from our point of entry."

Zaria gave a single nod, and he waited a moment to see whether she would interrupt. When she didn't say a word, Kane turned to Fletcher.

"Right," Fletcher said. "Once again, I'll be acting as security inside the Crystal Palace. Everything has been ironed out with Sergeant Price. Myself and his other trusted officers will be positioned closest to the Waterhouse exhibit."

"And you're just going to take this sergeant's word for it?" Zaria asked. "What makes you think those other coppers won't arrest us the moment we show up?"

It was a reasonable question, but it irked Kane nonetheless. He held up a hand, signaling that he was going to intervene. "*Trust* is a strong word. But if Price betrays me, it's mutually assured destruction. So, do I trust him insofar as to help us pull this off? Yes. It's in his best interests."

He watched Zaria's face as she tried and failed to come up with a way to counter that. In the end, she only said, "Fine."

That was good enough for Kane.

"Kane?" Fletcher said. "Tell Zaria what we need from her."

Kane could see how the word *need* sent Zaria's hackles up, but she didn't object and waited for him to speak.

"You already know I want the aleuite explosives," he began. "Powerful ones, since I'm going to require a good few minutes of uninterrupted time to get that lock open. Like I said at the private viewing of the Exhibition, I also need you to create a device that'll take out one of the glass panels since there's no exit nearby. I know there's a chemical that can do that—what's it called? Hydrate acid?"

"Hydrofluoric acid," Zaria said dryly. "Once it's bonded with soulsteel, you can manipulate the reaction to some extent as long as you understand the science. But remind me again why you can't just *smash* the glass?"

Kane shook his head. "Too many ways for that to go wrong. It could take several strikes, it would require us to smuggle another heavy object inside, and I don't want to worry about having to climb through broken glass when we're making our escape."

He forced his eyes away from Zaria's face as she chewed on her full lower lip. "I can make an atomizing adhesive, yes, assuming you can get me the supplies. The reaction isn't instantaneous, though. The glass needs time to weaken."

"How long?" Fletcher interjected.

"Thirty-six minutes."

That was, Kane thought, incredibly specific. He did a series of quick calculations in his mind. "Okay, we can make that work. Fletch, you can plant the adhesive on the window when the queen and prince consort arrive."

They would need fifteen minutes to get into the Exhibition—during which Kane would ensure they crossed paths with Henry Cole—and find their way to the Broadwood & Sons display that, all being well, should boast the exact pianoforte they'd stolen earlier tonight. He had ninety seconds to convince Julian Zhao to play the part he had in mind for him—there was no way the boy would let Zaria go alone. Four and a half minutes for Kane to play the Nocturne in C-sharp Minor on the pianoforte. Thirteen minutes for the rest, including bypassing the lock on the Waterhouse exhibit. That left two minutes for anything he hadn't foreseen. An ill-timed conversation, perhaps, or a few moments trapped behind a slow-moving crowd.

He turned back to Zaria. "Finally, when it comes to unlocking the exhibit itself, I need you to create a parautoptic key with fifteen self-arranging bits."

She blanched. "You need me to create a *what*?"

"I really don't know how to be clearer."

"Try."

Kane sighed, gesturing for Fletcher to pass him a fountain pen and the nearest scrap of paper. His pulse stuttered as he drew the outline of an admittedly peculiar key. Usually, he prepared to bypass a lock by studying the schematics if he had access to them, then practicing on a similar design. For once, though, Kane had limited faith in his lock-picking abilities. He hated to admit it, but he needed magical interference for this part. Everything relied on their ability to open this godforsaken display.

"I've never made something like that before," Zaria said incredulously. She squinted down at the sketch. "If the bits need to be self-arranging, the interior workings will have to be *tiny*. You're sure you can't pick the lock?"

"You heard what the bloke at the Exhibition said," Kane retorted. "It's supposed to be impenetrable. The combination of levers is manipulatable and subject to change."

Zaria gave a slow nod of her head. There was a glint in her eye he was coming to recognize—the one that appeared when she was met with a challenge. "I think I can do that. Having something adjust to its surroundings isn't the problem; it's the size that will be tricky." Her lips twisted to the side. "Just so I'm clear, you want the aleuite explosives to provide a distraction, a magical key to bypass the lock in that time, and an atomizing adhesive to facilitate an escape by the time you're done?"

"Correct."

"You ask so little." Her tone was wry.

Fletcher leaned back in his chair, holding up a hand. "Can we back up for a second? Purely out of curiosity, are these aleuite explosives...you know...harmful?"

"No," Kane said at the same time that Zaria shook her head.

"Aleuite can be used to create a number of different compounds. It's tricky to work with because it's highly reactive, but it's not flammable. It's through alchemology that I can turn it into an explosive, and once it goes off, it emits a dark smoke that fills a space within seconds."

Fletcher moved his jaw from side to side. "And it's safe to inhale?"

"I've never known anyone to experience lasting effects."

Kane took a drink, staring at Zaria over the rim of his glass. "So you say. Maybe you're just trying to find a way to kill me."

"Killing you would be counterproductive," she replied smoothly, then glanced down, severing a tension Kane hadn't realized was between them.

He cleared his throat. "Okay. Let's say that, for all intents and purposes, it works without a hitch. We release the explosives, and you make me a key that'll open the lock. Will the aleuite smoke be thick enough to conceal me from view?"

"It should be."

Fletcher cut in. "Not good enough."

Guilt stabbed through Kane's chest. He didn't deserve Fletcher's concern. It made him feel small, unworthy, and he longed to shrink and shrink until he could crawl inside himself and disappear. Eventually, one way or another, Fletcher would find out what Kane had done. When he did, he would regret each and every time he'd bothered to care about Kane. How could he not?

Zaria set her jaw. "I might be able to adjust the concentration so the resulting reaction is more intense."

"Good," Kane said, trying to steady his voice. "Do that."

"What I want to know is, how are we going to get the explosives into the Exhibition? They'll have to be relatively large if the smoke needs to be powerful enough to fill an entire section of the palace. Certainly far bigger than anything we could reasonably smuggle into the building in our pockets."

Fletcher shot Kane a meaningful look, tapping a mischievous finger against the square line of his chin.

Kane turned to Zaria. They'd already accounted for this; it was merely a matter of ensuring all the pieces came together. "Luckily for you, we've already orchestrated a plan to ensure everything we need will be at our disposal."

"Of course you have," Zaria grunted.

Kane ignored that. "I have one more request: What kind of weapon can you put together to disable anyone who gets in our way?"

Zaria was nonplussed. "You both have guns, don't you?"

"I said *disable*, not *murder*."

"Since when does it make any difference to you?"

God above, she was exasperating. Maybe he was being overcautious, and it certainly wasn't a crucial element of the plan, but why not take advantage of Zaria's skills while he had her on board? "Royalty is going to be present at the grand opening. Diplomats. Innocent civilians. We're trying to steal something, not start an international conflict. And I don't know about you, but if something *does* go wrong, I don't want to go down for homicide."

Fletcher nodded in agreement.

"Again," Zaria intoned, "since when are you opposed to homicide?"

"I didn't say I was opposed to it." Kane made the words clipped, short. "I said I don't want to get *caught* for it. And you can drop the judgmental act—it's not like you're some kind of pacifist."

"I've never murdered anyone, Kane."

"Maybe not directly. How about this for a hypothetical? Pretend a man asks you for your gun. He says he's planning to shoot someone in the head with it. Do you give it to him?"

Pink was rising in Zaria's cheeks. "Of course not."

"Except that you do. You *have*. It's quite literally your job." Kane drained the rest of his drink, knowing his show of apathy rankled. "So don't act like you're opposed to murder. If I wanted to put a magic bullet through someone's skull, you're stop number one."

"I am *not* responsible for what people do with the weapons they commission."

Kane shrugged. "Technically true. But you could always say no, Zaria, and you don't."

The charged silence that followed was agonizingly uncomfortable. Fletcher shook his head in exasperation.

Zaria appeared to be trying to collect herself. She released a long, unsteady breath, lifting her chin to look Kane in the eye. "Fine. You're right. I never claimed to be a good person, and maintaining a degree of separation doesn't make what I do any better. Now, tell me why the aleuite explosives aren't sufficient for disabling anyone who gets in our way?"

"That's not easily controllable," Kane said, shoving down the surprise he felt at her admission. "I want something like the dark market gun you made for Saville. Small and easily concealable but not lethal. We want this to go as smoothly as possible."

"What about a dart gun?"

"No. Causes far too much pain and would result in a scene. I want to incapacitate, not harm."

Zaria's expression was withering. "Dark market weapons *are* made to cause harm. So no, I've never created a gun that doesn't hurt people."

That was unfortunate, but it wasn't going to make or break Kane's plan. "Fine," he said. "Once I've managed to pick the lock and assuming everything goes according to plan, we'll want to replace the Waterhouse jewels. It'll help buy us more time to get as far away as we can. Leaving behind an empty display case would be more than a little conspicuous."

"And just where are you intending to find a display's worth of jewelry in less than a week?"

As she spoke, Fletcher rose, a grin playing at the edges of his mouth. Kane watched his friend yank open the wardrobe by the window, already knowing what was about to happen. Zaria tracked Fletcher's progress with grim distrust as he returned to the table with a linen bag.

When he upended it, her jaw dropped.

"Where did you *get* this?"

Kane surveyed the array of dazzling pieces with satisfaction. They might not have been as extravagant as the pieces in the Waterhouse display, but they were beautiful nonetheless. Of course, he had no intention of replacing the Waterhouse jewels—he'd simply been unable to leave these behind when he'd discovered them in the widow's home. If they could be used to cement Zaria's trust, though, all the better for him. "Same place we got the pianoforte."

She gave a slow shake of her head. "From a *dead woman*."

"Dead people don't care if you steal from them."

"It still seems a bit callous."

Kane wasn't about to argue. He pushed back from the table just as Fletcher, still standing, said in a strained voice, "Kane? There's someone outside."

22

ZARIA

ZARIA SCARCELY HAD TIME TO PROCESS FLETCHER'S WORDS before Kane was on his feet, extinguishing the candle between two fingers. The last image she had of his face was alarming: eyes hard, jaw soldered in a taut angle. She had the abrupt impression that this was how Kane Durante looked right before he killed somebody.

"Get up," he snapped, one hand already viselike around her arm as he assisted her to her feet. The next moment he had pushed her up against the exterior wall, out of view of anyone who might be looking in. Indignant at the impropriety of it all, Zaria shoved against him, but she was far too aware of the light pressure of his hand at her waist. The surprisingly nice scent of him and the twist of his lips as her eyes adjusted.

"Anyone could be out there," she hissed, trying to ignore the uneven cadence of her heart. "You don't live on a private street, you know."

"They were masked," Fletcher said solemnly, drawing a revolver from his waistband. "They must have followed us back from the warehouse."

Kane cursed. "They know she's here."

Ice shot through Zaria's veins. Her irritation evaporated, replaced by fear. At the same time, though, part of her was relieved that whoever it was had come here instead of to the pawnshop. When would this end?

Fletcher shook his head at Kane, who had withdrawn his gun as well. "I'm going alone."

"Like hell you are," Kane snarled, and his friend shot him an aggrieved look.

"We can't very well leave her by herself."

At that, Kane faltered, gaze flicking toward Zaria. She crossed her arms, feeling her face heat. "Don't talk about me like I'm not here."

They both ignored her. Fletcher was squinting out the window again. "I think they're gone anyway. They must have realized they were seen."

"How many?" Kane said.

"Two."

"Then let's find them."

"And risk them coming back for her while she's alone?"

Kane appeared to be fighting some internal battle with himself, his jaw working. Eventually, he said, "Fine. If you don't see anyone, come right back. Don't go looking for them without me."

"I don't think—" Zaria began, but something about his expression had her biting off what she'd been about to say. She didn't want Fletcher going out there alone, she realized, and not only because it would drive Kane mad. She was so very tired of putting other people at risk.

"I'll be careful," Fletcher assured Kane, then shot Zaria a crooked grin. "You really have a way of pissing people off, Miss Mendoza."

She rolled her eyes, but her stomach was in knots as he slipped out into the dark, the door latching shut behind him. Kane's face was stony as he swiped a hand through his hair. Zaria braced herself for his resentment, but it didn't come. He merely sighed, looking as tired as she'd seen him thus far. "Come on, then. You can have my room— I'll bunk with Fletcher."

She blanched. "What?"

"You're not going home, even with an escort. It's late, and whoever's after you clearly has instructions not to give up until you're dead." His lowered brow dared her to argue.

"But Jules—"

"Will be fine. No one's after him."

"He'll wonder where I am. I can't just *stay* here." The objection sounded weak even to her own ears. The reality was, she was terrified. Could this truly be about the faulty explosive device? Was that enough to make an attempt on her life? She could have made it work flawlessly if they'd only given her more time.

But perhaps that was the problem. She'd been given time, just like her father before her, and now she was out of it.

"Come on," Kane said again, this time with a touch of impatience, and Zaria realized he was standing at the bottom of a stairwell she hadn't noticed before. It was narrow, set back in the corner of the room, a distinct nod to the building's former purpose. She followed him to the next level. It looked more like a regular home than she'd anticipated, lacking the high ceilings and industrial beams of the ground floor. Former offices, if she had to guess, though the space into which Kane led her had been converted into a bedroom. This was evidenced only by the bed in the middle of the space—otherwise, it was simply…bare, save for a wardrobe pushed up against the wall opposite the door.

It could have been anyone's room. It could have been no one's.

"It's very clean." She was abruptly conscious of what Kane must have thought of the dingy, cluttered workspace that doubled as her sleeping area.

"I like things tidy" was his curt reply.

Zaria couldn't decide whether that fit with what she knew of him. Rather than meet his gaze, she kept her eyes on the bed, her cheeks warm. It felt inappropriate to be standing here with him, though of course that was absurd. "Will Fletcher be okay?"

Kane's face shuttered. "He'd better be."

Zaria thought of what Fletcher had told her earlier. "Do you think you worry about him too much?"

"Do you worry about Master Zhao too much?" Kane countered, a snide note to his voice. "I assume that's why you didn't bring him tonight."

She stiffened. "That isn't why."

"Oh?"

"If you must know, I finally told him the truth. About everything."

"I take it that didn't go splendidly."

"Insightful of you." Zaria went to sit on the edge of the bed, trying and failing to ignore the searing press of Kane's attention. "He's desperate to help me. He wants me to teach him alchemology."

Kane shrugged. "So do it."

"It's not that simple."

"Why not? You need help, and he wants to help. Seems sensible to me."

"First of all, you know full well it's horribly difficult to teach, not to mention learn. And second, I don't want him to suffer."

"But it's fine if you suffer."

"Yes," she snapped.

Kane leaned against the doorframe, arms crossed, brow quirked. "Sounds like you're being an idiot."

"You are *such* a hypocrite."

"No good could possibly come from my telling Fletcher about Ward's threats. But you—you would benefit from letting Julian help you. You're just being difficult about it."

"You don't understand," Zaria retorted. Kane couldn't fathom how much study went into alchemology. How many years it took to become even the slightest bit proficient and how it drained so much from a person. "Jules would feel the same if our situations were reversed. He worries about me, too—that's why he offered in the first place. In fact, he's probably worried about me now, seeing as I haven't arrived home."

It wasn't until she said it aloud that she realized how stressed her friend must be. Guilt surged through her. Their fight aside, she had just told Jules about the attempts on her life, and when she didn't return to the pawnshop tonight, he would surely assume the worst.

"I can get a message to him," Kane said, infuriatingly blasé.

"How?"

"Some of the younger guys are always running around on Ward's behalf, and they listen to me. I'll track one down when Fletch returns."

"Okay," Zaria said. "Thank you."

But she couldn't keep the edge out of her voice, and Kane let his arms fall to his sides, continuing to watch her far too closely for comfort. She was about to snap at him to stop staring but held her tongue. She'd already snapped at him too many times tonight, which was a fool's maneuver considering she needed him to trust her. However,

Zaria reasoned, he would undoubtedly know something was amiss if her demeanor toward him shifted with no explanation. She could see that now-familiar vulnerability in his face—maybe, if she could get him to open up like he had the other night, he might continue lowering his guard around her.

That was something she needed. *Not* something she wanted.

"I'll leave you to it, then," Kane said, pushing away from the door-frame. In his white button-down, lit only by the moonlight filtering in through the narrow window, he looked more like a memory than a real flesh-and-blood person.

"Wait." Zaria leapt to her feet as if to physically stop him, heart beating faster for no discernible reason. She felt the need to keep him talking, to crush this unbearable tension between them. "I... Fletcher said you're Ward's favorite. Why is that?"

The question appeared to knock Kane off-kilter. He recoiled, a scowl taking hold of his delicate features. "Because I'm the best he's got. What does it matter to you?"

"I'm only curious. We should probably start trusting each other a little more, shouldn't we?"

Kane's expression turned cold. Unfathomable. Then he seemed to get hold of himself, his shoulders lifting as he gave a single hard, silent laugh. "Seems I'd have a better chance of bringing you the moon than I do getting you to trust me."

"It doesn't seem as though you trust me much either," Zaria pointed out. "If you did, you'd tell me the truth."

"I'm trusting you to help me pull this off, aren't I? And you're trusting me to make sure we don't fail."

"I also trusted you when you told me that church was safe."

Kane tilted his head, mouth tightening. His hair wasn't quite as slick as usual: A lock had escaped to brush his temple, and something

about it made him look younger. "That was before I knew just how invested someone was in ensuring your untimely death."

She fought to conceal her flinch. "Forget it."

"You want trust?" He stepped fully into the room, approaching her until they were a mere handbreadth apart. Agitation seemed to radiate from his body. "I'm Ward's favorite because when he killed my parents, he made himself my father."

Silence stretched between them. The air was suddenly too heavy, too hard to breathe.

When Zaria spoke again, the words scraped the back of her throat. "What do you mean?"

"I was a child," Kane said very quietly. "So I let him. Pretty fucked-up, isn't it? I dream of killing him, you know, but I'm not sure I could ever truly go through with it. So sometimes, when I watch other people die, I imagine they wear his face." He leaned back, mouth a frozen, twisted grin. "Do you feel trusted now, Zaria?"

She didn't know what to say. She feared him this way, with that smile like a blade—sharp edged and dangerous. He'd been made into a terror of a boy, Kane Durante had, his past so slick with blood he now wore it like a victory shroud.

And then, completely unbidden, Zaria's head was full of Cecile's voice. What the woman had said to her in the belly of the crypt.

Then I saw them, lying on the floor of his office. A man. A woman. And—and a little boy.

A whole family slaughtered, Cecile had thought, but a wave of clarity swept through Zaria as the two stories fit together.

The little boy hadn't been dead, had he? He stood before her now, dark lashes casting crescent shadows on his cheekbones in the dim light. How was it that he managed to look at everything like a god surveying his kingdom?

A vengeful god. A crumbling kingdom.

"You don't have to be what Ward made you," Zaria said hoarsely. She had no idea how long she'd let the silence between them persist. She almost resented Kane for this—these feelings she didn't want—and yet she ought to have known all along that his story was a tragedy.

He turned unsmiling, unblinking, a shadow settling between his brows. "Ah, Miss Mendoza. It's far too late for that."

And though he walked out the door then, shutting it behind him, Zaria stood in his empty room feeling as if he'd never truly left.

KANE

THE BEGINNINGS OF A COMMOTION GREETED KANE AS HE MADE his way back downstairs. It was coming from outside—a series of muffled yells followed by a curse growled in a voice that he recognized as Fletcher's.

Panic speared through him, white-hot and urgent. It shattered the complicated haze of emotion his conversation with Zaria had unearthed. He lunged for the door, not bothering to don his coat or shoes. Cool wind buffeted his face as he swung his head from one side to the other, eyes slitted against the night, desperately seeking some sign of his friend.

A figure appeared around the side of the building, dragging a second, smaller one along behind it. Kane would have known Fletcher's outline anywhere. Relief and worry tangled in his chest as he sprinted toward the duo—Fletcher was upright, but that didn't mean he wasn't injured—and the latter dissipated as his friend shot him a wry grin. There was a bruise high on his cheek, bisected by the old scar there, but otherwise he appeared unharmed.

"Caught one of our Peeping Toms. You're not gonna believe this."

Kane frowned, and only then did his attention slide to the man Fletcher had hold of. Broad shoulders, light brown skin, and a handsome face in spite of the clearly broken nose and bloodied lip. Recognition shot through him, but he couldn't make the pieces fit together. "Anil?"

Anil Sahni gave an apprehensive twist of his mouth. Another of Ward's men, he had always been someone Kane had rather liked, if only because he could be counted on to say very little. True to form, the man uttered not a word as Kane's gaze flicked back to Fletcher. "What is this?"

Fletcher's hair was sweaty, his cheek already beginning to swell, but he looked pleased with himself. "Caught him a couple of streets over, still wearing that stupid mask. We had a bit of a skirmish. Nothing serious. I told him he could answer to you."

"You're sure he was the one outside the window?"

"Positive. He wasn't alone either, but the other guy got away."

Kane tracked a semicircle around Anil and Fletcher, head spinning. As far as he knew, Anil's loyalty was exclusively to Ward. He might have thought the man's spying unrelated to the attempts on Zaria's life, except that he'd *seen* Anil there, he realized with a jolt of certainty.

"You were in the church," Kane said, adopting the voice he used when he wanted someone to fear him. "You were the one I shot. I'm guessing that's why you didn't put up much of a fight tonight."

Understanding lit Fletcher's face, but he said nothing. Neither did Anil. Kane sighed, toeing the ground with his shoeless foot. "Who're you working for, Sahni?"

Anil tried to twist away from Fletcher, pain contorting his features. A moment later he wilted, going still. His dark eyes were guarded when they met Kane's. "You already know the answer to that."

"I sure as hell don't. You're supposed to be Ward's man. Are you working for a buyer who goes by the name Vaughan, or is it someone else entirely?"

"Am I supposed to know what the fuck that means?" Anil said. "I *am* Ward's man. His alone."

"Then what the hell are you playing at, trying to kill Zaria Mendoza?"

There was a beat during which Anil only stared at Kane, his brows lifted as if waiting for him to understand. And then abruptly, Kane did. His mouth went bone-dry.

"Ward is the one who wants her dead."

Anil mimed a round of applause. "I don't know what you're doing with her, Durante, but he doesn't like it."

"That doesn't make any sense," Kane ground out. Ward wanted the necklace. Zaria was helping Kane to steal the necklace. Sure, Ward had instructed him to tell no one but Fletcher about the assignment, but the kingpin had to see why Zaria was an asset. She certainly wasn't a threat.

Anil shrugged, the motion made awkward due to Fletcher's grip on his left arm. "I just do what I'm told."

"Which was what, exactly?"

"Get rid of the Mendoza girl and not say a word to you. Problem is, you keep getting in the way."

Fletcher tightened his grip on Anil, not seeming to notice the man's wince. "There's no reason for Ward to want Zaria dead."

Kane didn't doubt he and Fletcher were shuffling through the

same questions in their minds. *None* of this made sense. Why hadn't Ward said anything? How many others knew about it? Kane was sure it was what the rest of the men always dreamed of—that someday Ward's favorite boy, the one they both loathed and feared, would fall out of favor with the kingpin.

"Who else is in on this?" he demanded of Anil.

"Abe was spearheading it, but you killed him. Charlie Horowitz. Joey Egelton."

Kane couldn't conceal his surprise. Abe Walker was a nasty piece of work. Now that he looked back on it, the man he'd shot *had* sounded like Abe. It had been dark, the man's face mostly covered, but Kane ought to have recognized his voice. A pity he'd killed Abe without getting to enjoy it. Charlie, though, was a strange choice for the job. The guy was unerringly clever but not one for violence. And Joey Egelton was all of thirteen. "You truly have no idea why Ward gave you this assignment?"

Anil gave a rapid shake of his head. "You think I'm dumb enough to question him? He's annoyed with me as it is. That woman in the church wasn't supposed to be the one to die."

"So you were the one who pulled the trigger."

"I wasn't aiming for her. She got in the way."

As if that were somehow better. Kane pinched the bridge of his nose with his thumb and index finger, casting about for control. Zaria had nearly been killed by this man. She'd been forced to watch Cecile's life drain out of her and had blamed *him* for it. Fury licked through his veins and pooled in the back of his throat until he thought he might spew poison instead of words. When he spoke again, his voice was like metal on glass. "I ought to fucking shoot you right here, Sahni."

"I'm sorry!" Anil said, eyes wide as saucers. "I didn't know the girl

was important to you. I figured you were running some kind of con on her."

That struck Kane like a physical blow. Both things were true: Kane *was* running a con on Zaria. But also, no matter how he tried to convince himself otherwise, she was important to him.

Not just for the heist, though that should have been the only reason. He shouldn't be thinking about the way she'd looked standing in his bedroom, golden-brown hair coming loose from its intricate knot, expression so perfectly obstinate. He shouldn't like the way her dark eyes became a weapon when she was angry at him. He shouldn't be jealous of her friendship with Julian Zhao and how the boy interacted with her in an affectionate yet effortless way that Kane would never be able to achieve.

The idea of Anil Sahni shooting Zaria dead in the crypt of St. John's shouldn't make him want to rip the man's head off.

"This was my last chance," Anil continued when Kane said nothing, a note of pleading in his voice. "Ward was furious I let the Mendoza girl get away, and the only way to redeem myself was to kill her tonight. If I fail, he'll kill *me*."

Yes, that sounded like Ward. "He said that?"

"He didn't need to."

Fletcher shot Kane a look as if to say, *Fair enough.*

"Well then," Kane told Anil coolly. "You'd best leave town entirely. Because it sounds like Ward will murder you if you don't kill Zaria, and *I'll* murder you if you do. You can pass that along to your associates."

Fletcher's gaze burned into the side of his face, but Kane refused to meet it, opting instead to stare Anil down until the other man looked away.

"Fine," he grunted. "I'll leave before first light."

"See to it that you do."

The aftermath of Anil's confession was the quiet following an explosion.

They'd released the man into the night, and Kane had no doubts he would be gone by morning. Unlike most of Ward's crew, Anil had a family, though he'd never mentioned as much to Kane directly. He didn't need to. Ward had made reference to it once, but even if he hadn't, Kane could tell Anil was the type of man with something to fight for. He would pack up his loved ones and get the hell out.

Kane and Fletcher sat at the dining table, staring at each other without speaking. Fletcher's fingers drummed an uneven rhythm on the wood, and Kane's thoughts slammed into one another like bugs hitting a glass window.

"What do you think it means?" he said finally.

Fletcher swiped a hand along his jaw, which was sprouting a thin layer of barely visible scruff. "That Ward wants her dead?"

Kane gave a slow nod. He felt like a length of rope that had unraveled and been pulled too taut.

"Dunno. It means he's keeping an eye on us, for one, which I don't love."

"Then he has to know what Zaria's contributing to the heist. It doesn't make any sense that he wants to get rid of her, unless he wants me to fail, which I know he doesn't." That had been made abundantly clear to Kane.

"Maybe he's angry that you told her about the necklace?" Fletcher suggested. "You said you were supposed to keep it confidential."

"Then why not punish me? Why say nothing at all and quietly go after her?"

"He doesn't like to punish you."

Kane's laugh was a bitter, choking thing. "It hasn't stopped him before."

Fletcher crossed his arms. His light hair was in disarray, and the bruising on his face was beginning to deepen in color. Though he looked nothing like he had as a child, Kane was abruptly reminded of the first day they'd met. The defiant, determined look in his friend's blue eyes... it was too familiar. Kane knew Fletcher didn't like his relationship with Ward. He rarely said it, but it was evident in the way he stiffened whenever Kane relayed his interactions with the kingpin. If it came right down to it, Fletcher would get himself killed trying to protect Kane from Ward, and Kane couldn't have that.

Especially when he knew he'd never been the one truly in danger.

"Are we going to tell her?" Fletcher said, and Kane lifted his head.

"Beg pardon?"

"Zaria. Are we going to tell her Ward's the one who put a target on her back?"

Kane thought of Zaria upstairs in his bed, undoubtedly still awake. She never looked well rested. He imagined confusion and fear contorting her delicate features, and how her jaw would solder tight when she realized the very person trying to kill her was inextricably connected to Kane. She'd been right, hadn't she? Cecile's death *was* his fault.

He hated himself for what he said next.

"I'm not sure we should."

Fletcher's face contorted. "Why not?"

"She knows we work for Ward. If she finds out he's behind this,

she'll be even more hesitant to trust us. There's the threat of her pulling out of the deal entirely."

"It's her life," Fletcher objected, lowering his voice. "Don't you think she has the right to know?"

Kane tried not to flinch. "The Exhibition's in six days. If she backs out, we're fucked."

"Yeah." Fletcher pressed his index fingers into his temples. "Yeah, I guess that's true. It just feels wrong."

Kane clenched his teeth against the guilt that threatened to overwhelm him. If Fletcher understood why keeping Zaria in the dark was the better option, would the same apply when he learned what Kane had been keeping from *him*? Or would he look back on this conversation and feel even more betrayed?

He should come clean to Fletcher now. There might not be a better opportunity. If something went horribly wrong, and if all their planning amounted to nothing, then Fletcher needed to know he was in danger.

"Fletch?" Kane broke the silence, the single syllable quivering in space. "There's something I need to tell you."

Fletcher tilted his head, eyes wide and clear. It was evident in that look how much he trusted Kane. How he waited, expectant and unconcerned, no part of him anticipating the bomb that was about to drop. "Okay."

It was the *okay* that undid him—as if Fletcher were expecting Kane to unravel, not the other way around. All at once, Kane's conviction evaded him. He couldn't do it. He couldn't say the words. They were going to get this necklace one way or another, and Fletcher would never have to know. That was what Kane had been counting on from the start, wasn't it?

God, he was one sick son of a bitch.

"I need to sleep in your room tonight," Kane said, scrambling for something to say. "I didn't want Zaria going out, so she's in my bed."

Fletcher snorted. "Hell, Kane. You made it sound like you were going to confess a sin. I don't think you need to be embarrassed about having a girl in your bed if you're not in there with her."

The guilt was suddenly too much. Kane lurched to his feet, fully aware of how erratic he must look, and grabbed his coat where it hung beside the door. "I'm going to take a walk."

Fletcher stood. "Do you want me to come with you?"

"No," Kane said too quickly. "No," he repeated, steadier the second time. "I just need to clear my head. Don't wait up, okay?"

Fletcher followed him to the door anyway, his step light, still skeptical. "You're not going to visit Ward, are you?"

"Hell no."

"You sure?"

"I promise."

One side of Fletcher's mouth slipped up in a wry grin. "Yeah, but it's easy for you to lie."

It was clearly a joke, but Kane couldn't bring himself to return the smile. It felt like someone was sawing his insides apart with a rusty blade, and he immersed himself in the sensation, knowing he deserved it.

"Not to you, Fletch," he said quietly. "Not to you."

24

ZARIA

THE NEXT DAY, ZARIA WAS IN A FOUL MOOD.

She'd slept well, which was confounding given the altogether-too-*Kane* scent of the room. It made it impossible to forget where she was. Emerging in the morning had felt strangely embarrassing, though there was no reason for it. At first, Kane and Fletcher had been nowhere to be seen—which wasn't surprising given it was mid-morning when she finally awoke—but the moment Zaria tried to slink out of the house, she found herself face-to-face with a moody, freshly bathed Kane.

"And just where do you think you're going?"

She paused, lingering on the threshold, and blinked. The door was already open. In front of her stood Kane in a partial state of undress, which was to say he wore only trousers and a thin linen shirt he'd neglected to button fully. The arrow tattoo at his throat shifted when he tilted his head. Zaria forced her gaze to meet his, tearing it away from the triangle of his exposed sternum. "Home."

"No, you're not."

Her brows shot up. "Are you going to stop me?"

"Yes."

"I didn't realize I was a prisoner here."

Kane drew a hand over his chin. He looked like he hadn't slept, and there was an uneasiness about him, as though his thoughts were elsewhere. "You're not. But I have something to show you."

"I need to get back to the pawnshop." After a decent night's sleep, her frustration with Jules was dissipating.

"I told you I'd get a message there, and I did," Kane said dismissively. "Trust me. You'll like this."

"Somehow I doubt that."

"Humor me."

Zaria glanced past him into the street. The air was humid today, threatening rain, and the stench of the river carried over on the breeze. She bit down on the inside of her cheek as fury and curiosity warred within her.

"Fine," she conceded. "But if I'm not impressed, you're escorting me home."

"Deal."

Kane led her around the side of the factory to what appeared to be some kind of shed. The exterior was nondescript gray stone, the slanted roof visibly cracked in a few places. Zaria narrowed her eyes. "Is this where you're planning to kill me? Did you send Fletcher away so there wouldn't be any witnesses?"

One side of his face slipped up in a reluctant grin. "Fletcher's at work. And besides, he'd cover for me."

"Work?"

"He's a copper now, in case you forgot."

"Ah." Zaria gathered her loose hair into a knot, trying to lessen the heat. "I take it last night turned up nothing of interest."

Kane shrugged jerkily. "I'm afraid not."

She frowned in suspicion, intent on asking after his discomfort, but the next moment, he had shouldered the shed door open. All other thoughts fled. "What's this?"

He moved aside to grant her entry. "Cecile worked out of here for a while, back when she was in Ward's employ. I don't think it's been used since, but I tried to get everything you might need."

Zaria didn't quite know what to say as she looked around. In the middle of the space was a waist-high worktable covered with an organized assortment of alchemology supplies. On the wall farthest from the door were cabinets, some of them hanging off their hinges, but they had been stocked with vials and various tools. Zaria walked over to the table, dragging a finger across its surface until she found a jar of silvery powder. "This is soulsteel."

"It is." Kane sounded pleased with himself.

It was the most soulsteel Zaria had ever seen in her life. She turned away from it, her throat tightening. "This must have cost a fortune."

"This is what it's like to work for the kingpin." Kane shut the shop door, coming around to stand on the other side of the table. There were no windows, and he struck a match, using it to light a candle. It flared brilliantly to life, an orange glow climbing the column of his neck. He looked rather monstrous lit from beneath. "Can you get started today?"

"I'm already working on the aleuite explosives," she reminded him. "They're back at the pawnshop."

"I can have everything brought here."

She wanted to argue, but she had to admit that this place was… perfect. An alchemologist's dream. "All right then."

Kane rested his elbows on the table. "Can I watch you work for a bit?"

Zaria swallowed hard. She hadn't counted on being monitored. But it wasn't as though she was planning anything unsavory—not yet, at least. She could take this for what it was: the perfect opportunity to convince Kane he could trust her. When they finally carried out the heist, she would need his guard down as much as possible.

"I suppose." She opened the jar of soulsteel and let the glittering powder sift through her fingers. Kane remained quiet, his eyes tracking her movements as she added the soulsteel to the flame, trying not to let her hands shake. When she took her knife out, he stilled.

"Don't worry," she said, bemused. "I'm not going to stab you."

Kane let that one pass, watching as she pressed the tip into the skin of her arm. Blood welled, immediate and shining. It was only once she had let it drip into the flame that he said, "Why?"

"I don't have a primateria source, do I?" Zaria wiped the excess blood away with her sleeve. "I use my own life energy."

"I didn't realize it required a blood debt."

"Power demands payment." She slid her gaze up to his, tracking the minute shifts in his expression from beneath her lashes. "I'm sure you know that."

Kane tilted his head. A vein strained at his throat. "And that's why alchemologists die so quickly, is it?"

Zaria recoiled from the blunt question. "The effects are difficult to predict. But yes. It's an exchange of sorts."

"What if you used someone else's blood?"

"It wouldn't work."

"And why not?"

"Because," Zaria said, indignant at his myriad questions, "you don't just throw blood at a candle and then *boom*, magic. There's work to be done from within. You have to travel inside yourself and make it clear what you're willing to give up. You have to know exactly what you want to do. Then, finally, you have to be able to picture how it happens."

"Ah." He rocked back on his heels. "Does it make you go mad?"

"You're an idiot." She did her best to ignore him as she withdrew into herself, casting about for focus. It was harder with Kane there, wondering what he would see in her face as she struggled to find that place where creation thrived.

Perhaps Kane sensed that, because a moment later he had averted his gaze, fixing it instead on a piece of parchment Zaria hadn't seen him take out. She paused, her thoughts funneling back into the present as she tried to make out the design on the page before him.

"What is that?"

"Copy of the architectural blueprint for the Crystal Palace."

"Where did you get it?"

Kane shot her a withering look. Zaria took that to imply he had obtained the blueprint through unsavory means.

"There's no problem you can't solve with theft, is there?"

He adjusted the collar of his shirt, a hint of humor playing at his lips. "I like to think not. Now, are you going to get started or continue trying to stall?"

"I'm not stalling," she said. "You're … distracting."

"I suppose you'll just have to ignore me." Kane's voice suggested he knew exactly how difficult that would be. "Surely the great Itzal Mendoza taught you the importance of focus."

"He tried," Zaria said, though her face burned. How could she explain that in order to do this properly, she needed to latch on to the type of focus that regular people didn't seem to have?

"What does that mean?"

"I wasn't always a great student." The words were clipped. "I was all wrong in too many ways." She cleared her throat. "Will you at least move aside?"

Instead of retreating from the worktable, though, Kane stepped closer to her. His expression had lost its casual disdain, and there was apprehension in the line of his mouth. "You seem all right to me."

"You wouldn't know right from wrong if it were presented to you by God himself."

"Oh, I know the difference. I just don't shy away from the latter."

Zaria swallowed hard. Kane backed away, and for a moment, she thought he had finally decided to leave. But then, from the shadowy corner of the shed, he asked, "Why do you think you're all wrong?"

There was a strange edge to his voice, as if he desperately needed to know the answer. As if her reply would either tip the world or set it right.

She didn't care to explain herself to anyone, least of all Kane Durante. Even as she had the thought, however, the words bubbled up in her chest, slipping past her teeth before she could stop them.

"Isn't it obvious? I'm careless, but also very particular. I'm too easily frustrated. I'm terrible at connecting with people, so everyone assumes I don't like them, and I don't bother to change their minds. I don't *want* to change their minds because I'm terrified they'll decide I'm not good enough, and then I'll look like a fool. I'm constantly thinking fifteen thoughts at once, and yet I can't remember a single one of them. I say all the wrong things at the wrong times, and my father's entire business would fall apart if I didn't have Jules to help me stay organized. I'm a disaster. Are you happy now?"

She said this all very fast, her chest heaving, and didn't know why she was angrier for having given him the truth. Unwilling to hold his gaze, she stared into the glittering flame. By this point, the candle was beginning to burn lower, wax pooling on the table and collecting in the divots in the wood. Zaria wanted to melt into a puddle of wax herself. Kane still hadn't said a word, and she couldn't decide what would be worse: his pity or his derision.

She was surprised, then, when she didn't get either one.

"That doesn't make you wrong," Kane finally declared in a way that managed to be both soft and harsh. "You're exactly who you are."

Zaria gave a hollow laugh. It didn't sound like her. "That's sort of the problem."

"Maybe that's *why* you were able to master alchemology. It's about holding multiple points of focus, right? You see yourself as full of contradictions, but maybe having fifteen thoughts at once is a strength." Bemusement curved his lips. "Whatever it is about you that makes you feel like a disaster . . . maybe that's the reason you can do what so many other people can't. Did you ever think of that?"

"No," Zaria muttered, because she hadn't. She was so accustomed to holding feelings of shame, she'd never thought about anything of the sort. She bit the inside of her cheek as the glittering flame sputtered out, wisps of smoke curling up from the point of demise.

"Well," Kane said. "Maybe you should."

When she finally looked back up, he was gone.

It took Zaria far too long to refocus her attention, even without Kane to distract her. After hours spent fitting together the nonmagical parts of her creations, she finally managed to slow her racing pulse, sinking into something of a meditative state as she worked. Distantly,

she knew the day was slipping away from her. But she couldn't risk stopping now, or she might never find her way back into the project.

The first couple of primateria creations had gone easily enough. Exhaustion tugged at the edges of her consciousness, though she was able to ignore it. At some point, she'd realized there was a glass of water on the counter beneath one of the cabinets; Kane or Fletcher must have put it there ahead of time. She resolved to drink it after creating *one more*.

Shutting her eyes, she let her thoughts coalesce and settle like an alchemological compound. There was no sound but the *tap, tap* of her foot as she let the rhythm lull her into concentration. She beseeched the world to disappear, and this time it did, melting away and dragging her into oblivion. She imagined the precise interaction of materials she required and was ready for the tension, the subsequent rush.

But Zaria was not ready to open her eyes and feel her heart stop.

It restarted with a jolt as she fought back the dizziness, primateria clutched in her left hand. She couldn't remember plucking it from the candle or blowing out the flame. She must have, though, because tendrils of smoke unfurled in the air before her, partially obscuring Kane's face.

"Kane." His name on her tongue betrayed her shock. She tried and failed to push herself up. Where had he come from? She was certain he hadn't been there a moment prior.

He frowned, his dark brows drawing together. His hand was on her cheek, she realized, fingers cool against her burning face. "Christ. Are you okay? Your countenance is..."

"I'm fine." Nausea rose in the back of her throat as she struggled to fit the pieces of herself back together. She was bent over the work desk, she realized distantly, her other cheek pressed to the wood.

"Zaria."

The world tilted as he repeated her name. Another wave of dizziness crashed into her like an incoming tide, and her heart stuttered in that horrible, off-tempo rhythm as she pushed away from the table, from the primateria, from Kane. She was too aware of her body, and everything felt wrong. Black spotted the edges of her vision. "I need to leave."

"What?" Frustration laced his voice. He gestured to what she'd created so far. "Is this everything I requested?"

Was he mad? Didn't he recall how many magical items he'd asked her to come up with? And some of them, like the parautoptic key, were things she'd never so much as considered attempting before. "I'm not a machine, Kane. I've done enough for today, and I'm going home." She made to sidestep him, but he blocked her with ease.

"Sit *down*. You look like you're going to pass out again."

Her frustration mounted. She couldn't have Kane seeing her like this—weak and confused, her thoughts clouded. "Don't tell me what to do."

"I'm not trying to," he said blithely. "And I know you're not a machine. I was only trying to discern whether you'd overextended yourself."

"Pretending to care now, are we?"

"I have no need of pretending. I was half-worried I'd return to discover that you'd expired."

"And wouldn't that be inconvenient for you." To her relief, the nausea was already fading.

"What's that supposed to mean? It *would* be inconvenient, but—"

"I know you're only worried because of what you need me to do for you, Durante. Otherwise it'd make no difference to you whether I was dead or alive."

For some reason, Zaria realized belatedly, the accusation had been a mistake. Kane's eyes flashed, looking too large in the shadow-carved gauntness of his face.

"No *difference*?" he hissed. "Zaria, all I've done all week is try to keep you alive. What do my intentions matter? Why can't you just say *thank you*?"

They were good questions, and she resented that fact. Why did she care about Kane's reason for protecting her when what mattered was that he had? She suddenly felt very foolish. The dip in her stomach whenever he was near—like she was standing on a precipice overlooking some great height—was ill-advised. He was unbearable and dangerous. So why did she feel contorted into knots, full of held-breath anticipation as she waited for him to admit that there *was* another reason he kept saving her life?

For a moment, she thought he might do just that. His throat worked as he swallowed, and his focus on her intensified. But then he sighed, dragging fingers through his hair, and shook his head. "Forget it. It doesn't matter. If you can't take care of yourself, Fletcher is the one who'll suffer in the end."

Something inside Zaria soured. Right. This was about *Fletcher*. She blinked furiously back at Kane, her head finally clearing as she said, "So I've heard. And whose fault is that?"

"You think I wanted this?" Kane's voice was barely audible. It was more frightening than if he'd yelled. He relit the candle, then a second one. The flames flickered, turning his face skeletal. "You think it doesn't eat me alive? There is *nothing* I wouldn't do for Fletcher. Nothing."

"I thought you didn't care about death," Zaria scoffed. "Cecile's certainly didn't bother you."

"Cecile meant nothing to me."

"You're sick."

Kane took another slow step forward. "And what about you? You hadn't seen her in years. Were you truly weeping for her loss, or was it merely that her death meant you no longer had a way of getting what you wanted?"

The sensation of weakness faded, leaving Zaria with nothing but a burning fury. Kane didn't know her. He hadn't known the reasons Cecile was important to her or that Zaria *had* gotten what she wanted in the end. He didn't understand that for a few blissful moments she had finally, *finally*, felt a little less alone.

"Fuck you, Kane," she whispered.

He stood directly before her now, lithe and motionless as a specter. His teeth flashed as he gave a single, dismissive laugh. "You've convinced yourself that I'm callous, but I'm simply selective when it comes to other people. You're the same, aren't you? We both have one person we'd sacrifice everything for, and anyone else just gets in the way."

"What exactly are you sacrificing, Kane? Everything *you* do"—Zaria thrust a finger at his chest—"is to undo the damage you've already caused. So you can delude yourself into believing you're not a *shit* person who lies to anyone who's ever attempted to care about you."

She didn't know what made her say it. Perhaps it was the conversation she'd had with Fletcher and how he so desperately wanted Zaria to give Kane more grace than he deserved. Perhaps it was the expression on Jules's face when she'd left the pawnshop last night. Perhaps she merely wanted to see Kane hurt.

It must have worked, because something shuttered behind his eyes. They looked amber tonight, the same color and equally liquid as the whiskey he so often smelled like. She wished she knew what he was thinking. Why that muscle ticked in his jaw. There was an

unfamiliar hesitance in his body language as he searched her face, but there was also a certain *hunger* about him. She tensed, unable to stop her breath from turning shallow.

"You're treading dangerous ground, Miss Mendoza," Kane breathed. He was so close that she could feel the heat of his body. Saw the brief flick of his gaze down to her mouth, then back up again.

"And?" She challenged him, an animal hunger of her own clawing its way up her insides. Her skin was hot. Too hot. The fire between them burned from fury to lust until the two were all but indistinguishable. Kane lowered his face to hers, pulse fluttering in his throat as his jaw tensed, neck going taut. Zaria didn't move an inch.

It was nonsensical. She hated Kane in that moment. She *hated* him, and there was no part of him that was not wrong for her.

But she couldn't help the disappointment that lanced through her when he began to back away again.

"Coward," she hissed.

That was when he lunged and pulled her face to his.

Kane kissed her with feverish intensity, and Zaria didn't stop him. Her body went slack as he shoved her against the wall, his hand sliding up her rib cage and trailing over her shoulder to rest at her throat. Kissing Kane was not gentle. It was grasping fingers and bruising touch and the delicate skim of teeth. It was vicious collision and fury in the space between breathless gasps. It was the heady scent of smoke and the dizzying absence of all rational thought.

Kane's mouth brushed her jaw, and he hooked a finger in the collar of her jacket, wrenching it aside. Cool air danced along the exposed stretch of her collarbone as his hand tightened on her neck. He was *beautiful*, this dangerous boy, and Zaria resented it. Resented the way he was soft and firm in all the right places as he pressed against her. Resented the chill that danced across her skin as the pressure of his touch nearly undid her.

"What was it you called me?" Kane exhaled the words against the hollow of her throat.

Zaria pulled her lips back from her teeth, utterly motionless. *"Coward."*

Something rumbled in his chest—either a laugh or a growl—as he dragged his mouth back up to hers. Her hands fisted in the fabric of his shirt, drawing him closer, and lightning sparked behind her shuttered eyelids. Nothing existed that wasn't Kane.

She was a fool. She knew it even as her fingers trembled and her stomach tightened. She knew Kane was chaotic, charming, tragic, unpredictable. She knew trying to understand him was like trying to snatch raindrops from the air. She hadn't been lying when she said he was a mess, but she was something of a mess herself. They were too similar—perhaps that was the problem. They would break each other into unrecognizable pieces. They would set the world on fire purely by accident and watch as it burned down around them.

She was going to *betray* Kane. Would kissing him like this— like her very soul would crack if she pulled away—help her do that? Would it make him trust her more than he ought to if he believed she truly felt something for him?

And then, the thought that made Zaria's heart turn over: What if he was kissing her for the same reason?

Once the idea crossed her mind, she couldn't escape it. She ripped away from Kane, bracing both hands against his chest to shove him back. Confusion darkened his gaze as he stumbled, still breathing heavily, his hair mussed where she'd run her fingers through it.

"I have to go," Zaria huffed, ducking to the side as she made to leave.

Kane moved with impossible stealth, blocking her exit. He held the door shut, fingers splayed against the wood, veins in the back of his hand straining. "Stay. Just a little longer."

It wasn't a request but a command. He couldn't even ask her a question—he had to pose it as an order.

God, how had she allowed herself to soften toward him even for a second? Kane was using her. And she had all but asked for it, fool that she was.

Coward.

Well. She would use him right back, and they would see who cracked first.

"Good night, Kane," she said coolly, slapping his arm away and yanking the door open. "I'll be back tomorrow. Assuming I feel like it."

He didn't say another word as she swept past him out into the dusk.

25

KANE

This time, Kane didn't follow Zaria. He didn't need to. He knew she wouldn't be in danger tonight.

Tonight, the danger was here.

He'd requested a meeting with the kingpin and received word that he would pay a call later tonight. That was unusual. It wasn't often Ward deigned to meet anywhere other than the place he was currently conducting business from. As a result, Kane had needed Zaria to disappear. He'd gone out to the workshop with the intention of pissing her off, hoping that would compel her to leave of her own accord, but the state in which he'd found her had thrown him completely off track. He had forgotten to infuriate her. Instead, fool that he was, he'd tried to convince her that he cared about her.

And then he'd kissed her.

He shouldn't have let her goad him into it. He'd tried to tell himself it was convenient—that Zaria might trust him more if she thought he felt something for her—but he hadn't expected the raw, animal desire that ripped his chest open when their mouths met. Even now, he could still feel the heat of her lips. Could still taste the bittersweet flavor of her self-hatred. For that brief moment, Kane knew he would have done anything Zaria asked. He would have lain down in the dirt and let her walk the distance of the earth across his back.

Then she'd drawn away, severing the connection with a finality that hurt Kane like a physical blow.

He was so irrevocably fucked.

Fletcher had retired to bed a few hours ago, but Kane hadn't followed suit. If his friend noticed anything was amiss, he hadn't commented on it, though he'd lingered at the bottom of the stairs for longer than usual.

Kane stayed awake, balancing a glass of whiskey on the armrest of the chair he so often occupied. Waiting. The room grew cooler, but he didn't light a fire. The sky outside shifted to the navy hue of midnight, camouflaging the haze of smog, and still Kane didn't move. The lifting of the glass to his lips was automatic. His eyes fixed on nothing in the corner of the room, and his mind spun and spun until alcohol turned his thoughts into something less coherent. Until it softened the edges of whatever demon reared inside of him, snarling to get out.

Kane didn't know what time it was when the knock on the door came.

He was drunk enough at this point not to feel anything but a mild irritation as he pushed himself to stand, abandoning his drink. He swiped his gun off the table on his way to the door and shoved it into his waistband—a futile precaution. When he yanked the door open, it took a moment for the figure on the top step to swim into focus.

Kane's stomach churned. He didn't know why. It wasn't as if he was unprepared.

"Ward."

The kingpin's golden eyes found his, conveying mild disdain. He looked impeccable as always, not a hair out of place as he removed the hat poised atop his head. His black jacket was buttoned up to the throat. "Good evening, Kane."

The greeting was disarmingly pleasant, and Kane fought to gain control of himself as apprehension sunk its claws in. He regretted the whiskey now. He preferred to have all his wits about him when dealing with Ward.

"Aren't you going to invite me in?" Amusement lined the planes of Ward's face as his gaze sharpened.

"You certainly took your time."

"I did, yes."

Kane didn't know what to do with his body. He shuffled aside, feeling ungraceful in a way that he rarely did, and allowed the kingpin to enter.

Ward wrinkled his nose as he stepped inside, scouring the dark space before focusing back on Kane. "Have you been drinking?"

He didn't see why it mattered. He gave a noncommittal shrug, and Ward exhaled in disgust.

"Alone in the dark, at that. Where's Master Collins?"

Kane indicated with his chin. "Asleep upstairs. Can we get to the point? I take it you know what I wanted to discuss."

"I can guess." Ward's lips twisted, wry and cruel. "Does it have anything to do with the charming Miss Mendoza?"

Her name in the kingpin's mouth made Kane's blood run cold. "I don't know what you're playing at, but I *do* know you've been trying to have her killed."

"A hefty accusation."

"Don't you fucking touch her."

Perhaps it was the alcohol that made him bolder than usual. Either way, it was a mistake. Ward rotated to face the door, beckoning with a single finger, and the next moment two men filed into the entryway. They were enormous, seeming to take up much of the room. Kane recognized them immediately. Davies and Yardley tended to work alone, though they sometimes accompanied Ward to help him deal out his own personal form of justice. Kane had never liked the men, if only because they had never been frightened of him.

They advanced toward Kane, each taking hold of one of his arms, and shoved him into the nearest dining chair before his whiskey-addled mind could comprehend what was happening. His pulse skyrocketed as he struggled against their viselike grips.

"What the hell?" Kane spat, wildly seeking Ward's impassive face. "What is this?"

Ward watched the scene play out with icy disinterest. "You know, boy, I've been watching you. Making sure you don't step out of line. A good thing, too." He nodded to Davies, and the enormous, well-dressed man grasped Kane's jaw roughly with a hand.

Pain lanced down into his neck, cutting through the haze of intoxication. He attempted to turn his face away, teeth clenched, to no avail. "I haven't—*done* anything."

"Ah, but is that the truth, Kane?" Footsteps sounded beside him, and Ward's face came into view a moment later. His eyes were liquid malice. "Tell me, then: When I gave you this assignment, what was the main thing I requested of you?"

Panic spiked in Kane's blood, and he had the wild thought that he was glad not to be sober just now. "I don't—"

Ward held up a hand. "Before you proceed unwisely, I recommend you take a moment to consider your next words. If you lie to me, Kane, I will know, and it will be all the worse for you."

It was the truth. Ward had always known when Kane was lying. It was impossible to con the man who had made him so good at it.

The kingpin laid a hand on Kane's cheek. His skin was cold. Ward hadn't touched Kane like that in years, and Kane hated the *yearning* it instilled in him. He wanted to push the feeling away. To lock it up in a tiny box and throw away the key. He was not the boy he had once been, desperate for validation and tormented each time it was withheld. He was no longer the child who had so badly wanted a father figure.

That child was broken. Mangled by reality, crushed by false hopes, and bruised by disappointment.

Kane would have slapped Ward's hand away, but his arms were still restrained by Yardley and Davies. He settled for jerking his chin to the side. "I'm doing everything I can to bring you that damned necklace. If you're going to be picky about the circumstances under which I obtain it, perhaps you should have done it yourself."

He knew it was a mistake the moment he uttered the words. There was a reason Ward had brought these men with him: Dainty inked *x*'s weren't going to cut it. Not this time.

Yardley grabbed Kane by the throat, his thick fingers unyielding. Kane gasped and choked for breath, having no free hands with which to fight. Shadows began to fill the edges of his vision. His head throbbed and spun. For the first time in years, death seemed like a real, immediate possibility, not a threat looming in the distance.

He hated Ward. Hated him with a passion unmatched even by his desire to impress the man.

Sometimes, when I watch other people die, I imagine they wear his face.

It was what Kane had told Zaria in his bedroom. And yet it only seemed to be true half the time. Kane didn't know how to reconcile the two halves of himself that Ward had created.

"Enough." Ward's voice sliced through his fury. "I think he gets the point."

Kane glowered, straining against Yardley's grip.

"What did I make you promise me?" Ward asked. He tilted his head, surveying Kane as if he were a dissected specimen flayed open on a table. "When I ordered you to the steal the necklace, what did I say?"

There was a pause. The moment stretched until it circled the perimeter of the room, then tightened. Kane felt as though the space were getting smaller. His thoughts were a jumble, each one tinged with anger he had no means of expelling. Ward waited, cool and collected.

Through gritted teeth, Kane finally said, "You told me not to tell anyone about it. Nobody but Fletcher."

Ward's face turned sad. It was a false kind of sad, and it made Kane more nervous than anything. It was the face Ward made when he was about to do something cruel.

"That's right. And did you listen?"

"I—"

"Do you seek to infuriate me, or is it just that you are unable to follow the simplest of instructions?" Ward's fingers trailed Kane's cheek, nails scraping skin. This time Kane didn't flinch away. *"Did. You. Listen?"*

"I needed help! Once the necklace was moved to the Crystal Palace—"

Davies's fist hit him square in the jaw. Kane ought to have seen it coming, really. His head snapped to the side, and he let out a growl as he turned back to face Ward.

"No, okay?" he snarled. "No, I didn't listen."

"Right. And you didn't tell just anyone, did you? You told Zaria Mendoza."

"She's only a girl—"

"Only a girl?" Ward showed all of his teeth. "She's a dark market alchemologist. She's Itzal Mendoza's daughter."

Kane tried to exhale, but the air kept getting stuck somewhere along the way. When he finally replied, it sounded strained. "What does that matter?"

Ward's eyes flashed. "Oh, it matters."

"You leave her alone, or I'll—"

Davies's second blow connected with brutal efficiency. Ward watched Kane absorb it with disdain, golden eyes like chips of citrine. "Do not presume to give me orders, Canziano."

"Why do you want her dead?" Kane bit out. "Why try to kill her behind my back? I was already planning to double-cross her. This won't benefit her in the end."

There was a long pause. Ward seemed to turn the question over in his mind, and Kane knew even before the kingpin answered that he was going to lie.

"I was trying to protect you. I'm *always* trying to protect you, and the girl cannot be trusted. Her father was a swindler. A talented cheat. I hoped to dispose of her swiftly in a manner that wouldn't distract you. You're struggling enough as it is. And yet, as always, you evade my attempts to help. Abe Walker, dead in the street. Anil Sahni, run out of town."

"Abe wouldn't be dead if you'd told me the truth."

Ward waved a dismissive hand. "I don't care about Walker. I care only for your success."

Kane glared, the blood pounding in his ears. He felt disconnected from every aspect of himself—a toy on a shelf, watching a scene play out in slow motion. Present but not part of anything.

"Spare me the bullshit." His mouth was dry, but he mustered enough saliva to spit onto Ward's pressed coat. "You don't know what it is to care about another person."

This time it was Ward himself who threw the punch. It didn't have nearly as much force as the last two, but it left a searing ache along Kane's temple, and he knew Ward's ring had split the skin. A trail of hot blood slid down to his jaw, which he set, continuing to glare defiantly at the kingpin. Ward already looked chagrinned, the fury fading as quickly as it had come.

He grabbed Kane's chin and jerked it up, forcing him to meet his gaze. "Remember who you belong to," he breathed. He smelled like tobacco and patchouli. "I'd have preferred the Mendoza girl dead, but if you're so desperate to keep her alive, then cut ties with her yourself. Can you do that for me? Can I trust you to do better?"

Hating himself more than he had ever hated anyone else in his life, Kane nodded.

Ward released him. There was something regretful in the action. He waved an impatient hand, dismissing Yardley and Davies. Kane slumped forward in the chair as they disappeared back into the night. When the kingpin spoke again, his voice was changed. Softer.

"What have I taught you? If you want to rise above others, you have to be ruthless. I can feel us growing apart, and it's because you're no longer willing to let me guide you. Stop *fighting* me, Kane."

Kane's thoughts were muddled. How many times was he going to let Ward torture him and reel him back in?

But the man knew just what to say to make him stay.

People like you and me understand that the world owes us nothing, Ward had told Kane once. *We know to reach out and take what we can, because if we don't, someone else is going to do it.*

Kane had tried. He'd tried and tried, yet never felt he obtained anything of real worth. Not when Ward was there to snatch it from his fingertips.

The kingpin turned up the collar of his jacket, and then he was gone, a shadow melting into the dark.

Minutes slid past.

Kane didn't move. He simply sat there, anger sprouting from the devouring emptiness inside him. It twisted and lashed, a wild thing within his bones, leaving him tense and desperate for—*something.* He didn't know what, and it made him want to scream.

Before he knew what he was doing, Kane swiped a hand across the table and sent his glass crashing to the floor. He made no attempt to avoid the spray of crystal-like fragments. Didn't move at all, in fact. He only continued to stare blankly at the wall as second after agonizing second ticked by.

"Kane."

Someone grabbed him roughly by the shoulders, and Fletcher swam into view. To say he was a deep sleeper would have been an understatement—he must've woken at the sound of shattering glass. Kane tried to writhe away from his friend's hard stare, but Fletcher held him firmly in place.

"What happened?"

How was he supposed to answer that? Kane reached for the table again, that still-drunk part of him desperate for something else to break.

Fletcher caught his arm, face a tense mask. "Leave the fucking dishes alone."

A distant part of Kane was aware of his unhinged behavior, but the guilt that roiled within him was a secondary torment. He needed—

"A towel," Fletcher said. "I'll get a towel. You're covered in blood. Sit down."

Kane sat, tilting his head back to look up at the ceiling. "Sorry."

"Don't be."

"It was Ward."

"I figured as much." Fletcher disappeared around the corner, returning with a cloth that he pressed harshly to Kane's cheek. A long moment of silence stretched between them as Kane replaced Fletcher's hand with his own, feeling his pulse beneath the fabric.

"Okay," Fletcher said as they both relaxed by increments. "Talk."

"Ward wants us to cut ties with Zaria."

"Shit. What does he have against her?"

"He wouldn't explain."

"How long ago was he here?"

"You just missed him." Kane removed the towel, inhaling through his teeth. "I shouldn't have gotten her involved in the first place. I wasn't supposed to tell anyone about the necklace other than you."

Fletcher sank into the chair beside him. "Are she and Julian in danger?"

Wasn't anyone in danger once Ward had his eye on them? Even if Kane *did* cut her out of the plan, he didn't trust the kingpin to let her live. Not given what she knew. "Probably."

"And you hate that because you care about her."

Kane immediately stiffened, and he cut his friend a look. "We need her, Fletch. You know it as well as I do. So yes, I care what happens to her."

"That's not what I said." Fletcher crossed his arms, but something in his gaze had softened. "What are you not telling me?"

God, where to start? Kane pressed his thumb and forefinger to the bridge of his nose. His temples throbbed. Damn Fletcher's ability to read him so easily. Like the coward he was, he opted for the least important truth. "I kissed her."

Fletcher swatted his shoulder. Lightly but with enough sting that Kane gave an automatic wince of surprise.

"The hell was that for?"

"What in the world were you thinking?" Fletcher retorted. "How much more complicated are you intending to make this?"

"It's not that complicated."

"You're going to *betray* her, Kane."

"And now she'll see it coming even less."

Fletcher shook his head in disbelief. "What about you?"

"What *about* me?"

"You wouldn't kiss someone you didn't care about."

"Sure I would. Have you met me?" The lie bittered Kane's tongue. Maybe he did care about Zaria just a little. Maybe he'd allowed himself to enjoy that kiss before she pulled away and fled into the dark like something uncanny nipped at her heels. But what did it matter? The important thing was that it didn't make a fucking difference. He was going to betray her just like Fletcher said. Hell, he had nearly gotten her killed.

"We have to tell them."

Kane started at the change in subject. "What?"

"Zaria and Jules." Fletcher's brow flicked up. "We have to warn them about Ward. I realize it's a risk, but they deserve to know."

Kane leapt to his feet. He couldn't have this conversation again.

"I need to get some sleep." He threw down the towel, now spotted darkly crimson with blood from his split brow.

Fletcher stared at it a moment, his mouth tight. "All right."

They deserve to know. Fletcher's voice chided Kane all the way to his room. *They deserve to know.*

It was a relief when pain and intoxication gathered him into blissful unconsciousness.

26

ZARIA

Zaria didn't see Jules until the next morning.

She hadn't gone looking for him upon arriving home, instead collapsing into an exhausted heap on her bed and trying very hard not to think. And yet she'd found all she could *do* was think, until eventually she must have passed out with a pillow over her head and Kane's face behind her eyelids.

Now she stood outside Jules's bedroom door, fist poised to knock. It was still early, and the exhaustion from all she'd done yesterday made her feel vaguely hungover.

Or perhaps it was the sheer amount of self-disgust Zaria felt whenever she remembered Kane's lips on hers. Nothing good could come from what they'd done. Her body, though, hadn't wanted to listen to logic. Despite knowing with every facet of her being that she shouldn't be attracted to Kane Durante, she hadn't been able to resist goading him. She could lie to herself no longer. It wasn't his easy charm or his con man's grin but the tortured flash in his eyes whenever he said Fletcher's name. It was the way he'd shown her he was *human*.

Kane would give everything to protect his friend. And for a brief, foolish moment, Zaria had wondered if he'd been trying to protect her, too. If he'd wanted to keep her alive because he cared about her. Not her work—*her*. Some small, ridiculous part of her wanted to be important to someone like that. Someone who fought so hard to care for nothing and nobody but made an exception every so often.

It wasn't sensible. It wasn't healthy. Kane couldn't fix her desperate need to feel like she mattered. In the same vein, she couldn't mend whatever his veritable slew of issues were. They were both carrying too much.

What she needed to focus on right now was the one person to whom she *did* matter. The person who was forever trying to help her shoulder the weight of everything the world had thrust upon her and asked for nothing in return.

When she finally summoned the courage to knock, it took Jules a moment to respond. Zaria waited, oddly nervous, until she heard him say, "Yeah?"

It was close enough to an invitation. She opened the door, bracing herself for the anger she was sure to see written on Jules's face.

He didn't look angry, though. He only looked tired, his back curved against the wall where he sat on his bed with a book in hand. *Nicholas Nickleby*, Zaria read. It was nothing she was familiar with. That said, she didn't read much. She always found herself skimming the same passages again and again, her toes twitching incessantly, her mind led astray by a thousand other things.

"Can I come in?"

"Looks as though you already have."

Said by anyone else, it might have sounded rude, but Zaria knew

Jules well enough to hear the lightness in the words. She stepped farther into the small square room, taking in the familiar surroundings. Peeling walls and dusty floors. A bed much too narrow for two people but that they'd slept on in the past, shoulder to shoulder, more than once. A poorly built side table on which sat a stack of worn books and the last nub of a candle. It was all both comforting and miserable in its familiarity.

Zaria came to sit on the edge of the bed, and Jules didn't stop her.

"I'm sorry," she said, because his expression made it clear he would say nothing more until she did.

He set the book down, brows drawing together as he sat up. "For what?"

Of course he wouldn't let her get away with a vague apology. Jules wasn't like that. When they had a problem, he wanted to confront it head-on. It was one of the things she liked most about him. At the same time, though, it meant she needed to deliver the script she'd mentally prepared while lying in bed last night.

"I kept you in the dark when I shouldn't have and when I didn't need to. I was trying to protect you, but in doing so, I not only lied—I took away your right to make your own choices."

"Yeah," Jules said, swinging his legs over the side of the bed so his position mirrored hers. "You did. But that's not why I got upset. I was upset because you took away *my* ability to try to protect *you*."

Surprise caught Zaria's face in a frown. "I don't need you to—"

"Neither do I, Zaria!" Impatience edged his voice. "That's what I've been trying to tell you! Don't you see? We feel the same way, but for some reason, you can't seem to understand that." At her pained expression, he spoke more softly. "I know you sometimes feel you're no good at reading people. But you've always been able to read me, so you'll know I'm telling the truth when I say this: I feel the same

overwhelming drive to get us out of this place and keep you safe in the process." His mouth tilted up in a slight grin. "I'm just not quite as openly aggressive about it."

Zaria's chest ached. She wanted him to smile for real, but wasn't sure whether she'd earned it. She felt full of hairline fractures, each one having multiplied until she no longer trusted her strength.

"I'm sorry I didn't tell you the truth," she whispered. "About everything, I mean. It was inconceivably foolish."

Jules sighed. In that moment, Zaria wondered if he was fracturing a little bit, too. "Yeah, it was. But Zaria?"

"Hmm?"

"I'm sorry I compared you to your father. That wasn't fair, and it wasn't true. He never cared about anyone the way you do. Even when he was hunting for the primateria source, he was thinking only of himself. What he could do with it. You've never been like that."

She bit the inside of her lip hard. "Thanks, Jules."

His mouth tilted a little further. It still wasn't a real smile, but it was closer. "Sure. Now, can I ask you something?"

"Of course."

"Why the hell did a scrawny little chap turn up here night before last to tell me you wouldn't be coming home? Did Kane kidnap you?"

With a strangled laugh, Zaria began to tell him about meeting Kane and Fletcher, only to be whisked across the city to steal the pianoforte. About her conversation with Fletcher and the workshop Kane had set up for her. How she'd managed to create quite a bit of primateria but emerged from her stupor certain she was on the brink of death.

She didn't tell Jules about the kiss, though. She couldn't bring herself to say the words aloud, let alone weather the horrified reaction she knew would follow.

"Okay," he said slowly once she had finished. "So nothing we didn't already expect, then. But how are you going to create that key? I've never heard of anything like it."

We, he said. Because it was always the two of them, always together, no matter what the circumstances were. Relief spread through Zaria. That, at least, hadn't changed. "I don't know," she admitted. "I'm worried about that one. It might take me a few attempts."

The problem with primateria was that you had to know what you wanted from it. If it didn't work, you couldn't just stuff it in a different invention. You had to reconsider your plan and start over.

Jules ran a hand through his hair. "Kane is taking advantage of you, and you know it."

"Of course I do," Zaria said dryly. "That's the whole purpose of our agreement. He needs an alchemologist. We're not exactly common."

Jules stood, rage hardening the lines of his face. Zaria thought it was directed at her until he said, "Why the hell would your father teach you alchemology knowing full well what it does to a person? Why would he leave you with all his commissions? What kind of father does that to their only child?"

"It was his life," Zaria said after a brief moment of contemplation. She'd asked herself the same thing countless times. "I think... it was all he had to give me. To ensure I could make a living after he was gone. One that didn't involve the streets or the factories. Not to mention he needed my help while he was alive, especially after Cecile left." The walls around her heart seemed to tighten as she said the dead woman's name.

There was a beat of silence. Jules was breathing heavily, his chest rising and falling in quick succession. When he lifted his chin, his

gaze was sharp. "We need to get you out of London. Away from these commissions and whoever it is that wants to hurt you. And if that means working with Kane…" He shook his head, pressing his fists against his eyes. "I'm in."

"You are?"

"Yeah. Let me help you. For real, this time."

"You don't have to—"

"I want to," he said firmly. "We're positive the necklace is the source?"

She nodded.

"Well then. Someone's going to have to help you run from Kane when you steal that necklace out from under his nose." Jules appeared to relish the thought, a small grin ghosting his lips.

Zaria returned it, but his words made her think. Would Kane be desperate enough to get the necklace that he would be willing to kill her for it? Willing to kill Jules if he got in the way?

She already knew the answer. Nothing would stop Kane from doing whatever it took if he thought Fletcher's life was on the line. He'd already made that exceedingly clear. Would *she* be willing to kill *him*, though, if it came down to it? If it was her life or Kane's?

She didn't know. And that was both very stupid and very dangerous.

"It's going to be tricky," she warned Jules. "Ward threatened Fletcher's life if Kane doesn't bring him the necklace. Kane won't let it go easily."

Jules grimaced. "We'll just have to outsmart him, then."

Zaria spent the next two days in a blur of creation. And this time, she brought Jules with her.

She returned to Cecile's old workshop as promised, first completing the aleuite explosives, then the nonlethal ammunition Kane had requested. The latter was tricky: Primateria existed only in a certain form, and attempting to dilute its effects rather than exacerbate them was relatively foreign terrain to Zaria. Next, she worked on the atomizing adhesive, which would disintegrate the window.

Jules was by her side for much of it, and although she still refused to teach him to create primateria, she did show him how she created the inventions themselves. Soon he was handing her the tools and pieces she needed, and was even mixing chemicals with careful precision. He was more of a watch-and-learn type of person, which was a relief, because verbal explanations weren't Zaria's strong suit. It was slow work, mainly because he forced Zaria to pause whenever illness seemed to be creeping up on her, but in the end, it cut back on time spent dry heaving in the corner of the room.

Kane never showed up personally, and she didn't stop to think about why that might be. She was too busy being relieved. The last thing she needed was him distracting her from the tasks at hand.

On the last day before the Exhibition, Zaria came to the workshop alone. Jules had been needed at the pawnshop, and she'd told him she wanted to add the finishing touches to her inventions. In reality, she still had one last bit of primateria to create: the one that would finally make her parautoptic key work.

She hoped. She'd made several attempts so far, and none left her with enough confidence that she felt prepared to pass the key on to Kane. The problem, naturally, was that she had no way to test it. She was relying on a combination of guessing and gut instinct, but there was no way to be certain the thing would work when the time came.

Zaria took an unsteady breath, staring at the materials on the table in front of her. The past few days had left her worse off than she cared for Jules to know. She scarcely ate, and when she did, her body rejected it. Sleep was a hard-won thing, but once she found it, it was a struggle to rise again. More than once she'd emerged from the fog of creation forgetting where she was. Every so often, she would press a hand to the center of her chest, anticipating—and fearing— that she might feel the very moment when her heart decided to quit altogether.

And yet here she was, lighting a candle one last time. Blood already beaded on her arm, the pain of the cut lost in the agony that radiated through the rest of her body. Zaria let it drip into the flame. Her heart stuttered, off-kilter in a way that was becoming disturbingly familiar. Sweat beaded on her brow. She added the soulsteel with shaking hands and bit down on her tongue so hard that she tasted iron and salt.

Then she let go.

With all the practice she'd had this week, it should have been getting easier. And it was—at least in the beginning. She pictured her intentions with ease. The rush came shortly after, but the light that usually accompanied it was dimmer. Perhaps it was only Zaria's imagination, but darkness seemed to be growing, expanding inside of her. She clung to the fleeting high as she searched wildly for the hook, for the thing that would yank her back to the surface, but her mindscape was as dark and blank as a dreamless sleep.

She was drowning.

Even with her eyes closed, dizziness managed to take hold. It was the kind of dizziness that sent down lurching up and up lurching down, and there was only that horrible blankness as it spun and spun and spun around her.

Then there was nothing.

ZARIA

There was heat against her face.

Zaria squinted, then opened her eyes little by little as she tried to make sense of her surroundings. Cold ground. Paneled walls. She was lying on the floor of the workshop, head tilted to the side as she waited for it to stop spinning.

The warmth on her face disappeared, replaced by a lightly stinging tap. Zaria scowled, turning her head, and looked right into the bone-white face of Kane Durante.

"Are you *slapping* me awake?"

At least he had the grace to look abashed. "That wasn't a slap. I mean—I didn't know what else to do."

Though he'd quickly rearranged his expression, Zaria hadn't missed the flash of real, unmitigated concern there. She studied him more closely. He wore a white shirt unbuttoned at the throat, his hair slick as always. His face was a mess, though: Vicious bruising shadowed one cheek, and the skin around his left eyebrow had split. His upper lip was slightly swollen, and the shadows beneath his eyes seemed to have multiplied since she had seen him last. He looked as exhausted as she felt.

Nausea hit her like a gut punch, and she reeled away, retching. Kane recoiled, but nothing came up.

Stupid. Embarrassing. Zaria wiped her mouth with the back of her hand. "Can I help you with something?"

"You look like hell."

"You're one to talk. What happened to your face? Finally piss off the wrong person?"

The look he gave her was odd. "Don't worry about me. Is this because of the work you've been doing?"

"I'm not worried. And yes, as a matter of fact." Zaria gestured to the table, attempting at the same time to push herself to her feet. Kane reached out as if to help her, but then his arm snapped back to his side. Smart. "There's a reason not many people practice alchemology."

"You said it requires sacrifice."

"It does."

"And what exactly are you sacrificing?" he asked, watching as she finally managed to stand.

It had been easier not to think of Kane when she wasn't looking at him. Embarrassment flooded her like poison. She could remember how he felt against her, how he *tasted*, and it made her palms sweaty.

"Currently? My patience."

"Hmm." Kane turned away, pacing a slow semicircle around the worktable. For someone who must have arrived to find her unresponsive on the ground, he was relatively unruffled. He came to a halt, forefinger trailing over the tools she'd abandoned, and said, "Have you finished?"

Zaria pressed her dry lips together. "Yes, actually."

"And you didn't think to come and get me?"

"I was *unconscious*."

"Right." He smiled, but the shape of it was grim. "You cut it close, the grand opening being tomorrow and all."

It felt like a jab, and Zaria bristled. Thank goodness Kane couldn't keep his mouth shut, so she was forced to remember all the reasons she disliked him. It didn't matter how lovely and dangerous he looked in white, or how one side of his mouth creased whenever he grinned. It was a facade. A mask he used to trick people into doing what he wanted.

Zaria could only hope the confidence he stowed behind it would be his downfall.

"No matter," he said smoothly. "Let's drop it off, then, shall we?"

"Drop *what* off?"

Kane arched a brow. "Your handy inventions. Unless you'd planned to carry all this into the Exhibition in broad daylight."

Zaria hadn't planned anything of the sort. She hadn't truly thought about it. How *were* they going to get all this into the Crystal Palace? Aleuite explosives were small, but they weren't exactly inconspicuous, contained in fist-size vials as they were—and that wasn't even considering the other items.

"I suppose you have a plan for that," she said.

"I told you before that I do."

"Are you finally going to tell me what it is?"

Kane splayed his fingers on the surface of the worktable, considering them rather than looking at her. "You'll find out shortly. Now, do you have the key?"

Slightly apprehensive, Zaria handed him the final version of the parautoptic key. Kane's face tightened as he turned it over. She knew why: It looked distressingly ordinary. The handle was a little wider than most, designed to accommodate the primateria, but otherwise it could have been any old key.

"It should self-adjust to fit the parautoptic lock," she told Kane, whose frown deepened.

"Should?"

"It wasn't as though I had anything to test it on. You said yourself the only locks of its kind are displayed in the Exhibition."

He dragged his index finger along the key's metal bits, counting them. When he had ascertained there were fifteen, he said, "It better work."

Zaria straightened, suddenly defensive, though she had the same reservations. Her heart thrummed unsteadily. "How about *thank you*?"

"Thank you," Kane snapped. "Now help me gather this up."

He was worried, Zaria realized as she obliged. Worried something would go wrong and that Fletcher's life would be in jeopardy. He didn't want to dwell on the prospect of failure or allow for a margin of error.

That was all very well. She felt the same.

It was imperative that they succeeded.

To Zaria's confusion, Kane's plan involved leading her to the warehouse where they'd stashed the pianoforte.

"What are we doing *here*?" she demanded as he beckoned her inside, the heavy door giving a plaintive creak. Kane moved as if he'd

forgotten her presence: swiftly, a little too quietly, though he didn't seem to be trying for stealth. He ignored her question, leading her over to the instrument. At some point he must have covered it with a sheet, which he removed now with a flourish.

Zaria stared at him in confusion. "Are you going to play?"

Kane's grin was a wry, crooked sort of thing. "No."

Before she could ask, he forced the top of the pianoforte open, revealing the inner workings. Then he set the bag he'd been carrying inside.

"Now you," he said.

Zaria continued to stare. It must have begun to rain, because the pattering of drops against the tin roof abruptly drowned out her thoughts.

"Go ahead." Kane gestured into the pianoforte, indicating that she should copy him, and all at once, the pieces clicked into place.

"Oh my God," Zaria said. "You're Trojan horsing."

"That's not a verb."

"But you *are*, aren't you?" She walked around to the other side of the instrument, shaking her head in disbelief. No matter how she tried, she couldn't fathom how Kane planned to use a *pianoforte* to make everything they needed for the theft more accessible.

His upper lip curled. "If you insist, then yes. I am *Trojan horsing*. But don't worry, they're expecting it."

"Expecting what? And *who* is expecting it?"

"The Royal Commission."

Zaria couldn't abide his relaxed stance. The way he spoke in riddles and looked at the pianoforte instead of making eye contact. She was sure he'd already stopped thinking about the kiss—doubtless he believed he had her right where he wanted her.

Her cheeks burned at the prospect, but she kept her mouth shut.

Let Kane think whatever he wanted. Let him imagine her capable of truly falling for him. Let him underestimate her.

"The Royal Commission," she echoed, not comprehending. "What do they have to do with anything?"

Kane buttoned his jacket farther up his neck, flipping the collar to hide his tattoo. "They're expecting J. S. Garrett's contribution to the Broadwood & Sons display."

"Could I have that in English?"

"J. S. Garrett"—he pointed at himself—"was left a mess of expensive items when his father died. One of those items was this pianoforte."'

Zaria's brows shot up. "You can't seriously think you'll be allowed to enter it in the Exhibition."

"Oh, but I do. I just have to get it past the expert." Kane glanced down at his ever-present pocket watch. "I'd better go fetch them. If my information is correct, they're meeting nearby."

"*What* expert?" Zaria hurled the question at his retreating back as he made for the exit. "And who's meeting nearby?"

"Don't move," he called. "I'll be back shortly."

He was gone before she could argue, leaving her alone in the dim light with only an instrument for company.

Insufferable. For someone who considered her a crucial aspect of his plan, Kane certainly wasn't concerned with letting her in on it.

The minutes slid past as Zaria paced the floor, her steps echoing through the cavernous room. She wished she could have brought Jules along today; Kane was taking up too much space in her head. Hell, he was taking up too much space in her life.

It seemed like no time at all before he was back, accompanied by two well-dressed older men Zaria didn't recognize. Both glanced around the warehouse as if perturbed, taking in the high-beamed ceiling and wide expanse of unused space.

"It's in here?" one of the men said, brightening as he caught sight of Zaria and the pianoforte. "Ah! This must be your wife."

"Yes," Kane said, shrugging at Zaria behind the first man's back as the second one trailed a finger over the ivory keys. She shook her head in disbelief. "Anyway, what do you think, Mister Quincy?"

Quincy withdrew his hand. "Beautiful. Excellent craftsmanship, at least to my untrained eye. If it's what you say it is—"

"It is. I told Mister Roberts all about it."

The first man—Roberts, presumably—nodded. "The pianoforte Chopin practiced on before his last concert at Guildhall, nearly three years ago now. I'm sure it will make a fine addition to the Broadwood & Sons display. Of course, I'm not an expert."

Zaria tried not to react. They'd stolen this pianoforte from a recently deceased widow, and Kane was trying to say it had been played by Chopin? He was bold—she'd give him that. Bold, but possibly mad.

"I assume you brought one?" Kane said smoothly. "An expert, that is."

Quincy nodded. He was a stout little man, spectacles poised on the edge of his nose, facial hair obscuring his mouth. "Yes, yes. As I'm sure you can understand, the commission relies upon third-party expertise. Someone from Guildhall should be here shortly. He should be able to confirm that this is, in fact, the instrument you claim."

Horror settled in the pit of Zaria's stomach. She chanced a sideways look at Kane, but he appeared unconcerned. Why wasn't he concerned? Any so-called expert would know at once that he was lying.

"Speak of the devil," Roberts said, turning toward the entrance as a shadow loomed in the doorway. "Here's Mister Walsh now."

Zaria mimicked him, tension in every part of her body. Walsh was tall, broad shouldered, and something about the way he moved struck her as vaguely familiar. When he removed his hat, lifting his head, she understood why.

"Lovely to meet you," Quincy said to Walsh, who was, in fact, Fletcher Collins wearing an expensive suit.

Because *of course* it was.

Fletcher offered a tight-lipped smile, shaking Quincy's hand with a delicate air that was very unlike him. "Honored to be here. I'm rather short on time, though, so—is this the instrument?" After releasing Quincy, he clasped his hands behind his back, performing a slow walk around the pianoforte.

"So I hear." Roberts gestured to Kane. "This is Mister Garrett, whose late father was in possession of it."

Fletcher nodded thoughtfully. "It's definitely a Broadwood pianoforte. Recently made, rarely used." To Kane, he said, "A collector or a musician?"

Kane came to stand beside him, maintaining the distance of two people not yet well acquainted. "My father? Only a collector."

They were good at this. Eerily good.

Zaria tried not to be offended that Fletcher ignored her entirely. He placed his fingers over the keys, plunked out a chord that resounded through the warehouse, and nodded again. After that, he bent at the waist, squinting at what was surely the manufacturer's mark on the front of the instrument. He walked around to the other side, brow furrowed. "A collector's piece indeed. It's in excellent shape."

"Exhibition-worthy shape, though?" Quincy demanded. His

voice was rather nasal, Zaria noted for the first time. "We're tight on space, as I'm sure you can imagine."

Roberts held up a hand, silencing his partner. "More important, is it the instrument Mister Garrett claims? No offense intended." This last sentence was directed at Kane. Turning back to Fletcher, he said, "Mister Garrett believes it to be the instrument Chopin rehearsed on prior to his last concert. If that's the case, it would have stood in your practice hall a few years back."

Fletcher chuckled. "This is precisely the pianoforte Mister Garrett says it is. And frankly, gentlemen, I would consider it an offense if you *didn't* include it in the Exhibition."

Roberts's brows ascended toward his hairline, a feat considering how far it had receded. "Is that so? Well then. It's a late addition, to be sure, but consider it done. We'll have movers pick it up this evening."

"Excellent." Kane grinned broadly. "My father would be thrilled to know someone besides him will finally be able to appreciate the instrument's splendor. Wouldn't you agree, my darling?"

It took Zaria a moment to realize he was addressing her. "Oh— yes. Positively thrilled."

Quincy and Roberts each shook Kane's hand once again, nodded in Zaria's direction, then made their way to the exit. Roberts threw a glance over his shoulder at Fletcher, as if waiting for him to join them.

"Mister Walsh," Kane said loudly as Fletcher feigned walking away, "I'd love for you to stay a moment longer, should you be willing to let me pick your brain."

"Of course," Fletcher said, and his assent must have satisfied Quincy and Roberts, because the next moment they had disappeared. He blew out a breath. "It worked."

Zaria felt her shoulders relax as Kane said, "I knew it would."

She swatted him on the arm, barely hard enough to sting, but he scowled at her as though it had.

"The hell was that for?"

"What do you *think*?" she shot back. "You're lucky I happen to be half-decent at improvisation. Why can't you explain anything ahead of time?"

Kane blinked, apathetic. "We've been through this. Had I told you the plan beforehand, you would have gotten in your head about it."

"That's not true." The response leapt from her tongue automatically.

"The *important* thing," Fletcher said, shooting Kane a pointed look, "is that it worked. Now I only have to hope those two don't recognize me at the Exhibition."

Kane gave a flick of his wrist. "Even if they happen across you, which is unlikely, they won't make the connection. Nobody pays attention to what a copper looks like—they only see the uniform." He clapped his hands together, his energy abruptly shifting. "In any case, I'd say we're ready."

Fletcher flashed a mischievous grin, but Zaria felt her stomach hollow out.

One day and one chance.

That was all she had.

28

KANE

Later that evening, Kane, Fletcher, Zaria, and Jules all sat around the table in Kane and Fletcher's living area.

Perhaps it was the enormity of what tomorrow would bring, but Kane felt as if most of the tension had faded. Jules and Zaria sat on one side of the table, he and Fletcher on the other. Everyone watched him. Waiting for him to outline the plan one final time.

Zaria's eyes met Kane's through the candlelight. Her hair was loose around her shoulders, waves framing her jaw and collarbone. She still looked rather sickly, skin pale and cheekbones hollow, but her gaze was unflinching as ever. Kane could still taste the panic he'd felt upon finding her unresponsive on the floor of the workshop. It had risen in the back of his throat like bile, bitter and gag inducing. He couldn't lose her when they were so close to pulling off the heist. He needed her expertise. He needed her intelligence.

He needed to kiss her again.

He wasn't finished with her. Not even close. But Zaria Mendoza was not—could not be—for him. Especially when he was going to betray her so very soon.

What if you simply gave her what you promised? An especially frustrating corner of Kane's mind kept posing the question. He could steal the rest of the jewelry, he supposed, and avoid going back on his deal with Zaria, but it was just too risky. His focus was on saving Fletcher—that was the reason they were doing this. He wasn't going to thrust that into jeopardy by stealing the entire goddamned Waterhouse display. A missing necklace could be overlooked, but a missing exhibit could not. He'd already sold the jewels they'd stolen from the widow, having never intended for them to enter the walls of the Crystal Palace.

What did it matter if Zaria hated him more than she already did?

"Okay," he said when he could bear the silence no longer. "We go to the palace shortly before noon tomorrow—that's when the queen and prince consort are meant to be arriving, and they're each to make a speech. That'll draw the attention of the masses. We'll pay our fare like everyone else and enter through the main turnstiles. Fletcher will already be inside, having gotten Price to place him as close to the Waterhouse display as possible. The queen's entrance is his cue to plant the atomizing adhesive on the window."

Fletcher nodded once, his mouth a straight line. "Price knows the plan. He's not going to interfere."

Kane didn't expect him to. They'd made it very clear what was at stake should the sergeant decide to turn on them. "Once we get inside, things might get dicey. I wouldn't be surprised if tens of thousands of people attend. In a way, that's a positive, because it means more distractions. Nobody will be paying attention to us. Zhao, are you in, or are you only here for the hospitality?"

This he threw at Jules, who was surveying him with considerable distaste. The boy was fiercely loyal, evidenced by the fact that he was here at all, but he made no secret of the fact that he detested Kane. Jules appeared to be getting along with Fletcher, at least; the two had shaken hands when Jules and Zaria arrived, while Jules had avoided Kane's outstretched arm like the plague. Kane frankly didn't care whether Julian Zhao liked him or not, but it was irritating to be the only one making an effort.

"I'm in," Jules said stiffly.

"And if anything goes sideways," Zaria said, chiming in for the first time. "Jules and I won't be sticking around." She placed an easy hand on Jules's forearm. Kane's eyes latched on to it, that expression of obvious ease between the two of them. Acid stung the back of his throat, and he struggled to choke it down. Though he knew Zaria's relationship with Jules was purely platonic, a petty, immature part of him resented the other boy. But what was the point? Kane would do what he needed to, and then Zaria would be gone, never again speaking his name unless it was to curse it.

"Nothing is going to go sideways," he snapped, an edge to his voice that hadn't been there prior. "I'm confident we'll get into the Crystal Palace with no issues. Once inside, we obviously have to seek out the pianoforte. We know where the Broadwood exhibit is going to be, and I've mapped out the most efficient route. I've allotted fifteen minutes to get from point A to point B." He turned to address Zaria, his stomach flipping when she arched a brow at him. "Ideally, we get there before the queen's speech commences. Once we get the explosives, you and Jules will take them, and I'll deal with the rest. Meanwhile, Fletcher will ensure he's in position.

"When the queen starts speaking, you'll release a single vial of the aleuite. Fletcher will start to evacuate everyone away from the

Waterhouse display, and as he does, you'll release the second vial. We'll have to find a place where you and Jules can stay out of sight. Once the smoke spreads, that's when I swoop in to start picking the lock. All being well, it should only take me a few minutes to get to the necklace." Six minutes, to be precise. "I'll hand the rest of the jewelry off to you and Jules," Kane added quickly, aware that he had almost forgotten to mention the other items. Luckily, neither Zaria nor Jules appeared to catch his slip.

Kane wouldn't pass the jewelry off, though. He would utilize the fog to lose Zaria and Jules, escaping with Fletcher and the necklace as fast as possible. Once they figured out he had swindled them, they were welcome to linger and attempt to take the rest of the Waterhouse jewels, but he didn't envy their chances of success.

"At this point, the thirty-six minutes required for the atomizing adhesive to react should have passed. The glass of the window will have begun to disintegrate, but nobody should notice with the aleuite smoke. The moment we're outside, you release the third vial. We blend into the panicking crowd and disappear."

"It sounds simple when you put it like that," Zaria said, a note of dubiety in her tone.

Kane inclined his head. "It is. As long as everyone sticks to the plan, we shouldn't encounter any issues." At least they'd better not. There were only two spare minutes for anything he hadn't foreseen.

"I don't think it sounds simple at all," Jules grumbled. "There seems to be a lot of guesswork going into this."

Kane clicked his tongue. "Contrary to popular belief, Master Zhao, I am tragically unable to predict the future." The words came out more harshly than he'd expected—his voice twisted them into a drawl. "Now, would you stop scowling at me like I burned down your fucking house?"

Jules's eyebrows shot up, his thin shoulders tensing. For a moment, Kane wondered if the boy would rise, but he only said, "I wouldn't put it past you."

The words were laced with vitriol, and they rolled off Kane's back like nothing. He allowed a smirk to grace the sides of his mouth, then caught Zaria glaring at him in his periphery.

Coward.

Fletcher put a hand on Kane's arm, leaning across the table to address Jules. "I know it's stressful, but if we all stick to the plan, there's no reason it shouldn't work. Try to trust us."

He sounded so genuine, so sincere, that the crease between Jules's brows smoothed over. "I trust you well enough. It's *him* I don't trust."

That was obviously directed at Kane, who rolled his eyes. "Look, I don't want to get caught, and I'm assuming you don't, either. You can trust me enough to ensure that doesn't happen."

"He makes a point there," Zaria said, sharing a meaningful look with Jules that Kane was unable to interpret. Irritation tugged at his insides.

"All right. Any more questions?" It came out sounding like a threat, and he wasn't surprised when nobody said a word. Despite Jules's apprehension and Zaria's incessantly tapping fingers, Kane knew they had placed their confidence in him. They had no other option.

"We'll be going, then," Zaria murmured, rising to her feet in a single fluid movement. Kane stood at the same time, unable to help himself.

"Wait," Fletcher said, suddenly serious. "There's something you two need to know."

Zaria hesitated. Though it was Fletcher who had spoken, she stared unblinkingly at Kane as if daring him to elaborate.

Kane stared back. *God fucking damn it, Fletcher.* This—telling Zaria about Ward—felt riskier than everything they planned to do tomorrow. If she decided to back out, they were in trouble.

She won't, Fletcher had assured him yesterday when they'd discussed this very issue yet again. *She's not like that. She's more determined than she is afraid. And once we get Ward what he wants, he'll forget all about her.*

His friend had better be right.

"Whatever it is you don't want to say," Jules put in, eyeing Kane as if he could see right through him, "just say it."

Kane gritted his teeth until his jaw hurt. He cut a sidelong glance to Fletcher, who gave a marginal incline of his head. Finally, he locked gazes with Zaria. "It's Ward."

Confusion marred her delicate features. "What?"

"Ward. He's the one who wants you dead. I had no idea, and I still don't know the reason."

Zaria blinked. Kane got the sense she was fighting to wipe her expression clean. "How can you be sure?"

"He told me."

Jules took a step forward. "You son of a—"

Fletcher leapt between him and Kane, laughably out-sizing them both. "It's the truth," his friend said, his Irish accent more pronounced now that he was riled up. "Kane only just found out. Neither of us had any clue. We're telling you now so you go into tomorrow knowing all the risks."

Zaria still hadn't looked away from Kane. He was almost positive they were thinking the same thing: that what happened at the church *had* been because of him, no matter how indirectly. A muscle ticked in Zaria's brow, and she lifted her chin. "Why tell me at all? What if I decide it's not worth it?"

"You won't." It was Fletcher who had been convinced she wouldn't back out, but now, looking her directly in the eye, Kane knew it was true. She needed this. It was her only hope of saving the pawnshop, of saving Jules. Something soured in his stomach. When Zaria came away from this with nothing, there was a good chance Jules would be forced to join Ward's crew. It was unfortunate, but so what? He wouldn't necessarily die. And better Jules than Fletcher.

Zaria scoffed. "You think I have no sense of self-preservation."

"No," Kane said. "I just know you want it too badly."

She exchanged another look with Jules, who looked about ready to do something violent and inadvisable. When she spoke again, her voice held a note of fear. How odd that Kane was familiar enough with it to notice. "You really don't know why Ward wants me dead?"

He shook his head, fighting to ensure it looked genuine. Why was it so much harder to lie to her? "All I got from Ward is that he hated your father and seems to think you can't be trusted. That's why those men had their faces covered—they knew I would recognize them. As long as you stay with Fletcher and me, though, we can protect you. Anyone who works for Ward knows better than to mess with me."

It wasn't wholly true—Abe Walker had tried, after all. But Kane had established what would happen to anyone else who made the same mistake.

"We just thought you needed to know," Fletcher said seriously. "It's your life, after all."

Zaria shot Kane a hard, meaningful look. He felt laid bare by the accusation in her dark eyes but forced himself to nod.

"Well," Jules said, sounding vaguely disgusted. "I suppose it's too late to back out now anyway." He leveled a finger at Kane. "Count yourself lucky that we plan to get the hell out of this city after

tomorrow. Otherwise, there's no way we'd be risking our necks for this plot."

Kane said nothing to that. He led Jules and Zaria to the door and leaned against the frame, arms crossed.

"Good night," Zaria said coolly, sweeping past him.

Almost of its own volition, Kane's hand snapped out and took hold of her arm.

She stared down at it, frozen, before her eyes snapped up to meet his. Jules was already a few strides away, a lone figure against the night.

"We need to talk." Kane forced the words out with difficulty. They sounded strange. Guttural. "Alone."

Zaria snatched her arm away, a tendon straining in her throat. "We have nothing to talk about."

"I think we both know that's not true."

The evening wind was vicious, and it whipped Kane's collar away from his neck as he waited for Zaria's response. He could feel Fletcher's eyes on his back from inside the house, but he didn't care. By now Jules had backtracked and waited, immobile, in the middle of the street. Tension pulsed in the air.

And yet Kane didn't know what he would have said. What he would have told her, what difference it would have made, had Zaria not turned away. Had she not scoffed in the face of his last statement, the ghost of a bitter smile curling her lips. Perhaps he would have asked if she regretted it, that kiss. Perhaps he would have told her that *he* didn't. Perhaps he would have apologized in advance.

He might have told her something that surprised them both if she hadn't said merely, "Good night, Kane."

By then, it was too late.

29

ZARIA

Zaria spent that night thinking about the Exhibition. The more she did, the more her memory twisted the feats of industry into a garish, improbable maze. She had a single chance to ensure everything went according to plan—both Kane's plan and her own. In theory, it all seemed easily accomplished.

That was what worried her.

Zaria had seen that same worry reflected on Jules's face when she bid him good night. He hadn't asked about the awkwardness with Kane, and she was glad for it. She didn't have an explanation.

We have nothing to talk about.

I think we both know that's not true.

She refused to dwell on what Kane and Fletcher had said about Ward. Partially because being hunted by the kingpin was such a terrifying prospect, her mind couldn't seem to process it. It didn't seem real. Mostly, though, she couldn't think about how Kane *was* responsible for everything that had happened. For all the times she'd nearly been killed. If she thought about *that*, she wouldn't be able to focus on the role she needed to play.

So she fought to pretend none of it had happened, focusing instead on how tomorrow would be their last day in Devil's Acre. Soon, so soon, they would be free of London. Away from Alexander Ward and the terrible boy he both adored and tormented.

She slept restlessly, tossing and turning until the slow creep of dawn dragged her from her bed. Several hours later, she and Jules left the pawnshop in an unnatural silence, anticipation and foreboding like a taut wire between them.

They met Kane near the edge of the slum. It was a disarmingly nice day, though gray clouds threatened in the distance. Zaria wore an expensive-looking deep-red dress she'd procured from the pawnshop; its rightful owner wouldn't miss it before redemption day came back around. It was tight in the waist and lower in the front than she generally preferred, but at least she looked well-off. Jules, too, had managed to dig up a nice suit and hat.

As always, Kane looked impeccable. With his long coat and slicked-back hair, he looked like a businessman of questionable morals. The bruising on his face was worse today, his eye shadowed black, but he didn't shy from Zaria's stare as she neared. Their gazes locked, warring in the moment before they both glanced away.

"Good morning," he murmured, giving her and Jules each a once-over. "So you two *can* clean up relatively well."

Zaria supposed it was as close to a compliment as Kane ever gave. Rather than answering, she studied the lines of his injured face, searching for evidence of stress.

But Kane didn't appear nervous. His expression was cool and as undisturbed as still water, his shoulders free of obvious tension.

Zaria wished she could say the same. The sweat on her palms lingered no matter how many times she wiped them on her dress, and there was a tension in her stomach she couldn't dispel. Anticipation was a relentless thing. All she wanted was to get to the Exhibition and for this to be finally, mercifully over.

"You finally gonna tell us how you copped a mouse?" Jules said, indicating Kane's face. "I want to send the other guy a gift."

There was a note of teasing in his tone, though. Kane gave a sardonic smile, not bothering to bite back. He turned to Zaria. "You ready?"

She wasn't sure how to answer that. No, she wasn't ready. She wanted to return home, sink back into bed, and never emerge. But since that didn't seem a viable option, she said, "Yes."

The city was busier than she had ever seen it, and yet *busy* was a perilous understatement. The closer they drew to Hyde Park, the more people flooded the streets. The air was dense with palpable excitement, and it was impossible to move without being shuffled and shoved. The patrons were young and old, rich and working class, Londoners and not. For months, fearmongering gossips had warned of foreigners overtaking the city in their eagerness to visit the Exhibition, which made Zaria roll her eyes—not only were the claims loathsome, but today it was clear that most patrons were in fact British, their familiar accents audible all around her.

And it wasn't only people who occupied the park: An arrangement of oddities that must have been exhibits spilled out onto the lush grass. An enormous crowd had formed at the southern entrance, waiting to gain entry through one of the seven turnstiles, and intrigued onlookers gathered on balconies and clustered in the windows of nearby houses, watching the chaos unfold.

For a moment, Zaria forgot to be bitter, overwhelmed as she was. She wanted to see *everything*, but at the same time, she wanted nothing more than to avoid everyone in the vicinity. It was all just so *much*. Her breath caught in her chest, and she became jittery with discomfort. A light wind carried with it the stench of sweat combined with unnecessarily strong perfume. Zaria wrinkled her nose as a baby wailed nearby. It seemed like everyone in London was here and then some. Everyone who could afford it had worn their finest gowns and suits, and she was surprised to see that despite the diversity of the crowd in the park, those in the official line were overwhelmingly upper-class.

"I'm underdressed," she said to Kane under her breath.

He shook his head. "You're fine. Opening day is for those purchasing season tickets. The price will go down over the next week, and then more of the general public will be able to attend."

"I can't afford a season ticket!"

"That won't be a problem." He led her farther into the anarchic press of bodies, and it took an infuriatingly long time to reach an entry point. Zaria positioned herself as a buffer between Kane and Jules, relieved to be with people she knew. None of them spoke, and if they'd tried, they would surely have been forced to yell—the air around them hummed with the indecipherable cacophony of a thousand voices. Zaria's fingers fluttered at her sides, and without looking down at her, Kane grabbed them lightly in his own. It seemed an almost automatic response, and she stared at his hand on hers, as thankful for the grounding pressure of his touch as she was perplexed by it.

"Master Wright!"

A voice boomed above the rest, causing them all to turn. It took Zaria a moment to recall that Master Wright was, in fact, Kane. They watched a portly man shove his way over to them, the sheer magnitude of his confidence causing people to leap out of his path.

How in the world had he managed to pick Kane out among all these people?

Kane had already plastered a smile on his face. "Mister Cole! An honor to see you again, sir."

Right. Henry Cole. Zaria straightened, and beside her, Jules did the same.

"Don't tell me you're waiting in line," Cole said jovially. He sounded in much better spirits than the previous time they'd met. Perhaps it was the excitement of opening day, but somewhere along the line he'd evidently decided Kane deserved his respect. "At this rate, you risk missing the speeches. Follow me."

Zaria looked to Kane in dismay. They were working with a tight timeline and needed to get to the pianoforte before anything else. If she thought Kane would politely decline, however, she was disappointed. He smiled, managing to hide the tension she'd seen in his jaw only moments before.

"Mister Cole, you're far too kind."

Cole waved a dismissive hand. "Please, it's of no consequence!"

Zaria grabbed Kane's arm as he made to walk away, and he pivoted, frowning. "What?"

"We can't follow Cole around," she hissed. "We don't have time for that."

"We're skipping the queue, aren't we?"

"He'll talk forever if you let him."

Kane rolled his eyes, pulled away, and kept walking.

"Son of a bitch," Jules muttered under his breath. "Do we follow him?"

Zaria twined her fingers together, watching Kane and Cole navigate the crowd. "I don't think we have much of a choice."

Together they skirted the hordes of waiting patrons, making their

way to the turnstiles. Zaria fixed her gaze steadfastly on the back of Kane's head, trying not to lose sight of him while also attempting not to trip. She stepped on more than one foot, her mouth shut tightly against the stench of far too many bodies, but she caught up to Kane just as Cole escorted him through the entrance.

"Your fiancée, Master Wright!" Cole boomed, waving Zaria through. "And your—?"

"Friend," Kane said without missing a beat. "My very dear friend, Julian Sing."

Cole nodded, first to Jules and then to the men standing at the entrance, an indication that their party was with him. "Nice to make your acquaintance, Master Sing."

Jules accepted the fake surname with ease, though his polite smile was strained as he shook Cole's hand.

"You must let us pay," Kane said indulgently as he passed through the turnstile. Zaria arched a brow; he showed no sign of procuring any money. Besides, if they were being offered a free visit, why couldn't he keep his mouth shut? She elbowed him hard in the ribs. In response, or perhaps retaliation, he looped an arm through hers, setting her hand on top of his. Her shoulders stiffened, head spinning with the scent of him.

Cole looked positively affronted by Kane's request. "An apprentice of Charles Fox paying to enter the building he helped create? Absolutely not. I do say," he added, nose crinkling, "what in the world happened to your face?"

Zaria wondered how he hadn't noticed it earlier. But Kane gave an easy grin, a quick roll of his eyes, and said, "Would you believe I found myself in the middle of a pub fight? Too much drink for all parties involved, I'm afraid."

Cole guffawed. "I'd be lying if I said I hadn't had similar experiences."

Kane was good. Zaria didn't know how he managed to be so laid-back or how he read people so easily. She felt like an awkward accessory at his side without the vaguest idea of how to play at charm. Beside her, Jules moved in silence, hands clasped behind his back as Cole led them aimlessly toward the upper level of the Crystal Palace.

Zaria's insides seized. They couldn't make their way to a whole other level—not when everything they needed was on the main floor. Cole's voice faded into the background as excited chatter filled her ears. She caught a partial conversation between two women about when the queen and prince consort would arrive, though it was soon lost beneath the bellow of a wild-haired man with a stern brow.

"A brazen circus of commodity fetishism..."

"Karl, *please*—" the man's companion began, though Zaria didn't hear the rest of his appeal as Kane pulled her away.

They passed displays of beautiful artwork, each brushstroke more intricate than the next, then a working steam engine. A hydraulic press, a whole fire engine, and a number of various locomotives. Zaria skimmed over an array of furs and leathers to fixate on the most beautiful carriage she'd ever seen. It certainly wasn't the type of thing people took out in London's public streets. But her heart hammered in her chest all the while, and she couldn't focus on much of anything. Each beat was a ticking clock.

"Look." Jules grabbed Zaria's elbow, pointing over the balcony to the Exhibition's main entrance. His face was wan, his lips tight. "Is that the queen's procession?"

Zaria followed his gaze and realized he had to be right. Even from a distance, she could see the crowd parting, making way for a woman in an enormous dress with a tall man in black at her side. The queen and the prince consort. Her mouth went dry, and she dug her fingernails into the back of Kane's hand.

He grunted, pulling free of her grasp. Cole noticed, stopping midway through a monologue regarding his opinion of French furniture. "Are you quite all right, Master Wright?"

"Yes." Kane said smoothly. "I think my fiancée is impatient to see the musical instruments, though. There's a Broadwood pianoforte she's been quite enchanted with."

Cole nodded. "Perhaps Master Sing can accompany her? I'd love to engage yourself and Mister Fox, once he arrives."

Kane's mask slipped just enough for Zaria to make out his impatience. It snapped back into place a moment later, though his voice was edged as he said, "I would love that. Unfortunately, Eleanor doesn't get along very well with Master Sing."

Jules rolled his eyes where Cole couldn't see.

"Very well," Cole said, clicking his tongue and shaking his head in unison. "Women, am I right? I'll be certain to find you later, then."

Kane's grin was snakelike. "You do that."

Zaria waited until they were a distance away from the man before rounding on Kane. "Are you *trying* to waste time?"

He procured what looked like a small bronze coin, holding it between two fingers.

"What is that?" Jules asked before Zaria could.

"Exhibitor's medal," Kane said, handing it to Zaria. Sure enough, one side of the coin was inscribed with the word EXHIBITOR set against a tiny rendering of the globe. The other was a side-profile likeness of the prince consort. "Cole and the rest of the commission are giving them to the exhibitors that impress them most. He had them in his pocket."

Zaria frowned. "And that's why you let him hold us up?"

"I let him hold us up because he's the prince consort's adviser, and ignoring him would be rude. But yes, I had also planned for him to find us. You'll notice I'm wearing precisely the same outfit as the last time he saw me, which is useful in triggering someone's recognition. The medal is about to become important." Kane checked his pocket watch before guiding her down the steps leading back to the main floor, one arm outstretched to block patrons converging in the opposite direction. Then he glanced over his shoulder. "Julian, how do you feel about role-play?"

Jules hurried to catch up with them. "What kind of question is that?"

"A simple one." Kane's narrowed gaze swept the area. His hand was warm on the small of Zaria's back. It made her think unwittingly of how he'd skimmed those hands up her rib cage, his lips against her neck.

Wrong, wrong, wrong. In less than an hour, she was going to ruin his life and put Fletcher's in jeopardy. She didn't even *like* Kane. She only liked the way he smelled, the way his body fit against hers, the way his touch made her skin come alive. But she could get that from anyone, couldn't she? Any fool with two hands and a reasonably handsome face would do. It was only that Kane was the first one with the gall to kiss her with the kind of passion that stemmed only from fury. Had it been a regular kiss, Zaria didn't think she would have enjoyed it half as much.

"All right." Kane came to a halt, pressing the medal into Jules's hand. "The pianoforte is right over there." He pointed, though Zaria couldn't see over the crowd. "I suspect the gentleman with the red hair is the representative from Broadwood & Sons. Present this to him as a member of the Royal Commission."

Zaria blinked. "Why can't I distract the exhibitor?"

"There aren't any women on the commission."

"Well, there should be," she snapped.

Kane held up his hands. "You'll get no argument from me. Unfortunately, I don't make the rules. Mendoza, once we get the aleuite, I'll hand the vials off to you. Use the first one as soon as I've gotten everything ready. Fletcher is right"—he pivoted, scouring the hordes of people—"*there.*"

Indeed, Fletcher was tall enough that Zaria could see him standing at the edge of the space a short distance down the corridor. His face was an expressionless mask beneath his officer's hat as he stared out over the crowd. Zaria swallowed. Surely Ward wouldn't *actually* kill him for Kane's failure to steal the necklace, would he?

"Nobody will believe I'm a member of the commission," Jules said. "I don't look rich enough."

Kane gave a disgruntled sigh. "Well, start to believe you're rich enough."

"What does that even mean?"

"Cons only work if you're committed. Believe in your role so sincerely that no one will question you. It's all about the confidence. Believe you're a member of the commission. Believe you're a rich man, and so will everyone else. One thing you need to know about humanity, Master Zhao, is that we're suggestible fools."

Jules thrust his shoulders back, pursing his lips slightly. He adjusted his jacket with a flourish.

"See?" Kane said. "You look richer already."

"I'm trying to imagine I'm as much of an asshole as you."

"Whatever it takes."

All around them, people were beginning to move with considerable haste toward the center of the Exhibition. Zaria stayed as close as possible to the nearby display of a hydraulic press, keen not to be bowled over. Kane, on the other hand, had no such concerns: He stayed put, forcing the other patrons to step around him.

"It must be about time for the queen's speech," Zaria murmured. She had no desire to see the queen or the prince consort; really, she had no desire to see anyone at all. There were altogether too many people here, pushing and shoving and laughing and talking, each one of them unbearable.

"Yes," Kane said. "And *that* is my pianoforte."

He pointed to where a trio of pianos stood accompanied by various other instruments and pieces of furniture. Plush red curtains hung from the rafters on either side, delineating the display from the others nearby. The crowd around them was beginning to thin, but it was still busy enough that Zaria felt a jolt. How the hell were they going to get anywhere near the pianoforte without someone questioning them?

Jules must have had a similar thought, because he said to Kane, "There's no way we're going to pull this off."

Kane waved a hand, effectively shushing him. "Don't be so pessimistic. That'll be the exhibitor"—he pointed to a tall man wearing a coat of scarlet—"and you only need to distract him for all of thirty seconds. Fletcher's right down the corridor, as is the Waterhouse exhibit, so we'll be ready for the next phase."

"What am I supposed to talk to the exhibitor about?"

"You hand him the medal, Julian." Impatience edged into Kane's voice.

"I meant after that!"

Kane looked to Zaria as if appealing for her input. She shrugged. "Ask about the display. I don't know."

Jules chewed his lower lip. Stood up taller again. Narrowed his

eyes. "Okay. I'm a wealthy bastard from the Royal Commission. I can do this."

"Of course you can," Zaria said, having no idea whether it was true.

He loped confidently over to the exhibitor, and she and Kane watched in silence until Jules handed over the medal and the man cracked a smile. She had to admit, it appeared to be going well.

"Come on." Kane's voice was at her ear. He pulled her toward the red curtain at the edge of the exhibit, and together they slunk behind it. The fabric was ruched, which aided in their disappearing act, and Zaria inhaled sharply through her nose as Kane pressed against her.

"Don't," she hissed.

"Don't what?"

"Stand so close."

He pulled back, and she could hear his frown as he said, "I'm just trying to get this done, Mendoza. Though I must say, it's interesting to know where your head is at."

"My head isn't anywhere," she retorted.

Kane's laugh was silent. "Do you regret the kiss, Zaria?"

Zaria, this time. Not *Miss Mendoza*. "Of course I regret it. Don't you?"

There was a beat of quiet. She wondered if she'd offended him or whether he was merely considering her question. Eventually, he said, "Not for the reasons you might think."

"Well, that clears everything up."

He leaned closer, his next words released on a breath. "I like the way you're so determined to hate me even when your body betrays you. It makes things so very interesting."

Cocky bastard. Zaria made a humming sound in the back of her throat, allowing herself to soften into him. She heard his sharp inhalation as she brought *her* lips to *his* ear. "The only one betraying themselves here, Kane Durante, is you."

He backed away, knowing at once what she was referring to. A laugh rumbled in his chest. There wasn't a hint of embarrassment in his voice as he said, "Unyielding as always."

She ignored that, yanking the edge of the curtain aside to reveal the pianoforte. "Eyes on the prize."

30

KANE

KANE COULD SCARCELY REMEMBER FEELING MORE CONFLICT-ing emotions than he did right now. Zaria Mendoza drove him mad in so many ways. In another world, he might have spent the rest of his life following her just to see what she would do next.

But in this world, in less than half an hour, she would never speak to him again. He'd be lucky if she didn't try to kill him.

"Okay," he said to Zaria now. "I'll prop the back of the pianoforte up, and you check inside." Kane put a hand to the gun at his waist. The parautoptic key was just above the weapon, stowed safely within the lining of his coat.

Zaria nodded, expression solemn, and Kane slipped out from behind the curtain.

The pianoforte was only a few steps away, sleek and beautiful. Nobody appeared to be paying attention to him—not yet—but his heart rate kicked up a notch regardless. All around him, countless voices formed a veritable wave of sound, and a few meters away the exhibitor was still in conversation with Jules. All Kane's senses sharpened. This was it.

He beckoned Zaria out of the shadows, then wrapped his hands around the top of the instrument and pushed it open. He'd nearly forgotten how heavy it was. He didn't dare look out at the crowd, afraid that if he met someone's gaze, it might give him away. They were *supposed* to be here, he and Zaria, and he repeated that mantra a half-dozen times before she peered up at him from around the pianoforte, eyes wide and horrified.

"There's nothing in here."

Kane took a steadying inhale. "Okay."

She gaped. "What do you mean, *okay*? Not a single thing about this is okay. Are you sure this is the right piano?"

Was he *sure*? Of course he was sure. They'd dragged it through the streets, for God's sake. Kane would know it anywhere.

"Get over here," he snapped, scouring the area over his shoulder. Mercifully, the exhibitor was still turned away from them. Zaria scooted over to where Kane stood, and he motioned for her to replace his grip with her own. She did so, grunting slightly, and he took the opportunity to peer inside the pianoforte.

Zaria was right. There was nothing in there. Nothing but the dampers surrounded by rows of delicate strings.

Thank goodness.

Indicating for Zaria to transfer the top of the pianoforte back to him, Kane let it slam shut. The sound was deafening.

Zaria looked like a cornered animal. Her face was as white as bone. A number of patrons in the vicinity turned, as did the exhibitor. He broke away from Jules, adjusting his scarlet coat, and stalked toward them.

"Sir, please step *away* from the pianoforte!" the exhibitor implored, wringing his hands. Jules trailed along behind the man, his eyes full of panic.

"My apologies," Kane said calmly. "I only wanted to take a closer look before my performance. Anton Mikhailov." He thrust out a hand before gesturing to Zaria. "And this is Catharina Ivanova, my assistant. I've come to showcase the unmatched tone of the Broadwood. We intended to approach you first, but you were otherwise occupied."

The man gaped before appearing to gather himself, shaking Kane's hand. "Miss Ivanova and Mister Mikhailov, is it? I didn't think the Russians had made it to London. Seems to me I was told their vessels got stuck in the ice."

Zaria scoffed loudly enough that Jules started. "You can have a Russian surname without being *from* Russia, you fool. You offend us both. Now, is this performance going ahead or not?"

Kane worked to hide his bemusement. Regardless of how she might hate it, Zaria *did* work best when she was forced to improvise. She was surprisingly effective under sudden pressure. That, and he hadn't wanted to give too much of his plan away. His conversation with Ward kept replaying in his mind, and he couldn't forget the pure distrust on the kingpin's face whenever he'd spoken Zaria's name.

Kane wanted to trust her entirely. But he was nothing if not what Ward had made him.

The exhibitor looked to Jules, who luckily appeared to remember that he was meant to be a member of the Royal Commission. He gave a curt nod. "I seem to recall it *was* the wish of Broadwood & Sons that people be allowed to showcase the sound of their pianofortes. If Mister Mikhailov claims to have been invited, then let him perform. I can't see why he would lie."

The exhibitor muttered something to himself, procuring a silver timepiece and squinting down at it. "The queen is expected to make her speech at noon. If you're going to play something, you have five minutes."

Kane smiled widely. "I only need four and a half."

Despite having mentally prepared for this, he couldn't seem to relax his muscles. He hadn't played anything in years. Hadn't *wanted* to play anything, knowing it would remind him of his mother. Of her hands on his and the soft spill of notes she coaxed forth on cold nights.

He sat down on the bench. It had been long enough that only a single Chopin piece lived inside him. It was a miracle he still remembered it at all, but somehow it had taken up residence in his very blood, his bones, and he knew that if he only touched his fingers to the ivory keys, it would spill out before he could stop it.

Music was soft, Ward always said. A skill for women. Ironic, really, considering so many of the composers Kane knew were men. The point, though, was that Kane was not soft. He was bladed edges and tapered points. He was not the kind of man who sunk time into practicing music and feeling whatever came along with it.

This was a Broadwood, though. Perhaps not the one Chopin had practiced on, but it didn't make a difference to Kane. All at once he was desperate to touch the keys. To discover whether the music that still lived inside him would emerge sounding the way it did in his head.

So he played.

The piece started out soft, expressive, the notes rising and falling in a series of chromatic tones. The steady, grounded rhythm of the bass clef coaxed memories forth from his fingers. The melody slipped from minor to major, then back again, and when it shifted from the central motif, he found the trills still came easily enough. There were enough repetitive parts that the song didn't get away from him, and his throat tightened as his thoughts slipped away with the alternating tempo, taking him elsewhere.

He was in the living room in his old home, listening to this very piece. *Underappreciated*, his mother always said, because the nocturne was far from the best-known. *But I like the way this one feels so delicate. It leaves room to breathe.* Kane's mother always incorporated rubato, or freedom of tempo, in the way she believed Chopin had always intended. *The left hand stays steady, but the right hand can dance.*

And Kane did let it dance, slowing as he approached the run and adjusting the speed as he worked his way through. When the end came, it was quiet. So very quiet. It snuck up on him, and he scarcely realized he had reached the final chords until his hands stilled.

A small crowd had gathered, Kane realized with a start, and the exhibitor had tears in his eyes. The man clapped his hands together as Kane rose. He didn't know what to do. He felt as if he were in a dream, or perhaps trapped nearly a decade in the past. He rose, stalking past Zaria and Jules until he came to a halt at the exhibitor.

"Stunning," the exhibitor said hoarsely. "And one of my favorite pieces. You know, many performers of Chopin elect—"

"Nocturne in E-flat Major, yes," Kane said. "I'll admit I'm partial to a minor key."

His hands were shaking. He didn't know why. He squeezed them into fists in the hope that nobody would notice. Zaria cut him a sideways glance, clearly marking his behavior as strange, but she didn't comment on it.

Kane checked his pocket watch. Five minutes to retrieve the items.

He shook the exhibitor's hand again, waving away the man's ongoing slew of compliments. "Thank you for your assistance. We'd really rather be going, else we might miss the queen's speech."

The crowd that gathered during his performance had begun to disperse, and he stalked away from the display of instruments without checking to see whether Zaria and Jules followed.

"Now what?" Jules demanded in a hiss. "Looks to me like you didn't get the explosives."

"Well spotted, Julian. You're really quite astute."

Zaria forced her way to Kane's side, shoulders tense in a way he suspected had nothing to do with the empty pianoforte. Something about this place bothered her, and she cringed every time a particularly loud noise rang out over the crowds. He had the sudden absurd, aggressive desire to shield her from everyone else as she said, "Care to explain whatever the hell *that* was, Kane?"

He scanned their surroundings for a familiar tall figure. "That, my darling, was a nearly flawless performance of Chopin's Nocturne in C-sharp Minor."

"You know full well that's not what I—"

"The pianoforte was inspected upon being transferred here," Kane interrupted her. "The items were discovered and confiscated. And by confiscated, I mean that they were handed over to the police, which was always the plan. When I slammed the lid of the pianoforte, that was the sign for Fletcher to prepare to retrieve the items. From there, he knew he had four and a half minutes to get in and out of the coppers' temporary command center while most of the patrons were distracted by my performance." He inclined his head toward a discreet door a short distance away from the pianoforte exhibit. At the same time, apprehension roiled in the pit of his stomach. "Fletcher was only supposed to need three minutes. He should be here by now."

"What does that mean?" Zaria asked quietly.

Kane could feel her eyes on his face but didn't turn to meet them, knowing any sign of alarm would only set her on edge. He could feel the seconds slipping away, his sanity alongside them. If anything had happened to Fletcher, he was going to raise serious hell.

Tick. Tick.

"I'm going in there," he said.

Zaria stared at him as if he were mad. Beside her, Jules shifted his weight back and forth, performing an impatient little jig in place. "That's a terrible idea. You're not a copper."

Kane ignored them. He was already moving against the current of people, most of whom leapt out of his path. Somewhere, he could hear the echo of a woman's voice rising above the noise—the queen's speech?—and panic gnawed at his insides anew. In the back of his mind, the seconds continued to tick away.

When he reached the curtained-off area surrounding the door, he scowled at the exhibition worker standing guard. "Move."

The man straightened, a furrow appearing between his prominent eyebrows. His outfit marked him as volunteer security—not a member of the Metropolitan Police. "I think not. This is a private—"

Abruptly, Jules was at Kane's side, flashing the exhibitor's medal at the volunteer. For all intents and purposes, it meant absolutely nothing, but he did it with such authority that the man hesitated. He glanced between Jules and Kane with some trepidation. "I don't—"

"Oh, for God's sake," Kane barked, shoving the man aside and shouldering the door open.

Beyond it was a dark space that was evidently being used by the Metropolitan Police. He scanned the array of uniforms on makeshift racks, the rows of gleaming boots, before his eyes adjusted and he picked out three figures in the dim. One he recognized immediately as Fletcher. His friend was stiff-backed, his hands raised. The second man, Kane had never seen before. And the third was—

"Junior," Kane snarled, and Richard Price grinned.

Beside him, Zaria's eyes widened in understanding. She put a hand to her waist where she presumably kept her weapon.

"Keep your revolver up, Simon," Price barked at his colleague, then pointed his own gun at Kane. "Well, well. For a minute, I thought I was going to have to stand by and *let* you break the law. Instead, I'll get to say I'm the one who finally got Kane Hunt in darbies." He procured a pair of handcuffs as he spoke, his gaze roving over Zaria, then Jules. "I must say, I'm not impressed by your choice of accomplices."

Both Zaria and Jules were unmoving, perfectly silent. The former appeared to be trying to catch Kane's eye, but he refused to be distracted. In his periphery, Fletcher was stone-faced, hands still raised in surrender, a muscle flexing in his neck.

"Didn't think your lot carried firearms," Kane said mildly to Price even as his heart thundered. "Policing by consent and all that."

Price lifted his chin. "They're issued in special circumstances."

"I'm honored."

"Not because of *you*," the sergeant scoffed, disgust pinching his features. "Because of the Exhibition. This place is a dipper's dream."

Kane crooked a finger in his own gun's trigger guard, spinning the weapon around. "You don't want to mess this up for me, Junior. I can destroy your life. Your father's life. Your legacy in the force will be ruined like *that*." He snapped once with his free hand, the sound swallowed by the canopied space.

Price licked his upper lip, betraying a hint of fear. "And yet Ward contacted my father last night, keen to do business. Seems the Price family status is important to the kingpin of the dark market after all. So tell me, Hunt: How do you plan to take us down without his support?"

"Need I remind you that not everything I do requires Ward's support?" Kane set his jaw, fury and desperation unfurling in his blood. "I don't need him to make you sorry you crossed me."

"See, that's the thing," Price said. He began to pace, eyes narrowed, spots of color in his cheeks. "I think you do. I think you use Alexander Ward's name when it suits you, but that he's not behind you as much as you'd like everyone to believe." The sergeant's gaze traveled up to Kane's temple, and Kane realized he must be focused on the bruising there. "Not only will you *not* be stealing from the Exhibition today, but you're all under arrest for possessing dark market artifacts as well as conspiracy to commit a criminal offense."

Kane gave a prolonged, ungenuine laugh. "We're under arrest, are we? You're outnumbered, Junior."

Price shrugged, shifting his gun from Kane to Jules—the only one of them not armed. "You hand over your weapons in the next three seconds or your companion dies. Three."

Jules's eyes went wide, meeting Kane's. They communicated a horrified, silent plea, and for a moment, Kane was torn. In his periphery, he saw Zaria shifting farther and farther to his left; to his surprise, she hadn't said a word.

Had she not been here, Kane undoubtedly would have let Jules die. He was no longer terribly important to their plot, and if they failed, Fletcher's life was on the line. How could anyone begrudge Kane for choosing Fletcher over Jules? And yet if anything *did* happen to Jules, Kane knew without question that Zaria wouldn't continue.

"Two."

Price had spoken the truth, and it drove Kane mad. Ward *didn't*

have his back, and yet Kane dropped Ward's name whenever it suited him, trying to make it seem as though he did. What an inconvenient time for the young sergeant to finally wise up.

"One. Last chance, Hunt."

And Kane was still completely undecided. He heard Fletcher hiss his name under his breath.

A shot was fired, then another.

31

ZARIA

Z ARIA FIRED DIRECTLY AT PRICE'S CHEST.

Her second shot swept his companion off his feet, and then both were on the ground in an unseemly jumble of uniform-clad limbs.

Zaria blew soulsteel residue from her fingers as Kane, Jules, and Fletcher all spun to gape at her.

"What?" she demanded.

Jules was the first to speak. "Did you just *kill them*?"

Kane shook his head before Zaria could respond. "The shots weren't loud enough or bright enough. Look—there's not even any blood." He knelt down beside Price's prone form, his gaze flicking up to meet Zaria's. Hazel eyes glittered beneath long lashes. "You said dark market weapons were meant to be lethal. I took that as an indication you weren't going to fulfill my request."

Zaria shrugged. The idea of a weapon that looked lethal but

wasn't—a weapon that could intimidate without killing—had intrigued her. Creating it had been tricky, as she'd known it would be; predictably, everything hinged on having the exact right amount of each alchemological substance. But after firing more than one hole into the wall of the makeshift workshop Kane had provided her with, she'd eventually gotten it right. She just hadn't wanted to give one to *him*, afraid he'd ask questions she didn't care to answer.

"So what if I did?" The question was defensive. "You can't say it didn't come in handy."

Fletcher shook his head. "Son of a bitch. Even if they're not dead, you can't shoot a *copper*, let alone two."

Zaria chose to ignore this. "I thought this was a time-sensitive scenario."

"She's right." Kane considered Price and his companion with disdain. "Fletch, find the supplies and get back to your position. Zaria will release the first explosive the moment we walk out this door."

Fletcher nodded, then turned and disappeared into the shadows of the adjoining hall.

Jules was already poking around the perimeter of the space, and Zaria had a mind to join him when she felt Kane move closer. His wry grin flickered as she turned to face him.

"That was a good call," Kane said, softly enough that Jules didn't seem to hear. "I might even miss working with you once this is over, Mendoza."

Surely that was a lie, but the set of his mouth was serious. Almost grim.

Zaria didn't know how to respond, so she deftly sidestepped the topic. "You play very well. I guessed as much."

"What?"

"The pianoforte."

Kane's brows drew together. "I told you I didn't play at all."

"You did," she allowed. "But I knew you were lying. I could tell by the look on your face."

"What's that supposed to mean?"

For some inexplicable reason, she felt her cheeks heat. "You look at an instrument like a man who understands what it's capable of. Like a man who knows music."

Kane made a low hum in the back of his throat. "My mother taught me before she died. I hadn't touched one since, but I never forgot that song."

Zaria's heart thudded dully in her ears as she noted the tense set of Kane's shoulders. How many years had he refused to touch a pianoforte? How many years of melancholy had he injected into today's performance?

I might even miss working with you.

"Here," said Fletcher, making a sudden reappearance with his cheeks lightly flushed. In his arms were a number of items. He handed Kane a black leather package—his tools, Zaria supposed—then tossed her the aleuite explosives. She'd contained them within a couple of large vials, knowing the glass would shatter to dust the moment the reaction took hold. Nothing would be left unless someone knew what to look for.

She took the vials, immediately handing one off to Jules.

"We'll need to be quick," Kane said, checking his pocket watch yet again. "I allotted five minutes for us to retrieve everything. It's been eight, and we only had a two-minute buffer, which means I now have five minutes to pick the lock. Hopefully, it'll take even less time than that." He shot Zaria a meaningful look. "Ready?"

She forced herself to nod, though she wasn't ready. She wasn't certain she remembered what *ready* felt like.

Jules, by all appearances, felt much the same. He glanced at her from beneath worried brows, and Zaria saw the question in his eyes: *We're really going to do this?*

She gave a jerk of her chin. Jules's expression softened into resignation, and together they fell into step behind Fletcher and Kane as the former led them back out into the Exhibition. The volunteer who had been outside the door was gone, which struck Zaria as a bad sign.

This assessment was reinforced by Fletcher, who said solemnly, "Ten pounds says he heard the commotion and went to tell someone. Get out of here and be quick about it. We can't have that windowpane disintegrating before we're ready to go."

Though she knew it wasn't the case, Zaria felt as though everyone were looking in their direction as they headed for the Waterhouse exhibit. She fixed her gaze straight ahead, trying to mimic Kane's unhurried steps. If he shared her nerves, he didn't show it. The dull sound of distant applause sounded somewhere behind them—likely a reaction to the queen's speech. Not everyone had gathered to listen. A few people still milled about the exhibits, but far fewer than there had been prior to the royals' arrival. Zaria inhaled deeply to steady herself. She could see the necklace up ahead, the cage around it gleaming like a beacon in the light trickling through the glass walls.

Before they got any closer, Kane thrust out a hand. Zaria halted, nearly colliding with his arm.

Jules hissed, "What is it?"

Kane's eyes darted like a predator's around the area. They landed on Fletcher, still positioned at the edge of the space, then on the exhibitors that remained by their displays. Finally, he focused on the window behind the Waterhouse exhibit, which was beginning to

take on a distinctly cloudy look. The muscles of his jaw worked, going taut. "Set off the first one. Now."

"Here?" Jules blanched.

"Well, not in the middle of the fucking room."

There it is, Zaria thought. That flicker of stress. The single piece of evidence affirming Kane wasn't unshakably confident. She didn't know if it made her feel better or worse.

"If you want to get caught, that's not my business," Kane said, "but I'd recommend you go somewhere discreet. Duck into the furniture exhibit or something." He gestured with his chin before turning to Zaria. "Once Fletcher ushers everyone out of here, you set off the second one right beside the exhibit."

"Asshole," Jules muttered. "Lucky for you, I know where to go."

Zaria pivoted to watch him leave, but Kane spun her back around, fingers digging into her shoulder. "Don't look at him. Other people might follow your gaze."

She pursed her lips, knowing he was right. Her heart barreled against her ribs as she fixated on Kane's chest, not wanting to look him in the eye.

"Why are you so tense?" Kane murmured, using his grip on her shoulder to move her aside as another couple passed by. "You're about to get everything you ever wanted."

Zaria felt her mouth twist into a wry grin. The noise and sheen of the Exhibition spun around her. "Everything I ever wanted? You think a few Irish trinkets are *everything I ever wanted*?"

"Well," he amended. "Everything you wanted out of our deal." His eyes flashed as she finally looked up at him. "I daresay you have a veritable list of things you want, Zaria."

He wasn't wrong. But the things she wanted were so very foolish.

Then again, why shouldn't she want things? She stood amid an

impossible array of items that had only come into being because somebody, somewhere, had *wanted*.

Kane, she thought, wanted in the way of the British Empire. He yearned for what was not his, desired in the way of men with no regard for others, and was all the more a scoundrel for it. Perhaps that was why Zaria could barely stomach the thought of letting him have her. Perhaps it was why she tried so hard to forget the sensation of his lips on hers. More than anything else, she did not wish to be Kane Durante's conquest.

And yet her body was not in line with her brain.

"Kiss me again," Zaria said, because the only surefire way to avoid being conquered was to do the conquering yourself, was it not? She jutted her chin up, pleased by the look of shock that flickered across Kane's face. Confusion swiftly replaced it, settling between his dark brows.

He scanned her features as if searching for some kind of explanation there. "Why?"

"Because I asked you to."

"You regretted it last time, if I remember correctly." The tenor of Kane's voice dipped lower. Despite his words, he lifted a hand to the small of her back, guiding her closer. He released a breath by her ear. "You're leaving me with three and a half minutes to pick the lock."

Zaria felt her body stiffen at once. She was stupid, *selfish*, and yet it was only what Kane deserved. It didn't make sense for her to want him, just as it didn't make sense for him to want her back, but she didn't care. Not right now.

Kane leaned forward, eyes half-lidded. He pressed his lips to the base of her throat.

It was a featherlight brush, not at all reminiscent of the way he'd kissed her back at the workshop, and Zaria shivered beneath it.

Her thoughts fled, her pulse stuttering as Kane's lips moved up to the curve of her jaw. She was immobile, strands of her hair shifting gently with his exhale.

Then he moved away.

"There," Kane said, almost too soft to hear. There was an odd sort of sadness in his gaze, and his hand lingered on her back just a moment too long before he let it drop.

"That's not what I meant."

The ghost of a smile traced his mouth. "I know."

He brought two fingers beneath her chin, tilting it up, and lowered his face to hers.

Just like the first time, there was fire and hunger and desperation. It was softer this time, though, and there was the distinct taste of melancholy on his lips. It caught Zaria off guard the same way his music had. She had not known Kane Durante could be soft in a way that was not coercing. Had not known he could be melancholy in a way that did not scream of falsehood. As if in response, she felt the weight of her own sadness settle on her chest, and she kissed him harder.

That was when the smoke came.

It was preceded by a *bang* that made Zaria flinch and Kane go still. His body turned statue-like, and when he spoke, it was in a voice altogether different from the one he'd just used.

"I suppose that's our signal."

Zaria supposed it was.

Chaos reigned as the aleuite billowed, released from a place of unidentifiable origin. It was thick and impossibly dense as it swelled to fill the area. Tendrils crept out from a rapidly growing wall of slate-gray smoke. It looked lethal, Zaria noticed with no small amount of pride, as officers yelled panicked orders and footsteps slapped against the floor of the Exhibition. She could see Fletcher ushering wild-eyed men and women toward the exit, their faces masks of horror.

"If we don't move," Kane yelled into her ear over the clamor, "it's going to look mighty suspicious."

He had a point. Zaria allowed the wave of patrons to sweep her up, grimacing as bodies slammed into her own in a series of shoves and elbows. She hadn't realized how many people remained in this area until they'd all begun swarming to escape at once. Her ears rang with the frantic calls of women looking for their significant others, or perhaps their children, and the tang of aleuite grew identifiable in the air.

Kane had disappeared. Zaria knew he was here somewhere, heading for the Waterhouse exhibit the same way she was, but the back of his head wasn't distinctive enough for her to know whether he was in front of her. She tried not to think of his mouth—desperation on his lips, melancholy on his tongue—as she fumbled with her own explosive.

Nobody paid her any mind as she withdrew it from her pocket or as she fiddled with the wax sealing the vial shut. Why should they? They didn't notice when she broke away from the crowd, turning from the exit instead of shoving through it, and let the second aleuite bomb go.

The sound of the explosion was loud enough to set her teeth on edge, but it was the subsequent screeches that made Zaria wince. *Dramatic*, she thought, pulling a cloth kerchief from a pocket of her dress and holding it to her mouth as the smoke spread out. The fabric smelled of chemicals, having been thoroughly dipped in an alchemological solution the night before. Zaria hadn't lied to Kane and Fletcher: Nobody experienced lasting effects from aleuite.

The short-term ones, however, were something else entirely.

It had taken some trial and error, but Zaria had managed to adjust the concentration so a person could withstand the smoke for about five minutes before they would pass out—approximately the amount of time Kane said he needed to get the lock open. Given that they were behind schedule, she would need to delay him slightly.

There was a reason she hadn't told Kane about the nonlethal revolver she'd created. It utilized aleuite as well, but in a highly liquid concentration sure to knock someone unconscious once it found its way into their bloodstream. A tranquilizer of sorts. If he'd found out, he would have asked about it. And if she'd told him the truth, she might well have risked him making the connection.

Zaria squinted, but it was difficult to make out her hand in front of her face. She was forced to rely on memory as she picked her way toward the Waterhouse exhibit, eyes streaming. Her heartbeat was frantic, her breaths labored against the kerchief. The other patrons were being evacuated, which meant they would be fine. The officers, too, should be okay so long as they didn't venture into the denser parts of the smoke.

Eventually, she found Kane.

He was all but an outline, those skilled fingers working away at the lock on the cage. The only thing separating him from the item that would save Fletcher. His one friend. The one person he cared about. And yet he didn't know what he was after, did he? Ward did, surely, but Kane was oblivious. His frantic desperation was not for himself. It was not for magic, or money, or any of the other things most people cared so much about.

He didn't notice her at first, focused as he was on the lock. Zaria could tell by the way he kept shaking his head that the effects of the aleuite were already taking hold. The cacophony of the crowd faded into the distance, and for a moment, her mind was full only of the song he'd played. Sad and beautiful, just like him.

The good parts of him anyway.

She wanted to kiss him again, as many times as it took to understand who he was when the mask came off. But Zaria was under no illusions that he was fixable, and besides, it wasn't up to her to try. She knew what she wanted. She knew, and it was within her grasp, and Kane Durante was not the type of boy you gave things up for.

32

KANE

KANE SENSED ZARIA BEHIND HIM, BUT HE DIDN'T DARE TURN around. Even if he had, he doubted he would have been able to see her. His attention was on his hands as he struggled to insert the parautoptic key for the third time.

"This isn't working," he hissed, panic making him dizzy. He didn't understand what was happening; normally, he was calm and collected while committing a theft. It was crucial to keep yourself grounded. This time, however, he was starting to feel as though he might pass out.

Zaria's body was suddenly flush against his back, her hair brushing his cheek as she leaned forward. "What do you mean?"

Her voice was laced with urgency, though it sounded slightly muffled. Kane didn't look up at her—his gaze had started to swim, and the last thing he wanted was for Zaria to notice something was wrong.

"The key isn't *working*. You said it was supposed to adjust to fit the lock, right? Well, I've inserted it three times now, and nothing's happening."

There was a beat of silence that felt like an eternity. "But—that can't be," Zaria whispered, audibly shaken. "I created so many iterations, and this one is supposed to work. When it's in an enclosed metal space, the bits are meant to rearrange themselves to align with the levers."

"That's all very well, but that doesn't seem to be the case!" He inserted the key again. It rattled uselessly, and only then did he realize the problem. "There are more than fifteen levers."

"You said fifteen was the maximum, so I only created fifteen bits!"

It was true. It was *supposed* to be true. Kane swiped an unsteady hand across his brow. "This is impossible."

Zaria loosed an unsteady breath, and only then did Kane glance up to see a flash of white. Was she wearing some sort of scarf? He narrowed his eyes, then shook his head. He wasn't thinking straight. What mattered was that they needed to get this lock open.

"You'll need to arrange the bits yourself, then," Zaria said firmly. There was a rustling of fabric, and the next moment she had thrust what looked like a delicate pair of spectacles in front of Kane's face.

"What the hell are these?"

"Magnispecs. Put them on and use them to look into the keyhole. They're powerful enough that you should be able to see the levers inside. Once you know the arrangement, you can pick the lock the regular way. I assume you're capable of it."

Kane held the strange spectacles up to his eyes, feeling like a fool. It was difficult to see much of anything at all, but he pressed them against the keyhole as she'd suggested, waving her away with his free hand. "Leave this to me. Go check on our escape route."

He felt Zaria move away, which he took as assent. He didn't quite understand the mechanics of the atomizing adhesive, but he had to believe it would work. He'd timed everything around the moment when the device would apparently cause the glass wall panel to disintegrate, the pieces tiny enough that it would look as though nothing had ever been there at all. Once they escaped with the necklace, Fletcher would ensure any officers stationed at the exterior wouldn't interfere. The smoke would spill outside, and they could blend into the evacuated crowd, no one the wiser.

Kane's hands were sweating. His vision didn't seem to want to focus as he squinted through the magnispecs, trying to make out the levers inside the lock. Zaria was right: The magnispecs were inconceivably efficient. He adjusted them using the dial on one side. At the very least, the levers were somewhat visible. He counted quickly once, then again. There were *sixteen bits*. His heart thudded in his ears, seeming to echo strangely. Now the trouble lay in working out how they corresponded to the key he held. If he was correct, the first two bits of the parautoptic key needed to be quite short. With shaking hands, Kane removed each of the key bits, trying desperately not to let them fall to the floor. His dexterity was off, but he plugged two of the metal pieces back in, then pressed his eye back to the keyhole. A long bit next, then another short. Two medium-size ones of nearly the same length.

He had no idea how much time was passing. It could have been seconds or hours. His hands itched to check his pocket watch. At one point, he realized in horror that he was out of short bits and had to start all over again. Finally, however, he had an arrangement that made sense. The lock couldn't possibly require another combination.

"*Kane.*"

Zaria's voice seemed to emanate from somewhere far away. Kane felt as though his ears were stuffed with wool.

"Kane, the smoke will lift soon."

Her steps neared, and Kane inserted the key. Only then did he procure his smallest pick, inserting it so that it pressed against the sixteenth lever. Darkness crowded the edges of his vision. He might have been looking through something small and tube shaped. But he forced his body to stay upright, maintaining his grip on the key and lever as he turned them simultaneously.

The lock clicked.

Zaria's face swam into view at the narrowed apex of his vision. It *was* a scarf, Kane saw—or, rather, some kind of handkerchief. His thoughts were hazy, strings of logic coalescing as slowly as if they were being dragged through molasses. Horror dawned, acute and sobering, followed by realization.

Then rage.

She saw it, that rage, and something flickered in the depths of her gaze. "Kane—"

"Zaria," Kane spat.

It was all he said before he crumpled to the ground.

33

ZARIA

THE NECKLACE WAS WARM TO THE TOUCH.

Warmer than it should have been, sitting there upon its bed of cool velvet. Zaria shoved a few additional pieces of jewelry into her pockets for good measure, fastened the necklace around her throat beneath her high collar, and stepped over Kane's prone form in a daze. She swore she could feel the metal pulsing against her skin, almost as if it had a heartbeat of its own. Perhaps it was the magic that lived within awakening at the touch of someone who knew how to use it.

She hadn't expected to encounter any trouble with the lock, but it ended up providing precisely the delay she'd needed. The timing had been impeccable. She'd done it. The primateria source was hers so long as she could get out of here safely. Jules was supposed to meet her back at the pawnshop, and then they would leave London behind forever. They had to be fast about it if they were going to escape both Kane and Ward.

At her feet, Kane didn't stir. He wouldn't for a good half hour or so, assuming the smoke dissipated in time. Zaria could hear his voice in her mind, the dangerously furious tone of it as he whispered her name.

He'd said it like he'd known she was betraying him. She wondered what more he might have added had he not succumbed to unconsciousness. If he'd wake and think the second kiss was a ruse. If the gentler pieces of him she'd uncovered would evaporate. If he'd hunt her to the ends of the world for his revenge.

She supposed that this would become her life the moment she walked away from this place. An existence running from Kane Durante was surely a dangerous one, but it was a risk Zaria was willing to take. She would sleep with one eye open, a gun clasped in her hand. She could sell the rest of the jewelry and leave this wretched life behind. After all, the dark market was everywhere. Let Kane hunt her all he liked. She had survived this long. She was always, always willing to do whatever it took.

It was why they could never be together. Why it had never really been an option.

"Goodbye, Kane," she murmured, knowing he couldn't hear.

And she left him there to be devoured by the haze.

The glass panel nearest the Waterhouse exhibit was already gone, courtesy of Jules. Tiny fragments of glass were scattered on the floor, and more aleuite smoke billowed into the sky outside the palace. Based on its current density, she could estimate that Jules had released the final explosive less than five minutes ago. She darted through the jagged opening, careful to avoid the jut of the metal framing, and emerged, coughing, into Hyde Park.

Once she was mostly clear of the smoke, she tossed her handkerchief aside, letting the crowd swallow her up. The panicked

cacophony was too loud after the tense silence while Kane picked the lock. It was an assault on her ears. There were too many bodies, too many smells. She felt as though she were being squeezed through a veritable tube of humanity. She kept half an eye out for Fletcher but didn't see him among the officers she spotted. Thank God for that. Not only because she didn't want to be caught, but if she'd truly just doomed him, she didn't want to look him in the eye.

And yet she couldn't help but feel certain Kane would protect him. It was why she'd never considered that part of the equation with much concern: Kane would keep Fletcher alive no matter what it cost him. Zaria knew as much because she would have done the same for Jules.

She let the frantic wave of people engulf her, plastering a terrified look onto her own face as harried officers ushered them farther away from the Crystal Palace. Here, people milled around on the grass of Hyde Park, hollering for their families or exchanging panicked theories about what had happened. Zaria had no doubt that at least some of the patrons would've recognized the effects of aleuite, but to say as much was to admit a connection to the dark market, and thus she suspected it would be a while before the mystery was solved.

The sky above had turned a uniform gray, a colorless drape tossed over the heavens. She paused a moment, allowing herself to be buffeted by the cool wind. Her mouth was dry, her heart beating a relentless countdown. Once she returned to the pawnshop, Jules would be prepared to go, either with George or without him. Zaria would grab her alchemology supplies, and then they would start over someplace else. Someplace she could build a new reputation for herself. Someplace she could deal in magic only if and when she wanted to. She would have to go by a different name, of course, but that was no matter.

Her blood thrummed in her veins. Everything felt surreal. The day she'd been anticipating for so long was finally here.

The pawnshop was eerily quiet when she arrived. The trio of golden orbs swayed above the entrance as the wind picked up, the stench of piss and impending rain on the air. As she wrenched her hair out of its updo and shoved open the door, Zaria hoped it was one of the last times she'd ever smell this place. The last time she'd skirt reeking puddles and dirty, wailing children. The last time her chest would clench painfully as she tried to avert her gaze from the hopeless ones staring back.

She couldn't save any of them. London's working poor had to fend for themselves, and they all knew it.

Neither Jules nor George was in the front of the shop, but Zaria could hear footsteps upstairs. She doubted George would agree to leaving. It would break Jules's heart, but he'd conceded that if it came to it, they would leave his father behind. He could make his own choices.

She drew a finger along one of the dusty shelves before turning into the hallway. She thought of how she'd led Kane down here, his own gun pressed against his back. How calm he'd been, that self-satisfied grin making him look devilishly, frustratingly handsome.

Something horribly close to guilt roiled in the pit of her stomach, and she shoved it aside. Nothing Kane did had been for her—it had all been for himself. He had merely been helping her to help him.

Zaria knew as much, and yet the thought of Kane brought back the mental image of him lying motionless on the Exhibition floor. They were enemies now, she realized. Honest-to-God enemies.

She didn't know how to feel about that.

In another life, perhaps they could have worked well together. Could have pulled off countless heists with her skills and his cunning. A formidable team for more than just a week, had they chosen it.

But Zaria had made her choices. And if there was one thing she'd always been good at, it was following through.

She pushed the door to her workshop ajar. It was dark inside, and she felt her way over to the table as her eyes fought to adjust. The place was painfully familiar; she knew there were candles around here somewhere.

As she had the thought, one flickered to life just in front of her.

Zaria froze, her mouth going bone-dry. Kane couldn't have found her already. There was no way for him to have gotten here before her. By now, he should have barely regained consciousness.

But it was not Kane's voice that echoed in the room around her.

"Good afternoon, Miss Mendoza."

Zaria turned and looked directly into the face of Alexander Ward.

She'd only seen him once before—at a dark market exchange she'd attended with her father back when she was all of twelve—but she couldn't forget those eyes. They had an oddly metallic sheen to them, and there was something feline about the way he blinked far too infrequently. They were the eyes of a man who did not *feel* the way most people did. In fact, Zaria suspected they were the eyes of a man who did not feel at all.

For a moment, she couldn't speak. Every muscle in her body

tensed. She was tempted to flee, but she knew instinctively that Ward would be able to stop her. Besides, Jules and his father were right upstairs. Her gaze flicked up to the ceiling as she mentally urged them both to stay put. As her thoughts realigned themselves, she reached for the gun at her waist.

She saw too late that Ward was already holding one of his own, and he pointed it right at her.

"Put it down," he said calmly, almost politely, "and take a seat. I realize that, of the two of us, only one of our weapons is lethal, but wouldn't it be nicer if we could chat like civilized folk?"

Fear spiked in Zaria's blood. "How did you—"

"Price works for *me*. Not Kane. Put the gun down." Ward took a slow step, then another, beginning to circle her like an animal circling its prey. Zaria's head spun, but she couldn't foresee an outcome where she managed to shoot Ward before he shot her first. She dropped the gun. It felt like the worst kind of surrender. Everything she'd dreamed of only moments ago suddenly felt out of reach again.

Because of course she knew why Ward was here: He wanted the necklace. The primateria source. Forget leaving the city—Zaria would be lucky if she left this room alive.

"Say what you came to say." Her voice sounded dead, little inflection to it. She sank numbly into the chair by her desk.

Ward gave a breathy chuckle as he grabbed her gun, setting it aside. It didn't make Zaria feel any less trapped. He was lovely, this man, with a face befitting a sought-after suitor. He looked precisely the same as he had six years ago, not a line creasing the smooth skin of his face. Zaria thought she understood why he was so good at getting what he wanted—why *Kane* was so good at getting what he wanted. They were cut from the same cloth whether Kane had allowed it to happen willingly or not.

"When I found out Kane had gotten involved with Itzal Mendoza's daughter, I was certain you had to know he was after the primateria source. Why else would you have agreed to help him seek it out? I knew you'd betray him. I tried to get rid of you, but he turned out to be annoyingly gallant." Ward tilted his head to the side, surveying Zaria with mild interest. "I told him to cut ties with you and let him think I'd dropped the matter. But no matter how apt a thief my boy may be, you're far cleverer. I figured you'd be the one to end up with the necklace." He stretched out a hand, a pleasant smile gracing his lips. "Now give it to me." Zaria swallowed hard. The kingpin was clever. He'd read the situation perfectly and had predicted each one of her movements. But he was wrong about the first thing he'd said—she hadn't known the necklace was a primateria source at first. She hadn't known, and she'd been desperate enough to help Kane anyway.

It was strange, looking at Ward and knowing he'd made Kane what he was. She couldn't imagine being fathered by the man who'd killed your parents. Zaria wondered what sort of things Kane had carved out of himself to make space for the lessons Ward taught him.

"You destroyed his life," she found herself saying, her voice hoarse. She didn't know where it had come from, the emotion that now swelled in the cavity of her chest, but she let it grow. "You destroyed his life. He was a *child*."

Ward's brows shot upward, and something like understanding crossed his face. "You care about him."

She didn't respond.

"And yet you still betrayed him." This time Ward's laugh was the real thing. It sent goose bumps climbing Zaria's arms. "How boldly you claim *I'm* the monster, Miss Mendoza."

She wasn't about to get backed into that corner. "You don't even care that the people in Devil's Acre are suffering, do you? You make demands of them while knowing they have nothing. You ruin lives with no thought for it. And all the while you're bleeding boys of their humanity, turning them into monsters just like you." Her mouth twisted on the last sentence, and they both knew she was only referring to one boy in particular.

Ward clicked his tongue. "I *saved* Canziano's life. I could have killed him, and I didn't."

"Canziano?"

Ward's mouth twisted. "The name Kane's mother gave him."

It didn't suit Kane at all. Was that why he'd left it behind? Zaria tried to imagine him as the child he'd once been: a watchful, well-mannered little creature. Slender hands made for music, not murder. She wondered if his parents' deaths were what had broken him or if he'd already been starting to crack.

"Give me the necklace," Ward repeated, malice edging into his tone.

She took a step back, knowing it was pointless. "No."

He looked almost bored. "You have five seconds to hand it to me, or I fire a bullet into your pretty little skull."

Zaria could picture very well what damage a dark market gun would to do her head. Magic would shred the flesh, burrow into her brain, then disintegrate from the inside out. She'd be dead before she realized Ward had pulled the trigger. But was she supposed to simply...give it up? She had risked everything for the primateria source. It was all she'd wanted since her father's death. It was the one thing that was supposed to change her life.

It couldn't do that, though, if she was dead. And what about Jules? Would Ward leave her cooling body here for him to find, crushing his heart and hope for the future in one fell swoop? Or would he take Jules for his crew without ever explaining what had happened?

Hands shaking, gaze as hard as flint, Zaria reached up and unclasped the necklace.

She'd worn it only a short while, but giving it to Ward felt like handing over a piece of her soul. She watched it dangle between her fingers, glinting vermilion in the firelight, before he reached out and snatched it. Greed sharpened the angular planes of his face, and his lips parted.

"Beautiful," he whispered.

Ward's gun was still raised, but his attention was no longer on Zaria. If she could move fast enough to retrieve her gun from where it sat atop the worktable, she might be able to get a shot off. Maybe. It was a chance she needed to take before the moment passed her by.

Zaria lunged.

At the same moment, someone burst through the doorway into her workshop.

34

KANE

ZARIA HAD BETRAYED HIM.

Kane ought to have known. She wasn't the type to let herself be easily manipulated. He'd given her far too much leeway. Had trusted her to believe him when he said he could give her what she wanted. After all, he was accustomed to people wanting to trust him, wasn't he? Zaria shouldn't have been any different.

He'd been a goddamned fool, though, and let himself get pulled in too deep. Fletcher had been right all along.

Kane thought unwittingly of Zaria's face. The way she'd looked when she'd asked him to kiss her again. How the feeble light creeping through the glass windows of the Crystal Palace made her look more goddess than girl. He'd known he was in trouble then. Because for the second time in his pathetic life, he'd found someone he couldn't bear to let down.

He had planned to take more than just the necklace from the

Waterhouse exhibit. It wasn't quite what he'd promised, but it was better than nothing. How could he leave Zaria with nothing after all she'd done?

Kane hadn't known what was wrong with him—why he suddenly couldn't bear the thought of doing exactly as he'd planned from the very beginning. Maybe he was becoming too soft. Maybe he'd let her in just a little too far. He'd made it a habit of caring for no one but Fletcher, and that was the way he ought to have left it.

Part of him had known what was happening when he'd heard Zaria's footsteps. When she'd whispered his name like an incantation into the smoke.

All he could do was murmur hers in return, a furious rebuttal.

Then he'd felt nothing at all.

He was shaken awake a short while later, having been dragged away from the display—and then to his feet—by a panicked-looking Fletcher. A splitting headache had settled itself behind his temples, and he found himself unable to form words as he looked into his friend's worried face. In the background, he could vaguely make out the shape of a suspended canoe, which had to mean they were near Canada's exhibit.

"Kane. God, are you okay?" Fletcher had slapped him lightly on the cheek, but Kane scarcely felt it. All his focus was on remaining upright. "What happened?"

What was there to say? All along he'd been planning to betray Zaria, and then *she'd* betrayed *him*. The rage that uncoiled in his chest was unlike any he'd felt before. It was akin only to the type of fury Ward sometimes managed to ignite within him. His mouth tasted like bile.

Fletcher had given a dismayed shake of his head at Kane's lack of response, grabbing Kane's arm and flinging it over his shoulders with ease. "We need to get out of here, and not through the window—coppers are swarming on both sides. Can you walk? You're gray."

Kane's strength was coming back in increments, but it took a few steps for him to get his legs back under him. *No lasting effects*, Zaria had claimed. He might have laughed if he hadn't been so mutinous.

"Zaria" was the only thing he'd been able to force out. Her name sounded like a curse. It tasted like poison on his tongue.

Fletcher released an uneven breath, guiding him along a corridor toward what Kane hoped was an exit. "What about her? Speaking of which, where are she and Jules? Do you have the necklace? You're lucky I was the first to find you—you passed out right beside the display."

Kane loved his friend, but sometimes Fletcher excelled at missing the obvious. He stopped walking, forcing them to halt. "*Fletch.* Zaria's long gone, and no, I don't have the necklace. It's no coincidence I keeled over when I did." He tensed, lowering his voice as a handful of agitated coppers approached, but the copper nearest them only nodded at Fletcher.

"Any more where he came from?"

Fletcher shook his head. "Not that I could see. He must have been especially sensitive to the smoke. Found him passed out between Canada and Ireland."

They were talking about *him*, Kane realized, and the nonchalant manner in which the other man addressed Fletcher must have meant Price hadn't gotten to him yet. If the sergeant was still unconscious in the back room, he was bound to wake up soon. Especially if whatever Zaria had used to incapacitate him was similar to aleuite.

The thought had brought Kane up short, and he'd clenched his teeth together so tightly that it verged on painful. *That* was why she hadn't told him about the guns. More likely than not, they used aleuite to incapacitate, and she hadn't wanted him to make the connection.

"You're having me on," Fletcher hissed, pulling Kane toward the entrance. As they passed through the turnstiles, he added, "You really didn't get the necklace?"

"No. Like I said, my passing out wasn't a coincidence. She planned this, Fletch. All of it. The aleuite smoke was never safe to inhale for a prolonged period."

Fletcher had paled, then reddened, his voice turning thunderous. "That little—"

Kane gave a limp wave of his hand. He wasn't interested in hearing the myriad names he was sure Fletcher was about to call Zaria. "No point. We need to find her before she gets too far. I managed to get the display case open, so I'm certain she has the necklace." And had entirely compromised their escape plan in the process. "Now let me go—I can walk."

Fletcher obliged but watched Kane closely as he righted himself. When he seemed satisfied Kane wasn't about to fall over, he said, "Why would she want it?"

It had been a good question. Why *would* Zaria want the necklace? Perhaps she'd somehow found out Kane was planning to double-cross her, and this was her way of making him regret it. It would be very like her to do something simply to infuriate him.

That said, she had also known Fletcher's life was on the line. And though Zaria was a lot of things, she wasn't the type of person to doom anyone in the name of retribution. There had to be another reason. A more important one. How long had she been planning this?

"I don't know," Kane admitted. "What matters is finding her. I need to get that necklace to Ward as soon as possible."

Fletcher grimaced. "Her goal was to get out of London, right?"

"What are you suggesting?" Kane snapped, then bit down on the inside of his cheek. This wasn't Fletcher's fault. No, it was *his* fault. His own idiotic fault for putting his trust in someone he shouldn't have. And if Fletcher paid the price for it—

Well. Zaria already thought Kane terrible. She would find out just *how* terrible he could truly be.

"I'm just saying," Fletcher hedged, "what if she's already gone?"

"No." Kane snarled the reply. He took a breath in another attempt to calm himself. "She can't be gone. She won't go without Julian, and I'm willing to bet he won't go without his father. We need to check the pawnshop before we do anything else."

"Then what are we waiting for?"

And that was how Kane found himself outside the building where he'd first met Zaria, his heart in his throat.

Every piece of him hurt in different ways. Combined, it was enough to hollow him out completely. He'd only wanted to make Ward happy. He'd only wanted to win Fletcher's freedom. And in the very end, he'd only wished he could give Zaria what he'd promised her. Kane supposed that was what happened when you allowed yourself to care for people: It destroyed you.

It was with that hopeless thought that he finally gathered the courage to kick open the door.

The pawnshop was empty. Everything smelled like must and impending decay. Fletcher filed in behind him, eyes narrowed, and pointed wordlessly at the ceiling. On the second floor, Kane could hear the distinct sound of two men arguing. Jules and his father, most likely. His lip curled in grim satisfaction—they hadn't gotten very far, then.

"We'll corner them upstairs," he whispered to Fletcher. "Follow me."

Before he could start toward the stairwell, however, he suddenly heard a third male voice.

Kane's blood turned to ice, prickling along his veins. He knew that voice as well as he knew himself. It featured in all his nightmares, both waking and sleeping. Snapping around to look at Fletcher, he saw his own acute horror reflected in his friend's gaze.

Ward? Fletcher mouthed, the question mark implied, and Kane nodded slowly. It didn't make sense that the kingpin was here, and yet the light tenor was unmistakable.

Or *did* it make sense? After all, Ward had told Kane to cut ties with Zaria, and he'd refused. Ward had turned Price against them. He'd been meddling in Kane's plans from the very start. Why shouldn't he know that Zaria had been the one to end up with the necklace? Why wouldn't he have come to see things through himself?

Kane's horror multiplied tenfold as a woman answered, barely audible. By now he was intimately familiar with Zaria's voice as well. His fury with her was bordering on mutinous, but it was *his*. Not Ward's. The kingpin did not get to kill her. Not if Kane had anything to say about it.

"Stay here," he told Fletcher on a quiet exhale. "If Jules comes down, grab him."

"But Ward—"

"Won't hurt me. *Stay here.* Promise me, Fletch."

There was a long pause, but then his friend dipped his head.

Kane was around the corner and down the corridor in a half-dozen steps that echoed ominously in the narrow space. The door at the end was open, and he barreled through it without stopping to think.

The world turned on its head.

He saw Ward, the necklace in one hand, a dark market revolver in the other. He saw Zaria, bent at the waist as if midway through rising. Time seemed to stretch taut, then unraveled as she met Kane's eyes. Hers were full of true, genuine fear.

Now he understood. Ward had read Zaria in a way Kane had failed to do. If the kingpin was good at anything, it was understanding people. He predicted their steps and guessed at their desires with shocking accuracy. He'd assumed Zaria was going to betray Kane, hadn't he? That was why he'd referenced Itzal Mendoza's penchant for deception. *That* was why he'd wanted her dead.

Kane barely glanced at Ward, though. His focus was on Zaria.

If Ward had backed her into a corner, then Kane was the one who held her there. The mere sight of her sent his rage surging to near-apoplectic levels. She stared defiantly back at him, willful and tight-lipped. It was the very expression he'd become so familiar with. But where she'd always been unflinching in his presence, this time she recoiled from what he said next.

"Didn't make it very far, did we, Mendoza?"

Kane heard the deadly, absolute calm in his own voice, and understood her reaction. He sounded softly condescending. Utterly unfeeling.

He sounded like Ward.

Zaria looked past him to the door, seeking an escape where they both knew there was none. Meanwhile, Ward watched them with mild interest, eyes glittering in the dim.

"Don't tell me you wouldn't have betrayed me first," Zaria said, almost too quietly to discern. "Don't tell me you wouldn't have if you'd gotten the chance."

Kane took a step forward. His brain felt disconnected from the rest of his body. Like somebody else was coordinating the movement and he was merely along for the ride.

"I thought about it," he said, deciding honesty would cut deepest. "But in the end, I couldn't do it. Not to you."

He couldn't tell whether Zaria believed him. Something like pain sparked behind her eyes, though it was gone before he could be sure he'd seen it at all.

"I had no choice," she said. "Kane, the necklace, it's—"

"Powerful." This from Ward, staring at them from behind the trinket. He held it in front of his face, which was set in a hungry expression. The stone glinted in the candlelight as it swung back and forth, back and forth. "Yes," he continued, perhaps in response to Kane's bewilderment. "*Very* powerful, in fact. You see, it's a primateria source."

It all made sense then. Revelation after revelation struck Kane like physical blows. Why Ward had been so desperate for the necklace and why the stakes seemed so high. Why Zaria had agreed to help him and why she stuck around despite her apparent desire to be anywhere else. Kane had thought himself in control when this whole time he'd been at the center of a game he hadn't fully understood. He felt *sick*. Sick right down to his very core, until anger bloomed to replace it once more.

That was when he finally relaxed. Anger was a feeling with which he was familiar. Anger he could trust.

"Anyone who knows what the necklace truly is would understand why I wanted it," Ward said, a response to Kane's unspoken question. "So I couldn't very well steal it myself, could I?"

It struck Kane as a foolish thing to say. Ward didn't do anything himself regardless.

"You're not even an alchemologist," Zaria spat. "What use is it to you?"

Ward pivoted slowly in place. "What use is it? What *use*? You of all people should know the power of a magic source, Miss Mendoza. In the hands of a skilled alchemologist, the possibilities are limitless. In the hands of a man such as myself, well…" Ward paused to clasp the necklace around his neck. It looked rather odd there, a little too ostentatious, perhaps, but he slipped it under the fold of his collared shirt. "Some say a primateria source not only lends magic to the user but also brings power to the possessor. I'll admit I became very intrigued when I heard one was discovered in Ireland, and even more so when my sources revealed it had become part of a piece of jewelry in George Waterhouse's display.

"I was put out, you know," Ward said to Zaria, "when your father didn't manage to find one. I had my eye on him, and he let me down. I considered hiring him, forcing him to continue his search, but he was rather a disaster of a man, wasn't he? So much gambling. Far too much debt. A difficult child to deal with. Not to mention his reputation for being…less than trustworthy." The kingpin scoffed. "And so I hired Cecile Meurdrac instead."

Kane couldn't help watching Zaria's face as Ward spoke. She paled ever so slightly, her mouth tightening further, but did not reply. Smart of her.

"Anyway," Ward said, straightening with businesslike haste. "I think we'd best be getting on with it. Ah, here's Master Collins."

Kane turned, abject horror flooding him as Fletcher appeared in the doorway of the workshop.

"Fletcher," Kane snarled. His heart hammered against the cage of his ribs, threatening to escape. "Get the hell out of here."

But Ward beckoned Fletcher inside. His pleasant smile was back, wide and dangerous. "Isn't this convenient! Thank you for coming, Collins. It saves me having to track you down, and I do so love efficiency."

Even Zaria had gone pale, understanding what his arrival could mean. Only Fletcher himself was unaware, Kane realized in dismay. His friend surveyed the room in confusion, taking in the scene before his gaze came to rest on the kingpin. "What is this?"

Kane made a final, desperate attempt. "Fletcher, *go*."

Fletcher raised a brow, tilting his head at Ward as if to tell Kane, *Careful*.

Amusement played at the corners of the kingpin's mouth. "He doesn't know what's going on, does he? Oh *dear*. Canziano, I think you'd best explain."

"Explain what?" Fletcher took a step back. "Kane, what's he talking about?"

But Kane couldn't speak. Didn't know that he would ever be able to speak again. He gave a helpless shake of his head as Ward pointed his gun directly at Fletcher's chest.

He had no idea what would happen next. If Ward was only threatening Fletcher or if he truly intended to kill him. After all, Kane hadn't completed the task, had he? He'd failed to steal the necklace. And although Ward had gotten it in the end, he was not the kind of man who forgave inadequacies.

Ward clicked his tongue. "Don't move, Master Collins. If your friend won't explain, I suppose I'll do the honors. You see, when I told Kane to steal the necklace, we had a little deal. He succeeds, and you get to go free, no longer obliged to work for me. He fails, and...well." Ward twirled the gun between his fingers, demonstrating his absolute ease, knowing what it would do to Kane. "You die."

Fletcher's lips parted. His eyes widened, then narrowed. Bewilderment and disbelief traced every line of his face as he turned to Kane. "That's not true."

It was a statement, but there was a hint of questioning to it. As if part of Fletcher knew there was every possibility Kane would have betrayed him like this. As if he knew better than to trust him fully, even now.

"I—" Kane began, then cut off. He could feel his insides fracturing piece by piece. Could see Fletcher's sheer horror, and over his friend's shoulder, Zaria's dismay. She'd frozen in place, watching the scene play out. Watching Kane break his best friend's heart.

Just as he'd always known he would.

The pale light of hope in Fletcher's eyes dissolved as he watched Kane struggle for words. What was he to say? It wasn't as though he could defend himself. He was guilty, guilty of it all. Trapped between the boy he'd betrayed and the girl who had betrayed him. Watched by the man who had murdered his parents, stolen his life, and squashed what little goodness he'd once possessed.

But this wasn't entirely Ward's fault. Kane had known better. He had known all along that he would hurt Fletcher, and he had done it anyway.

"I only wanted you to be able to leave this place." He forced the words out with difficulty. They sounded mangled, scratchy, like nails scraping wood. "I brought you here, and I only wanted to free you."

When he met Fletcher's eyes, he regretted it. Kane had never seen such rage on his friend's face. Fletcher's expression was tense, cold. Empty. It was an expression Kane only knew from looking in the mirror. He'd never in his wildest dreams expected to see such wrath in the good-natured gaze he knew so well.

"How many times have I told you, you don't get to decide what's good for me?" Fletcher hissed. "I told you I didn't want to leave. I *told you*. And you never, ever listened. Somehow you couldn't fathom the idea that I might want something other than what you wanted *for* me." He swallowed, his throat shifting in a way that looked painful. "Fuck you, Kane."

Kane couldn't feel his limbs. He couldn't feel anything at all. Pieces of him were splintering, falling away. First Zaria, then Fletcher. They were stripped back, leaving him bare. Vulnerable.

Perhaps this was merely the way he was always meant to be. Bitter and broken, with nothing and no one save Ward.

"Terrible, isn't it?" Ward murmured, though Kane had the sense that he was enjoying this. That he enjoyed watching as everything was ripped away from Kane so he would be forced to rely on the kingpin alone. "He runs a good con, my boy. I'll give him that."

Kane gave a jerking shake of his head. "I'm not your boy."

Ward ignored that. He leveled the gun at Fletcher, false sadness in the line of his mouth. When he spoke, however, it was to Kane. "We had an agreement. You knew what would happen if you failed."

"You got what you wanted," Kane croaked. He felt so very ill. It scraped against the shell of his already-empty chest. He'd been turned inside out and scooped clean. "You got the primateria source. He gets to live."

"That wasn't the deal. You were to bring the necklace to me, and you didn't." Ward's eyes shifted to Kane, then narrowed. "What the hell do you think you're doing?"

Kane grasped his own gun with trembling hands, pointing it at Ward. He'd grabbed it almost without thinking. "Don't you hurt him."

"*Kane*," Fletcher snarled, the single syllable laced with a fear Kane didn't deserve.

Ward laughed, a genuinely surprised sound. "You make any move to pull that trigger, and by the time you do, Master Collins will already be dead."

Kane's wild gaze found Zaria's again—just for a moment—and he watched the rest of the color drain from her face. He wondered what his own looked like.

"Canziano." Ward's voice was sharp now. "Do not *move*."

Kane didn't move.

"That's what I thought," Ward said, the calm lightness returning as quickly as it had fled. "Now put the gun down. Control your emotions. I taught you better than this, didn't I?"

Kane did not put down the gun. He thought about what he'd said to Zaria the night before he'd first kissed her.

I dream of killing him, you know....Sometimes, when I watch other people die, I imagine they wear his face.

Resentment flared in Kane anew, intertwining with a wild energy. He felt unstoppable. Time ticked to a halt, and consequences ceased to mean anything. When he spoke, he scarcely recognized his own voice.

"You think you can shoot before I do?"

It was as much a challenge as a threat, and in his periphery, he saw Fletcher blanch. Ward, however, frowned. "Stop this, Canziano."

"Answer the question."

"Do I think I can shoot before you do?" The kingpin gave another harsh laugh. "Of course I do, fool boy. You should have seen how quickly I shot your traitor parents. Now, say goodbye to—"

But Kane never heard Ward say Fletcher's name.

He shot first.

35

ZARIA

ARIA CRINGED AS LIGHT STREAKED THROUGH HER WORKSHOP. She turned away from the scene before her, knowing she wouldn't be able to stomach watching Fletcher die. It would be *her fault* if Ward killed him. She'd been willing to take the risk, horrible person that she was, but having to see it was something else entirely. She'd never imagined being here to watch it happen. She was supposed to be long gone by now.

But it wasn't Fletcher whom the magic ripped apart.

It was Ward.

Her back was pressed into the wooden chair so firmly that it was beginning to ache, though Zaria barely felt it. An acrid scent filled the air. She found herself unable to move as Ward gasped, a hand snapping to clutch his chest as blood spilled from the wound. His widened eyes fixed on Kane, betrayal and disbelief etched into every line of his face. For the barest slip of a moment, Zaria could almost imagine he was a father staring at his son. A father who hadn't known how to love and now was forced to confront what he'd created. His expression was one Zaria would never forget.

Then he collapsed to the floor. Crimson pooled around him, leaking toward the place where Zaria stood. She stared over his body into a wholly different face—one she no longer recognized.

Kane's jaw was taut, the veins in his neck stark and bruise-like. There was something cadaverous about him in the candlelight. It coaxed flames into his black, black eyes and contoured his body in furious orange. He still held the gun out before him, though his hand no longer shook.

Zaria was struck by the sudden realization that she was going to be next.

"Kane, *no.*" No sooner had acceptance replaced the fear than Fletcher's voice cut through the oppressive silence. He shoved Kane aside, moving to stand in front of Zaria. Kane stumbled slightly, but his expression didn't change. It was as if a mask of impassivity had been painted onto his face. He still hadn't looked down at Ward.

Zaria straightened, heart pounding. She couldn't understand why Fletcher was stopping Kane from shooting her, and she didn't ask.

Because it was Fletcher, though, Kane faltered.

She watched as he crouched down, his gaze roving over his adoptive father's motionless form. Watched as his fingers curved clawlike toward the kingpin's neck.

He snatched the pendant away, knuckles straining as he clenched it tightly in a fist. Then he straightened and pointed the revolver in her direction once more. "Get out."

The words were deadly, leaving no room for argument. Zaria crept to Fletcher's side, trying to make herself small. Desperate to leave this place before Kane changed his mind. There was no hope of getting the primateria source—not now.

She couldn't reconcile this terrifying man with the boy who had kissed her. That evening, in twin candlelight, he'd grasped her hips and pressed his mouth to her neck.

What was it you called me?

She had told him he was a coward. It wasn't true, though.

He was a monster.

"Kane," she said hoarsely, a last-ditch attempt. She hated the expression on his face. Hated that this was all her fault, even if she knew she wouldn't have done it differently. It shouldn't have ended this way. When it came right down to it, all she'd wanted was to take the necklace from Kane. Instead, she'd taken everything from him.

She stepped around Fletcher, pushing past the hand he thrust out to dissuade her. Kane was motionless as he watched her approach. But his throat worked, a muscle leaping in his jaw. He let her come to him, a cruel sort of tilt to his mouth.

"I'm sorry," Zaria whispered. "You might deserve this, but that doesn't make what I did any less terrible. I never intended for any of it to happen like this."

His face slackened, and for a single, fleeting moment, Zaria thought she'd gotten through to him. The next moment, however, she realized the truth: Her words hadn't calmed him. They'd only made him shut down entirely. A final nail in the coffin of his fraying composure. Now he was about to explode.

"*OUT!*" Kane roared the word, swiping a hand across the surface of the worktable. The items there clattered to the ground, metal clanging and glass spraying. The candle, too, fell with a crash. It rolled over to where Zaria stood, the tiny column of orange fire undulating wildly, igniting the parchment that already littered the floor.

She had left them there, Zaria realized, as she always did.

Discarded designs for the parautoptic key that, in the end, hadn't even worked. The edges blackened and curled, the evidence of her sleepless nights shrinking down to ash. The rest of the notes were her father's: fragments of his life's work, his passion, and everything she had to remember him by. She watched in disbelieving horror as they, too, were consumed by fire. A scream built in her throat. She lunged for the nearest pages, hands clawed in desperation, but she recoiled just as quickly when the overwhelming heat touched her skin. Her vision blurred. She tried to stamp out the flames closest to her, but it was futile.

The old pawnshop never stood a chance. The fire spread quickly, licking across the floor. Smoke pressed in, searing Zaria's nostrils, and light flared. Flames crept up the walls in columns of impossible heat. Resignation washed over her alongside the panic, and finally she ran. Ran like the devil was on her heels, dragging Fletcher with her, because he'd frozen as if he might never move again. He bellowed Kane's name in a ragged voice, and she shrieked for Jules, eyes streaming from smoke or anguish or both. She had no idea if either of them would hear. All other sounds were swallowed by the *snap* of rapidly burning wood.

Kane did not run.

They left him there, surrounded by the flames, in a hell of his own making.

Jules was already outside when Zaria burst into the street, heaving labored breaths. He was at her side in an instant, smelling of smoke—or perhaps that was her—and taking her firmly by the shoulders. To anyone else, it might have seemed rough, but Zaria was desperate for the familiar, grounding contact. She leaned into him, blinking tears from her eyes.

Tears from the smoke, nothing more. She would not cry for the place she'd wanted so desperately to leave or for the pieces of her father that had littered the space. She would not cry for her half-finished commissions, her sketches and lists, her tools and materials.

She would not cry for Kane Durante, even as her heart seemed to rend itself in two.

"Your father," she gasped to Jules through lungs that felt scorched. It wasn't quite a question, but he understood. The muscles of his neck tautened, his grip on her arms becoming painful.

"I don't know."

"What—"

"I don't *know*, Zaria. I haven't seen him. We were arguing about... well, you know, and then..." Jules's voice cracked. "I have to go find him."

He started forward, but Zaria dragged him back again, her heels skidding on the dusty ground. "Don't you dare, Jules! You might not come back out again."

"What even *happened*?"

"It was Ward," she told him, low enough that no one else save Fletcher would hear. "He was here, waiting for me in my workshop. He wanted the necklace. He threatened to shoot Fletcher, and Kane...Kane shot him first."

Jules started, blinking at Fletcher as if noticing him for the first time. Wariness crossed his features. "I'm not even going to ask. Not yet anyway." He leveled an unsteady finger at the other boy. "Zaria did what she had to do."

Fletcher said nothing. He wasn't looking at either of them. His mouth was a firm line, his eyes dim. Zaria recognized that look—he was retreating deep within himself. She wondered if he was in shock. He hadn't said a word since emerging from the pawnshop, his gaze fixed on something in the middle distance.

"Fletcher," she said, and he turned to face her without much interest.

"What?" A single hollow word.

"I'm so sorry."

Fletcher shrugged, staring back into the flames. A large crowd had begun to gather, and the air around them was rent with shrieks and urgent chatter, but neither of them paid it any mind. "He's not dead. He will have escaped."

Kane, he must have meant. Zaria frowned, realizing she'd subconsciously come to the same conclusion. She peeled Jules's hand away from her bicep, lacing her fingers through his and squeezing. His mouth was a tense line as his gaze bored into Fletcher.

"Kane's like a cat that can't help but land on its feet," Fletcher continued, "even when he wants to let himself break."

Zaria followed his bleak stare, watching the flames lick up what remained of the pawnshop. At some point, the golden orbs had detached from the entrance, and one of them rolled across the street to settle a short distance from where they stood.

"I just don't understand," she said. "Ward didn't *need* a primateria source. He's already powerful. There has to be more to it, especially given what he was willing to do. I mean, I thought he favored Kane. Why would he hurt him by threatening your life?"

"Ward may have thought he loved Kane," Fletcher said sharply, "but his love was toxic. He used pain and threats to get what he wanted. Kane loved Ward, too, even though he shouldn't have. I don't think he could help it. This ... this will destroy him, Zaria. He'll self-destruct, and he'll try to take everyone and everything else down with him. Kane, when he's angry, is dangerous, but Kane when he's grieving? That's a catastrophe."

Zaria swallowed past her raw throat. She thought of the boy who'd played the pianoforte at the Exhibition. The way he'd pressed his lips to her throat like she was something delicate and infinitely precious. The rueful sadness in his eyes when he pulled away. She thought about the story of the little boy who'd watched his parents die in front of him and how hearing it had made her burn with a furious protectiveness.

But she could not protect Kane. Nobody could—least of all himself.

She was spared from having to respond by the appearance of George Zhao covered in soot and looking as distressed as she'd ever seen him. He fought his way through the crowd, chest heaving as he wheezed and cursed at those who stood in his way. Jules inhaled sharply and released Zaria's hand, sprinting toward his father, only to stiffen with uncertainty when he reached him.

"My boy," George rasped, more a declaration to the crowd than a greeting to Jules. And then the man Zaria had never once seen show any outward affection threw his arms around his son.

She smiled faintly as Jules hugged George back. She felt at once filled with joy and like her insides were being forced through a very small opening. It hurt to watch when all she had to remember her own father by was currently smoldering around them.

"Did you know?" Fletcher's low voice sounded by her ear, and Zaria started. She hadn't realized he'd moved closer.

"Did I know what?"

"That Ward told Kane he would kill me."

"Yes," she admitted heavily. She was so tired of lying. "I don't think he wanted to tell me, but he needed me to understand why the job was so important to him."

Fletcher snorted, dragging a hand through his unruly hair. "And you double-crossed him anyway."

Zaria winced. "I didn't feel good about it. But alchemology killed my father, Fletcher. It drained the life right out of him. If I wanted to continue his work in any capacity, I needed that primateria source."

"So you knew it was a source all along."

"No. I only learned of it the night I met up with Cecile."

"The woman who died," Fletcher confirmed.

It hurt to hear the words. Zaria was still trying not to dwell on the events of that particular evening, but the memories prodded at her relentlessly. In a roundabout way, Cecile had given her life for that meeting, and what difference had it made? She felt like such a pivotal part of Zaria's life, and in the end, she was just as Fletcher said—a woman who had died.

"Yes." The word seemed to stick in Zaria's throat. "That's the one."

The pawnshop continued to slowly burn—no fire brigade would come to put it out, though locals were already endeavoring to assist with buckets of foul water. Nobody cared if the slum burned. Zaria stared into the flames until they burned an imprint behind her eyelids, listening to the soft crackle of the weakening joists. Jules and George had joined the extinguishing effort, and the latter was yelling instructions while his son ran back and forth delivering buckets. At this point, the pressing concern was ensuring the fire didn't spread to the neighboring houses.

"Hope you didn't have anything explosive in that workshop of yours," Fletcher said, watching the scene play out.

She cut him a sidelong glance. "I'd be a pretty shit alchemologist if I didn't have flame-resistant containers." Before she could think better of it, she blurted out, "Aren't you angry with me?"

"For what?"

"The bit where I let Kane pass out and stole the necklace from under his nose comes to mind."

Fletcher's responding laugh was hollow. "If I'm being honest, I'm so angry at him that you're not really my main concern. Besides, we were going to double-cross you, too."

"You were?"

"Yeah. Kane never had any intention of stealing the other Waterhouse jewels."

They looked at each other a moment. Then Zaria couldn't help it—she laughed. It came out much as Fletcher's had, the sound twisted and strange. Of *course* Kane had been conning her from the start. She'd known exactly who he was, what he did, and had decided to trust him anyway. "Well then. Fuck you."

"You were prepared to let me be killed," Fletcher reminded her, and she blew out a sigh.

"What a mess."

"I'll say. For what it's worth, though, I'm sorry about Cecile."

"It's not worth a lot, but I appreciate it."

They were silent another long moment. Then Fletcher asked, "What are you going to do now?"

Zaria recoiled from the question. It felt too big somehow. "I don't know. I mean, Jules and I have to get out of here. Kane will come after me, Fletcher. Assuming the coppers don't find me first." After all, she still had the other pieces she'd stolen from the Waterhouse display. "The plan was always to leave London."

"Fair enough. Kane will take some time to regroup, though,

before he makes his next move. Despite everything, he's not impulsive. You should have at least a few days." Fletcher cut her a sidelong glance. "And you'll need it. You sound like you've spent fifty years blowing clouds."

Zaria mustered a tight grin, accepting his advice as the olive branch she suspected it was. Cautiously extended, but a peace offering nonetheless. "What about you? What's your plan?"

Fletcher sighed. He looked impossibly tired, his light hair askew and his brow furrowed. "I'm not sure," he admitted. "You know, I always thought Kane would break free from Ward. I never thought he'd end up being like him. I should have seen it coming."

She felt herself soften. It couldn't have been clearer that Fletcher, despite his faults, was not like Kane. Still, as much as she wanted to, Zaria couldn't say she agreed with him. She could see perfectly well the similarities between Kane and the very man he'd hated. Had seen that depravity in him from the very beginning.

It should have been enough to deter her, but it hadn't. Even now, after all that had happened, some twisted part of her balked at the thought of never seeing him again.

She pushed that part aside, deftly and with finality, locking it up in a very small box. She would try to forget about Kane Durante. The look on his face as he snatched the necklace from Ward's neck and the way his voice had wavered, nearly imperceptibly, as he'd bellowed for them to leave.

This wasn't the way she'd pictured leaving London: no primateria source in hand, running from the boy whose face she knew she would see each time she closed her eyes.

"Excuse me," she told Fletcher, throat tightening. He nodded, and Zaria ducked to the back of the murmuring crowd, the noise a dull buzzing in her ears. She needed silence. A moment's reprieve from the commotion in the street and in her head. She hoped Jules would understand when he looked around and saw her absence.

"Zaria Mendoza?"

Her own name sounded from behind her, and she spun around, finding herself face-to-face with another girl. It took her a heartbeat to place the muscular frame, dark eyes, and reddish-blonde hair. When she did, her pulse kicked up another notch. "Can I help you?"

The girl smiled, and not kindly. Last Zaria had seen her, she'd been holding a magical explosive. A *defunct* one.

"You can, actually," the girl said, drawing a tiny sleek revolver from the folds of her gray skirt. "You see, Mister Vaughan isn't very happy with you."

"There *is* no Mister Vaughan," Zaria snapped back, remembering what Kane had told her. How he'd attempted to look into her client, only to find that he didn't exist.

One side of the girl's mouth curved up. "I'll be sure to tell him that. Now start moving."

Zaria complied but not before glancing around anxiously for Jules. Relieved when he was nowhere to be seen, she began a slow, unsteady walk to the end of Horseferry Road. There was a stagecoach waiting there, she saw, drawn by two sleek black horses. Her stomach churned.

"Faster," the girl hissed, sounding at once too close and strangely far away.

Zaria's thoughts were a tempest. What was she going to tell this Mister Vaughan, whoever he was? She ought to have known she would answer for this eventually. Somehow, with everything that had happened since, the troubles associated with her outstanding commissions had seemed so far away.

The stagecoach loomed ahead, the door thrust open by a single

gloved hand. Letting out a shaky breath, Zaria slid her own hand into the pocket of her dress, a desperate attempt to conceal her fluttering fingers.

Then she froze.

The cold press of a delicate metal chain met her fingertips.

EPILOGUE

KANE

Kane swept into Ward's most recent place of residence as dusk stole across the rooftops of London.

A few of the kingpin's cronies still surrounded the building, but not a single one spoke as he shoved past them. Perhaps it was the blood on his shirt, the scent of smoke, or the air of unsteadiness about him. Perhaps they could already guess what had happened.

His footsteps echoed along the gilded walls as he made his way to Ward's office. Poured a glass of the finest whiskey and tossed it back like a man seeking water in the dead of summer. Slammed it down on the bookshelf, then took a seat.

With his ankles crossed on top of Ward's desk, he could finally think.

He was alone. No Ward. No Fletcher. No Zaria. Who was there to stop him from doing whatever the hell he wanted? Ward had paid for what he'd done, and if killing him had knocked any sort of emotion loose in Kane, he hadn't felt it yet.

Maybe Fletcher would come find him. Maybe he wouldn't. Maybe it was better that everyone understood precisely what and who he was now. There were no more secrets.

He leaned back in the chair as the door creaked open.

A man in an onyx hat and lapel appeared in the entrance to the office. Well-dressed. A dark market contact, no doubt. Tom, Ward's doorman, appeared just behind the man's shoulder.

"Sorry, Durante, but he insisted—"

"It's fine." Kane waved a hand. "You can go, Tommy." He lit his pipe, peering at the man through the smoke between half-slitted eyes. Tom backed away, shutting the door behind him.

"Sit," Kane said to the man, who frowned.

"I'm meant to be meeting with Alexander Ward. Who are you?"

"Who am I?" Kane echoed, and the laugh that clawed its way out of him was more *Ward* than any other answer he could have given. "Who am *I*?"

The man's expression shifted to one of wariness. Kane grinned widely, interlacing his hands behind his neck.

"I'm the goddamned kingpin of Devil's Acre."

ACKNOWLEDGMENTS

This is my third published novel, but it feels like the book version of my firstborn child. I penned the first words of this story over eight years ago, so as you can imagine, I have nearly a decade's worth of people to thank.

To my agent, Claire Friedman: I think this is the first manuscript of mine you ever read. You saw something in the earliest version of *Thieves*, back when it looked so very different (and far less coherent!). Even before you were my agent, your feedback convinced me not to shelve the book completely, and I am forever grateful for that. Thank you for always being the best advocate! To my editor, Nikki Garcia, and assistant editor, Milena Blue Spruce: I'm so happy we could collaborate again on this. Your ideas always take a story to the next level, and you're both truly wonderful to work with. It's such a comfort to know you're there when I get stuck. Thank you so much—you work way too hard! To Kelly Moran: Thank you for everything you did to help this book succeed out there in the real world. You are so wonderful and appreciated. Thank you as well to Jake Regier, David Hough, Stefanie Hoffman, Savannah Kennelly, Christie Michel, Tara Rayers, and Jenn Baker for your hard work and contributions. To Jenny Kimura, Sasha Illingworth, and cover artist Christin Engelberth: Thank you so much for ensuring I got the beautiful, historically accurate cover of my dreams!

A novel of mine would not be published without several breakdowns along the way, so infinite thanks to Emily Miner, Page Powars,

Kelly Andrew, and Jen Carnelian, all of whom have the misfortune of being in a group chat with me. I love you guys so much, and I genuinely don't know what I would do without you. To the rest of my publishing-adjacent friends and fellow authors: You know who you are, and I'm so grateful we connected. Thank you for watching my chaotic Close Friends stories on Instagram (or skipping past them, which is so very understandable). A specific thank-you to Carlyn Greenwald, who pulled this book out of her Author Mentor Match slush pile and was the first to believe in it: You changed everything for me, and I owe you huge. To each and every member of my family: Thank you for supporting me, celebrating with me, and bragging about me (even when I desperately wish you would stop). Not everyone is lucky enough to have such a huge circle of people to rely on, and I don't take it for granted. A special thanks to my British papa, without whom I suspect I would have found this book much more difficult to write. As always, my final thanks to Edward, who believes in me more than I believe in myself. Thank you for the undying love and support, and for the infinite iced coffees. You're the kind of guy people write books about. Not me, because my fictional romances are unhinged, but other people, probably.

Turn the page for a sneak preview of

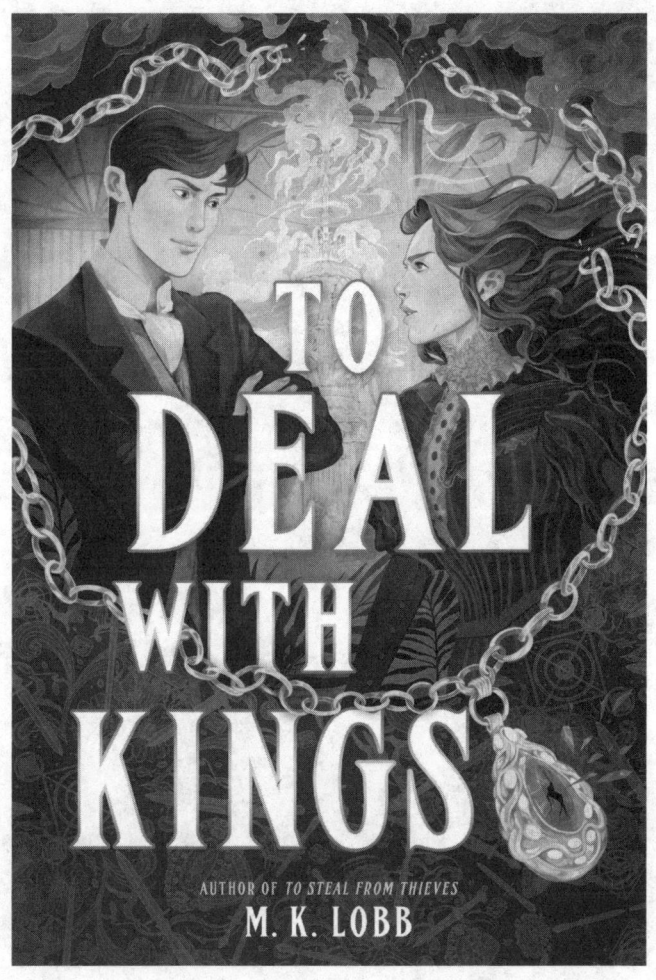

TO DEAL WITH KINGS

AUTHOR OF *TO STEAL FROM THIEVES*

M. K. LOBB

AVAILABLE MARCH 2026!

PROLOGUE

MOONLIGHT FELL IN SHATTERED INCREMENTS ACROSS THE floor of the Crystal Palace.

The exhibits were dark, echoes of the day's excitement and chatter having long since faded into obscurity. The bustle of innumerable patrons had given way to stillness; even the steam-powered machines had ground to a halt. The only noise came from the dull, intermittent thud of polished black boots as the coppers made their rounds.

There was more security than originally planned. The Exhibition had closed early that day—*opening* day—giving time for shards of glass to be swept away and the aleuite smoke to dissipate. The queen and prince consort had been less than pleased to receive the news: A priceless artifact, stolen from right under the commission's noses during broad daylight. The ire of George Waterhouse, the Irish jeweler who'd supplied the necklace that now was missing. Most infuriating and disturbing of all, however, was what they knew about the thief. The means by which they had pulled off their daring heist.

Alchemology. A collision of magic and science that had proven impossible to understand—let alone regulate—and thus had been outlawed in Europe for the better part of the century. Alchemologists didn't often rear their heads amid polite society, thus sparing most from giving the illegal study much consideration, but England's rulers knew enough to recognize the devilry when they saw it. The Royal Commission for the Exhibition had been left humiliated and bewildered, every member with the same questions on their tongue: Who could possibly have managed to pull off such a feat? How had they gotten in and out without anyone being the wiser? Perhaps most curious of all, *why* had they taken a single item? The necklace had been far from the only priceless piece in the Waterhouse exhibit, yet the rest of the jewelry remained untouched.

It was convenient, then, that these questions distracted commission members and police constables alike as they circled the unlocked display, paced the exterior of the building, and stood at attention beside the gaping hole where a panel of glass had yet to be replaced on the ground floor of the Crystal Palace.

They didn't see that while one item might have been missing from the Exhibition, a new one had appeared. They wouldn't know its function, nor that it had been carefully placed and meticulously designed. They couldn't possibly understand that in due time, everything—*everything*—was about to change.

Not yet.

But they would.

ZARIA

THREE DAYS EARLIER

Zaria Mendoza had been held at gunpoint far too many times for one day.

It was an absurd thought to have as she approached the stage-coach waiting at the end of Horseferry Road, but her mind had long since stopped processing things logically. The fear settling in her chest was accompanied by a not-insignificant amount of resentment. First she'd stolen from London's Great Exhibition, betraying Kane in the process. Then she'd returned to the pawnshop only to find Alexander Ward waiting there. And *then* she'd watched Kane kill Ward—the man he'd both hated and loved—only to come unhinged and set the pawnshop on fire.

All of that was to say, the last thing she needed was for the stint she'd pulled on a former client to catch up with her.

"In." The girl at Zaria's back jammed the barrel of the gun between her shoulder blades. Zaria started, eyes fixed on the gloved hand of whomever was waiting inside the stagecoach. Mister Vaughan, no doubt. The man to whom she'd delivered a faulty explosive. He was holding the stagecoach door ajar, and though she couldn't yet see his face, she could only imagine the expression there. After everything, was this to be the end for her? It seemed almost unbearably unfair.

She clenched her fingers more firmly around the necklace in her pocket. Though she hadn't yet taken it out, she could tell what it was by the way it seemed to pulse against her skin. Somehow—for some reason—Kane had given her the primateria source. It didn't make any sense. He was adept at sleight of hand, sure, but Zaria couldn't recall being close to him in the moments after he'd snatched the necklace from Ward's cooling body. More to the point, why would he want her to have it? After everything she'd done, she couldn't see a single reason for Kane to help her.

Because the source *would* help her. It was why she'd snatched it from under his nose in the first place. It was the only way she could keep practicing alchemology without destroying herself in the process, and Kane knew as much.

She was still reeling as she sank onto the firm leather seat of the stagecoach, the girl with the gun clambering in behind her. With her broad shoulders and muscled arms, she was more imposing than the slight man who now sat across from them.

"Miss Mendoza." The man removed his hat and extended a hand. "A pleasure to finally make your acquaintance."

Zaria shoved her apprehension aside, arranging her face into an expression of cool confidence. It was the demeanor she adopted whenever she engaged in business dealings, and though it was certain to be of little help here, she let it wash over her with practiced ease. Finally relinquishing the necklace, she grasped the man's gloved fingers. "Likewise. Mister Vaughan, I take it?"

The man's smile was tight-lipped, not quite reaching his blue eyes. He looked to be in his forties, with prominent features, pale skin, and dark hair that was starting to gray. If the stagecoach hadn't marked him as someone of status, his outfit would have done the trick; he was dressed according to the latest fashions, his black ensemble uncreased and well-made. Zaria disliked him at once.

This fact was only cemented when he said, "You've found yourself in all sorts of trouble now, haven't you?"

She didn't answer, glancing out the tiny window. Gray clouds still billowed into the air above Horseferry—eighteen years of her life and work up in smoke alongside George Zhao's smoldering pawnshop. The acrid scent of it infiltrated the stagecoach.

"I'm Evan Pritchard," the man continued. "Mister Vaughan's most trusted, as it were. Don't roll your eyes, Maisie," he snapped, attention suddenly flicking to the girl at Zaria's side, whose lips were pursed. Collecting himself once more, Pritchard folded his gloved hands in his lap. "Vaughan is far too busy to chase after those who have disappointed him. And you *have* disappointed him, Miss Mendoza. An explosive meant to destroy only organic matter—is that not what he commissioned from you?"

Zaria inclined her chin. "Yes, but—"

"You can imagine his disappointment, then, when the detonation of the faulty device caused quite a scene. And if there's one thing my employer doesn't like, it's being disappointed."

"My intention was not to disappoint," Zaria said, keeping her voice measured. "The explosive wasn't faulty. I know what I'm doing, Mister Pritchard. But alchemological supplies are expensive, and I didn't have the soulsteel required to properly complete the job. I knew I wouldn't be granted another extension, so I delivered what I had."

"Which was nothing but a regular bomb," the girl—Maisie—snapped. A pink flush had crept into her lightly freckled cheeks. "You're lucky I didn't shoot you the moment I tracked you down. Do you know how it made *me* look? Delivering a device that didn't work as promised?"

Zaria had a vague recollection of Maisie inspecting the commission the night she'd come to collect it on Vaughan's behalf. It was obvious then that the girl was familiar with alchemology, even if she hadn't been able to identify any issues. And why should she? Zaria was careful. She knew how the dark market worked, and how the most impressive magical items were those indistinguishable from their nonmagical counterparts.

"Oddly enough, your reputation didn't factor into my decision," Zaria retorted, irritation prickling along her spine. She knew it wasn't smart, speaking this way to someone holding a gun, but she was just so *tired*. "Like I said, I didn't have the supplies I needed. It had nothing to do with my inability to create what Mister Vaughan was asking for. Please pass along my sincerest apologies."

Maisie let out a disbelieving snort, and Pritchard silenced her with a look. To Zaria, he said, "Vaughan is well aware of your capabilities. That's part of the reason he was so disappointed. There are precious few alchemologists in London as it is, which I'm sure you know, and most are highly specialized. You, though—you can create a wide variety of items, like your father. That's why he's willing to give you a second chance."

Rather than feeling relieved, Zaria tensed in her seat. "What do you mean?"

"Did you think Vaughan wouldn't recognize aleuite when he sees it?" Maisie cut in. "Everyone's talking about what went down at the Exhibition. They're already trying to pass it off as a malfunction with one of the displayed steam engines, but anyone with dark market connections knows what really happened."

"You caused quite the stir, Miss Mendoza," Pritchard said smoothly. Then, in response to her look of horror: "Yes, Vaughan knows it was you. I understand the Waterhouse exhibit was left in quite a state, too."

"*How* does he know all this?"

"That's not important."

Zaria brought her teeth together, then spoke through them. "I'd never even heard of your employer until I saw his name in my father's list of commissions. His alias, that is," she amended, remembering how Kane had looked into the matter and discovered nobody involved in the dark market went by that name.

"Regardless, Vaughan knows what you're capable of, and you interest him." Pritchard tilted his head to one side. Deciding how much to tell her, no doubt. "You see, he's made considerable strides when it comes to his status in this city. One might even call him the kingpin of the Covent Garden area."

"You mean Seven Dials," Zaria said, referring to the slum in London's West End. She'd rarely had occasion to go there, but she knew it wasn't dissimilar to Devil's Acre, which meant Vaughan was undoubtedly the Alexander Ward of that area. The thought made her uneasy. "So you're part of his crew."

Maisie's expression tightened further, but Pritchard smiled again. "Something like that. As I said, considerable strides. My employer's influence is growing, Miss Mendoza. He's clever. He understands an asset when he sees one, and he isn't so quickly moved to violence. A relief for you, I would imagine."

Zaria gave a noncommittal shrug, unable to ascertain where this was going.

"If one wants to extend that sphere of influence to the dark market, it's imperative that one participate in it, no?"

"I suppose."

Maisie let out a harsh sigh. "Get to the point, Evan. She's obviously not going to make it there on her own."

Pritchard waved Maisie's words away, his impassive gaze locked with Zaria's suspicious one. "Vaughan is aware of your allegiance to Alexander Ward, and his offer involves changing that allegiance. Rather drastically, I might add."

"I'm not—" Zaria began, then stopped herself. Admitting she was not, in fact, connected to Ward might well mean the difference between getting shot and leaving this stagecoach alive. In the same vein, it didn't strike her as prudent to reveal that Ward was currently dead beneath the rubble of the pawnshop. "I'm listening."

"Mister Vaughan wishes to continue to grow his influence even further. As a result, what he requires most is information."

Zaria had been shifting in her seat, fingers roaming the vertical stitching. At Pritchard's words, however, she froze, a harsh laugh bursting from her lips. "Are you asking me to *spy* on the dark market kingpin?"

"I wouldn't call it spying."

"Just because you wouldn't call it that doesn't mean it's not."

Pritchard leaned forward. His smile was a brittle, ingenuine thing. In that moment, the polite, amicable demeanor slipped away, and Zaria realized she was looking at a man who could be very dangerous indeed. "We're aware of your relationship with Kane Hunt, Miss Mendoza. And although he may try to maintain a low profile, we know he holds a considerable amount of influence among Ward's crew."

"Then why don't you ask *him* to spy for you?" Zaria bit out. "Why don't you ask one of the other crew members? Why me?"

"Because Mister Vaughan doesn't want Mister Hunt or any of the other members. He specifically requested you, and there's a reason you might want to please him."

That made Zaria's insides turn cold, as if ice water had been shot into her veins. When she replied, it was through a dry mouth. "And that reason is what, exactly?"

Maisie rolled her eyes, and Pritchard surveyed Zaria in a way that suggested he thought she was being purposefully obtuse. "Why, he could reveal your culpability in what happened at the Exhibition today. Am I correct in assuming you don't want that?"

The necklace in her pocket suddenly seemed to weigh a ton. "You don't have any proof."

"Do you truly believe we need it? Mister Vaughan is a powerful man in London. And you? You're a girl who lives in a slum and deals in illegal items." Pritchard's lips twisted. "Whose word do you think the authorities will give more weight?"

Was it possible, Zaria wondered, to so thoroughly detest a man you'd only just met? Either way, she couldn't let Pritchard's ultimatum rattle her. She had a primateria source. And although that was the only thing she'd taken from the Waterhouse exhibit in her haste, she and Jules still had plans to leave this city behind. All she had to do was appease Pritchard in this current conversation, then get the hell out of London before Vaughan could wise up to the fact that Ward was dead, Kane hated her, and this entire scheme was moot.

Still, she made one last-ditch effort. "Look, I just really don't think I'm the best person for the job."

Maisie pivoted her entire upper body to face Zaria. Her dark eyes were disdainful, and one hand still clutched the gun in her lap, barrel facing outward. "When Vaughan wants you to work for him, you say yes. There is no other option. You take the job, and you thank God for the opportunity."

"Is that what you did?" Zaria demanded before she could stop herself.

"Wouldn't you like to know."

Pritchard *tsk*ed, unclasping his hands. "Miss Ó Coileáin, if you can't learn to adopt some patience, I'm going to request we aren't partnered again. God help us." He turned back to Zaria coolly. "Here's the bottom line, Miss Mendoza. Your options are twofold: You can accept Vaughan's offer and rise alongside him as he wrests command of the dark market. *Or* he can tell the authorities and the Exhibition's Royal Commission what he knows of your involvement in today's events. Perhaps you and your friends can get a row of cells at Newgate Prison. Assuming you manage to escape execution, of course."

Zaria felt the blood drain from her face. Threatening to turn her in was one thing, but the rest of them? Kane might escape arrest, slippery as he was, but what about Fletcher? If she and Jules ran, would Vaughan go after the two of them? Did she *care*? That was something she would need to decide, and quickly. "What kind of information is Mister Vaughan looking for?"

"For now, collect as many names as you can of those associated with Alexander Ward. Not only his lackeys, but clients he frequently works with. Aristocrats who consider him an ally. Coppers under his thumb. That sort of thing. I'll expect a report…oh, shall we say by Monday? That gives you an entire weekend."

"That's not very much time." It sounded like the words had been shaken out of her. Zaria's mind, though, was elsewhere. Trying to decide on a course of action. Trying to imagine how quickly she and Jules could get out of London.

Pritchard gave that empty smile again. "I think you'll be able to make it work."

"We know full well that your loyalty to the kingpin runs shallow," Maisie said, her posture suggesting she'd been about to rise but decided against it. "Surely you must be paying him dues, and no doubt he threatened you to gain your compliance in the first place." Perceiving Zaria's guarded expression as affirmation, she added, "I think you'll find Vaughan is a much better man to have on your side. Besides, prison is hardly your only concern. In the meantime, do you really want people to know you sold a paying client a faulty explosive? That could really damage one's reputation."

Zaria met the other girl's malicious gaze and held it. "I've proven my reputation through my work. It'll take more than idle gossip to ruin it."

"So you hope," Maisie said coolly.

"Enough," snapped Pritchard. "Bring us quality information, and you won't need to worry about such things." He indicated the door. "Now, get out."

Zaria didn't need to be told twice. She scrambled to do so, awkwardly contorting her body to avoid Maisie's tall form.

"Oh, and Miss Mendoza?"

This was Pritchard again. Zaria turned, half-hunched where she stood framed by the stagecoach door. "Yes?"

His eyes held a warning behind their icy amusement. "*Don't* try to skip town."

M. K. LOBB

is a fantasy writer with a love of all things dark—whether literature, humor, or general aesthetic. She is the author of *Seven Faceless Saints, Disciples of Chaos, To Steal from Thieves,* and *To Deal with Kings.* She lives in Ontario with her partner and cats, and she invites you to visit her online at mklobb.com and follow her @mk_lobb.

CELEBRATING 100 YEARS OF PUBLISHING

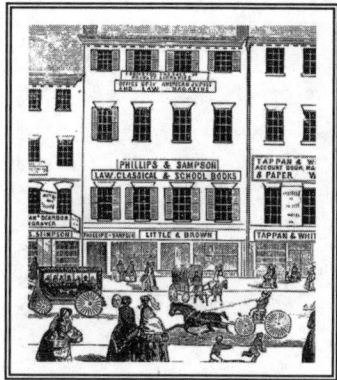

Dear Reader,

You may have noticed the words "Little, Brown and Company" on the title page of this book and wondered what they mean. Well, Charles C. Little and James Brown were the founders of this publishing house, and the "and Company" is all the editors, designers, marketers, publicists, salespeople, and more who help produce each book and bring it to readers like you. Little, Brown was founded in Boston, Massachusetts, in 1837, and some of its early publications included *The Writings of George Washington* and *The Works of Benjamin Franklin*. The catalog grew to feature works by Emily Dickinson and Louisa May Alcott, among many other notable authors. In 1926, recognizing that the literature we read when we are young has a deep and lasting influence and requires expert curation, the company appointed an editor to lead a dedicated children's department.

In 2026, Little, Brown Books for Young Readers celebrates one hundred years of excellence in publishing. Today, we are a division of Hachette Livre, the third-largest publisher in the world, and we are based in New York City. Our staff has grown from a team of two to more than one hundred people. And with the changes in technology, our books are read by more readers, in more ways, and in more countries than ever before. However, one thing has not changed: our commitment to providing a supportive home for all creators and superb stories for all readers. Thank you for being one of them.

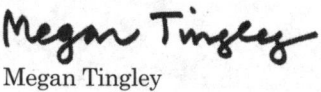

Megan Tingley
President and Publisher

LITTLE, BROWN AND COMPANY
BOOKS FOR YOUNG READERS

To learn more about Little, Brown's history, authors, and books, please visit LBYR.com.

More dark and daring novels from M. K. Lobb

SEVEN FACELESS SAINTS

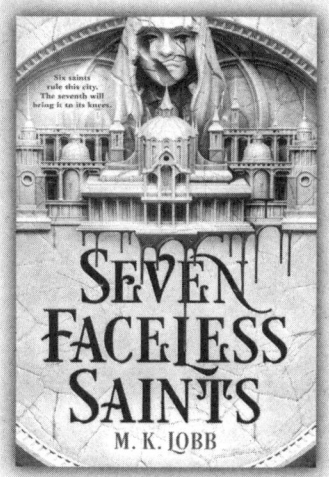

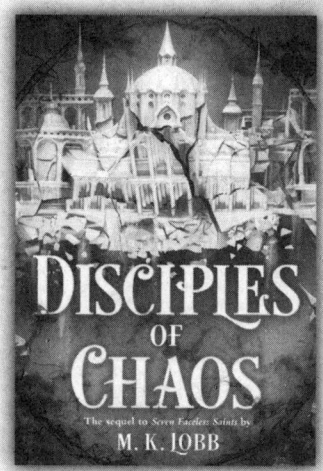

THIEVES & KINGS

BOBI254

 theNOVL.com